Sam Clarke

The Twelfth Ring

First published in 2017

CHAPTER 1

The black cab was outside our house. Much to the driver's joy, the metre was running and we were late. Mum had forced me to wear my smart suit because I had to make a good impression on a bunch of virtual strangers: the flight crew, the custom officials and my biological father. For a change, instead of algebra, I was battling a tie with a mind of its own. I had been booked on a special programme for minors travelling alone, which felt a lot like a prison transfer. I would be handed over to the British Airways crew in Heathrow airport and they would release me into my father's care once we got to Nassau. Like a prisoner, I had no choice in the matter.

Thirteen pounds later – at least according to the meter – we were cruising along the rainy streets of London. Mum was absorbed in her emails. I still couldn't believe that she had traded her role as a cardiothoracic surgeon in a London clinic for a six-month volunteering position in a Lebanese field hospital. We didn't get along, but the idea of not seeing her for such a long time made me feel strange. The idea of seeing my father for such a long time made me feel even stranger. After ignoring me for the best part of fifteen years, he had unexpectedly agreed to look after me while she was gone. Apparently, he wanted to get to know me better. His spur of the moment decision, coupled with the fact that he lived in another country, had plunged me into my current predicament. Six months away from school meant six months away from Cressida Rothschild, the most beautiful girl to ever walk this earth. She had been in my class for the last three years and we were like two planets sharing the same universe, but travelling on completely different orbits. She was popular, I wasn't. In an ideal world, she would throw her arms around me and beg me to stay; in the real one, a taller-than-average speed bump tore me from her imaginary embrace and brought me back to earth. My mother was studying me with such intensity that I felt like bacteria under a microscope. She couldn't possibly read my mind, where Cressida was waiting for my return in an outfit mum would never have approved of, but I blushed anyway. Unfortunately, my mother is first and foremost a doctor, constantly on the lookout for symptoms to diagnose. She leaned forward and squinted her eyes. 'You're red.'

I felt myself go even redder. 'I'm fine.'

'It's doesn't look like a rash. Is it itchy?'

Before I could answer, she had grabbed my wrist and was taking my pulse.

I snatched my arm back. 'Mum, please, leave it.'

She began poking my face instead. 'I need to identify the origin of the problem.'

'Maybe it was the yoghurt I ate for breakfast,' I said, in a desperate attempt to get her away from me. 'It had a bit of a funny smell.'

Typically, my excuse backfired. She straightened her back against the seat, like a cobra ready to strike. 'You ate expired food right before your flight? Are you trying to make yourself sick not to get on that plane? It's not going to work, Noah! We agreed that you would spend some time getting to know your father, it's too late to change your mind now.'

Considering that I had found out about her plan to get rid of me only two days before, "we" was a stretch to say the least. I kept my thoughts to myself. I had learnt from experience that there was no point in defying the Cobra, in particular when she was in attack-mode. At least she had stopped poking my face.

'I know I have to go, but I'm kind of nervous. Dad seemed nice enough whenever he visited, but I have met him thirteen times in my whole life. What if we don't get along? What if I don't like living on his barge?'

She glided over my first question. 'I may have been a bit hasty when I described it as a barge. It is a fairly nice vessel. I don't necessarily approve of his nomadic lifestyle, but I'm sure you'll like it.'

'Maybe, but... my life is here. My friends—'

'You don't have any friends. Unless you're referring to that underachiever you play videogames with.'

'Tom isn't an underachiever, he's dyslexic!' I protested.

'At least he has an excuse for his poor grades. Unlike you.'

'My grades are not poor, they're average.'

'Mediocrity is nothing to be proud of.' Thinking of my grades made her face even sourer. 'In any case, solitude won't be a problem. There is another girl of your age living on the boat and her tutor has agreed to take you on.' She glanced at an incoming text and continued. 'Look, I understand your hesitations, but your father has assured me that he will act sensibly and responsibly. I have made it very clear to him that failure to meet you at the airport or comply with my instructions will result in a lawsuit, so you really have nothing to worry about.'

My jaw dropped. The thought of not being picked up hadn't even crossed my mind.

'The rash has faded,' she said. 'As a precaution, I will get you some antihistamines when we get to the airport.'

She returned to her emails, a clear sign that our conversation was over. I switched my I-pad on and googled my destination. The Bahamas, an archipelago of over seven hundred islands, enjoyed three international airports – the odds of meeting my father weren't in my favour. On the plus side, it used to be a cool place. In the late sixteenth century, its waters were infested with pirates and buccaneers. The harbour of its capital city, Nassau, was a particularly notorious hotspot. I've always been a sucker for pirate stories, probably because my life is so incredibly dull. I wondered if mum was writing to Jean-Claude, her super-secret French boyfriend who I wasn't supposed to know about. Despite seeing her every day at work (he was a doctor at the same hospital), he rang more often than a life-insurance salesman. I suspected him to be the driving force behind her Lebanese adventure, because I had accidentally discovered that he would be going along. *Médecins Sans Frontières* had left a message on our answerphone confirming details of their joint accommodation in Beirut.

'Mum?'

She briefly lifted her eyes from the email she was composing. 'Yes?'

'Before the divorce, dad was a scientist, right?'

She pursed her lips in annoyed expression. She hated acknowledging that he had done something right. 'That's correct. Technically, he still is. As I told you before, he holds a PhD in Marine Biology and a master degree in Archaeology.'

'It's just that on his website—'

She nearly dropped her phone. 'Has he got a website?'

'Sort of. Most pages are under construction.'

'Does he mention me?'

I hoped not to hurt her feelings. 'No.'

'Thank goodness! What is this site called?'

'Magnuslarsson.com.'

'He uses his real name?' she asked in disbelief.

I typed the website address and handed over my I-pad. My father's face appeared on the screen. Dad's originally from Sweden and definitely has a Nordic look about him. Blond hair, blue eyes, nice smile and regular features. Despite being forty-one, he's a good-looking guy – if one can ignore his long hair and goatee beard, which are often styled in Viking plaits. With a hammer in his hand he could pass for a Thor impersonator. Or a Viking handyman. I could never decide if he was totally cool or utterly embarrassing. How he and mum ever decided to get married remains a mystery. A droid and a hippy would be more compatible.

'On his *About Me* page,' I said, tapping the correct tab, 'it says that he's an archaeologist and creep… a crypt… a zoo…'

'A cryptozoologist,' she said, taking me out of my misery and shaking her head in disapproval at either my father or myself. Or maybe both, she loved multi-tasking.

'What does it mean?'

'It's another word for time-waster.'

'Mum, I'm fifteen now and I deserve to be treated like an adult! You never talked about dad and I respected your choice.

4

I always accepted your version of the events and I never challenged your requests to be present at our meetings. You never gave me a chance to figure him out and now, all of a sudden, I have to spend six months with him. I don't know who he is, mum, I really need some straight answers.'

I had never challenged her so openly. The taxi was engulfed by an icy silence. She was expecting an apology but, this time, I wasn't going to budge. I meant what I said. We both waited for the other to make the first move.

'Cryptozoology is the study of animals whose existence has not been proven,' said the taxi driver who, up to then, hadn't proffered a word. 'Like Bigfoot or the Loch Ness Monster.'

I gaped, mum stiffened, the driver found an empty parking space in the drop off area. 'Welcome to Heathrow Terminal 5,' he said, pocketing his fare, 'the Bermuda Triangle of suitcases.'

Mum tipped him and he winked back. Thankfully she didn't notice and he narrowly escaped an eye examination. We entered the airport and silently made our way to the British Airways desk. We handed my papers to a friendly hostess who commented on how smart I looked in my suit and tie. She was rewarded with the most approving smile my mother could muster at such short notice and I had to do with one of her "I told you so" looks. The hostess stepped away to give us the chance to say goodbye. I wasn't sure what to expect, but I did know what not to expect: hugs, answers or a couple of tears.

Mum spoke first. 'About our conversation in the car…'

'Yes?'

'Why your father chose to become a cryptozoologist is beyond me. When we met, he was a promising and respected academic, his papers were regularly published and universities were fighting over him. He threw it all away and devoted himself to a pseudo-science. Cryptozoology is not based on concrete evidence, it relies on unproven sightings, old legends and local folklore. I never thought your father would go down that route. I'm sure you understand the repercussions of his choice on his career and on our marriage.'

5

'Is that why you divorced him?'

'It was the final straw. But there were other reasons which, as I've said many times before, I'd rather not discuss.' She straightened my tie and, for once, didn't speak my name confrontationally. 'Noah, I would like you to use these six months to get to know your father, but do not get carried away with his ridiculous theories. With hindsight, I should have been less interfering when he came to visit, but I didn't want him to put any of his preposterous ideas into your head.'

She took a step closer and, to my astonishment, hugged me. It wasn't exactly a warm embrace, more of a mechanical one, but her displays of affection were so limited that I was grateful all the same. I hugged her back. 'Bye mum.'

'Goodbye, Noah.'

She dusted my already clean shoulders and gestured to the British Airways lady to come over. Before stepping through security, I turned to wave, but she was already gone.

CHAPTER 2

The plane touched down in Nassau at 3:00pm local time. Fiona, the charming hostess who had acted as my guardian for the last nine hours, cleared all the formalities and escorted me to the arrivals hall. 'I'm sure he'll be here soon,' she said, for the fifth time, in the soothing voice of a professional trained to deal with emergency situations. I wasn't convinced and she didn't believe it either, she was checking her phone much too frequently. Someone cursed. Fiona and I turned. My father was elbowing waiting drivers out of the way.

'I'm so sorry I'm late! Traffic was a nightmare,' he said, rushing towards me. His bear hug was bordering on a headlock, I gasped for air. He then noticed Fiona and blatantly checked her out. 'I got your messages, Fiona. I tried to call back, but my phone died.'

Fiona smiled. 'It's all right, Mr Larsson.'

'Please, call me Magnus.'

'What a noble sounding name. Your wife, or is it ex-wife…?' she enquired, fluttering her eyelashes.

'Very ex,' confirmed my father, much to Fiona's delight. 'I never remarried. I'm free on Saturday, by the way.'

Was he hitting on the hostess right in front of me? Fiona didn't seem to mind. She giggled and adjusted her perfect hair. 'Right, well, I'll bear that in mind. Your ex-wife wants you to know that Noah was a bit red this morning.'

'I'm not surprised,' said my father, eyeing my tie. 'He's got a noose around his neck.'

So much for making a good impression! I was too jet lagged to be embarrassed.

'Before I release him, I will need to see some ID, please,' said Fiona.

My father produced a Swedish passport. She checked his details and asked him to sign a few sheets.

'Perfect,' she said, returning the passport. 'Noah, it was very nice to meet you. Magnus, when your phone recovers…'

He reached for her business card, gave her a smile that could have lit up a third-world country and herded me towards the exit.

Outside the terminal, the humidity hit me like a wet sponge. 'Did you come straight from a wedding?' asked my father, unwrapping the phone charger that he had bought from an airport shop.

'No.'

'Funeral? Graduation? Christening?'

'Mum made me wear the suit.'

'She always had a thing for ties,' he said, throwing my suitcase in the back of a battered pick-up truck.

I climbed in. The heat was stifling and my polyester suit felt like a shoal of wet fishes. 'Can you put the air-con on?'

He lowered the windows, not exactly what I had in mind. 'Music?' he offered.

'Sure.'

He flicked the glove compartment open. It was overflowing with prehistoric cassette tapes.

'Do you have anything more… recent?' I asked.

He plugged the charger into the cigarette lighter slot and connected his phone. 'Nobody sells tapes anymore, so my collection ends around 1995. There's always the radio.'

He found a station that, reception permitting, played the latest tunes. The wind and the radio pretty much killed the conversation, which suited me fine because we had never been alone before and I had no idea what to say to him. He hid behind a pair of sunglasses and I wondered if he felt as uncomfortable as I did. He was going quite fast, or at least much faster than mum had ever driven. One of his hands was holding the steering wheel and the other was fiddling with his beard, which was roughly four centimetres long and tied into a thin plait finished with a white bead. His shirt and shorts were an indistinct shade of greenish-grey, probably the result of too many washes at the wrong cycle. The t-shirt had a faded design on it, I had seen Tudor tapestries in better condition during a school trip to Hampton Court. His fingers were covered in silver rings and his totally out of place high-tech watch was swamped by a bunch of mismatched bracelets. We drove past Nassau harbour and eventually took an unpaved road leading to a secluded bay. A huge electronic gate protected the cove from unwanted visitors. My father leaned out of the window and punched the correct sequence in the access panel. The gate obediently opened. He drove through, parked his truck underneath a tamarind tree and killed the engine. I could see nothing but thick vegetation and a vast a number of security cameras. 'Where's your ship?

'Not far. She's called Valhalla. How's your Norse mythology?'

There was no point in pretending I was a straight-A student. Since he had never tried to impress me as a father, I figured I didn't have to try to impress him as a son. 'As bad as my Greek.'

He chuckled. 'In Norse mythology, Valhalla is the place where the souls of great warriors travel after death. It's ruled over by Odin and—'

'The Viking god?'

'In person. So, Valhalla is this cool place where the warriors can eat, drink and have some good old Viking fun while they await the arrival of Ragnarok, when they'll fight an epic battle—'

Norse mythology and jet lag didn't mix well. 'Ragna-what?'

'Ragnarok, the Viking equivalent of doomsday.'

'Oh, charming.'

He took the hint. Or maybe he noticed that my eyes were beginning to close. 'Words don't do Valhalla any justice,' he said. 'Come and see for yourself.'

We strolled down a twisty sandy path. With each step, my father kicked back some sand which inevitably stuck to my dark trousers. By the end of our walk, I could have passed for a miller.

When Valhalla came into view, I was lost for words. I stared. I blinked. I gaped. Nine hours of plane food made me appreciate the crunchy texture of the bug that flew into my open mouth.

9

Valhalla was an absolutely mind-blowing frigate, just like the ones you see in pirates' films. My gaze went up her three masts, flew over the crow's nests, rested on her folded white sails and came back down over the ratlines. A flag depicting a snake biting its tail flapped in the breeze from the top of the main mast. 'Is this where I'm going to live?' I asked, picking up my jaw from the floor.

He smiled. 'Yes, come on board.'

I had just stepped on the main deck when a girl came to meet us or, rather, to confront us. Her brown hair was cut into a long bob and her athletic build made you think that she excelled at every sport she tried. Her hand sat on her hip, resting on an invisible revolver. 'Is this him?' she asked.

I detected a slight French accent. And plenty of hostility.

'Yes, Isabelle, this is Noah,' replied my father.

My sandy suit attracted a disgusted stare. Or maybe I did. A male voice from somewhere down below reminded her, in no uncertain terms, that she had to finish her homework. She vanished in a cloud of huffs and puffs. 'Is she going to be my school buddy?' I asked, with a sense of foreboding.

'I'm afraid so,' replied my father, 'but don't worry, your tutor keeps her in line. He's ex-Israeli Special Forces.'

'Ex-Israeli Special Forces?' I echoed, more nervously than I had intended.

'He can teach you Krav Maga,' said my father, throwing a sidekick to an imaginary enemy. 'In fact, that's what we'll do tomorrow morning.'

'Is it a martial art?'

'Not exactly, it's a self-defence system devised for the Israeli army. It focuses on simple, natural movements.'

I had always wanted to learn a fighting technique, but mum had strictly forbidden it on the grounds that A&E departments across the country were congested enough.

'Does mum know about Krav Maga?' I asked.

'She probably knows more about Pilates.'

'I meant, does she know I'll be taught Krav Maga?'

'She said to keep you active. Do you think she'll disapprove?'

I couldn't tell if he was dumb or naïve, but learning Krav Maga suited me fine, so I didn't investigate further.

We walked across Valhalla's deck from bow to stern, where my father slept. He occupied the best room on the ship, the Captain's Cabin, and I hoped I wouldn't be assigned a dirty hammock in the hold. His cabin spanned the width of the stern and the slanted windows running along most of its perimeter provided a lot of natural light. The cabin was large, comfortable and... incredibly chaotic. His unmade double-bed was pushed into a corner of the room. A lamp was suicidally perched on top of a pile of thick books which acted as a bedside table, their well-worn spines a testament to the fulfilling career they had enjoyed before being downgraded to furniture. A number of greenish-greyish garments were trying to escape from a tall chest of (badly closed) drawers. A lucky sock had made it all the way to the floor and a t-shirt was about to follow suit. A tornado of Post-It notes had come and gone, leaving a sea of sticky squares on his cluttered desk. Overlapping layers of pictures covered the wooden panels between the windows. Two glittering swords framed an enlarged photo of my smiling father and a male friend riding a horse together. The horse didn't look too happy and I wondered why they couldn't have hired two separate ones. A dented cuckoo clock tried to tell the time, but the tiny doors wouldn't open and the bird kept on smacking against them from the inside. I was completely speechless. Thankfully he mistook my shock for admiration. He gave me a satisfied grin and beckoned me to follow him below deck. We stood in a long, thin corridor with eight doors at either side. 'Here,' he said, 'we've got the sleeping quarters and the living areas. Down below, kitchen, control room, lab, engine room —'

'Lab?'

'Yes, despite popular belief, I'm a legitimate scientist. This is your room.'

My cabin was quite small, but way better than the dirty hammock I had pictured. I had a built-in wardrobe, a bedside table and a desk with a chair. Outside my porthole, the sea and the sky melted into a vast expanse of blue. Someone had taken care of my luggage, my suitcase was resting on my single bed.

'Bathroom's here,' said my father, sliding a thin door. I stuck my head in the confined space: a toilet, a tiny basin with a mirror and an overhead shower. He returned to the corridor and pointed to the various doors. 'The cabin with the butterfly stickers on the door is Isabelle's, so keep clear. Her father, Miguel, sleeps next door. Third cabin is Ariel's, your tutor, and the one with the *Keep Out* sign belongs to Viggo, my… aide, but he only puts the sign up when Isabelle's around. The rest are spare cabins for when we have a sailing crew.' He faced the opposite side. 'More spare cabins, two big bathrooms and the lounge and dining area.'

The living area was very big and welcoming. One end was occupied by a long dining table, the other was set up as a cinema room. A large TV screen hung in front of a massive corner sofa surmounted by the framed poster of my favourite film: *Star Wars*. In a corner of the ceiling, I noticed a cluster of security cameras. My father's phone beeped. He checked the screen. A curt message from someone called Knut ordered him to phone him back immediately – no please, no thank you. Dad's reply was equally curt: "off-duty." He returned the phone to his pocket and glanced at his watch. 'There is somewhere I need to be,' he said. 'I'll see you at dinner. Feel free to explore.'

CHAPTER 3

Something didn't add up. Mum had always said that my father didn't have a penny to his name, but he was living on an awesome frigate anchored in a private marina. I wasn't sure if I should broach the subject, adults are notoriously cagey about their financial affairs, in particular around Christmas and birthdays. I hung the miller suit in the wardrobe, packed the rest of my clothes in the drawers underneath the bed and changed into a plain white t-shirt and dark cargo shorts. The end of my neck and the beginning of my t-shirt were a blurred line, I was in desperate need of a tan. I was dying to explore the rest of Valhalla, so I left my I-pad to recharge and headed for the bottom level. The layout was similar to that of the half deck. The closest door led to an industrial kitchen that could have doubled as a morgue – everything was stainless steel. A tall young man with an overgrown, shaggy haircut was chopping vegetables on the kitchen island. He could have been on his way to a surfing competition, his Hawaiian board shorts reached right below his knee and his blond, wavy hair stood out against the red of his t-shirt, which bore the name of an energy drink. He was barely into his twenties, with an affable smile and deep blue eyes. He introduced himself as Viggo. His Nordic name didn't go with his Californian accent which, he explained, was the remnant of a student exchange program with a San Diego high school.

'We're having stir fry tonight,' he said. 'Feel like slicing some vegetables?'

I didn't, but I'm a nice guy and I had nothing better to do. 'Sure.'

The way he handled the chopping knife unsettled me. Before passing it over, he made it fly from one hand to the other with a smooth controlled movement. When he did the same with a carrot, I decided I was being paranoid. 'Have you been here long?' I asked.

'About a year. I was studying medicine at Uppsala University in Sweden, but I couldn't get archaeology out of my head. One of my professors got me in touch with Magnus and I took some time off to reassess my priorities. I do plan to go back. Eventually.'

'I bet your parents gave you a hard time.'

'About what?'

'Dropping out.'

'Not really, but Magnus coming from such a well-respected family had a lot to do with it.'

I had no idea what he was referring to. I knew zilch about my father's family. They had never displayed any interest in my life either and had been collectively awarded a spot on mum's black-book of underserving human beings. We finished slicing the vegetables. Viggo washed his hands and dried them on his shirt. 'Have you met Isabelle yet?' he asked.

'Yes,' I replied, as neutrally as I could.

'Poor you! Her parents are divorced and she spends every school holiday here. Honestly, she gets more demanding by the hour! Sometimes I hide in the control room just to escape her!'

If my school-buddy could drive someone into hiding, I was in serious trouble. 'You'd better show me where the control room is. Sounds like I may need it.'

'Sure, but you'll have to find a different hiding place. You're not allowed in there alone. Magnus's rules,' he added apologetically.

'Any other rules I should know about?'

'Just a few. Your father's cabin is off limits too and we're not allowed girlfriends on board. Is that going to be a problem?'

I wished! Being an accidental monk wasn't fun. 'No, I'm... um... single at the moment.'

'I'm afraid it's going to stay that way, then. Sorry, dude.'

The unmistakable sound of shattering glass interrupted our conversation. We rushed across the corridor into what could have been a modern alchemist's workshop. Ampoules, petri dishes, graduated beakers, centrifuges, microscopes and other machines which I did not recognise covered every available surface. The alchemist himself was dusting glass fragments off his lab coat. I recognised him immediately as the man riding the shared-horse with my father. He was a full head shorter than me and his black hair was going grey at the temples.

'Jesus, Miguel!' said Viggo, bending down to pick up a tea bag and what was left of a graduated beaker. 'Why can't you make your tea in the kitchen like everyone else? Are you trying to avoid your own daughter?'

Miguel laughed raucously. 'Guilty as charged. I love her with all my heart, but sometimes she sucks the life out of me.' He then noticed me and attempted some damage control. 'She's not that bad, we're just joking. Aren't we, Viggo?'

'Speak for yourself!' replied Viggo, with a cheeky grin. 'Can I leave Noah with you while I check the CCTV monitors in the control room? I know you're itching to tell him your life story: born in Madrid, graduated at Cambridge, moved to Paris, got a post as an archaeology researcher at La Sorbonne, fathered the most difficult girl on earth...'

Miguel chuckled and threw a crumpled piece of paper in his direction. 'Get out of here, I'll give Noah a tour of the lab and I don't want you cramping my style.'

'What style?' asked Viggo, scampering out before Miguel could locate something else to throw at him. A book on undiscovered shipwrecks caught my eye. The cover was stained with overlapping coffee circles. 'What are you working on?' I asked, picking it up.

'Nothing much,' replied Miguel. 'Your father is trying to keep his workload to a minimum until you settle in. We've got a dive planned for tomorrow. You're welcome to join us.'

'I can't dive.'

'This is your lucky day, my friend,' he announced, clapping my shoulder. 'I've just booked a diving instructor for Isabelle. You can do the course together.'

Lucky day? As a fortune teller, he would have starved. 'That should be... fun,' I stammered.

'I'll ask Viggo to update your schedules.'

'Schedules?'

15

'We're not as disorganised as we seem. You and Isabelle will start each day with a Krav Maga session, followed by academic lessons and homework. Ariel, your tutor, will tell you when you can break for lunch. Talking about food… it's nearly dinner time. I hope it's not going to be stir fry again!'

The table in the living area had been laid informally. Viggo was dishing out the stir fry we had prepared earlier and Isabelle was doing her very best to ignore me.

'How did your meeting go?' asked Miguel, sitting in front of my father and eyeing the stir-fry with resigned desperation.

Dad chucked his phone on the table. He had fourteen missed calls from Knut, the rude guy who had texted earlier. 'Not bad,' he replied. 'I got a good lead on a sunken ship. I should get more details within the hour.'

'A good lead on a sunken ship?' I asked, trying to make sense of his words.

'Don't get too carried away, Noah,' said Isabelle in a condescending tone. 'Magnus has a fascination with undiscovered shipwrecks. He will get fixated on a particular vessel, waste days and days researching its cargo and hypothetical location and eventually start diving here and there in the hope of discovering a sunken treasure. But he will fail, miserably, as he always does. And don't even get me started on his hunts for sea serpents or other imaginary animals…'

Her grim predictions washed right over him, but Viggo gave her a dirty look. I turned to my father, fork in mid-air. 'Is this what you do? Are you a treasure hunter?'

'Not exactly,' he replied. 'I run a small archaeological and cryptozoological consultancy. I locate and retrieve items for private clients, but in my spare time I pursue my own projects. Sometimes, that includes treasure hunting or chasing mysterious creatures.'

I was barely able to contain my excitement. 'Can I be involved in your next search? Whatever it is?'

He beamed. 'Of course.'

'Is that a promise?'

He formally raised his right hand. 'I solemnly promise that you'll be included in my next search. Now eat, tomorrow is your first day on Valhalla and you've got an early start.'

As I tucked into my stir-fry, his ringtone came to life. It couldn't have been Knut, because he jumped to his feet and slid his finger across the screen. 'Any news?' he said into the phone. He paused to let the caller speak, walked to the other side of the room and reached for pen and paper. 'Got it, Wednesday 24th, 4:00pm, 51 George Street. Yes, I know the place. It's downtown Nassau. Have you personally seen the item?' He caught me looking at him and lowered his tone. 'I see. I'm on my personal phone, give me five minutes and I'll call you back on a secure line.'

He ended the call and left the room. I did some calculations in my head: Wednesday 24th was exactly two weeks from now. I wasn't sure what to make of it, but Isabelle leaned towards me and gave me a sly smile. 'Looks like you got your wish,' she whispered. 'The next search is on.'

CHAPTER 4

I didn't hear my alarm and arrived on deck late. The Krav Maga lesson was well on its way. I got my first glimpse of Ariel and wished I could return to the safety of my cabin. My tutor was a tall, bald, clean shaven man whose perfect posture wouldn't have looked out of place in a chiropractor's window. He acknowledged me with a brief nod. He exuded that "do not mess with me" attitude that I had never been able to master. Viggo was mistreating his punch bag with a vengeance; my father and Miguel were sparring together, working on their side and front kicks. Their moves were fluid, but powerful. They were drenched in sweat, but neither was willing to give up. Isabelle must have hated Krav Maga more than she hated me, because she didn't have the strength to blank me. The blow came out of nowhere, I was sprawled across the deck.

'Never lose focus,' thundered a Zeus-like Ariel from somewhere above me. I hadn't lost focus, but I had certainly lost face. It wasn't the first time and I handled my failure with a certain aplomb – I got up, rubbed my sore cheek and introduced myself as if I had been vertical all along. I braced myself for one of Isabelle's sarcastic remarks, but she didn't utter a single word or produce a single sneer. My father was right – Ariel kept her in line.

'Krav Maga,' boomed Ariel, 'from the Hebrew *krav* meaning battle, and *maga*, contact. The discipline encourages students to avoid confrontation, but if we can't, we fight. Krav Maga is not for show offs, its aim is to finish a fight as quickly as possible. The longer an attack lasts, the longer we prolong the danger. That's why, when we attack, we aim for the most vulnerable parts of the body. Your training will be hard and demanding, but you will get through it.'

'I'll do my best.'

'It wasn't an encouragement, it was an order,' boomed Ariel, before getting me warm up and showing me some basic exercises. By the time we finished I was completely wiped out, but my relentless tutor kept us on schedule. Academic lessons

18

were held on deck, not as a favour to the students, but as an endurance test. If we could concentrate in the heat and tempted by numerous distractions, we would be able to concentrate anywhere. Unfortunately, I was failing miserably. The jet ski that had just been delivered commanded all of my attention. I had recognised it from an article in the in-flight magazine: Kawasaki's latest model, the fastest jet ski in the world. Its powerful engine came with a hefty price tag. I watched my father run his hands over the jet ski's V-shaped hull and wondered, for the umpteenth time, what on earth had gone wrong between him and mum. He couldn't possibly be as broke as she made him, so why not come and visit more often? Why not make a bigger effort to be part of my life? I was his only son for God's sake! Unaware of my silent recriminations, he and Viggo chatted away in Swedish and lowered the jet ski in the water. Despite the age gap, they seemed to get on really well. Would my father and I ever be that close?

The following two weeks were a total blast. Academic lessons aside, I was having the time of my life. Viggo and I totally clicked and spent every afternoon paddle boarding or jet-skiing. When I got to meet Hope, my diving instructor, things hit a new high. She was an insanely attractive girl in her mid-twenties who Isabelle disliked immediately. Hope's long hair was permanently scrunched up in a messy bun and her smile was so contagious it should have come with a health warning. Whenever she was in the vicinity, I blushed – she even asked if I was doing something about my sunburnt face – and Viggo, an already expert diver, hung around more often than usual. She was so out of my league that I wasn't even jealous when they swapped phone numbers. My father and I were still a bit awkward around each other. We exchanged some pleasant chats, but any mention of George Street caused him to vanish on the spot. It kind of hurt because he had promised I would be part of his next search, but I was so desperate to bond with him that I decided to drop the subject until Wednesday 24th, which happened to be today. He still hadn't asked me to accompany him to Nassau and I had resolved to take the bull by the horns. I was half-way down the steps leading to the bottom deck, when I heard voices arguing in the lab.

'If it was about the twelfth ring, it would be different,' my father was saying. 'But he wants me to go on a stupid job when I've made it perfectly clear to him that I'm taking time off.'

Miguel sighed. 'It wouldn't be the first holiday Knut's asking you to cut short. It's never been a problem before. He knows something's up. Maybe you should tell him about Noah.'

'You know he doesn't like kids around. He's fine with Isabelle because you can send her back to her mother at the drop of a hat, but I can't send Noah to Lebanon, can I?'

'Dodging his calls isn't the answer.'

'I'll work something out,' said my father. 'Let's concentrate on the George Street business for now. If the item is genuine, you can swap your jeep for a limited-edition Lamborghini Diablo.'

I shifted position. The sole of one of my flip-flops squeaked against the floor. The sound was barely audible but, before I knew it, my father was standing in front of me with a suspicious look on his face. I was so startled that I forgot to look guilty. 'Hi dad, I was looking for you,' I said, with a smile that nearly split my face in half. 'What time are you leaving for Nassau?'

He didn't answer and tried to decipher my smile, which could have been anything from pure innocence to the start of a stroke. I hoped he wouldn't take too long because my face was beginning to hurt. To my relief, he didn't accuse of me of anything and checked his watch instead. 'Half an hour.'

'Cool, I'll be ready. Where shall we meet?'

'You're not coming,' he replied, without the slightest hesitation.

Disappointment spread over my face. 'But… you promised I'd be part of your next search.'

'And you will be,' he said, matter-of-factly. 'This is just a pick-up. Nothing exciting.'

The limited-edition Lamborghini Diablo sounded exciting enough to me, but bringing it up would have meant coming clean about my eavesdropping, and I didn't want us to start off on the wrong foot. Or on the squeaky one. He sensed my hesitation and spread his hands upwards. 'There's nothing going on here, Noah. You can trust me, I'm your father.'

I could have told him that trust and biological fatherhood do not necessarily go hand in hand, but I was still hoping to go to Nassau, so I held back. My silence baffled him. 'Is trusting me such an improbable thought?' he asked.

In a nutshell, yes, but I didn't want to offend him and ventured down the tortuous path of diplomacy. 'No, of course not, but... um... well... how can I put it...'

'Give it me to straight, Noah. I won't get angry.'

'That's exactly what mum says right before turning into the Hulk.'

'Try me.'

'I don't think you'll like my answer.'

'By now, I don't think so either. Spit it out.'

I scratched my head. 'Look, don't take this the wrong way but... trusting you is kind of hard. I mean... I still don't know why mum hates you so much and I have absolutely no idea where you've been for the past fifteen years.'

He kept his cool and didn't turn green. 'I know coming here was difficult for you,' he said, after a brief silence. 'And I know I owe you some answers, but this isn't the time.'

'When, then?' I pushed. 'Tomorrow? The next day? I really need to know what happened, dad. I really need to know... you.'

He opened his mouth to say something, but changed his mind at the last moment. He dropped his gaze. 'I should go. I'll see you at dinner.'

He clapped my shoulder and walked off. I headed for my cabin, my mood darkening with every step. He was as bad as mum, I would never get any answers out of him either. If I wanted to discover what had ripped my family apart, I would have to do it by myself. I just didn't know how. With my trip to Nassau up in smoke, I decided to make a start on my homework. Ariel had been very clear: every missed deadline would result in a hundred push-ups in the midday heat. Isabelle's door was open, she was laying on her front, flicking through a glossy magazine. She saw me and broke into a charming smile. When a pretty girl gives me that kind of smile, she always expects something in return. Usually something I'd rather keep. 'I can make it happen,' she said, 'but it's going to cost you a hundred Bahamian dollars.'

I sighed. I wasn't in the mood for games. 'What is?'

She snapped her magazine closed, it was a tattered copy of *Teen Vogue*. 'I can get you to George Street.'

Now she had my attention. I took one step inside her cabin, crossed my arms over my chest and tried not to look as interested as I was. 'Have you been spying on me?'

She rolled her eyes. 'I'd rather spy on a lonely seagull. I was spying on Magnus and you happened to come along. And get caught. One of these days I'll have to teach you how to eavesdrop properly,' she added, as if she regularly held workshops for MI6 agents. 'So, how about George Street?'

Price aside, her proposition was incredibly tempting. 'It depends. Can you get me there by 4:00pm this afternoon?'

Another "charming" smile followed. 'I can, but if Magnus catches us snooping around, we're going to be grounded on Valhalla for the next twenty years. The higher the risk, the higher the price.'

She was a natural born haggler, but my meagre pocket money had taught me how to drive a hard bargain. 'I'm not going to pay you anything. You want to know what they're picking up as much as I do.'

'Maybe, but I'm skint and I can't afford to take you for free. I know how to get a passage into town and you don't. You do the maths.'

She returned to her magazine. I cursed inwardly. I had never been past the front gate and had no idea how to get to Nassau. I needed her. 'I'll buy you a new *Teen Vogue*,' I said.

'And an ice-cream.'

I exhaled. 'Fine. Single scoop.'

'And you'll do my algebra homework for a week.'

She obviously didn't know how much I sucked at algebra. I shrugged. 'If that's what you want…'

We shook hands. I hoped I wasn't digging myself into a deep hole. 'So,' I said, lowering my voice to a whisper, 'how much is this passage going to cost us? Is your contact reliable?'

She giggled. 'You watch too much TV, Noah. Viggo goes grocery shopping every Wednesday afternoon. We'll tag along.'

My face fell. 'Your passage is *Viggo*?'

'Who did you expect? Ron Weasley in his flying car?'

'No, but I had pictured something a bit more… adventurous.'

'If you wanted adventure you should have stayed in London. Valhalla is the dullest place on the planet. Anyway, when we get to the supermarket, do exactly as I say. I'll take care of the rest.'

CHAPTER 5

I was on deck with time to spare, all I had to do was put my trainers on. My father, Ariel and Miguel had already left. Viggo, who had been locked in a never-ending texting session with Hope since they had exchanged phone numbers, had taken a short break to pore over a shopping list. By the time Isabelle showed up, I had cleared three more levels in my farming game. The reason for her delay was pretty obvious. She had undergone a major make-over, I just wasn't sure about the results. Her lips were a strange shade of pink and if her eyelashes got any longer they could have kept flies at bay. She had applied a magic potion to her face because her cute freckles had mysteriously disappeared. Her low-cut top made her look older than her years and her tiny handbag couldn't have contained anything bigger than a hamster. She walked right past me and made a beeline for Viggo. He threw her an absent glance and, for no apparent reason, winked. Her cheeks turned crimson. She recovered quickly but, as a serial blusher, I knew what I had seen. Her allergy to Hope finally made sense: she had a crush on my father's aide. I decided not to tease her about it unless strictly necessary, partly because I'm a sweet guy and partly because I had no idea how to get to George Street by myself.

The drive to Nassau was a pleasant affair. We had borrowed Miguel's jeep and Viggo – who was more responsible than my father when it came to sticking to speed limits – managed to ignore his beeping phone until we reached our unexciting final destination, Super Value Food Store. I was barely out of the car when Isabelle grabbed me by the arm. 'See you later, then,' she said, waving her manicured hand at Viggo.

He frowned. 'Hang on. I thought you were coming to Super Value.'

She fluttered her extra-long eyelashes. For a very brief moment, she was the picture of innocence. 'This is Noah's first trip to Nassau. Magnus said we could hop on a jitney and do some sightseeing while you do the food shopping. Didn't he, Noah?'

I hoped a jitney wasn't a wild animal, but I couldn't stand food shopping and was willing to take the risk. 'Yes, he... he did.'

Viggo slammed the jeep door closed and leaned against it, undecided. He rubbed his forehead, as if he wanted to warm up his brain. He was about to say something, when his phone beeped. His hand flew to his pocket at supersonic speed. He read his message and curled his lips into a cheeky grin. We could have burst into flames and he wouldn't have noticed. This was our chance. 'Can we go then?' I asked.

'Um... alright,' he said, without looking up from his phone. 'But you've got to be back here in exactly two hours. Don't be late.'

Isabelle dragged me across the street and flagged down an ancient looking bus. In comparison, my father's truck looked new. 'Jitneys are the easiest way to get around town,' she said, after we got to our seats. 'Pity they don't come all the way to our marina.'

As far as I could tell, nothing came (or was allowed to come) all the way to our marina. I glanced at my watch. Twenty to four. I bit my nail. I hadn't done it in a while, not since mum had found a disgusting varnish to stop nail biting that would put anyone off anything. I wasn't sure what was worse, the taste of the offending varnish or having to paint my nails in front of her. 'How far are we from George Street?' I asked.

Isabelle pushed her nose against the window to get her bearings. 'Not far, if we get off at the next stop we can buy my magazine on the way. The newsagent is right next to an ice-cream parlour. What's with the nail biting, are you having second thoughts?'

I was so tense that I could feel my nerves pulling inside me. 'No. I don't know. Maybe.'

'If you're afraid of getting caught, we can turn back. But you still have to pay me.'

I shook my head. 'I want to know what my father is up to.'

'You'll find out very soon. This is our stop.'

Ten minutes later, we were strolling down a side street. Isabelle, ice-cream in one hand and fashion magazine in the other, was rambling on about the stray dog that she had recently adopted in Paris. I couldn't make her out, most of the time she was incredibly irritating, but every now and then a sweeter version of her emerged and forced me to doubt my judgement. Or maybe I was being extra-lenient because she was so pretty. We had just turned into George Street when a series of loud bangs distracted me from Isabelle's multiple personalities. I had never heard gunfire before, but I instinctively pushed her to the ground. As her ice-cream splattered on to the pavement, I learnt my first French curse. 'Stay down,' I said. 'Gunshots.'

In the distance, I caught a glimpse of a man running for his life. He got closer. A pair of battered Converse trainers darted in my field of vision. A red cross, its four arms of equal length and wider at the ends, was tattooed on the owner's left calf. I blinked, refusing to believe what I was seeing. I looked up, I had to make sure. The cargo shorts, the mismatched bracelets, the greenish-greyish t-shirt: my father! He completely missed us and bolted down the road with a strange tube in his hand. Without thinking, I got up and started running after him. Isabelle was right behind me.

'Dad,' I shouted. 'Dad!'

He kept running. He trained regularly and was incredibly fast. Isabelle and I struggled to keep up. A hairless wasp whizzed past me at supersonic speed. Or maybe it was a bullet.

'Dad,' I shouted again, but he didn't stop. And then I realised that it was the last name he would answer to. After all, he wasn't used to having a son. 'Magnus!'

It worked. He turned one hundred and eighty degrees, shock chiselled into his every feature. Just then, his truck came to a screeching halt beside him. Ariel climbed out of the passenger side, extended his arm, pointed a gun at a pursuer who had nearly caught up with Isabelle, and fired. The man screamed and rolled on the ground holding his knee. My heart missed a beat, but my legs kept running. My father grabbed me by the shoulders and bundled me into the back of his truck. I crouched between the seats, next to Isabelle. Somehow, she had managed to save her magazine. The cylindrical leather tube that my father had been carrying a moment earlier was lying on the floor between us, I tried not to squash it. Miguel, both hands on the steering wheel, urged us to stay put. My father dived in, slammed the door and flattened himself against the seat. Police sirens howled in the distance and mixed with the passers-by's panicked screams. Ariel fired two more shots and jumped in. Miguel hit the accelerator – he was swerving so hard, I wished for a sick bag. After an eternity that must have lasted less than five minutes, Ariel barked that it was safe to come up. Isabelle and I slid onto the backseat next to my completely flabbergasted father. She reached for a tissue in the hamster-bag and dabbed at her perfectly dry eyes. By the time I realised what was going on, she had stabbed me in the back with the efficiency of a Ninja. 'It was Noah's idea,' she fake-sobbed. 'I wanted to go food shopping, but he insisted on coming to George Street.'

Her performance was incredibly convincing. For a split second, I nearly believed her myself. My father gave me a look that could have permanently killed a phoenix. 'Dad, that's not how it happened,' I began.

'Save your breath for Valhalla, Noah,' he replied curtly. 'You have a lot of explaining to do.'

I could have said the same to him, but decided to keep my mouth shut – arguing with an angry parent never ends well.

CHAPTER 6

I raised my hand to knock on my father's door and lowered it again, angry at my own hesitation. He had been locked in his cabin for the past two hours and had suddenly requested my presence. I presumed he had finally come up with a suitable punishment. And I also presumed I wasn't going to like it. The door swung opened and revealed my father's lean frame. 'How long are you going to stand there for?' he asked, more surprised than irritated. Without bullets flying past, he seemed to have reverted to his old self, but the mischievous twinkle that inhabited his eyes twenty-four-seven was gone.

'I just got here,' I replied.

'Your feet preceded you. They've been under my door for the last five minutes.'

I looked down, the gap between the door and the floor was tall enough for a cat to go through. He stood aside to let me in and gestured towards one of the chairs in front of his desk. Some of the clutter had been pushed aside to make room for two glasses of iced water. We sat down. I wasn't thirsty, but I didn't know what to do, so I reached for one of them anyway. He leaned forward and placed his elbows on his knees. His rage seemed to have evaporated, or maybe he had realised that, all things considered, his position was as sticky as mine. He skipped the small talk altogether and got straight to the point. A point I hadn't considered. 'If I send you back with a criminal record,' he began, 'your mother is going to skin me alive with her favourite scalpel. Luckily, I'm on good terms with the local police so you don't have to worry about getting arrested.'

Getting arrested? Criminal record? The water went down the wrong way and I coughed repeatedly to clear my airways. Unperturbed by his only son choking in front of him, he carried on. 'What you witnessed today was... a huge misunderstanding. It's not unusual for pick-ups to get messy, that's why I didn't want you to come to George Street in the first place. Your safety is my top priority.' I kept coughing, he kept talking. 'If we're going to spend the next six months together, we must lay down some ground rules. In the future, if I ask you not to do something and cannot explain why, I expect you to comply. I'll try not to do it often, but in my line of work things aren't always straightforward. For my part, I will try to be as open as I can.' He rubbed the back of his neck. 'I really don't want things to be awkward between us. How about we put it all behind us and move on, what do you say? Deal?'

He stretched his hand, eager to seal his proposal, but I kept mine firmly attached to the side of the chair. 'Are you in some kind of trouble?' I asked.

'No.'

'Why were those men chasing you?'

He stroked his beard. The moment of truth, would he treat me like a child or would he dignify me with a decent explanation? I hoped he wasn't going to invent anything too ridiculous. 'If I tell you,' he said gravely, 'you must promise not to speak about it to anyone outside of Valhalla, in particular your mother.'

'That's easy, we never talk about you anyway.'

'Never?'

'Anything to do with you puts her in a foul mood.'

'Still?'

'Still.'

He sighed. 'I see. In any case, when you give your word, it must be done properly.'

I found his obsession with ancient formalities bizarre, but I raised my right hand and solemnly promised that I would keep his secret. Satisfied with my performance, he reached for the cylindrical leather tube, unscrewed one end and emptied the contents onto the table.

'This is what I got today,' he said, putting on a pair of surgical gloves and unrolling a parchment across his desk. 'I bought it through an intermediary. We had agreed to a price weeks ago and I had already wired the first half of the money, but there was suddenly talk of another buyer willing to pay more. The intermediary backtracked and refused to return my deposit.

Nobody likes being double-crossed, so I grabbed the scroll and made a run for it. The rest you more or less know.'

I put two and two together. 'Is this the good lead on a sunken ship you mentioned when I first got here?'

'Yes.' He pulled his desk lamp closer. 'This map allegedly shows the resting location of the *Nuestra Señora de Begoña*. Ever heard of it?'

I shook my head.

'It was part of *Terra Firma* fleet which left Cartagena, in current Colombia, in 1605. They were headed for Spain and hurricane season was theoretically over. As the fleet passed the Serranilla Bank, it was struck by a spectacular surprise storm. One ship returned to Cartagena, two kept going and eventually got to Jamaica, but four galleons, carrying a cargo of gold, silver and emeralds, didn't make it. The remains of the galleons are scattered over a very wide area, but the wreck of the *Nuestra Señora* hasn't been located yet. I was hoping to make a play for it...'

I stretched my neck to get a better view. I was no expert, but the map certainly looked old. It was ragged at the sides and the ink had faded in various points. The parchment depicted an unnamed coastline. An area in the middle of the sea and two unspecified locations along the coast were marked by three separate crosses. A large section of the bottom right hand corner was missing, but the ship's resting location was clearly marked, therefore I presumed it made little difference. At the very top of the page, in neat handwriting, were the words *Nuestra Señora de Begoña*.

'Don't you need a license to salvage sunken ships?' I asked.

'In a nutshell, yes, but the Serranilla Bank is in international waters. There may be some leeway.'

The gunshots were still ringing in my ears. 'Legal leeway?'

He pushed the lamp away. 'We'll worry about technicalities later. First we need to scan the map and run some tests.'

He returned the scroll to the tube and threw it in my direction. I wasn't ready to catch it and it fell to the floor with a mighty thud. 'Give it to Viggo,' he said. 'He'll know what to do. And while you're at it, apologise to him. When you didn't return to Super Value, he drove all over town trying to find you.'

'It's alright. We're cool.'

We really were. Viggo had blamed my jitney-escapade on Isabelle's bad influence and I hadn't felt the need to tell him otherwise. The sound of the *Imperial March* suddenly filled the room. I glanced at my father's phone, curious to find out who had been assigned such an ominous ringtone. I half-expected it to be mum, but wasn't too surprised to see Knut's name on the screen. 'Who is he?' I asked, while my father rejected the call.

His jaw twitched. 'He's... a client.'

'You don't seem to like him very much. I hear the *Imperial March* quite often and you never pick up.'

He fiddled with a mean-looking military knife that he kept in his pencil holder and avoided eye-contact. 'Don't keep Viggo waiting.'

I picked up the tube and made for the door. As I closed it behind me, the *Imperial March* resonated in the background.

I found Viggo in the lab, slurping the leftovers of a graduated beaker with a suspicious look on his face. 'Miguel's mint tea tastes a hell of a lot like mojito. No wonder he and Magnus spent so much time in the lab last night!' I handed him the tube. He ditched the beaker and lit up like a supernova. 'The map?'

I nodded. 'My father says you'll know what to do.'

He unrolled the scroll, placed it on the glass plate of a nearby high-tech scanner and altered some parameters. The machine produced a concert of angry beeps. 'I'm changing the settings to get the best possible picture without damaging the scroll,' he explained. 'With the right equipment, you can scan pretty much anything these days: vellum, paper, papyrus, even your own face. The plate gets quite hot so it's kind of uncomfortable, but the result is great. Like a prehistoric selfie.' He elbowed me. 'You should try it.'

31

I chuckled. 'Yeah, right. And then you'll plaster my prehistoric selfie all over the web.'

'C'mon, I'd never do that. I'll send the image directly to your inbox. If you don't want it to see the light of day, hit the delete button.' He removed the map from the plate and gave me a mischievous grin. 'How about we do it together? It could be a dude-bonding exercise. I trust you with my stupidity and you trust me with yours.'

I don't know why, but I wholeheartedly embraced his idiotic proposal. The next few minutes were a blur of blinding lights, throbbing cheeks and hysterical laughter. I had never had so much fun with a scanner. When our faces could no longer take it, we returned the scroll to the plate and sent the image to a nearby computer. Viggo opened a program called *MappaMundi*. 'This software will compare our map to existing ones, new and old,' he said. 'It should help us identify the area of the modern world the scroll refers to.'

'Should?'

'It doesn't always work, in particular with maps like these.'

'What's wrong with it?'

'Nothing, but it's too basic to have been done by a cartographer. There are no obvious markers. *Mappamundi* will struggle.'

He returned the map to the tube, walked to a messy counter covered in ampoules and beakers and placed his finger in a dirty petri dish. I thought he would sample more of Miguel's concoctions, but the glass colour changed to light blue and a sensor read his fingerprint. A secret door at knee height clicked open. Viggo bent down, inserted the tube in the secret compartment and gently shut it. His phone vibrated against the counter – Hope had sent him a barrage of emojicons. 'It looks important,' he said with a straight face. 'Catch you later?'

I could tell when I wasn't wanted, but I was too excited to be offended. Secret compartments? Mysterious maps? 007 petri dishes? All in all, this had been the coolest day of my life.

CHAPTER 7

I was completely deflated. Viggo's predictions had come true – *MappaMundi* had hit a dead-end. I glanced at the full moon outside my porthole and sighed. The internet connection had become slower than a creep of tortoises and I was wasting my youth uploading pictures on my Instagram page. Pixel by pixel. I yawned and considered calling it a night. It was so hot, I hadn't bothered to shut the door. Suddenly, Viggo darted across the corridor. And back again. A wet toothbrush was sticking out of his back pocket and a strange phone, much chunkier than a standard smartphone, was pressed to his ear. 'Hey, what's up?' I called.

'Noah, where's your father?' he asked urgently, wiping some barely dry toothpaste from the corners of his mouth.

'Last I saw him he was off to the lab to have "tea" with Miguel. But it was a while ago.'

He pointed to the phone and whispered, 'Knut.'

Isabelle emerged from her cabin. I had been giving her the cold shoulder since she had back-stabbed me in the car, but she was still half-way through her magazine and I wasn't sure she had noticed. She offered to check the lab and rushed downstairs.

This Knut was really beginning to get on my nerves. I couldn't understand how someone could generate so much panic with a single phone call. I heard his voice bark something through the receiver. Viggo clapped a hand to his forehead and mouthed a curse. 'Yes, sir, that's what I said,' he replied. 'Noah is… um… he's here too.'

I frowned. How on earth did Knut know my name? Flip-flops echoed across the floor. Isabelle had returned with my father. He was rushed, but not panicked. Viggo handed him the fat phone. 'He knows about Noah,' he whispered.

My father's expression darkened. 'How?'

'I'm sorry,' replied Viggo, visibly upset, 'I let it slip.'

They exchanged apprehensive glances. My father slapped him on the back a couple of times, as if to cheer him up, and vanished into the nearest cabin. I resented their silent conversations, in particular when they were about me, but most of all I resented the deep bond that they seemed to share. We retreated to the lounge with the enthusiasm of a defeated army. I still didn't know why we were so upset. Viggo plonked himself on the corner sofa. 'I'm such an idiot!' he said. 'Knut wasn't supposed to know about Noah yet.'

My frustration got the best of me. 'Why not? What's it to him whether I'm on Valhalla or not? And who the hell is this Knut anyway?'

Two pairs of astonished eyeballs focused on me, as if I had arrived from Saturn in a Fiat Cinquecento. Viggo produced an incredulous half-smile, Isabelle blatantly laughed in my face. I went as sour as a lemon. 'Well, I'm glad you're having such a good time at my expense. Ha, ha so funny. So, who is he?'

If Isabelle laughed any harder, she would be recorded on the Richter scale. Viggo chuckled softly. 'Dude, unless you bumped your head in the last twelve hours, you need a serious memory upgrade. Last I checked, he was your grandfather.'

I stared back blankly. Viggo waited for me to laugh along, but I just swallowed a mixture of saliva and humiliation. My mother had always refused to disclose my grandfather's name in fear that I might track him down. I honestly wasn't planning to, in particular considering the amount of effort that he had put into missing my entire existence, but my assurances hadn't swayed her. I felt a surge of anger towards my father. He had had a golden opportunity to tell me who Knut really was and had fed me the client-story instead. Isabelle's teasing brought me back to the room. 'Your pallor is finally explained, you spent the last fifteen years living under a rock! Have you truly never heard of Knut Larsson?'

I shrugged. The name meant nothing to me.

She cocked her head in surprise. 'You haven't? Really? How about Alvastra Corporation?'

'Of course I've heard of Alvastra,' I said. 'It's a huge business conglomerate famous for its business ethics. What's your point?'

She and Viggo exchanged puzzled glances. 'Oh – my – God!' she shrieked, simultaneously shocked and excited. 'You seriously don't know who your grandfather is?'

I looked away in embarrassment. 'We've never met.'

Her curiosity was unleashed – my utter mortification wouldn't stand in her way. 'Why not?'

I bit my lip. 'It was his choice. When my parents divorced, he cut me out of his life.'

'Why would he do that?'

'I don't know,' I said, more angrily than I had intended. 'Not everyone's got a perfect family.'

This time she stopped laughing and Viggo suddenly found something of interest at the bottom of his glass of water. 'Dude, I had no idea things were that bad,' he said, when he found the nerve to look up. 'All Magnus said was to keep you secret from Knut for the time being. He never offered an explanation and, well... I never asked.'

An awkward silence followed. Their baffled stares unsettled me. Even Isabelle seemed to feel genuinely sorry for me, which said it all. This was too much, I was an outcast within my own family and I didn't even know why! It was hard enough to accept it when it was just me and mum, but having to admit it in front of other people was downright humiliating. I made for the door. Isabelle tried to grab my arm, but I shook her off.

'Let him go,' said Viggo from behind. 'He needs to blow off some steam.'

To add insult to injury, I was on a ship, I had nowhere to run. I came across the Krav Maga training area. I kicked and hit the punch bag so hard that my knuckles bled. I'm not sure how long I was there for, but a furtive noise got my attention. I rotated on the balls of my feet. It was pitch black, apart from... the glare of a tablet, opened on a Wikipedia page.

Knut Eskil Larsson (Stockholm, 1952) is a Swedish business magnate and philanthropist. The Larssons are a prominent family noted for a variety of accomplishments in the financial world. Despite being the head of one of Sweden's oldest families and enjoying global recognition, Knut Larsson is notably an extremely private individual.

Knut Larsson has been the Chairman and CEO of Alvastra Corporation for over twenty-seven years. Privately owned Alvastra consists of more than 350 subsidiaries and prides itself on its ethical investments.

I read Knut's estimated net worth and nearly fell off my chair. I scrolled through his academic history, outstanding achievements and list of awards he had received so far. It was certainly remarkable, but also quite boring. I examined the black-and-white photo of my grandfather in a smart suit, sitting at a shiny desk. He could have been anyone. I felt absolutely nothing for him. I shut the tablet and surrendered to self-pity. Having to use the internet to find out about one's family is pretty sad. It wasn't the first time either. I had googled my father in the past, but his relatively common name (at least by Swedish standards) had made it impossible to narrow down which entries were actually about him. I had come across his website purely by luck and recognised his picture. All I knew about him could fit on a single-sided sheet of paper: he had enjoyed a trouble-free childhood in his native Stockholm. At thirteen, shortly after the death of his mother, he had been sent to a British boarding school to complete his secondary education. After accepting a coveted place at Cambridge University, he had spent the subsequent five years accumulating two degrees, archaeology and marine biology. He had continued his studies at Harvard where, aged twenty-three, he and my mother had crossed paths. Cupid must have been shooting arrows with his eyes closed because, somehow, they fell in love and were married less than a year later. Unfortunately, other than myself, their union only produced grief. What hurt the most was that he had never opposed her request for full custody and had pretty much cut all ties with me. And, even though I couldn't fathom why, so had the rest of his family. At least, unlike Knut, he was trying to make amends. The more I thought about Knut, the tighter the knot at the pit of my stomach. Why was he so dead set against me? Could he somehow have forced my father to keep away from me all this time? Whatever my grandfather's problem, I had to know what it was. And there was only one person who could tell me. Before hesitation had a chance to kick in, I grabbed the I-pad and strode towards the stern, climbing the steps to the quarterdeck two at a time. The light in my father's cabin was on. I stormed in without knocking, but my grand entrance was ill-timed: dad was nowhere in sight. Viggo – the only person on Valhalla allowed in his cabin unsupervised – was rummaging through his desk and cursing away in Swedish. He looked up and sighed. 'He lost his driving license. Again. Third time this week.'

'I'll help you find it,' I said, taking a step closer. On top of a pile of sheets, partially covered by a book on mythological sea serpents, was the picture of an ancient ring. Could it be the twelfth ring that my father and Miguel had referred to when I had accidentally spied on them? Before I could take a better look, Viggo dumped another book on top of the image and put his arm up, as if I was en evil spirit he was trying to ward off. 'Sorry dude, I can't let you near his desk.'

Something stirred within me: jealousy. I hated feeling resentful towards Viggo because he was such a nice guy, but I couldn't help it. I should be the one with full-access to my father's life. Not him. I buried my hands in my pockets and pretended not to care. 'Where is he anyway?' I asked.

'Downtown.'

'Without driving license?'

'The girl he's having drinks with must be worth the fine,' he said, with a grin that stretched from ear to ear. 'She's only in town for one night. A hostess. Fiona or something.'

Great, I desperately needed to make sense of my life and he had gone on a casual date with a hostess he barely knew. His priorities spoke volumes. 'Did he say when he'll be back?'

The grin got wider. 'I wouldn't wait up. Is there anything I can help you with?'

'Not really,' I said, handing him his I-pad. 'But thanks for leaving Knut's bio, it was a nice gesture.'

He pointed to the small butterfly sticker on the tablet's protective cover. 'It wasn't me, dude. That's Isabelle's.' He paused. 'It's unusual for her to be so nice.'

I studied the butterfly. 'Should I be flattered?'

He chuckled. 'You should be scared.'

CHAPTER 8

I kept my eyes shut, shifted position, got rid of the sheets and put them back on – sleep avoided me like a good-looking girl. The sun rose out of the waves, but the amazing sight did nothing to cheer me up. A heavy knock on the door startled me. I checked the clock, 5:25am. I didn't feel like seeing anyone, let alone that early and in my old *Scooby Doo* pyjamas. 'Police, open up,' commanded a voice from outside.

I kicked my legs over the side of the bed and twisted the door knob with my now sweaty palms. A golden badge of the Nassau County Police Department was shoved in my face. I barely registered the insignia, too busy picturing the rough interior of the Bahamian prison where I would spend the rest of my holiday for fleeing a crime scene. The policeman, a scrawny young man with nicotine stained teeth, promptly identified himself. 'Detective Thompson, NCPD. Step outside please, sir.' I did as I was told. He scanned the inside of my cabin. 'Anyone else in here?'

'Like who?'

'Girlfriend?' He then noticed my Scooby Doo pyjamas and answered his own question. 'I guess not.'

I was too nervous to be embarrassed. Detective Thompson flipped his notebook open. His spiky handwriting reminded me of an ECG. 'Are you Noah Larsson?'

'Yes.'

Detective Thompson crossed my name off his list. 'Come with me.'

'Am I under arrest?' I asked, fighting the urge to bite my nails. It wasn't just about being taken into custody – if my *Scooby Doo* pyjamas showed in the mugshots, I would have gone viral overnight. Isabelle's door swung open. Valhalla's master-eavesdropper had used Detective Thompson's visit to hone her skills. 'Noah, don't say a word until your lawyer gets here,' she said.

I had no idea which lawyer she was referring to, but I nodded back and tried hard not to stare her pale-blue nightie, which clung in all the wrong places. Or the right ones. Something was seriously wrong with me. Since hitting puberty I couldn't help being attracted to every girl I met, including the ones I didn't like. Detective Thompson forced me to concentrate on more pressing problems. 'Nobody's under arrest. Not yet, at least,' he said, with a yellow smile that made Isabelle's lips curl in disgust. He then put his hand on my shoulder and pushed me forward. 'Go through to the lounge, young man. I'll explain everything when your father gets here.'

I mechanically put one foot in front of the other and begged every god I could think of to get me out of this mess. Isabelle grabbed her zip-up sweatshirt and followed us. In the lounge, Viggo, Miguel and Ariel were clustered around a second detective. Judging by their topic of conversation – beer-making techniques in medieval Germany – the possibility of a stint in prison didn't scare them in the slightest. Viggo, who started each day with an early morning swim, had come directly from the sea. He was still in his shorty-wetsuit and water had started to pool around his bare feet.

'Is Noah the last man on board?' asked Detective Thompson.

'Anatomically speaking, yes,' boomed Ariel. 'But a real man would rather die than be seen in that outfit.'

I wanted to glare at him, but my survival instincts knew better. I plopped myself on the sofa and crossed my arms over my chest to cover *Scooby Doo* as best as I could. And that's when my father rushed in, shirt back to front and inside out. The bead at the bottom of his beard was gone and the green bracelet wrapped around his wrist identified him as a guest of the Reef Atlantis hotel. He scowled at the yellow-toothed detective, with whom he was on a first name basis. 'Edward, is this really necessary?'

'I'm afraid so,' replied Detective Thompson apologetically. 'It's about the firearms that were discharged in George Street on Wednesday. An eye-witness has just placed your truck and your crew at the crime scene. I need to bring you in for questioning.'

'It's six o'clock in the morning!' thundered my father.

'I'm aware of that, but the NCPD cannot be seen ignoring such a serious accusation.' Detective Thompson lit up a cigarette and took a deep drag. His yellow teeth were obviously a work in progress. 'Magnus, it's just a formality. The captain will take care of everything. As long as your alibi checks out, you have nothing to worry about. You have an alibi which fits the circumstances, don't you?'

My father nodded. 'Joe's Bar. We spent the afternoon playing pool and left in a hurry when we heard the gunshots.'

Detective Thompson let out a cloud of smoke and allowed himself a smile. As I later found out, along with a vast selection of cheap beers, Joe's Bar provided affordable alibis to criminals in need. 'Very well,' he continued. 'I'm sure Joe will corroborate your statement. As well as your number plate, my witness provided partial descriptions of four men leaving the scene.'

Isabelle gave me a triumphant smile. The visually-impaired witness had saved her a trip to the police station. Detective Thompson leafed through his notes. 'The descriptions are vague enough, but I need four of you to come down to the station and give a statement.'

'Noah is a minor and I only have temporary custody,' said my father. 'Can you leave my ex-wife out of this?'

Detective Thompson winced. 'If she's the main guardian, she will have to be notified.'

The other policeman stepped forward. 'Magnus, minors generate a truckload of paperwork. You should keep things simple.'

My father chewed his lip and nodded. 'I'll need a few minutes.'

'We'll wait in the car,' said Detective Thompson, flicking some ash in an empty mug. 'Come out when you're ready.'

As soon as the detectives had left, my father turned to Viggo. 'Get changed. You'll take Noah's place.'

His aide sploshed out of the room without a peep. I may not be the bravest guy in the world, but I'm not a coward. 'Dad, this isn't right,' I protested. 'Viggo is the only person in this room

41

who wasn't in George Street! And even if mum gets to hear about this, so what? She's in Lebanon. There's nothing she can do.'

'*Nothing she can do?*' he echoed. 'Use your brain, Noah! You're underage and my alibi would place you in a sleazy bar in the middle of the afternoon. When your mother gets wind of it, she'll revoke the custody agreement on the spot. If you had gone to Super Value instead of playing detective, we wouldn't be in this situation.'

He may have been a newbie at fatherhood, but telling me off in front of everyone was totally uncalled for. I stormed out, embarrassed and furious, and followed Viggo's wet footprints to his cabin. The door was open and he was towel-drying his hair with the t-shirt he had been wearing the day before. 'My father's out of order,' I said. 'I won't let you take the fall for me.'

He dumped his t-shirt on the bed. 'Dude, chill, it's just a statement.'

His calm unnerved me. 'But you're innocent! You should never have been dragged into this!'

He unzipped his wetsuit and exposed the incredibly fit torso that had left Isabelle speechless on more than one occasion. 'Seriously, don't feel bad about it. If anything, you're doing me a favour.'

I frowned. 'How?'

'Dude, I'd much rather spend the morning at the police station than on my own with Isabelle. Hardened criminals, I can handle; bored girls, not so much.'

He turned to rummage through his wardrobe and I did a double-take. He practically lived in his rash vest and I had never noticed the small, vermilion cross tattooed on his right shoulder. It was identical to the design on my father's calf. Weird coincidence or buy-one-get-one-free at the local tattoo parlour?

My father and his crew left with Detective Thompson; Isabelle and I retreated to our respective cabins. I showered, threw my Scooby-Doo pyjamas in the bin, took them out again and fired up my laptop. My inbox was inundated with promises of cheap degrees from dubious universities and requests to confirm security details of bank accounts I didn't have. And then I saw it: *New message from Cressida Rothschild*. I blinked, twice, the message was definitely there.

Hi Noah,
I'm sorry we didn't get a chance to say goodbye.
Keep in touch,
Cressida.

I re-read it over and over. Cressida, the über-popular Cressida, was asking *me* to keep in touch. I cursed her timing. Lame as it sounds, this was the type of message I would have killed for when the distance between Cressida and I was measured in something other than nautical miles. I checked the date stamp to make sure I wasn't replying too soon, I didn't want to appear needy, or too late, I didn't want to appear rude.

'Uh-lah-la, who's Cressida?' asked Isabelle from behind.

I quickly shut the computer and she tried to force it open. 'Stop it. She's just a friend.'

My stance was far too defensive and the fact that I was willing to squash her fingers inside my laptop didn't exactly help my case.

'Isn't watercressida a type of lettuce?' she asked, trying to snatch the computer with her free hand.

I groaned. 'You're thinking of watercress.'

'Is she your girlfriend then? Or did she dump you when she saw your pyjamas?'

Viggo was right. I had drawn the short straw after all. A high-pitched sound saved me from answering. Pity it was the last sound I wanted to hear: the gate alarm. Isabelle let go of my laptop and took a step back. 'Someone must have entered the wrong access code three times in a row,' she said.

I checked the time on my phone. It was too soon for the rest of the guys to be back and they would never enter the incorrect code so many times. Something wasn't right. 'I'll check things out in the control room,' I said. 'It's probably a short circuit.'

I had no idea what I was talking about. My knowledge of electrical matters had come to a premature end when I had accidentally electrocuted myself during a D&T lesson. I rushed downstairs, Isabelle's flip-flops squeaking behind me. The CCTV monitors displayed two men. If it wasn't for the guns slung over their shoulders, they would have been completely unremarkable. One of them had plugged a hand-held device into the gate's control panel and was attempting to override the system. Isabelle brought her hand to her mouth. 'Oh my God! They're going to break in!'

I was nervous enough as it was, her gloomy predictions weren't helping. I doubted that my father and Miguel would be allowed to keep their phones on during their mock police interview, but I tried them anyway and it went straight to voicemail. At the fourth attempt, I left a brief message. I hoped we would be alive by the time they picked it up. Unless we wanted to walk into the intruders' burly arms, exiting via the main gate wasn't an option. We had nowhere to run. My heart was thumping so hard I thought it would crack a couple of ribs. Slowly, panic started to set in. Panic. The word kick-started my brain and I remembered the health and safety tour that Viggo had given me when I'd first set foot on Valhalla. 'The panic room,' I said to Isabelle. 'We'll hide in the panic room until everyone gets back. Viggo programmed the retina scanner to recognise my eyes too.'

She didn't react, but I was too engrossed with my plan to be bothered by her lack of enthusiasm. I moved to a panelled corner of the control room. The panels were secured in place with metal bolts. I counted them, found the one I was looking for and put my eyeball in front of it. The retina scanner kicked into action – a concealed door opened with a click and a hiss. I crawled through it. The windowless panic room was only a fraction bigger than my cabin. 'What are you waiting for?' I yelled to Isabelle.

'I… I think I'll stay here, thank you for asking,' came the unusually polite reply.

I partially crawled out. 'Are you crazy? This is the safest place in the whole ship. The access door is thirty-five centimetres thick. Get in here.'

'No.'

I pointed at the monitors behind her. The intruders had made it past the main gate. 'This would be a good time to reconsider.'

She stared at the armed men striding down the sandy path and kept on twisting her hands, as if she was washing them under an imaginary tap.

'C'mon,' I urged her. Without a word, she went down on all fours and slowly crawled through. I pulled the door behind us. As it clicked into place, I felt some of the tension leave my body. The panic room contained a single security monitor. I switched it on and fiddled with the controls until I was able to adjust the camera angles. The intruders were ransacking the place, but they seemed more interested in exploring every nook and cranny than in raiding expensive electronics. This wasn't a random robbery. They were looking for something specific and it didn't take a genius to figure out what it was.

'They're after the map,' I said to Isabelle. Strangely enough, she displayed no interest in what was going on. She remained in her corner, as quiet as a mouse, her fingers digging deeply into her fists. The intruders got to the control room and switched the camera feeds off. The monitor went black. They were close, I could just about hear their muffled voices. I pressed my ear to the door – all I heard was a whimpering sound coming from Isabelle's corner. Her forehead was covered in beads of sweat and I noticed a trickle of blood where her nails had dug into her palms. I moved away from the door and gently pried her hands open. 'What's up?'

'I'm claustrophobic,' she whispered. 'I'm OK if there's a window, but I can't do spaces like this. I just… can't.'

She snapped her fingers closed. If she didn't stop digging her palms, she would have no hands left by the time the others returned.

'There must be something you can do to keep your fear under control,' I said. 'Maybe we could try a visualisation technique. I read about it in one of my mum's medical journals. I'll describe a place, you'll imagine it in your head and believe that you're there instead of here.'

The look she gave me spoke a thousand insults. 'Great, I'm locked in a windowless room with a delusional Jedi!'

'At least give it a try,' I said. 'It must be better than carving your palms!'

She grabbed my t-shirt with both hands and pulled me towards her. I wasn't sure whether to expect a kiss or a head-butt. I got neither. 'You've got to get me out of here, Noah!' she screeched. Or sobbed. Or both. 'I'm about to have a panic attack.'

Her breath was now coming in great heavy gasps. 'Sit under the air-shaft,' I said. 'There's a bit of a draft. It will make you feel better.'

If the air-shaft hadn't been by the door, it could have been a perfect plan. As it turned out, I had just shot myself in the foot. With a bazooka. She briefly sat under the air-vent, mumbled something about the walls getting closer, pulled the manual door-release lever and rolled herself out. I rushed after her to pull her back inside but she was already in the corridor, rooted to the spot in front of the lab door. The place had been turned inside out and one of the intruders was fidgeting with the scanner. His back was turned and I definitely didn't want to find out what his face looked like. Isabelle's breathing was calmer, but still laboured. Dragging her back to the panic room could have back-fired, the only way was up. I pointed to stairs and mouthed "upper deck". She nodded in return. We tip-toed upstairs and managed to reach the main deck without any unwanted encounters. 'We can't leave by the main gate,' I whispered. 'They may have a getaway driver waiting for them.'

'How do we get off Valhalla then?'

I leaned over the gunwale and looked down. The jet ski was bobbing gently over the waves, tied to one of the purpose-built hooks affixed to Valhalla's hull. Isabelle followed my gaze and shook her head. 'I'm not sure, Noah. We've never dived from this height before.'

'Viggo does it all the time.'

'Viggo swims better than Poseidon.'

'We're good swimmers too.'

'What if the water isn't deep enough?'

'If it's deep enough for Valhalla, it's deep enough for us. C'mon, let's do it.' I heaved myself up and swung my legs over the gunwale. I was trying to assess the height of the jump, when I felt a hard jab between my shoulder blades. I turned around, slowly, picturing the gun before I even saw it. The intruder who was holding it offered a crooked smile. Despite being outnumbered, he didn't seem worried, but then he was armed and we weren't. He signalled for me to get off the gunwale and spoke into his two-way radio in a language I didn't know. In return, he got enough static to make the hair at the back of my neck stand even straighter. I slid off the gunwale and slowly raised my hands in the air. The back of my foot hit something hard. I looked down, the double-paddle of Viggo's kayak was lying on the deck boards. The intruder kept on trying to reach his accomplice and momentarily lowered his gun to adjust his radio channel. It was a golden opportunity to display my substandard fighting skills. I picked up the double-paddle with both hands and smashed it into the side of his face as hard as I could. Something cracked. It wasn't the paddle. The intruder tumbled forward, clutching the side of his head, his other hand frantically searching for the gun that he had dropped. I was transfixed by the blood – trickling through his fingers, dripping on the deck boards, sliding down the paddle…

Isabelle's scream woke me from my crimson trance. 'Snap out of it, Noah!'

I ditched the paddle. We scrambled on the gunwale and dived feet first. The drop was longer than expected, if I hadn't been airborne in the company of a girl, I would have screamed my lungs out. Isabelle had no such qualms. Her shrieks probably perforated what was left of the intruder's eardrums. The water opened beneath my feet and closed over my head. I was engulfed by silence and bubbles. The salty water stung my eyes, but I forced them to stay open. Isabelle was already swimming towards the jet ski's hull. I equalised and kicked-up after her. We climbed on. The starter key was hanging from the handlebar, where Viggo usually left it. I slid it into place, wrapped the safety strap around my wrist, put the jet ski in forward mode and squeezed the trigger throttle. The engine responded with a huge burst of acceleration and the jet ski flew over the water at incredible speed. I zig-zagged across the waves to avoid the bullets that were now being fired in our direction. They disappeared underwater like mini-torpedoes. The rain of bullets eventually stopped – either we were out of range or the intruder had run out of ammo. There was a third possibility too, but I refused to consider it and kept going. When Valhalla was nothing but a distant blur, I put the jet ski in neutral position and scanned the surroundings. Sea and more sea. I swung round to face Isabelle. 'I have no idea where we are,' I said, wiping water off my face with my forearm.

She pointed to my right. 'Pirate Cove is that way.'

'What's in Pirate Cove?'

'Hope's dive shop. She'll help us out.'

I nodded. 'Alright. Pirate Cove it is.'

Something warm coiled around my wrist. I instinctively yanked it back. Isabelle, completely startled by my reaction, released her gentle grip. I withered inside. When it came to girls I was a total loser, now she knew it too. I patiently waited for the dig that never came. 'I just wanted to say thank you,' she said instead. 'When I ran out of the panic room, you rushed after me. Most of the boys I know would have stayed put.'

I fidgeted with the safety strap to keep awkwardness at bay. 'Maybe you hang out with the wrong kind of boys,' I mumbled.

She produced a snort of superiority. 'Actually, they're the coolest boys in my school.'

I stopped fidgeting and made eye-contact. 'If they don't look out for their friends, they're not that cool.'

She pushed a strand of hair behind her ear. 'You looked out for me today. Does that mean we're friends?'

I gave her a non-committal shrug, unsure how to handle her soft and polite version. 'We could be. We're stuck in Nassau for the foreseeable future, maybe we should bury the hatchet and make the most of it.'

She thought about it. 'How about a secret trial friendship?'

I frowned. And not because the sun was shining straight into my eyes. 'A what?'

'We bury the hatchet for two weeks and see how we get on. Social medias aren't part of the deal, though. No selfies, no tagging and no following each other. If the friendship doesn't work out, I would have to ban you from my profiles and banning someone after such a short time always leads to rumours. We don't want our friends to think that we dated for two weeks before I dumped you, do we?'

If anything, being virtually dumped by such a good-looking girlfriend would have done wonders for my reputation, but I pretended to agree with her. 'No, we definitely don't want that. So, when does this trial start?'

A rare, genuine smile crossed her lips. 'Now?'

CHAPTER 9

By the time we got to Hope's shop, I was a total wreck. With my life no longer in danger, the adrenaline surge had been replaced by a ton of guilt. The third possibility I had so far refused to consider was gaining ground, at least in my head: I had never hit anyone before, let alone with a double-paddle, and I had convinced myself of having accidentally murdered the intruder. Isabelle took her new role as a friend extremely seriously and spent a whole four seconds trying to cheer me up. When her attempt failed, she huffed and ordered me to stop moaning. Hope was on her way out with a group of Japanese divers and bought our story about the jet ski running out of fuel. She lent me her phone to call my father and didn't ask too many questions – the few she asked were about Viggo, but I had no idea about his star sign. Or about star signs in general.

An hour later, my father's truck pulled up outside her shop and hooted. In spite of my recent brush with the Grim Reaper, he hadn't even bothered to come and get me in person. I climbed inside – feet first, long face afterwards – and didn't make much of an effort to return Viggo's smile. 'Magnus really wanted to be here,' he said. 'He couldn't get away.'

I slammed the door shut. 'Couldn't or wouldn't?'

He immediately jumped to my father's defence. 'Dude, he was worried sick, but things are pretty hectic on Valhalla at the moment – this is the first time we've had a breach.' He flicked the indicator on and joined the traffic. 'The good news is that the map is still in the safe, so no harm was done.'

The guy I had hit with the paddle would beg to differ. I scraped together enough courage to ask about the intruders. When Viggo repeatedly assured me that no dead bodies had been thrown overboard, I breathed a sigh of relief. 'Any idea who they were?' I asked.

'Two Russian dudes recovering the map on behalf of their boss,' he replied. 'We got their first names from the security video – Yuri and Vladimir. They tracked us down through the intermediary, reported us to the police to get us off Valhalla and broke in. If they hadn't miscalculated the size of our crew, they would have walked out with the map while we were in custody. Luckily for us, you bumped into them.'

I certainly had. More literally than I would have wanted to. 'Who did I...?'

I couldn't bring myself to finish the sentence. I wasn't even sure which verb to use. Viggo helped on both counts. 'You paddled Vladimir,' he said, stopping at a non-existent zebra crossing to let a pretty girl through.

Images of Vladimir's blood flashed through my head and threatened to bring up the breakfast I hadn't eaten. I forced my mind to move forward. 'Who's their boss, then?'

Viggo winked at the hot pedestrian. 'No idea. The intruders refer to him often enough throughout the CCTV video, but never by name. Or at least that's what Ariel says. Since he's the only Russian speaker on-board, we'll have to take his word for it.'

Somehow, I wasn't surprised my tutor spoke Russian. He would have looked quite at home in an unwelcoming Siberian tavern, where vodka was cheap and conversation frowned upon.

'Viggo, concentrate on the road,' snapped Isabelle, giving the pretty pedestrian the death stare. 'The cars in front are slowing down.'

He tapped on the brakes. The dashboard doll – a headless hula girl – swayed her hips accordingly. Her performance was cut short by a sudden traffic jam. Within seconds, hips and car had come to a total standstill. A policeman warned us to expect some delays – a water pipe had burst and traffic was being re-routed. I hoped it wouldn't be a long wait, my father's truck was already hotter than a furnace. Viggo shifted the gear into neutral, whipped out his phone and caught up with his messages. I wished I could do the same, but my handset was lying on the floor of the panic room. Isabelle and I were so bored that we ended up having a semi-decent conversation: I talked football, she talked footballers. The traffic eventually started to move. Whatever Viggo was typing had to be pretty interesting, because he didn't notice. The cars behind hooted wildly and forced him back to our dimension with a start. His phone slipped out of his hand and landed at my feet. I bent forward to pick it up.

'Dude, leave it,' he said, an edge of panic in his voice. His reaction startled me. If he hadn't freaked out, I would never have glanced at the screen. It displayed a picturesque chateau overlooking a peaceful lake – the kind of idyllic setting that dormant prehistoric monsters tend to favour in horror films. The snow-capped mountains in the background froze my brain and it took me a while to realise that I was staring at the website of an all-boys boarding school somewhere in Switzerland. A half-filled contact form asked about entry requirements for a fifteen-year-old British student. I turned to Viggo, shell-shocked. He shot me an anxious glance. 'Dude, it's not what it looks like…'

Confusion and disappointment made way for absolute anger. I pushed the phone in front of his nose. 'Why are you booking me into a boarding school?'

He didn't flinch. Clearly unimpressed by my weapon of choice. 'You should ask Magnus.'

'I'm asking *you*.'

He dropped his gaze. 'It's not my place to say. Speak to Magnus.'

'So he can feed me more lies? He didn't even tell me that Knut was my grandfather! You may worship the ground he walks on, but I can't trust a word he says!' Anger turned to bitterness. 'I thought I could trust *you*, though.'

He looked up. 'You can. I'm your friend.'

'Then prove it, for God's sake! Tell me what the hell is going on! Why is my father getting rid of me? Is it something I've done?'

'Dude, Magnus had nothing to do with this!'

His loyalty was beginning to border on the pathetic. 'Stop covering for him!' I yelled.

'I'm not lying!' he yelled back. 'Don't you get it? It's not Magnus who's trying to get rid of you!'

The penny finally dropped. 'It's Knut.'

Viggo bit his lip and nodded. 'The boarding school was his idea. Magnus agreed to look into it just to keep him off his back.'

I punched the dashboard in frustration. 'Knut has avoided me for fifteen years! He has no right to choose where I live!'

'Take it easy,' said Viggo. 'You're not going anywhere. Magnus will fight your corner.'

Isabelle's head snaked between the seats. 'Don't give him false hopes, Viggo. What Knut wants, Knut gets.' She squeezed my shoulder. 'I'll help you pack.'

My tear ducts were at bursting point. I sank back into my seat and spent the rest of the journey pretending to sleep.

By the time we arrived at our marina, I had come up with seven different ways to wipe Knut off the face of the earth; none of them particularly humane. Viggo grumbled something about his to-do list being longer than a reticulated python and disappeared in the bowels of the ship. Isabelle and I headed for the lounge, which had been turned into a war room that Churchill would have approved of. The blueprints of Valhalla's security system were pinned to the wall, next to the blown-up images of the intruders and of the device that they had plugged into the access panel. Ariel was barking in Hebrew in a funny-looking phone, similar to the one that Viggo was holding when Knut rang. In spite of the dining table between them, my father and Miguel were at each other's throats. They were so engrossed in their verbal onslaught that they failed to register our presence. My father was yelling at the top of his voice. 'Drop it! I'll tell Knut when I'm good and ready.'

Miguel threw his arms up. 'You're being unreasonable! They're Russians! It could be Dragomirov!'

My father's snort of disagreement could have put out a minor fire. 'Dragomirov goes for different finds, very specific esoteric artefacts. Treasure hunting is not his style. He has enough money to buy a small country, he wouldn't care for common gold.'

'Agreed,' said Miguel, 'but if it is Dragomirov, Knut would want to know.'

'I never understood his obsession with Dragomirov,' said my father, with a powerful shrug. 'He's just another billionaire with more money than sense. If dung was a status symbol, he'd buy it by the ton.'

As curious as I was about this Dragomirov guy, being caught snooping wasn't an option. With the boarding school looming in the background, I had to be on my best behaviour. Much to Isabelle's annoyance, I stepped further inside the room and brought our espionage mission to an end. She cursed my good manners and flew into Miguel's arms with unnatural spontaneity. My father kicked his chair back and rushed towards me. He cupped my chin in his hand and lifted my face to look at me properly. There was no need, I was nearly as tall as he was, but he kept on squashing my jaws, and my dignity, between his fingers. 'Are you hurt?' he asked. 'We found a tooth on the main deck.'

I went weak at the knees. *A tooth?* My first physical confrontation and the guy loses *a tooth*? I heard myself say that it wasn't mine. My father released my face and grilled me about the break-in. I did my best to fill in the blanks. 'I'm so sorry you had to go through something like that,' he said. 'Valhalla is a fortress. She's equipped with the best security money can buy. I'm about to meet with a team of surveillance experts to get to the bottom of this.'

Ariel finished his call and marched towards my father. 'My contact at the Special Forces confirmed that intruders' equipment is latest generation, military issue,' he said.

'As good as ours?' asked my father in disbelief.

'As good as ours,' confirmed Ariel. 'Whoever they work for must be pretty wealthy. This stuff doesn't come cheap.'

I lit up. 'If these guys went through so much trouble to get the map back, it must be real.'

'My main concern at the moment is figuring out how they breached our security system,' said my father flatly. 'All the rest can wait.'

His indifference rasped on my nerves. A bit more enthusiasm towards our search wouldn't have gone amiss. 'We may be sitting on an authentic treasure map!' I protested. 'The scroll should be our priority. We should re-examine it, see if we missed anything. We can't wait around; the Russians have already tried to steal it once...' My voice trailed off. A shiver made its way down my spine. I suddenly realised why he was so paranoid about the security system. 'You think they'll come back for it, don't you?'

He stroked his beard, which had been fairly skew since his rendezvous with Fiona. 'I'd be a fool not to consider the possibility. Which is why it would be best if you went away for a while.'

'Away?' I breathed. I couldn't believe that it had taken him less than a morning to give in to Knut's demands. Isabelle had been right after all: what Knut wanted, Knut got.

'Yeah,' he said, 'I have a great place in mind. Are you alright? You look a bit... flustered.'

I struggled to think of a polite answer. Viggo rushed in holding my phone. 'Dude, I found it in the panic room. It won't stop ringing. You've got a bunch of missed calls from your mum.'

I blanched. Missing mum's calls resulted in astronomical fines which she automatically deducted from my pocket money. 'How many?' I asked.

'Nine.'

I was officially destitute. I took the phone and thumbed my way to the Skype icon. 'I'd better call her back.'

'Not yet,' said my father, snatching the phone out of my hand.

'I missed our weekly call. In her book, it's pretty serious stuff.'

My desperation didn't sway him. 'Have you thought about what you're going to say?' he asked.

'Not really, but I may have to grovel. It won't be pretty.'

He wet his lips. 'I don't usually ask people to lie for me, but you can't tell her what happened. If she finds out about the break-in, she's going to unleash her lawyer on me.' He gestured towards the war room and gave me a helpless look. 'I really could do without the extra hassle…'

His aversion to my mother's sabre-toothed lawyer was justified. For the right fee, the man could have reduced Satan to tears. 'Don't worry,' I grumbled. 'Even if I told her the truth, she'd never believe me. I'll think of something.'

He returned my phone and gave me the thumbs up.

'But you owe me,' I added.

My threat amused him, which was kind of humiliating. He rummaged through his pockets and produced a crumpled banknote. 'Will this do?' he asked, handing me twenty Bahamian dollars. 'I've never bribed a teenager before so I'll have to trust you on the going rate.'

His carefree attitude was the straw that broke the camel's back. How could he be so chilled when he was about to ship me off to a Swiss boarding school? I snatched the note out of his hand and threw it back at him. It fluttered to the floor like a graceless butterfly. 'I'm not for sale,' I said, through gritted teeth.

His forehead creased in confusion. 'C'mon, I didn't mean it like that. It was just a joke.'

'To you everything is, isn't it?' He made to speak, but I didn't let him. 'You *promised* I would be part of your next search and this is it. You cannot pack me off to Switzerland when things start to get interesting. I won't tell mum about the Russians, but I want to be involved in anything even vaguely related to the map. And I want to stay here. With you. Whether your "client", or whatever you want to call Knut, likes it or not. You'd better stick to your word or… or…'

His eyes turned to ice. 'Or what?'

I had never threatened anyone before. I had no idea what to say next. 'I... um...'

He squared up to me. Eyes to eyes, nose to nose. His voice cut through the air like a deadly blade. 'Save your empty threats for the playground, Noah. I *never* break a promise.'

He turned on his heels and slammed the door behind him. The hinges shook. Inside, I did too. I looked around the room, Miguel was the only person who met my gaze. He blew his cheeks out. 'When you lose it, you certainly lose it like a Larsson.'

I'm pretty sure he didn't mean it as a compliment. 'I don't want to go to Switzerland,' I grumbled.

'Where did the obsession with Switzerland come from? Magnus had booked you into a beach-front hotel in Pirate Cove.'

My voice rose an octave. '*Pirate Cove*? Is that where he wanted to send me?'

'Yeah,' said Miguel, 'he thought you'd be happy to spend a couple days larking about with Viggo and Isabelle while we got Valhalla sorted out.'

I slid my hand in front of my eyes and wished for the floorboards to swallow me there and then. When Ariel strode up to me, I wished even harder. He crossed his arms over his muscular chest and gave me a slight nod. I tensed – Ariel would rather be hit with a stun grenade than have a conversation with me. 'Attacking an armed opponent with a double-paddle was a bold move,' he said, throwing me a measuring stare. 'As of tomorrow, you'll train longer and harder. If there is a latent fighter loitering within you, I will smoke him out and whip him into shape.'

And when I thought my day couldn't get any worse, my mother rang.

CHAPTER 10

Before locking himself in a meeting with the security experts, my father had issued everyone on board with a to-do list. Isabelle and I were supposed to help Viggo clear up the chaos left behind by the Russians. Unfortunately, any type of work sent her argumentative side into overdrive. Viggo's patience was running wafer-thin. 'Princess, pick any cabin you want and pack stuff away. Magnus said so, giving me attitude won't change things.'

'Then I'll start from *his* cabin,' she said, thrusting her chest out. I'm pretty sure she meant it as a defiant gesture, but I was momentarily distracted by the outline of her breasts.

Viggo didn't even notice them. 'You know the rules: nobody can stay in Magnus's cabin alone. Noah will go with you.' He turned to me. 'Dude, you're in charge. You've got to be in and out in fifteen minutes. Make sure the floor is clear and keep well away from his desk. If she gives you a hard time, call me.'

'I survived a whole afternoon at the Chelsea Flower Show with my mother,' I replied. 'Fifteen minutes with Isabelle won't kill me.'

Her glare implied the contrary, but I hit back with one of her favourite weapons, the blanking. Shortly afterwards, we were entering my father's cabin. Chaos reigned supreme, but I wasn't sure it had been burgled at all. Isabelle, who had never set foot in his cabin before, gaped in astonishment. 'My God! They searched everywhere!'

A part of me wanted to come clean, but I was undeniably keen to have a good snoop around. Something on his bed caught my eye. Sticking out from under a pillow was the same fat phone that Viggo was holding when Knut rang. I picked it up – dark, bigger than normal, with thick buttons and a retractable antenna. 'Is it charged?' asked Isabelle expectantly. 'I'm nearly out of credit and my father won't top me up.'

I pressed a few buttons. 'Completely flat. What's so special about it?'

'It's an Iridium.' In her world brand names were self-explanatory. Apple, Calvin Klein, Iridium, McDonalds... I was none the wiser. She enjoyed her moment of superiority. 'Noah Larsson, you truly are clueless.'

'We only have fifteen minutes. Can you skip the insults and get straight to the explanation?'

She spoke slowly, as if I was a complete idiot, which she probably thought I was. 'An Iridium is a satellite phone. It's much sturdier than the average smartphone and can be used pretty much everywhere because it uses satellites, instead of phone masts, to get a signal. There are four handsets on Valhalla and whenever they ring, it's some sort of emergency.'

'Are they more secure than standard smartphones?'

'The Valhalla ones are. They've been programmed to bounce over a number of satellites, making them very hard to trace, but you haven't heard it from me. By the way, they don't float. Last month your father threw one overboard in a fit of rage and it sank like a stone.' She squinted her eyes and focused on the wall behind me. 'That's curious, my dad has the exact same picture hanging in his study.' She walked up to the photo of our fathers and the horse. 'It was taken in Jordan. They look quite young, don't you think?'

'There's a date stamp at the bottom.'

She peered at the tiny orange print. 'Oh yes, 15th August. Can't read the year.'

She giggled.

'What's so funny?' I asked.

'Your father picked the hottest, most torrid time of the year to go to Jordan.'

'Maybe *your* father picked it.'

She gave me a knowing smile. 'C'mon Noah, by now you've figured out that Magnus is the one calling the shots.'

I had indeed figured out an unofficial hierarchy. Knut was top dog and my father was reporting directly to him. Miguel ranked slightly below dad and Viggo answered to everyone –

including the door and the phone. I couldn't place Ariel, he seemed to be his own agent.

'Don't tell me you haven't wondered what the hell is going on with our fathers,' she continued in a provoking tone.

Our friendship hadn't made it past the trial period yet, so I took the defensive route – fight a question with a question. 'Have you?'

She didn't answer, too busy pulling the wall apart. 'How cute, baby Noah with mummy and daddy. Hey, you never said your mum was pretty!'

'I never knew she was,' I muttered.

She handed me a battered picture that I had never seen before. Mum was smiling, properly, and my father was holding a tiny version of me in his arms. I had hardly seen any pictures of the first two years of my life. Mum and I had moved back to England soon after the divorce and the removal company had conveniently misplaced the computer containing our photo files which, inexplicably, she had failed to back-up.

'There's something on the back,' said Isabelle. I turned the image over. She read the smudged one-liner aloud. '"Noah's second birthday – Happy Times."'

My response was full of bile. 'Yeah, very happy! That's the year they divorced!'

I plonked myself on the corner of the bed, eyes glued to the picture. I simply couldn't comprehend how we could be a happy family in December and two completely separate entities less than seven months later. Isabelle sat next to me and studied the image. 'If you like it, you should keep it,' she said, as if it was hers to give away. 'I won't tell.'

'Was it under many layers?'

'Yes, but don't take it personally. I think they're in some sort of chronological order. If you keep digging, you'll find Magnus on his first day at school.'

I looked her in the eye. 'Thank you.'

She pushed a strand of hair behind her ear. She usually did it when she was embarrassed. 'For what?'

'Trying to cheer me up.'

She pushed more hair behind her ears and got to her feet. 'Let's pick a different cabin, this one's a nightmare.'

I nodded and slipped the photo into my pocket. I doubted my father would notice it was gone.

CHAPTER 11

Valhalla's new surveillance system had to be up and running by the end of the day. The security experts – nine ex-militaries vetted by Ariel in person – were fighting against time. Judging by their collection of scars and missing digits, they had met worse enemies. With Ariel busy supervising the security upgrade, Isabelle and I had been left to our own devices. As a result, our social media pages were updated in real-time. Ironically, not being in school seemed to have made me more popular. People who had routinely ignored me in the past were suddenly keen to be friends with someone who lived on a cool frigate. Cressida had commented on one of my photos and suggested we should catch up when I got back to London. My heart skipped a few beats. I immediately made a beeline for the mirror. The daily physical training had added some definition to my body. I was nowhere near Viggo's sculpted appearance, but I was fitter than I'd ever been. I also had a half-decent tan, but my sun-bleached hair was in desperate need of a cut. All in all, I wasn't totally dissatisfied with my appearance. I didn't look like the pasty schoolboy who had left London two weeks before. I was just as lost, but at least there had been a mild improvement in the looks department.

Valhalla was swarming with security experts, but we decided not to cancel our diving lesson. Our first confined dive was two days away and we desperately needed to revise. Hope had reserved the pool of a nearby hotel and, as far as I was concerned, the dive couldn't have come fast enough. Viggo was itching for it too – with Isabelle and I fully submerged, he would get to enjoy Hope's undivided attention for a couple of hours. I was learning about BCDs (Buoyancy Control Device) and SPGs (Submersible Pressure Gauge) when his I-pad pinged. He removed his sunglasses, concentrated on the message and scrunched his face. He gave Hope a longing look and jumped off the gunwale. If something could tear him away from my diving instructor, it had to be pretty amazing. I earmarked the paragraph I was studying and trotted after him to my father's cabin. Dad, eyes closed, was sitting on the floor in the Lotus position. He hadn't cracked a smile since our confrontation, but had been forced to address me on a couple of occasions and had been civil enough. Viggo cleared his throat. The Lotus opened a suspicious eye.

'Carbon dating,' said Viggo, 'the results are back.' He handed over his tablet. 'Not what we expected.'

My father threw me a fleeting glance, focused on the screen and frowned. 'It can't be! Do you trust your source?'

'Completely,' said Viggo. 'It's Miguel's research team back in Paris. They ran the test twice just in case, but it produced the same result.'

I was filled with curiosity from my toes to my scalp. 'What is it?'

My father handed me the I-pad. A brief email from the Sorbonne University stated that the map strip they had analysed dated back to 1315 AD. A full report was attached. 'It's medieval,' I said.

'It is,' said my father pensively.

Viggo continued. 'The less conclusive tests we ordered agree with the dating provided by Miguel's team. We're still waiting on palaeography, but I wouldn't expect any major revelations, there wasn't much to work on.'

I briefly wondered if they had switched to Swedish. 'Palaeo-what?'

'Palaeography,' said my father. 'It's a technique which can be used to date historical documents. It's more of an art than a science, but I like it. It consists of analysing handwriting while taking into account the writing methods and cultural context. It ultimately relies on the ability of the expert, so it's very subjective. Who did you contact?'

'Professor Madison, at the Smithsonian,' replied Viggo.

'Professor *Linda* Madison?' asked my father.

'Yeah,' said Viggo. 'She came highly recommended, but she's taking her time.'

Dad sighed. 'We'll be at the bottom of her pile. I stood her up on Valentine's Day two years ago to investigate the sighting of a sea serpent and she hasn't spoken to me since. Anyway, where were we? Ah, yes 1315 AD...'

I was mystified by their lack of enthusiasm. 'I thought the scroll being authentic would be good news,' I said.

'It is,' replied my father. 'Pity it precedes the sinking of our ship by a few hundred years. According to official records the *Nuestra Señora de Begoña* sunk in 1605.'

He intertwined his hands behind his head and searched the ceiling for divine inspiration. Or cobwebs. 'What do you think, Noah? How can someone draw the resting location of a ship which hasn't yet sunk?'

It was the first time he had ever asked for my opinion. For a nanosecond, I felt like a man. I cleared my throat and hoped not make a fool of myself. 'Well, it boils down to two options. Either the map is a good hoax drawn on an old parchment, or there are two *Nuestra Señora de Begoña*.'

He nodded in agreement. 'We need to start over. We were hunting for a very specific *Nuestra Señora de Begoña*, now we must do some digging for her older sister. Viggo, show Noah how to run a basic search. He's part of this treasure hunt, he should start helping out.'

I gaped. Given my earlier outburst, I had assumed that my days on Valhalla were numbered. 'Seriously? Am I still in?'

'I made you a promise, didn't I?'

'And you'll stick to it? Even if I bit your head off?'

He sank his blue eyes into mine. 'I *never* break a promise, Noah. The sooner you accept it, the sooner you'll get to know me.'

I wanted to hug him, but it didn't strike me as a manly thing to do, so I settled for an idiotic grin that would have made the hug utterly dignified.

CHAPTER 12

Viggo and I set up our workstation in one of the empty cabins and began our hunt for the 1315 *Nuestra Señora de Begoña*. So far, we had agreed that she had to be Spanish and guessed that her voyage must have started from somewhere in Europe – the Americas hadn't been discovered until much later. The *Ship Wreck Registry* website was a dead-end and Viggo was contacting similar organisations in the hope that their archives would offer better leads. I was going through a list of major medieval Spanish ports, but very few were able to provide records of the vessels which had moored there in the distant past. At first, we had refused Isabelle's demands to join our project, but she had unleashed a tantrum of epic proportions. In the end, we had to cave in for her own safety: her outburst had pushed Ariel to the limit and he had threatened to throw her overboard. On the jetty side. Her victorious smile disappeared the moment she walked into our cabin – she would be expected to work and I already occupied the seat next to Viggo. He handed her a list of minor Spanish ports. She was supposed to call them and find out if they were operational in medieval times. 'This is ridiculous,' she said three minutes into her tedious task. And huffed. And puffed. Viggo and I exchanged resigned looks. Our boring but peaceful haven had been forever shattered.

My father barged in without knocking. He and mum had something in common after all. 'Any developments?'

'Not yet,' replied Viggo.

'You're hopeless.'

Viggo glared at him. 'We're going as fast as we can, but it's kind of hard when you don't know where to look.'

Dad chuckled. 'Sorry, bad joke. I couldn't resist. I meant that Hope has left. She asked about your star sign, but couldn't have cared less about mine. Anything going on between you two?'

Viggo gave him a cheeky grin. 'Not yet.'

Isabelle wasn't strong enough to snap her pencil in half, but she came scarily close. My father surveyed our work area and sighed. 'This is taking too long. Let's try something bolder.'

Given the last twenty-four hours, I wasn't sure there was any boldness left within me, but I leaned back and waited for him to announce his master plan. He rubbed his hands together, eyes glinting with excitement. 'How do you feel about going to a monastery?'

As a single teenage boy, utterly devastated, but I forced myself to see the bright side: I still hadn't found the right time to ask him about Knut and the dreariness of a monastery could have provided the perfect opportunity. Viggo's voice derailed my train of thought. 'You mean the monastery where the map was found? It isn't exactly around the corner.'

'I know,' said my father, flicking through my list of medieval ports, 'but it beats ringing every harbour master in Spain.'

I stared at him in total disbelief. 'You actually know where the scroll comes from?'

'Of course,' he replied. 'Buying black-market items without enquiring about their provenance would be utterly idiotic.' He sat on the corner of the desk and started re-braiding his beard. 'The map was recovered in the library of an ancient monastery, hidden inside a medieval book. Given the mix-up with the dating, I would like to take a better look at it. I have already spoken to Brother Felipe —'

Isabelle frowned. 'Brother who?'

'Brother Felipe,' replied my father. 'The monastery's abbot.'

Viggo winced. 'I know the intermediary tried to rip you off, but approaching sellers directly is a serious breach of black market etiquette. If word gets out, your reputation will be tarnished.'

'One more stain won't kill me,' said my father, matter-of-factly. 'Anyway, Brother Felipe claims that the intermediary acted alone. He never authorised him to double-cross us.'

'And you believe him?' I asked.

'Not sure. He was reluctant to discuss anything over the phone, but he has agreed to meet us in person and show us the book.' He handed Viggo a Post-It note. 'Here's Brother Felipe's number. Make the travel arrangements and call him to confirm a time. We're too many for one car and I want us to travel together. Get a people carrier.'

Three hours later, we climbed into our newly rented minivan. My father adjusted the position of the driving seat and frowned at the dashboard. 'I'm sorry,' said Viggo. 'I did ask for a people carrier with a cassette player, but they don't make them anymore.'

Dad sighed, crestfallen. 'It's fine, as long as we don't play *Placido Domingo*.'

Miguel quietly returned his *Placido Domingo* CD to the front pocket of his backpack. My father turned the key in the ignition. The minivan was a big upgrade from his truck and even had working air-con. The movement made me drowsy and I slid into a dreamless sleep. When I woke up, the outline of a small hangar stood out against the horizon. We drove through a guarded barrier and parked in front of a *Learjet 75*. My jaw dropped, was the eight-seater plane our ride? I would have pinched my arm, but Isabelle had already done it for me. 'I'm *so* telling my friends about this!' she gushed, before pinching me again, which was totally unnecessary.

We clipped into our seats, the pilot carried out his safety checks and, flight plan in hand, came to my father. 'Is the destination unchanged?' he asked. 'I'd rather know now than in mid-air.'

'No changes,' confirmed my father.

The pilot nodded. 'We'll be leaving shortly. All phones and electronic devices must be switched off during take-off and landing.'

There was a flurry of gadgets. My father retrieved his phone from the side pocket of his seat. I was right next to him and couldn't resist a quick peek at the screen. My blood ran cold – twenty missed calls from Knut. He showed it to Viggo, muttered something in Swedish and powered it off. The pilot returned to his cabin and taxied the *Learjet* to the take-off strip.

CHAPTER 13

I had never expected the monastery to be in another country. After a short flight, we touched down in a small airport in the Yucatán Peninsula. Mexico was either very welcoming or very lax, because no-one came on-board to check our papers. A non-branded airport car met us on the landing strip and whisked us off to a waiting minivan, similar to the one that we had rented in the Bahamas, and also lacking a cassette player. Viggo took the wheel and typed some coordinates in the navigator. We were off to San Alejandro, an old catholic monastery on the outskirts of San Juan. 'When will Brother Felipe see us?' I asked, glancing at the stars outside my windows.

'Tomorrow morning,' said my father, putting his phone on silent and chucking it in the glove compartment. 'We'll spend the night at El Castillo, San Juan's finest hotel, and head for San Alejandro after breakfast. Viggo got us a great last-minute deal.'

Learjets and finest hotels? I spent the rest of the journey feeling like the premiership footballer that I would never be. And then we reached El Castillo. I groaned inwardly, Isabelle outwardly. San Juan's finest hotel was shabby and dated. Its walls seemed infected by a deadly virus which forced them to shed their own paint and it was hard to tell if the reception desk had been left temporarily unattended or permanently abandoned. Isabelle pushed past me and made for the bell sitting on the counter. Her manicured hand hit it a couple of times. '*Garçon?*'

Great, we were in a dump in San Juan and she behaved as if she was at The Ritz in Paris. Her haughty command went unanswered. She attacked the bell again, relentlessly. A creaky door announced the arrival of our receptionist, who didn't even bother to greet us. Either her parents wanted a boy or she was wearing someone else's badge because her name tag said "Manolo." She sat behind the check-in desk and threw some registration cards in our direction. They were stained with overlapping coffee circles. Viggo reached for a chewed pencil and began completing the proxy-coasters. 'We have a reservation under Magnus Larsson,' he said. 'Three adjoining rooms with bathroom.'

The receptionist grunted and produced four keys. The simple act of lifting them from their hooks generated a series of grimaces. She wasn't pretty to begin with, her facial gymnastics didn't help. Viggo counted the keys and raised three fingers in the air. 'Three adjoining rooms with bathroom,' he repeated politely, returning the fourth key.

'Three rooms,' said the she-Manolo, pushing three keys back to him, 'with bathroom.' She then pushed the fourth key.

It took me a couple of seconds to realise that the fourth key unlocked our shared bathroom. Isabelle wasn't going to settle for a communal bathroom without a fight. She slammed her hand on the desk and demanded to see the manager.

'Manolooooo…' howled the she-Manolo. I doubted she was invoking her own name. The door creaked again and, this time, revealed a moustached man in his fifties, an off-white vest stretched across his abundant paunch. He remained stationary under the *No Smoking* sign, a lit cigarillo in his left hand and a beer in the other. I coughed, he sneered. The Manolos exchanged a few words in Spanish, Miguel translated. 'He's saying it's Viggo's fault. He should have asked for three rooms with bathrooms.'

'Bathrooms? Plural?' said Viggo in disbelief. 'Is it even grammatically correct?'

My father dusted some paint peel off his shoulder. 'It's just for one night, we'll make it work.'

Nobody showed us to our rooms – three adjoining cupboards separated by very thin walls. I was careful not to lean against them in case they collapsed. Viggo and I were allocated a wobbly bunk bed with concave mattresses. I had slept on sturdier hammocks. He went for a shower. I heard him unlock the bathroom door and gasp. I joined him on the threshold. The bathroom was a potential hot-bed for mutant life-forms. Mould patches as big as continents floated on the uneven walls and the taps dripped constantly, as if they were in tears. A lonely cockroach – I prayed it was the only specimen – scuttled across the sticky linoleum floor. Viggo took a cautions step back. 'Dude, are cockroaches carnivorous?'

'No, but there's no way I'm setting foot in this contamination chamber. I'll skip showering.'

'I'd do the same, but I'm out of deodorant.' He winced. 'I guess I could rub the car's air freshener under my armpits, but the last time it gave me a hell of a rash.'

His resourcefulness was on a par with his idiocy. 'Leave the Magic Tree alone, you can borrow my deodorant.'

Viggo had gone to the nearest petrol station to fill up the van. I had stupidly forgotten to pack my phone and he was letting me play with his while he was gone. I was busy destroying an enemy spaceship when it began to ring. The caller ID displayed a withheld number. 'Hello?' I answered.

'Who is this?' asked a polite voice.

'Noah. Are you looking for Viggo?'

Silence.

'Hello?' I repeated.

'May I speak to Magnus?'

He hadn't introduced himself, but I instinctively knew who he was. My voice quavered. 'Who's calling?'

'This is Knut Larsson.'

I froze. Just then, Viggo returned. He chucked the minivan keys on the night table and pointed at the phone. 'Hope?' he whispered.

I shook my head. One look at my face and he understood. He took the phone from my trembling hand and rushed next door.

Minutes later, I could hear my father through the thin MDF walls that separated our bedrooms. Viggo was sitting next to me on the bottom bunk, elbows on his knees, hands cupped around his face. I assumed the same disheartened position. 'I messed up big time,' I said. 'I've handed my father to Knut on a silver plate.'

'It's alright, dude, they had to talk sooner or later.'

'Why are they speaking English instead of Swedish?' I asked, mildly curious.

'Knut wanted Magnus to be bilingual and always spoke English to him. The habit stuck.'

I hated feeling resentful, but I couldn't stand that Viggo knew my family better than I did. I also struggled to believe that my grandfather and I had spoken for the first time and he had intentionally ignored who I was. Next door the conversation changed tack. Sparks were beginning to fly.

'I will *not* send him back now. I told Katie he could stay,' yelled my father. A brief silence followed. 'I'm not trying to defy you, or the organisation, you know I wouldn't do that! My loyalty shouldn't even be questioned! This is a personal matter!'

'Which organisation are they talking about?' I whispered.

'Um… Alvastra, Knut's company,' mumbled Viggo.

Did he really think I was that stupid? I couldn't challenge him – not without missing my father's conversation – so I kept quiet. My father didn't. 'That's unfair and you know it,' he roared. 'Do *not* talk to me about sacrifices. I've always done what was expected of me.' There was a long pause. 'Well I'm not as perfect as Fredrik! Never was, never will be! Sorry to disappoint you! I'm in Mexico on a personal project right now, nothing you'd be interested in. I'll bring you up to speed when I return to Valhalla.'

Fredrik was my uncle – unsurprisingly, I had never met him either. Mum had mentioned him once, branded him as a total idiot, and promptly returned him to oblivion. The paper-thin partition shook like a loose sail in a strong wind. Viggo buried his face in his hands. 'Dude, he smashed my phone against the wall!'

I hardly reacted, too shaken by the conversation that had just taken place. I bit my nails. This couldn't go on, I had to find out why Knut hated me so much. My father stepped in and handed Viggo his newly cracked phone. 'I'll get you a new one,' he muttered.

Gadgets hate being replaced: the phone rose from the dead with a loud ring. My father snatched it from Viggo's hand and slid his finger across the screen. 'What now?' he growled, then his tone mellowed. 'No, this isn't Viggo Gustafsson, this is Magnus Larsson.'

He had unintentionally pushed the speaker button and we were able to hear the caller.

'Magnus Larsson?' echoed a female voice in an American accent. 'This is Professor Madison.'

I recognised the name. She was the lady my father had stood up on Valentine's Day in favour of the sea serpent. He sounded happy to hear from her. 'Linda, long time no see!'

'Not long enough,' replied Linda Madison. Her frostiness reminded me of mum. 'Your assistant sent me a high-resolution image of a scroll for palaeography testing.'

'That's right. I truly appreciate you taking the time to —'

'I didn't do it for you, Magnus.' Her iciness could have sunk the Titanic. 'It's my job. You'll be invoiced for my time.'

'Of course, I never —'

She interrupted again, keen to end the call as quickly as possible. 'There wasn't much information for a full palaeography test, but I wanted to flag that the words "*Nuestra Señora de Begoña*" have been tampered with.'

The conversation had just got a lot more interesting. 'Tell me more,' said my father, eyes alive with curiosity.

'The words "*de Begoña*" have been added subsequently. The handwriting is similar to the rest of the map, it's a decent attempt, but it has been done in a different hand and with a different writing implement. I would love to see the original, I'm sure an ink analysis would corroborate my theory, if there is enough ink, of course. Where did you get it from?'

My father hesitated. 'Maybe it's best if you don't know.'

Linda Madison lowered her tone. 'Are you still purchasing artefacts on the black market?'

His silence spoke volumes.

'You're beyond help,' she said, with a loud sigh. 'I can't believe I dated you for three months. Whose name should I put on the invoice?'

'Kraken Limited.'

'Kraken?' she spat. 'As in the legendary creature rumoured to dwell off the coast of Norway? You should stop playing with your imaginary zoo and get a real job!'

The line went dead.

CHAPTER 14

We couldn't stomach breakfast at El Castillo, so we bought some sweet rolls from a bakery and ate them on the way to the monastery. Isabelle couldn't stomach breakfast in the car either. She was sitting between Viggo and I and her sense of smell was in agony. The deodorant I had packed in a hurry had turned out to be a sun protection stick and no amount of UVB protection could mask the fact that we hadn't showered. She inched towards Viggo and bravely inhaled. 'Is this you?' she asked.

'Of course this is me,' he replied. 'Who did you think I was?'

She was temporarily disarmed by the stupidity of the answer. She inhaled again. 'Do you stink like this?'

'Like what? To provide you with an accurate answer, I need a reference value.'

I swallowed a smile. He had the power to deliver the most imbecilic answers with the utmost dignity. They bickered about smell benchmarks all the way to San Alejandro. The monastery was a pretty disappointing sight – it was old and crumbling. As I stepped out of the van, the sound of the church bells sent a shiver down my spine. A toll, a pause, a toll, a pause, the unmistakeable soundtrack of a funeral. Inside, a simple coffin lay in front of the altar. The pews were packed, as if the whole village had congregated to say their final goodbyes to the departed. Arriving late for a funeral is never respectful, arriving late and dressed in beachwear takes the bar to a new low. I had never been on the receiving end of so many disapproving looks.

'We shouldn't be here,' whispered Isabelle. Oddly, we were in agreement. Viggo casually dipped his fingers in the holy water, crossed himself and squeezed into a pew next to a large Mexican lady, forcing her to shuffle along. A priest in funeral attire was addressing the congregation and I was able to follow. My decent grasp of Spanish was all down to Carmen, mum's South American cleaning lady. She streamed Mexican soaps while she ironed and we religiously watched them together every Tuesday afternoon. Our tradition was a well-guarded secret. The priest began extoling the virtues of the deceased.

'Brother Felipe will be sorely missed,' he said. 'San Alejandro couldn't have wished for a better abbot.'

I felt queasy. Brother Felipe had agreed to show us the book and now, less than a day later, he was dead. I had an inkling his sudden departure wasn't accidental. Miguel and my father exchanged a few worried words and ushered us outside. In under ten minutes, Viggo had somehow worked his charm on the large Mexican lady. He excused himself in broken Spanish and she offered him a mint, which he readily accepted. He seemed completely unware of his effect on the female population and later claimed that Mexican funerary traditions include sharing mints with strangers.

Outside the church, the temperature was hotter than Death Valley. 'I wonder what happened,' said Viggo, slurping his mint and attracting a disgusted stare from Isabelle. 'Brother Felipe seemed fine when I spoke to him yesterday.'

'Can I borrow your phone?' I asked him.

'Why?'

'To check the local news. The church is at bursting point. Brother Felipe's death must have made the headlines.'

'Good thinking,' said my father. He then bumped Ariel's elbow. 'I told you he had a brain!'

My tutor didn't look convinced, but let it slide. Cheesy as it sounds, I felt absolutely overwhelmed. My intellect – along with everything else about me – often went undetected. Viggo handed me his cracked phone. According to the *Diario de San Juan*, Brother Felipe had been murdered in a botched burglary. The perpetrators had fled the scene. 'They buried him pretty quickly,' I said. 'I mean… he only died yesterday.'

'They had to,' said Isabelle, twitching her nose. 'A decomposing body in this heat would stink more than you and Viggo put together. Did you shower last night?'

I pretended not to hear. Luckily, my father had no interest in my personal hygiene. 'Our timing's terrible,' he said, 'but we're not leaving without seeing the medieval book. Let's look for the library.'

We entered the monastery via an unlocked side gate. The library was as disappointing as the rest of the building: it housed books, various species of spider and the occasional mouse. The books had been allocated their space on a first come, first serve basis and it was impossible to make sense of the place. 'There's an old computer here,' squealed Isabelle, studying a prehistoric monitor. 'It must contain the library's catalogue. What was the book called again?' My father opened his mouth to speak, but she didn't let him. 'Thank goodness you brought me along, you'd be lost without me!'

Undaunted by the obvious lack of keyboard or computer tower, she switched it on. The familiar faces of *Amor Prohibido*, Carmen's favourite soap, appeared on the ancient TV screen and exchanged honeyed words. Isabelle was mortified, Viggo laughing in her face didn't exactly help. 'The monks never disclosed the name of the book,' said my father, switching the TV off, 'but this place is filled to the brim with cheap paperbacks. Finding a medieval volume shouldn't be too hard. Let's check every shelf for ancient-looking books, ideally in Latin.'

We split in different directions. I started from the bottom shelves, Isabelle climbed a rickety ladder and studied the top ones. Time flew by. She was trying to dislodge a particularly stubborn volume when she lost her footing and fell backwards. Viggo happened to be right behind her and caught her in his arms. 'Are you OK?' he asked, with genuine concern.

She clumsily leant against his chest and failed to answer. Colouring aside, she was in a state of pure bliss. She didn't even notice the puffy-eyed monk entering the library. At first, I thought that a hairy caterpillar was crawling across his forehead, but it was just his bushy eyebrows joining together above his nose. The two monks that followed him couldn't have been more different: the first, a young man with a mop of curly hair, the second, the clone of Emperor Palpatine – hood included. Viggo's career as a superhero was short-lived. He dumped Isabelle on the floor without batting an eyelid and rushed to shake the hand of the uni-browed monk. 'Hi, we had an appointment with Brother Felipe. Since he's... um... unavailable, we were hoping that someone else could assist us.'

'I'm Brother Ignacio, prior of San Alejandro,' said the monk, returning a limp handshake. 'Brother Felipe was looking forward to your meeting. He saw it as a chance to atone for his sins.' We exchanged puzzled looks. Brother Ignacio continued. 'I will do my best to honour his last wish. Which one of you is Magnus Larsson?'

'I am,' said my father. He ditched the book on feathered serpents that he had been perusing for the last hour and stood up. 'Please accept our sincere condolences for the loss of your brother.'

'Thank you,' murmured Brother Ignacio. 'I understand you had a few questions about the map.'

My father nodded. 'That's right. Forgive my bluntness, but I'll get straight the point. The map you sold us has nothing to do with the *Nuestra Señora de Begoña*. The wording has been tampered with and the dating doesn't add up.'

Brother Ignacio didn't seem surprised. He let out a soft sigh. 'If I tell you what happened, can you guarantee that no harm will come to me or my brothers?'

'You have nothing to fear. As I've told Brother Felipe, our intentions are good. All we want is the truth.'

Brother Ignacio invited us to sit down. Isabelle was still on the floor so I offered her my hand. Her cheeks were back to a normal colour, but her ego was likely to be as bruised as her backside. We joined Viggo on an uneven bench that would have made a passable see-saw. Brother Ignacio introduced Palpatine as Brother Fernando and the curly-haired monk as Brother Cristobal.

'Brother Cristobal has only recently joined us,' said the prior, 'and has been tasked with reorganising our library.'

The librarian reaped a few sympathetic glances.

'A few months ago,' continued the prior, 'he came across an old book of Latin prayers dedicated to the Virgin Mary. The last three pages were not part of the original volume. Two were in Arabic, the third was a map showing the resting location of a ship called *Nuestra Señora*.'

An excited Viggo elbowed me in the stomach and nearly winded me. While I gasped for air, Brother Cristobal took over: instead of informing the dioceses about their discovery, the monks had put the *Nuestra Señora* map on the black market to raise funds for San Alejandro's much-needed repairs. The scroll had piqued the curiosity of a Bahamian buyer, who wanted to know if it was linked to the *Nuestra Señora de Begoña*. 'We had never heard of the ship or its treasure,' said Brother Ignacio to my father, 'but you were our only buyer and we couldn't afford to lose you. We retouched the scroll and added the words "*de Begoña*" to the existing "*Nuestra Señora.*" Our intermediary finalised the deal and flew to Nassau to meet you. On the day of the exchange, out of the blue, another buyer made contact. He was after the original map and was willing to pay a premium for it.'

'The original?' asked my father.

'Yes,' said Brother Ignacio. 'Yuri had no interest in the *Nuestra Señora de Begoña*.'

The sweaty hair at the back of my neck stood straight. The namesake was too much of a coincidence. 'Yuri? Russian? Dark hair, brown eyes?'

The caterpillar curled into a frown. 'That's right. How did you know?'

My father scrolled through his phone until he found Yuri's picture. 'This Yuri?'

Brother Ignacio crossed himself, puffy eyes wide with terror. 'That's him. He struck some sort of deal with our intermediary to stop the sale of the map at the last minute, but you snatched it and ran.' The prior clasped my father's hands into his. 'Mr Larsson, I don't know what the map means to you, but I beg you: forget you ever came across it.'

'I can't.'

'You *must*. Yuri will stop at nothing to get his hands on it. *Nothing.*'

'Did he kill Brother Felipe?'

The words had left my mouth before I could stop myself. The monks shuffled on their bench as if it was on fire. None of them ridiculed my suggestion, which was kind of worrying. To make things worse, Brother Ignacio broke down in tears.

'Yuri showed up yesterday with our intermediary,' said Brother Cristobal, handing a white handkerchief to Brother Ignacio. 'He held us at gunpoint and demanded the book where the map came from. Brother Felipe, may his soul rest in peace, put up a fight and Yuri...'

'Shot him before our very eyes,' cried Brother Ignacio. 'If we didn't surrender the book, we would suffer the same fate. We had no choice. We handed over the volume and made up the robbery story to avoid any issues with the police. We're not proud of our actions, but we didn't know what to do.'

'What was the book called?' asked my father.

'We can't remember,' said Brother Ignacio, a little too soon and avoiding eye-contact.

'You mentioned pages in Arabic,' persisted my father. 'What did they say?'

Palpatine emerged from his hood. '*Señor* Larsson, you lucky we speak *un poquito de* English, we no speak Arabic too. Book with no name, gone, Arabic pages, gone. Maybe time for you and your friends to be gone too.'

I often caught him staring at the TV set and suspected he wanted to get rid of us to view the next episode of *Amor Prohibido*.

Brother Ignacio stood up. 'We have told you all we know. If Yuri crosses your path again, do not underestimate him. That man is Lucifer personified.'

CHAPTER 15

Viggo had just turned the key in the ignition when Brother Cristobal rushed out of the church waving his arms in the air, as if he was drowning in the troposphere. Palpatine was right behind him, but his old age slowed him down and he struggled to keep up. Viggo lowered the driver's window and stuck his elbow out.

'Mr Larsson, you forgot your cardigan,' screamed the drowning monk.

Isabelle had never appreciated my father's fashion sense and he had just disappointed her further. 'You wear *cardigans*?'

'I did during the *Grunge* years. Even your father owned a couple back then. How he switched from *Pearl Jam* to *Placido Domingo* remains a mystery...'

Miguel chuckled. 'Get over it, Magnus, I like Placido.'

Brother Cristobal approached the minivan. Without warning, he pushed his head inside the driver's window. Viggo leaned back and barely escaped a kiss. 'The book was called *Domina Nostra Hierosolymitana*,' whispered the monk. 'Brother Ignacio has ordered us to forget about it and move on, but I don't want Brother Felipe's death to be in vain. I have a good feeling about you and I think you should know. Perhaps some good will come out of all this.'

Palpatine caught up and Cristobal quickly changed the subject. 'I'm glad you enjoy the Gospel of Matthew, I also like the Sermon on the Mount.'

Before taking his leave, he handed Viggo a woolly, pink garment, complete with a colony of moths. Isabelle shuddered at the sight and the moths eagerly joined us in the van. The cardigan was clearly an excuse to come and talk to us, but Brother Cristobal couldn't have picked an uglier garment if he had tried. Viggo studied the dreadful bundle with a critical eye. 'Do you think Hope will like it?'

'She'll *love* it,' replied Isabelle, chasing a moth from her face.

He turned to my father with an expectant smile. 'Can I keep it?'

His question went ignored. Dad and Miguel were locked in a staring competition. 'Was the book called…?' began Miguel.

'It was,' said my father, glumly.

His reaction threw me. 'Have you heard of it before?'

'No,' he grumbled, shoving Miguel's CD in the car stereo. His grumpiness mystified me. All in all, our trip had been pretty successful: the mysterious *Nuestra Señora* ship depicted on our scroll may not have been the *Nuestra Señora de Begoña*, but she was undeniably important – Yuri wouldn't have gone through such trouble to get hold of a useless map. All we had to do was find out why. *Placido Domingo*'s operatic singing suddenly filled the van. The tenor made it impossible to have a proper conversation and I suspected he was being played for that very reason. Isabelle was immersed in a word search puzzle. I borrowed her pen and scribbled "What was the book called?" at the edge of her magazine. She jotted down "Domina Nostra Hierosolymitana." Crikey, her Latin was pretty good, she had no hesitation in spelling the extremely long word. I frowned, she gave me a superior smile and wrote "Our Lady of Jerusalem." She then pointed to the chewing-gums sticking out of my pocket and turned her palm up.

We landed in Nassau late in the evening and headed for Magic Sunset, a beach front restaurant which offered a cheap and cheerful, eat-as-much-as-you-like buffet. Isabelle would have preferred something more upmarket, but she was too hungry to protest. The buffet was Viggo's idea of heaven, he had so much mango chicken that I thought he would grow feathers. The manager eventually asked him to restrain himself or pay an extra charge. My father and Miguel entertained us with some of their treasure hunting adventures and even managed to make Ariel smile. Once. One blink and you missed it. The restaurant manager found out that I was a huge pirate fan and took me to his office to give me directions to the *Pirate Museum*. When I returned, my father and Miguel were no longer at the table. Isabelle and Viggo were bickering wildly, she was still allowed in the vicinity of the buffet and he was trying to convince her to get him more chicken.

I was super keen to visit the *Pirate Museum* and pictured how different the beachfront must have looked four hundred years before. I was dotting the horizon with galleons and sloops when I noticed two figures in the midst of an animated discussion. There were no fists flying, but my father and Miguel were clearly in disagreement about something. The Spaniard eventually threw his arms in the air and stomped back, my father remained on the beach – completely alone. It was the perfect opportunity to ask him about Knut. I took a deep breath and stood up to join him, but a flying bread roll hit me square in the face. 'My next shot will be harder,' said Ariel, throwing a pineapple from one hand to the other, as if he wanted to determine its weight.

I hesitated. Being knocked-down by an organic weapon wasn't on my bucket list. 'I want to talk to my father.'

'Give him ten minutes. He's sitting in the Lotus position, he's... meditating.'

He spat the word as if it was a crime against humanity. I hated being told when I could see my own father, but defying Ariel, with or without a pineapple, was suicidal.

Ten minutes later my bare feet were sinking in the soft white sand, the fine grains trickling between my toes – the pleasant, relaxing feeling did nothing to curb my anxiety. My father was still sitting in the same spot, hypnotised by the ocean. I sat next to him and crossed my legs. He acknowledged me with a terse smile. 'Are you scouting for the sea serpent?' I asked, to break the ice.

He chuckled and messed my hair in an affectionate gesture, as if I was a dog he really liked. His bracelets chimed. 'I'm enjoying the view. I love the sea, that's why I chose to live on it.'

'I love it too. Mum took me every year.'

'She did?'

I detected a veil of sadness, as if he was sorry not to have been there. 'Salty air is highly beneficial to the respiratory system,' I replied, mimicking mum's austere voice. We burst out laughing.

'How's your mother, really?' he asked, switching to a more serious tone.

I wasn't sure what he meant, physically? Psychologically? As a doctor? As a parent? I opted for a non-committal British answer. 'She's fine, thank you for asking.'

'Yeah? Is she? What's the deal with this Lebanon thing then? Is she having some mid-life crisis or something?'

He didn't sound judgemental, just curious and, maybe, a bit... worried? I didn't want him to waste time on the Cobra, so I decided to come clean. 'She's absolutely fine. In fact, I'm not even supposed to know, but...'

He looked at me sideways, his lips stretched into a mischievous smile, the twinkle in his eyes alive and kicking. 'But?'

'She has a boyfriend.'

The smile was gone. 'Since when?'

'Not sure.'

'Is it serious?'

I was actually hoping to find out why Knut hated me, rather than discussing my mother's secret love life with her estranged ex-husband. 'I think so, they're in Lebanon together. He's a doctor too, French.'

'Good-looking?'

'Don't know, I've never met him.'

He feigned suspicion. 'Are you sure he exists? Has he got a name?'

'Jean-Claude Olivier.'

'Wow, *two* names! She picked well!' He moved his gaze back to the ocean, deep in thought. 'That's good,' he finally said more to himself than to me, without sounding terribly pleased. 'I'm glad. Katie deserves to be happy.'

I was confused. Why was he wasting time worrying about her? Did he know what she had put me through all these years?

'*She* deserves to be happy? Have you got any idea who mum really is? I'll tell you, because while you were doing whatever it is that you do, I was the one who had to live with her for fifteen years! She's the most insensitive person you'll ever meet, totally incapable of feelings or emotions. She is first and foremost a doctor. To her, tears are watery fluid secreted by the lacrimal glands and laughter is a psycho-physiological reflex! I can count the number of times she hugged me on one hand! Sometimes I wonder if she's even human! I honestly have no idea what possessed you to marry her, did you lose a bet? Were you high or something?'

He was taken aback by my explosive reaction. He opened his mouth to speak, but nothing came out. He turned his palms upwards, as if he was trying to explain something, and then lowered them again. He then wet his lips, played with his beard and, finally, produced a sentence. 'Noah, your mum, she…' he hesitated, looking for the right words. 'She wasn't always… like she is now. She used to be different.'

'Different?'

'She always was first and foremost a doctor,' he added, as if to reassure me, 'but the divorce changed her. A lot.'

I raised two sceptical eyebrows. 'You mean she used to be *nice*?'

He sniffed nervously. 'Yes, she was warm, enthusiastic…'

'OK, so what happened? Did she bump her head? Had a personality transplant?'

He stroked his chin, he was incredibly uncomfortable. 'Of course not. I… well, I…'

'You what?' I pushed.

'I guess you're old enough to know.'

'Old enough to know *what*?'

'I broke her heart,' he said wistfully. 'And then she changed.'

I stared at him, dumbfounded. The only way I could picture my mother with a broken heart was in an operating theatre fixing someone else's. She had never properly explained the reasons behind their separation. The court documents cited irreconcilable differences and (his) erratic behaviour. When his foolishness had started to damage her public profile, she had called it a day.

'*You* broke her heart?'

'Yes.'

'Was there another woman?'

He looked genuinely offended. 'No, I was never unfaithful. Is that what you think of me?'

'I don't know what to think! Nobody ever tells me anything! I only recently found out that you becoming a cryptozoologist played a major part in your divorce!'

He sighed at the memory. 'Destroying my career was something she never approved of...'

'Look,' I said, 'for argument's sake, let's say that you broke her heart by embarking on a debatable career, couldn't she just deal with it? Why did she have to file for divorce? Why did she have to split us up? Why did she have to *destroy* our family?'

Being able to voice the resentment I had harboured towards her for my whole life felt exceptionally liberating. My father tilted his head back and exhaled. 'She didn't destroy anything, Noah,' he said, looking me in the eyes. His voice was mellow, nearly soothing. 'It was *me*. I was the one who asked for a divorce. I was the one who... who...'

He stopped, the coward couldn't even say it! He was the one who broke our family up! My world came crashing down around me, his voice like static noise in the background.

He wet his lips. 'When I left her, she was hurt, humiliated. Her friends had warned her against marrying me, they thought I was too unreliable, but she followed her heart and did it anyway. Less than three years later, I proved everyone right. She's a proud woman, she wanted to come out of the marriage with her dignity intact, so we agreed that she would file for divorce and show the world that she had come to her senses. It was the least I could do. Since then, as you know, we haven't been the best of friends.'

I struggled to control the maelstrom of feelings that was rising within me. All these years I had blamed mum for the break-up of our family and all along it was down to him. I should have known, all the signs were there, but I had chosen to ignore them. What sort of father wouldn't try to be in his son's life? What sort of father would give up every right to his child without a fight? What sort of father would be happy with visiting his son once a year under supervision? He sensed my internal struggle and put his hand on my arm, but I angrily pushed him away. I walked back to our table in a zombie-like state. Viggo was mumbling something about parking in a restricted area and urging us to make a move unless we wanted to walk back to Valhalla. If I had known the way, I would have.

CHAPTER 16

Sitting at the bottom of the pool was exactly what I needed. With the regulator in my mouth, I didn't have to talk to anyone, and with my diving companion in the same position, I didn't have to listen to her either. Through my diving mask, I could see Hope and Viggo sitting by the edge of the pool, legs dangling in the water. He had taken the trouble to wear a new shirt and she was sipping the double shot soya latte with extra caramel that he had just bought her.

Isabelle and I were supposed to keep an eye on our SPGs to check the level of air in our tanks. Later we would learn how to empty water out of our masks without resurfacing (I wasn't convinced it was possible) and how to share air in an emergency. The latter would involve using a single regulator and she had demanded a written statement confirming that I would gargle extensively before the lesson. Hope had given us whiteboards and markers to chat underwater. I totally ignored mine, but it wasn't long before Isabelle's sweet message appeared in my field of vision. "What the hell is wrong with you?"

I shrugged, hoping she would leave me alone, but she pushed her whiteboard closer and gave me a questioning stare from behind her mask. She must have huffed, because the amount of bubbles around her suddenly increased. In spite of my aloofness, she wiped her board clear and composed another message. "What an idiot! I hope he catches a verruca."

I presumed she was referring to Viggo, whose submerged foot was casually brushing against Hope's. I was still shaken by my conversation with my father. I desperately needed a friend to talk to. I wished I could open up to Viggo, but he was too close to dad. Isabelle would have to do.

I grabbed my board. "Bad day, talk later?"

She gave me the OK sign.

By the time we inflated our BCDs and resurfaced, Viggo and Hope were checking calendars to schedule our next dive. 'No, that doesn't work either.' Hope's face was pretty even when she was frowning. 'We'll have to do another date.'

'I'd love to do another date,' replied Viggo, cheekily implying something of a more romantic nature. Hope smiled alluringly and I briefly wished I was him.

'She was talking about a dive, Viggo.' Isabelle's untimely intervention annihilated their flirty exchange. Hope excused herself and Isabelle headed for the changing rooms.

Viggo was fuming. 'What's wrong with her? I practically had a date in my pocket!'

I shrugged. His love life wasn't at the top of my priority list. He took a step closer. 'Dude, I know it's none of my business, but you seemed pretty down last night. Anything I can do?'

It felt good to be asked. 'Not exactly, you're too loyal to my father.'

He didn't contradict me. 'I have sworn loyalty to Magnus, but you're my friend. If you need me, I'm here.'

He slapped me on the shoulder, threw me off balance in the process, and ran after Hope. His peculiar choice of words kept ringing in my head. I wasn't an expert in naval employment laws, but I had never heard of deckhands swearing loyalty to their employers.

As soon as we returned to Valhalla, we joined Ariel at the study table. 'Today we'll talk about Galileo Galilei,' he boomed, 'the father of modern science and observational astronomy. Galileo had a personal instrument maker…'

With the corner of my eye, I noticed my father on deck. He briefly conferred with Viggo, who was taking care of our diving equipment, and made a beeline for us. His mere presence infuriated me, I pretended not to see him. 'Noah, do you have a minute?' he said.

I cursed inwardly, couldn't he take a hint? 'Not really, this lesson on Galileo is very interesting.'

Ariel got a quarter of an inch straighter, either out of pride or suspicion.

My father pushed his lips together. 'Fine, have it your way.' He sauntered off.

'Since you appreciate him so much,' said Ariel, 'you will be working on a special assignment on Galileo. It must include discoveries, historical setting and hand-drawn portrait.'

'Can we work on it together?' chirped Isabelle, whose idea of hell was spending time alone with Ariel. 'Galileo is my favourite scientist.'

My tutor squinted his eyes. 'Your enthusiasm is disturbing, but I would be a fool to pass on an opportunity to get rid of you for a few hours. Don't make me regret my decision.'

Isabelle and I headed for my cabin. I fired up my laptop and opened up a search page. She straightened her shorts and sat on my desk. I tried hard not to stare at her naked legs and wondered if they felt as smooth as they looked. And then I thought of Cressida's legs and my mind started to wander.

'Why are you giving Magnus attitude?' she asked, bringing me back to earth. Sometimes she could be as direct as my father. I fiddled with the mouse, the cursor moved aimlessly across the screen.

'It was him,' I said bitterly.

'Can you be a bit more specific?' she asked, painting her nails with my Tipp-Ex.

'The divorce, the break-up of my family, it was all down to him! He admitted it! I spent my whole life blaming my mother for something she didn't do. I always pictured him as a casualty of her decisions, but he never was, was he? All along, he did exactly what he wanted, when he wanted it, without giving us… without giving *me*, a second thought!'

My outpour didn't shake her one bit. She kept on painting her nails with the dedication of a medieval miniaturist. 'It's all too blurred. You need to dissect the situation. Magnus is certainly at fault, but if your mother's so innocent, why didn't she tell you the truth?'

'She didn't want people to know he had dumped her. He said he broke her heart.'

'Was there another woman?'

'No, apparently becoming a cryptozoologist was the last straw.'

'It's hardly romantic,' said the miniaturist, admiring her handiwork, 'but to end a marriage for a change of career is a bit extreme. There must be more.'

I put my head in my hands, upset, the discovery too raw for me to view things rationally. I knew I had to talk to my father sooner or later, but I wasn't ready to face him. Right now, all I could see was how he had let me, and my mother, down. 'What do you know about his company?' I asked.

'Kraken?' She produced a condescending snort. 'It's not Fortune 500 material, more like Misfortune 500. Why do you ask?'

'Because I need to know where I stand. The very little I know about him doesn't make any sense. My mother always said that he was too skint to visit, but he owns a company, lives on Valhalla and travels on private jets.'

'I wouldn't be surprised if he billed his crazy expenses back to Knut. If you want to see how well Magnus is doing in his own right, you can buy Kraken's accounts off the internet. Do you have a credit card?'

'Nope. You?'

'Yes, but it's maxed.' She drummed her freshly painted fingers on my desk. 'How badly do you want to know?'

I sensed trouble, but I didn't care. 'Badly enough. What do you have in mind?'

'I love tapping into your dark side,' she said, with a mischievous smile. 'Viggo has access to Kraken's bank account. If we can get hold of his password, we should be able to take a peek.'

'Let's do it.'

CHAPTER 17

Before concentrating on our espionage mission, we had to get our Galileo assignment out of the way. The hand-drawn portraits were proving particularly difficult. Mine resembled Santa, Isabelle's was still a work in progress, and the progress was slow. She huffed and threw her pencil to one side. 'We're wasting time. Let's print an image and trace.'

'Isn't that cheating?' I asked, while Santa glared mercilessly from the sketch pad.

She rolled her eyes and copied an image of Galileo onto a memory stick. 'We'll use the printer in the control room.'

Against my better judgment, I followed her. Half-way down the stairs, she turned and signalled to be quiet. The lab door was open, my father and Miguel were arguing.

'You haven't told him yet?' yelled Miguel

'No, but I will,' replied my father.

'Magnus, this is serious! You know we have to report any Jerusalem-related findings, no matter how small or insignificant. *Domina Nostra Hierosolymitana* falls in that category.'

'Relax! It's just a book, and we don't even have it!'

'I always stood by you, but this is going too far. It may be just a book, and it's probably going to be a dead-end, but we *must* call it in. It's our duty. You cannot let personal matters interfere with your obligations. We knew that having Noah here could potentially complicate things. Viggo and I respected your decision because you're a brother to us, but we all took an oath and we must stay true to it.'

Jesus Christ! What were they involved in? Isabelle and I exchanged confused looks. No matter how much we wanted to, we couldn't stay there much longer. My father and Miguel could have come out at any moment. The control room was about ten metres away. We removed our flip-flops and, one at a time, made a dash for it. We hadn't planned on Viggo being there. 'To what do I owe the honour?' he asked, from the comfort of his swivel chair.

'We need the printer,' said Isabelle, fanning herself with the memory stick.

'Princess, you know the rules. You're not supposed to sneak in here. Leave the memory stick, I'll print it when I'm done.'

'We'll wait,' she said, implying that the only way to get rid of her was to give her what she wanted.

Viggo's phone beeped. Whoever said that men cannot multi-task had never met Viggo Gustafsson. He composed a message with one hand and typed his computer password with the other. Doing two things at a time slowed him down and I was able to see which keys he tapped. He plugged the memory stick in and opened Galileo's jpeg. 'How many copies do you…?'

He stopped midsentence and looked over my shoulder. I was suddenly aware of my father standing behind me. I got ready to blank him, but he didn't even try to acknowledge my presence. He ordered Viggo to schedule a call with Knut and left without waiting for his reply.

My father and Ariel were practicing Krav Maga on the main deck. Dad was usually an excellent fighter, but today Ariel was destroying him.

'You're not concentrating, Magnus. Your movements are slow and predictable.' Ariel easily blocked a few more hits. 'Focus on the fight, you're too distracted. This is exactly what we feared would happen. A true warrior never loses concentration, never misses a chance to anticipate his opponent. You must channel your energy properly, be aware of your surroundings. Hello Noah.'

My father briefly turned and, wham, with one swift move Ariel had him horizontal on deck. He rested his foot against dad's throat. 'I haven't crushed a windpipe in a while.'

'Let's keep it that way,' replied my father, remaining perfectly still.

'Maybe you should try some of that chanting you do with the yoga teacher,' suggested Ariel with a hint of disgust. 'At least you won't get hurt.'

My father wasn't offended in the slightest. 'Maybe I should, I need to realign myself.'

Ariel removed his foot. 'If you keep on fighting this badly, you'll be realigned by your opponent. Bone by bone.'

My father got up and rubbed his neck, he was out of breath. A part of me took solace in the fact that our fight had shaken him so badly. He glanced in my direction. 'Want to talk?'

Each time he spoke, I couldn't escape the wave of resentment. 'No thanks,' I muttered politely, but coldly.

He nodded, hand on his hip, slightly hunched over. Ariel's hits must have been powerful ones. 'Noah?'

'Uhu?'

'I'll stop reaching out because it's not working. When you're ready to talk, come and find me. I treated you like an adult and, maybe, it was too soon. I'm sorry, I'm not used to dealing with kids.'

It was the most offensive apology I had ever heard. I watched him limp towards his cabin and reflected on my actions. All I ever wanted was the truth and yet, on the one occasion where he had been open and straightforward, I had shut him out. We were at a turning point in our relationship and my behaviour was going to be the deal breaker. If I could put aside my resentment and my anger, maybe I could get the answers I so badly needed. I inhaled and practically smelled my own fear. What I had discovered so far had created a lot of internal turmoil. Was I ready for more?

CHAPTER 18

I woke up to the sound of the waves lapping against the side of the ship. My schedule for the week had been delivered. Viggo punctually slipped an updated version under my door each Monday morning. I studied the A4 sheet, our second confined dive had been confirmed. Viggo's password was still embedded in my head. I really wanted to access his computer to find out more about Kraken, but I didn't want to land him in any trouble. Isabelle didn't share my hesitation – her copy of *Teen Vogue* had started to fall apart and she desperately needed a diversion.

My father's disappointing Krav Maga performance had resulted in extra training. In terms of abilities, Viggo was his best match so Ariel had decided that they should fight each other. Isabelle and I watched them spar on the quarter deck. They were concentrating very hard and paid us no attention. 'Let's check the computer now,' she whispered. 'They'll fight for at least forty-five minutes.'

We sneaked down below. The control room was open. Viggo never bothered to lock it because he trusted everyone on board. I sat on his swivel chair and guilt seeped into my bones.

'Don't feel bad, he'll never know.' Isabelle sounded like a self-help audio-book for hesitant criminals. 'You're just going to take a look. You deserve the truth, you know you do.'

I'm ashamed to say I didn't need much encouragement. I entered the password and the computer unlocked. Viggo hadn't bothered to log off properly – his mailbox and other applications remained open, including the web page of a small financial institution which prided itself on its ethical investments. It couldn't be a coincidence. I clicked on the client log-in button and was redirected to a menu asking for an access key. We rummaged through the drawers and uncovered a security key generator. My shaky fingers entered the code; Kraken's bank statement appeared on the screen. Isabelle produced a well-tuned builder's whistle. 'Chasing imaginary animals pays pretty well!'

'It doesn't. Look closely. The balance is healthy, but all the transactions are in debit.' I paused. 'All but one.'

She peered at the screen. Each month, a regular benefactor credited the same large sum: Knut Larsson. 'Well, at least your mother wasn't lying,' she said, 'Magnus is totally skint. Without Knut, Kraken would go bust.'

I checked the balance again. 'He's got more than enough for a few trips to London, though. First class.'

'If Knut's pulling the strings, he may not be allowed to visit you. Talking about Knut, did you figure out why he hates you so much?'

'Not yet. How are we doing for time?' I asked, nervously biting my already chewed fingernail.

She checked the timer on her phone. 'Ten minutes left.'

'Maybe we should pack it in, just to be safe.'

'Agreed.'

I locked the computer. As I pushed the swivel chair back, I accidently hit Isabelle's foot. She lost her balance and fell forward. I tried to catch her before she hit the desk and she somehow landed in my lap. We were locked in an incredibly clumsy embrace when the door flew open and Viggo walked in.

'Dude!' He clasped his hand over his eyes. 'I'm sorry, I didn't mean to… eer… interrupt?' He lowered his temporary shield, his face the picture of shock and embarrassment. 'Are you guys together or something?'

Isabelle sprang to her feet and rejected the idea so fiercely I was nearly offended. 'Of course not,' she said, oozing repulsion from every pore.

'But you were sitting on him and—'

'Do you really think I would look twice at someone like Noah? I go for more… manly types.' She gazed intensely into his eyes. He didn't get the hint and stared back vacantly. She exhaled, defeated. 'I fell in his lap.'

'That's handy,' he said with a snort.

I was now quite amused, but Isabelle didn't find the situation funny in the slightest. If Viggo believed she had feelings for me, her hopes of achieving whatever she hoped to achieve with him would be incinerated. I was an expert on unrequited love and felt I had a duty to put things right. 'She's telling the truth. She did fall in my lap completely by accident, it's all a huge misunderstanding.'

His shocked expression made way for a suspicious one. 'And what were you doing here in the first place?'

My mind went blank. I already regretted betraying his trust, but it was too late to come clean without getting into a lot of trouble. Isabelle was strangely quiet, a tell-tale sign that she was also stuck for ideas. His eyes scanned the room and focused on the computer, I freaked out. 'It's true,' I heard myself say. 'We wanted to be alone.'

'Noah!' screamed Isabelle, her mouth twisted in a revolted snare.

Viggo remained very serious. 'First of all, the control room is off limits unless I'm here.' He shifted uncomfortably. 'Secondly, I'm trying to be delicate here but… you guys make a terrible couple.'

Had we nodded with more vigour, we would have sustained whiplash injuries. 'Will you tell my father?' I asked.

He thought about it and shook his head. 'It would be too awkward, but it's not your father you have to worry about.'

'Meaning?'

'Dude, I'm not sure how Miguel would react if he knew you were snogging his only daughter in the control room.'

The colour drained from Isabelle's face. Images of my own funeral flashed before my eyes. 'Look,' said Viggo, 'I'll let you off, but you must promise that, from now on, you'll behave properly. No romance, are we clear?'

'Absolutely,' we concurred.

He pointed to the door. 'Get out. I need some time to recover. Noah, Magnus is waiting for you. Your mother has requested an urgent Skype meeting.'

'I told you I hadn't lost him,' said my father through gritted teeth as I entered his cabin. Mum's face was already on the laptop screen and, clearly, they had squeezed in a quick virtual fight. 'Here he is,' continued my father, 'Noah Larsson in the flesh. Noah, why don't you pick up a newspaper showing today's date and put it next to your face? Once your mother is satisfied that you're not a hologram, she will hopefully tell us why we had to drop everything to come and see her. I can't imagine anything being so urgent.'

I sat down in front of the camera. I wasn't sure if he was serious about the newspaper thing, but I couldn't see one. There was something slightly different about my mother, she looked... excited?

'Hello mum,' I began mechanically, 'how are you?'

'I'm fine, thank you.' She paused. She nearly smiled. 'Actually, I'm great.'

Something was horribly wrong. Happiness wasn't part of my mother's world. Her generic stance was that feelings, like volatile substances, were too unstable to deal with. She slowly lifted her left hand and positioned it in front of the camera. My father jumped up. 'Are you engaged?' he asked, completely astounded.

'I am.' The Cobra was trying really hard to smile properly. 'I know this may come as a shock, Noah, but I have been seeing someone for the last eight months, his name is Jean-Claude. Last night he went down on one knee, luckily his joints are perfectly healthy, and asked for my hand. Of course, I agreed.'

'Of course,' spluttered my father, his arms defensively crossed over his chest. 'Who wouldn't want to marry a man with perfectly healthy joints? It's the epitome of romanticism.'

He stepped back from the screen and plopped himself on his unmade bed. The news was unexpected, but I really didn't think he would sulk. Did he still harbour some feelings for her? He was the one who had asked for a divorce, so it was highly unlikely, but his reaction threw me.

'Noah, are you pleased?' asked my mother, implying that there was only one correct answer.

'Um… yeah.' It's not that I wasn't pleased, but I didn't know Jean-Claude and now he would be moving in with us. 'Congratulations.'

'Thank you. We will celebrate the wedding when we return to London. This time I will do it *properly*.'

'There was nothing *improper* about getting married in Vegas,' snorted my father in the background.

'You got married in Vegas?' I asked in disbelief. 'Like rock-stars and crazy people?'

'Magnus!' screamed mum, as if he had given away details that could compromise national security.

His very mature response amounted to a shrug that she didn't even get to see.

'It's all right, mum, you don't need to keep things from me. I'm not a child anymore…'

She gave me a look that could have killed the Grim Reaper and I decided to put my speech on hold. 'I should go,' she said, pursing her lips. 'Magnus, if you are there, don't forget that you signed a non-disclosure agreement with regard to certain aspects of our life. You *must* observe it. Goodbye Noah.'

I wondered how much stuff my father wasn't supposed to disclose. Her face vanished from the screen and I turned towards him. 'Vegas?'

The memory made him smile. 'We eloped.'

'Mum? Eloped?'

He nodded. 'Before the wedding, she gave an Elvis impersonator a lecture on the dangers of high-cholesterol.'

I burst out laughing. In spite of the recent, unsettling revelations, I had laughed more often in a short stay with him, than in a lifetime with mum. This was a perfect opportunity for rebuilding bridges. 'I'm sorry about the other night.'

'And I'm sorry I wasn't a good father.'

Typical dad, simple and straight to the point. Awkwardness lingered in the air, but I was glad we had re-established a connection. He fiddled with a paperclip, I pulled at a loose thread in my t-shirt. 'Why didn't you tell me about Knut?' I asked, as non-confrontationally as possible.

He chewed his lip. 'I was going to. I just wanted to get to know you better first, give you a chance to settle in properly. The timing of his call was unfortunate.'

'As was the timing of your date with Fiona,' I blurted. 'I had a thousand questions, dad! And you bailed out on me!'

'I needed some time. I wasn't ready to tell you about him yet. You had been in the dark for so long that I didn't think a few more days would have made a difference.'

Mum was right, he was the most insensitive man on the planet. 'Are you ready now?'

'Knut's expecting my call,' he said, opening his desk drawer and reaching for the Iridium. 'When I'm done, I'm all yours.'

CHAPTER 19

'By the time you finish your training, we'll need a new deck,' bellowed Ariel. I sprang up and rubbed my permanently sore face. Pain aside, I was in a good mood. Since clearing the air with my father, I felt a lot better. The map was back in my thoughts and I was dying to work on it. Isabelle was snubbing me for letting Viggo believe that there was something between us, but my colossal blunder was playing in her favour. To prevent our non-existent romance from blossoming, he was suddenly spending a lot more time in our company.

My father stormed on deck and raised his arm over his head. Before anyone could stop him, he had thrown the sat-phone overboard. Isabelle was right – they didn't float. 'You really have to stop doing that,' said Miguel, looking up from his paper, 'those phones are expensive.'

'Did something happen?' I managed to ask, before being horizontal again.

My father helped me up and cast a worried eye over the boards. 'Knut's coming over tomorrow.'

My breath got shallower. 'What? Why?'

'He's interested in the *Nuestra Señora* map.'

'Like the Russians?'

'Like the Russians.' He exhaled a curse. 'We should get Valhalla ready.'

'How many cabins do you need?' asked Viggo.

'Three. One for Knut and two for his security guards. Get Noah and Isabelle to help.'

I swallowed. 'Am I going to be a problem?'

'No,' said my father, 'he knows you're here.'

'He just doesn't want me around,' I added bluntly.

He patted me on the back of the head. 'Don't take it personally.'

I wasn't sure how else to take it.

Back home I was expected to look after my room according to my mother's strict standards, therefore I prepared the cabin for Knut's security guard in record time. I popped in next door. Isabelle was entangled in a sheet, trying to figure out the purpose of the fitted corners. 'I have never made a bed before,' she said, giving me an imploring look.

I freed her, stretched the sheet across the bed and tucked a fitted corner under the mattress. 'Have you ever met Knut?'

'A few times.' She sensed my agitation. 'Relax, we won't see him much. He'll spend all his time with Magnus.'

I tucked the second corner. 'Why do you think he's interested in the map?'

'He's big on ancient stuff. Sometimes he acquires artefacts to donate to museums and sometimes he adds them to his private collection. He's very keen on some of the crusades.'

I tucked in the last two corners. 'Just some?'

'He can't be that concerned with the first – Magnus always says that anything pre-1119 keeps Knut off his back.'

'1119?'

'Yeah, like the tattoos.'

I frowned. 'Which tattoos?'

She unfolded the top sheet. 'Magnus has a super-tiny *MCXIX* inked on the inside of his forearm. You probably never saw it because it's covered by all the bracelets. My dad's got one too, next to his vermillion cross, but without a machete to hack away at his chest hair you'll never see either of them.'

'That's 1119 in Roman numerals,' I said, making a mental note about Miguel's cross tattoo.

'Duh!' she replied from under the sheet. 'I challenged them about the matching *MCXIX* tattoos. They claim it was the name of their secret fraternity at university, but I don't buy it. Fraternities are an American thing and they both studied at Cambridge. Also, fraternities' names are usually made up of Greek letters, not Roman numerals. I've googled this mysterious *MCXIX* fraternity and nothing came up.'

'If the fraternity was secret, it wouldn't be publicised.'

She rolled her eyes. 'Oh God! You sound just like them!'

Viggo barged in, his tense demeanour relaxed when he saw that Isabelle and I were at opposite ends of the cabin. 'I'm picking up Knut tomorrow morning,' he announced. 'I'll leave early, so you'll have to make your own breakfast.'

The knot in my stomach tightened. I was running out of time, I had to find out why my grandfather hated me so much.

My father had a rare gift for disappearing when I needed him the most: this time, he had gone for a swim. Ariel, arms crossed over his chest, was standing by the rope ladder dangling over the side of Valhalla, Viggo was removing his t-shirt. 'Why didn't he wait for me?' he asked, slightly resentful.

'He did,' replied Ariel, 'but you were texting a novel and he wanted to go before Christmas. He dares you to catch up.'

'I can take it easy then,' said Viggo with a wicked smile, before twist-diving into the water. He covered an incredibly long distance in a very short time.

I couldn't get my father's tattoo out of my head. While I waited for them to return, I did an internet search on 1119. It had been a busy year, but I couldn't discern which particular event, if any, had left its mark on my father. A series of weary huffs announced Isabelle's arrival. I wondered what sort of bed she had made, but it would be for Knut's security guard to find out. 'I feel like Hercules after his ten labours,' she said.

'Twelve labours,' corrected Ariel. 'Unlike you, he didn't cut corners.'

'I never cut…'

Her words lingered in the air, Viggo had flung his athletic frame on deck, leaving her completely thunderstruck. He could have passed for a Greek God: his hair was pushed back, highlighting a bone structure worthy of a fashion model and his sculpted body, covered in water droplets, glinted in the sun. He shook his hair to get rid of excess water and thoroughly sprayed her, but she was too stunned to complain. My father climbed on board next. Viggo, hands on his hips, slapped him with a victorious grin. 'I beat you.' He panted. 'Again.'

My father panted back. 'I'm twice your age.'

'I'll get you a new hip for your birthday. Then you'll have no excuses.'

My father exploded in a boisterous laugh and I wondered if the two of us would ever reach that level of camaraderie. He tied a towel around his waist and brushed past me on his way to his cabin. 'Come. It's time.'

I followed him.

'This is Knut,' said my father, peeling a yellowed photo off the wall and tapping his index finger in the centre. 'The picture's a bit old, but he looks very much the same. Add a few more lines and take away some hair.'

I studied the portrait. It had been taken somewhere on a ski slope and my stern grandfather was surrounded by two young men whose grins could have circled the earth. I immediately recognised a much younger and clean-shaven version of my father. The second guy was hugging a Burton snowboard the way I was planning to hug my girlfriend – if I ever got one. I had never met him, but his familiar features left no doubt as to who he was: the other family member who had shunned my existence for no apparent reason. 'Is this your big brother?' I asked, pointing at the snowboard's boyfriend.

'Yeah, that's Fredrik. Did your mother say anything about him?'

'Only that he's an idiot.'

He chuckled. 'He can be. But most of the time he's a great guy. He bought you a snowboard before you were even born. He was dying to take you on the slopes.'

'Well, clearly, he got a better offer,' I said, trying to sound detached and coming across as petulant. 'I've been living at the same address for over thirteen years and he never showed up.'

His face darkened. 'After the accident, he had a hard time adjusting.'

I knew I had put my foot in it, I just wasn't sure how deep. 'Mum never mentioned any accidents...'

'When you were little, Fredrik was in a serious car crash and sustained a spinal cord injury. He can't walk anymore, let alone snowboard.' He paused. 'The recovery wasn't easy. By the time he got better, your mother and I were in the final stages of our divorce. She had taken you back to England and we were barely on speaking terms. He thought it best to stay out of it.'

'Where is he now?'

He shrugged. 'Not sure, he's a busy man, he didn't let his disability hold him back. He sits on the board of Alvastra and will take the reins from Knut when the time comes. Don't feel sorry for him, he hates that. He's a Larsson, he's a fighter.' He took the photo back. 'Look, I know that having Knut around is going to be a bit weird, but ride it out, he won't stay long.'

The cuckoo clock emitted a series of grating noises, the poor bird was trying to scratch his way out. My father punched it a couple of times and the cuckoo went quiet.

'Why does he hate me so much?' I asked, annoyed by the quaver in my voice.

'Knut doesn't hate you. Not at all.'

'He certainly doesn't love me,' I snorted.

As usual he opened his mouth to say something, but didn't utter a single word. He put both hands on my shoulders. 'It's complicated.'

'Tell me about it!'

He glided over my sarcasm. 'I will, but what I'm about to say isn't easy and must stay strictly between us. Not a word to your mother. Do I have your promise?'

Given his obsession for this promise business, I complied. 'Fredrik's crash wasn't an accident,' he began. A shiver ran down my spine. 'The expert we hired to go over the remains of his car discovered a remotely operated device that had caused the failure of the braking system. It was triggered when Fredrik was travelling at top speed on the motorway. It was an attempt on his life, Noah. Someone wanted him dead.'

The hair at the back at my neck stood straight, my father rubbed his eyes. He wasn't crying, but recalling the accident had a profound effect on him.

'Do you know who did it?' I asked.

He shook his head. 'Our private investigators didn't come up with anything. I don't have to tell you how badly this shook my family, most of all Knut.'

The adjective knifed through me: *his* family, not *ours*.

'To this day,' he continued, 'he considers himself responsible for what happened to Fredrik. Not being able to protect him nearly destroyed him. It was a very dark time, Noah, and Knut made some drastic adjustments to his life. Believe me, he never hated you, but he felt that the less contact he had with you, the safer you were.'

I let his words sink in. Was Knut's hostile attitude truly a precautionary measure? Did he really believe that ignoring my existence would keep me safer? And from what? His paranoid stance could have explained why my father had gone to such lengths to keep my presence hidden. In a way, thinking that Knut hated me, was much more straightforward.

Revelations aside, I felt a sense of relief. My father had been open and honest. He pushed his feet into his Converse trainers and picked up a t-shirt from the floor. 'There's somewhere I need to be. I'll see you later.'

He slammed the door behind him and left me alone in his cabin. No-one, apart from Viggo, enjoyed the same right. Was he beginning to trust me or had he left in a hurry to dodge all my other questions?

CHAPTER 20

'Did someone harvest your brain last night?' boomed Ariel, unrolling a physical map of Scandinavia in my face. Concentrating on the geography lesson was harder than usual – I hadn't slept a wink, too nervous about meeting Knut.

'Um… no,' I replied, considering his question for a second too long.

He drummed his lethal fingers on the Baltic Sea. 'Prove it. What did I just say?'

I tried to push Knut out of my head. He didn't budge. 'Something about Norway being the second least populated country in Europe.'

'Correct,' said Ariel. 'Whenever you meet Viggo you should count yourself lucky. He may have grown up in Sweden, but he's half-Norwegian, therefore he's a rare sight.'

The description was certainly befitting. I wondered if exercising with Viggo on a regular basis would have turned me into a rare sight too. Ariel asked us to locate Bergen, Viggo's birthplace, on the map. Isabelle's geography was as bad as my algebra: she began her search for Bergen by going over Denmark with a fine-toothed comb. The boards creaked under my father's steps. He had made an effort with his appearance. His hair was tied back, his goatee freshly braided and he had even bothered to lace up his trainers. His right hand was in the air, fingers at full stretch. Ariel read his sign, rolled up the map and tied an elastic band around it. 'Your next assignment will be a project on Norway. It must include a defence plan in case of an attack from Finland. Knut will be here in five minutes, get in position.'

Nobody had warned me we would be playing army, but five minutes later we were standing on the main deck, arranged over three rows – a mini-military parade awaiting the arrival of a minor king. My father and Miguel, arms flat at their sides, were at the front. Ariel was right behind them, Isabelle and I had been relegated to third row and instructed to be quiet until spoken to. The formation wasn't accidental, we were organised in order of importance and I didn't rank high.

Steps echoed on the metal gangway, each thud bringing my grandfather a little bit closer. He stepped on deck: tall, lean, light beige chino trousers, white linen shirt and a wide-brimmed straw hat that reminded me of an upside-down nest. He had brought his own portable fort, two gargantuan security guards who may have been distant cousins of the Minotaur. Viggo lined up next to Ariel. Knut acknowledged us with a brief nod. The adults bowed their heads in return. Shortly afterwards, the military ranks were broken and Knut gave my father a warm hug. 'Magnus, it has been a long time.'

His voice commanded authority, but I didn't detect the slightest hint of arrogance. My father returned the hug. 'It has, *pappa.*'

Knut gestured towards his security guards. 'I'm sure you remember Moshe and Gunnar.'

Seriously? A security guard called Gunnar? The size of Knut's guards confirmed my theory, the man was paranoid about safety. Moshe was Ariel's spitting image – big, bald and dangerous to know; Gunnar's bulging biceps stretched the short sleeves of his shirt to breaking point. The guards were dressed smartly and neither made an effort to remove their sunglasses. Their earpieces were discreet, but noticeable. Gunnar stepped forward and spoke to the emptiness in front of him. 'We need to sanitise the ship.'

'There's no need,' said my father. 'She's got a brand-new security system.'

'We need to sanitise the ship,' repeated Gunnar.

'Go ahead,' said my father, 'but you're wasting your time.'

Gunnar vanished downstairs, Moshe handed Ariel an earpiece. 'Stay with Mr Larsson while we complete the inspection.'

Ariel stepped aside and left me totally exposed. I could feel Knut's eyes on me and decided that staring at my feet wouldn't have made a great first impression. I gingerly lifted my head. Yep, Knut was staring at me with unsettling intensity. My father gave him a terse smile which Knut didn't return. 'He shouldn't be here, Magnus,' he said. Not a good start. He studied me for another couple of minutes. 'He's got something of Fredrik.'

'He does,' agreed my father, 'but he's a lot smarter.'

Knut chuckled at the joke, but quickly returned to his sombre mode. 'We'll talk about this later.'

It didn't bode well, he wanted me off Valhalla and was talking as if I wasn't there. I pretended to look uninterested, but inside I was hurting big time. I was flabbergasted when a wrinkly hand appeared in my field of vision. I removed my arm from behind my back and reached to shake it. His grip was firm and stronger than I expected from a man his age. 'Knut Larsson,' he said, without betraying any emotions.

'Noah,' I replied softly.

'You may call me Knut,' he said formally. 'Or grandfather, if you so wish.'

He calmly retrieved his hand and, unexpectedly, gave my father a light pat on his shoulder. This time, they exchanged the briefest smiles. I had been under the impression that there was no love lost between them, but their body language told a different story. Despite their seemingly perennial divergence of opinions, they appeared to have a strong bond.

'If Valhalla is as tight as you say, it shouldn't take Moshe and Gunnar long to give her the all clear,' said Knut, making his way towards the study table and taking Ariel's chair. My tutor followed him like a shadow, but Knut didn't seem to notice his presence. Miguel and Isabelle excused themselves and I made to leave too, but my father pushed me down into an empty chair. Viggo, who I hadn't even noticed leaving, reappeared carrying a tray laden with ornate china cups and a steamy tea pot. He was evidently familiar with Knut's habits because my grandfather hadn't asked for anything. Small talk wasn't Knut's forte either. 'Where's the map?' he said, airing himself with his straw nest.

'As soon as your Rottweilers clear Valhalla, I'll take you to it,' answered my father. 'I'm surprised by your interest, though, it's not the type of thing you usually go for.'

Knut filled his cup with the dark brew, dropped a sliced lemon in it and glanced uncomfortably in my direction.

'Don't worry,' said my father. 'Noah's been involved with the map since day one, it's our little project.'

'As I mentioned earlier, we will discuss later, in private, whether Noah can stay.' Knut sounded quite annoyed at having to repeat himself. 'And I'm afraid you will have to put your little project on hold. At least for the time being.'

'That could be difficult, I promised Noah we'd work on it together.'

Knut stiffened. 'You did what?'

'I promised,' confirmed my father unperturbed. 'And you know that a promise cannot—'

'I'm totally aware of what a promise entails,' said Knut, smashing the cup on its saucer. The expensive looking china produced a refined clink of protest. 'Noah, leave us.'

I made to stand, but my father stopped me. 'If it's about the map, he should stay.'

'He was about to leave. Unlike you, he can do as he's told,' said my grandfather frostily. He then turned towards me. 'Please, Noah, sit. Since your father is being so obstructive, we'll have a nice talk about the weather.'

My father didn't take kindly to the wry comment. 'You, of all people, cannot accuse me of—'

'I'd love to talk about the weather,' said Viggo, topping up Knut's cup. 'Nassau is very humid, but the sea and the sand certainly make up for it. Having said that, I really do miss those nice, crisp Swedish winter days. I also miss my horse, he's an Arabian.'

His remarks were, as usual, the embodiment of idiocy, but served their purpose and prevented my father and Knut from exchanging harsh words. Gunnar and Moshe returned and reported to their boss. 'Everything's in order, sir. We have swept your cabin and all communal areas for bugging devices. The ship is clear. For health and safety reasons, I would advise caution when entering Magnus's cabin.'

My father was very slightly embarrassed, but stoically held Knut's scolding gaze.

'Sir,' continued Gunnar, 'we cannot guarantee any privacy above deck. I would suggest holding any sensitive conversations in a more secure environment. If you can let us know in advance which room you are going to use, we'll take the necessary precautions.'

'Very well.' Knut stood up. 'We'll meet in the main lounge in one hour. Magnus, bring the map.'

Moshe escorted Knut downstairs and Gunnar walked straight up to Viggo. 'Who did you hire to make my bed? A trained monkey?'

The carbon fibre kayak glided over the crystal-clear waters. To keep me out of Knut's way, Viggo had taken me on a surprise trip. When we were far enough from Valhalla, we took turns diving in. Viggo was an excellent swimmer – he had been part of his high-school's swim squad and still trained every day before breakfast. 'I'm a mermaid-dude,' he said, diving under the kayak and emerging at the other side. 'I can stay under for a long time. All I have to do is learn to sing and then I'll woo the ladies with my melodic voice.'

I laughed, my gaze fell on his cross tattoo. It was a smallish design, three by three centimetres, and the colouring was still bright. 'Where did you get your inking done?' I asked with a certain aplomb, not that I had ever set foot in a tattoo parlour.

'In Cyprus, during a holiday.'

'Did it hurt?'

'Dude, imagine a hedgehog rolling back and forth on your shoulder, he finally leaves, you breathe a sigh of relief, and the hedgehog comes back and rolls some more!'

'How did you choose the design?' I asked between chuckles.

His head bobbed among the waves. 'It sounds crazy, but I didn't choose it. It chose me.'

I raised my eyebrows, only Viggo could have a mystical experience in a tattoo parlour. 'My father has the exact same design,' I said, struggling not to imply too much.

An inscrutable expression came over him. He kept on bobbing up and down and managed to shrug his shoulders while treading water. 'Isn't that a funny coincidence?' His simplistic answer deserved an applause. He swam closer and held onto the side of the kayak. 'Can you keep a secret?'

I leaned over, optimistically hoping that he would shed some light on the curious case of double-inking. I overbalanced and nearly capsized. He pushed me back and prevented me from falling in the water. 'Hope texted,' he said. A grin spread over his face. 'She's free tomorrow evening. I know the timing sucks, with Knut being here and everything, but I really hope I can get the night off. I could take her somewhere romantic, like that buffet we went to the other night. I have a discount coupon, we can get twenty percent off if we go early. I may need to bring my own candle, though, I didn't see any when we went,' he added pensively.

His ideas on how to make a girl feel special certainly didn't conform to the usual standards. I wasn't an expert on romantic dinners, but I was pretty sure that cheap buffets aimed at the tourist trade didn't qualify as such. He heaved himself onto the kayak. 'You can't say anything to Isabelle. I stole the coupon from one of her magazines. I know you two are, ahem, close, but we can keep dude stuff between us, right?'

I don't know how girls do it, but you speak of them and they appear out of nowhere. Isabelle was steering a jet ski in our direction. She expertly carved the water and parked next to our wobbly kayak. She was distressed, agitated, and hadn't even bothered wearing a life-vest. 'Guys, I overheard the most incredible conversation between Magnus and Knut,' she panted.

Viggo hooked the jet ski with his arm to keep it close. 'You shouldn't eavesdrop.'

'It wasn't intentional.' For a change, she sounded sincere. 'They were fighting and—'

Viggo dismissed her protests with a wave of his hand. 'I'm sorry, I'll have to tell your father.'

'But—'

'Make space,' he said, climbing on the jet ski and getting hold of the handlebar. 'I'm taking you back to Valhalla. Dude, are you OK to start rowing on your own? I'll come back for you.'

'Yeah, sure.'

I was so stunned by his overreaction that I forgot to check how far we'd come. Isabelle eavesdropping wasn't big news, but each time Knut was involved, everything got blown out of proportion. 'Hold me tight,' he said to Isabelle, positioning his thumb on the green button that would start the jet ski. His command went unanswered, she was spellbound by his trapezius muscle. Viggo pushed his hair back. In preparation for Knut's visit he had given himself a DIY haircut. The difference was barely noticeable, it was only slightly shorter. Isabelle pushed her nose closer to the trapezius muscle, then turned in my direction and pointed to the nape of his neck. His self-inflicted haircut had uncovered a minuscule tattoo. I could just about make it out: MCXIX. I blinked, I wasn't dreaming, it was definitely there. Viggo, completely unaware that his neck was generating so much interest, was growing impatient. 'C'mon Isabelle, hold me tight.'

She clumsily wrapped her arms around his torso. He glanced over his shoulder. 'Unless you want to fly off this thing, you'll have to hold me a hell of a lot tighter. Pretend I'm your boyfriend.'

She probably did it on regular basis! She tightened her embrace and they disappeared into the distance. I followed their foam trail, unable to put the matching tattoos out of my head.

CHAPTER 22

Viggo did not come back for me. I reached Valhalla, completely wiped out, and shouted for someone to help. Ariel leaned over the gunwale. 'Oh Romeo, Romeo. Wherefore art thou Romeo,' he droned, without a hint of passion, before lowering the rope ladder. I secured the kayak to one of the purpose-built hooks and climbed towards my bald and burly Juliet.

Viggo jogged towards me and handed me a towel. 'Sorry I didn't come back for you, Magnus needed me.'

I gestured towards Isabelle sulking on the gunwale. 'Is she OK?'

He gave me a noncommittal shrug. On a scale of one to ten, his current interest in her plight was minus twenty. 'Miguel dealt with her, it turned out she was exaggerating as usual and hadn't heard much. You should probably change into dry clothes, the map meeting starts in fifteen minutes and Knut doesn't like to be kept waiting.'

'Am I invited?' I asked, dumbfounded. 'Did Knut say so?'

He winked and smiled. Without giving sulking Isabelle a second thought, I dived into the shower and rinsed the salt off my skin. Five minutes later, my hair barely dry, I was standing outside the main lounge. Gunnar ran a metal detector over me and cleared me to enter. Aside from my father and Isabelle, who wasn't supposed to attend anyway, everyone was already there, including Knut. Pathetic as it sounds, I was chuffed when he nodded in my direction.

The near-religious silence was shattered by a concert of angry beeps coming from the corridor. Viggo and Miguel stifled smiles. Outside, Gunnar had the nerve to ask my father if he had anything metallic on him. Knut exhaled and spoke loudly enough for Gunnar to hear him. 'I take it Magnus has graced us with his presence?'

'Affirmative, sir, but he's covered in metallic objects,' came the proficient reply.

'Objects!' My father snorted. 'They're bracelets.'

'In my opinion they do not constitute a threat, sir,' advised Gunnar. 'Should he remove them all or would you rather start your meeting on time?'

Knut sighed with resignation. 'If he has the scroll, let him through.'

My father entered with the plastic container where we usually kept the breakfast biscuits. It was packed with surgical gloves, magnifying glasses and crumbs. The tube with the *Nuestra Señora* map was tucked under his arm. He threw the gloves in Knut's direction. My grandfather shook some crumbs off and slipped them on. The rimless reading glasses went from his breast pocket to his nose. He unrolled the map.

'Tell me everything,' he demanded, without taking his eyes off the scroll. My father complied, but conveniently failed to mention the shooting in downtown Nassau or the fact that we were aboard Valhalla when the Russians came. The played-down version of the burglary didn't sit well with Knut. 'Get Gunnar to run the facial recognition software on the images of the burglars,' he said. 'I want to know if they are linked to Dragomirov.'

I knew better than to ask for clarifications. My father must have gone out on a limb to have me present and I wanted to see how these meetings played out before making any contributions.

Knut kept on studying the image. 'There isn't much detail. Are you positive about the dating?'

'My team is one hundred percent reliable,' said Miguel.

'And are there absolutely no leads on the pages in Arabic mentioned by the monks?' asked Knut.

My father shook his head. 'Not unless we find out who these Russians are and go after them, but it will involve risks.'

He threw a nervous glance in my direction.

'If the facial recognition software identifies them, we *will* go after the Russians. I want those pages.' Knut focused on my father and Miguel. 'If we get a lead, you will have to find a secure location for your children, preferably in a European boarding school, or I will be forced to assign the task to another team.'

'But *we* found the map!' protested my father. 'And I promised Noah we'd work on it together.'

Knut shot him a silencing look. 'I'm aware of that, but tracking the Russians with minors in tow would be too dangerous. I won't allow it.'

'Then you'd better take me off the project,' said my father defiantly. 'I'm staying with Noah.'

Knut clasped his hands. 'Even if it means missing out on the twelfth ring?'

My father's resolve melted like an ice-cube in the sun. 'You never said this was about the twelfth ring.'

'I have reason to believe that the map may lead to it,' said Knut, removing his reading glasses and rubbing the bridge of his nose. 'The ring's last sighting was recorded in 1318, when the owner boarded a ship from Valencia to Cyprus. Unfortunately, the ship never made it to its destination and vanished somewhere along the way, most likely at the bottom of the sea.'

'I've heard the story a million times,' said my father dismissively. 'But unless you know something I don't, I can't see a connection with our map.'

A fleeting smile crossed Knut's thin lips. 'I do know something you don't, Magnus: the ship was called *Nuestra Señora*.' He paused for effect and went in for the kill. 'And I also know that the ring's owner happened to be fluent in Arabic. In all likelihood, he's the author of the missing pages.'

My father lit up like a Christmas tree. This was the type of adventure he lived for. Our eyes met and his expression changed to a downcast one: I was in his way.

'What's so special about this ring?' I asked, breaking my silence. If I was being traded for a medieval trinket, I wanted to know what it was.

All eyes were on Knut. He took a while to answer. 'It is an extremely rare medieval piece. Only a handful were forged. It entitles the bearer to certain…' he hesitated, looking for a vague enough word, 'certain rights. It's part of a set of twelve and I happen to have the other pieces. I cannot go into specifics, but it would be disastrous if the twelfth ring ended up in the wrong hands.'

'What rights—?'

He cut me off. 'Magnus, the Russians have the Arabic pages, but not the map, correct?'

'Correct.'

'Could they have acquired a copy?' continued Knut, making notes on a legal pad.

'I can't see how. The original is still in our possession.'

'Did they ever refer to the ring in the security footage?'

'No, but very few people know about it. I would work under the assumption that they're after the map for other reasons.'

'You're becoming complacent,' said Knut, sternly. 'It is a grave error.'

My father dropped his gaze. Knut made a few more notes and put the pen down. 'Until we hear from Gunnar, the meeting is adjourned. Dismissed.'

CHAPTER 23

Gunnar's military computer came in a sturdy case that could withstand an overweight T-rex on a sugar rush stomping on it. I tried to picture Gunnar on a sugar rush and scared myself to death. Viggo handed him a memory stick with the pictures of Yuri and Vladimir. Gunnar uploaded the files and selected a number of databases from a list. I managed to read *Interpol*, but the screen changed before I could make out any of the others. An emerald green progress bar appeared in the middle of the screen, moving slower than a drowsy snail. 'It will take a while,' barked Gunnar the genius. 'Lock the control room when you leave.'

Viggo failed to answer, too busy licking his fingertips and running them along his eyebrows to smooth them down. This ape-like grooming routine was a sure sign that Hope was on her way. I was also looking forward to seeing her, the meeting had left me pretty unsettled and I yearned for a diversion. If my father decided to go after this mysterious ring, I would be shipped off to a boarding school until mum's return. I doubted she would leave her newly-acquired fiancée behind and come back to London to make me feel better. It suddenly hit me that their marriage could make my life ten times worse. What if Jean-Claude and I didn't get along? What if they decided to have a baby? I paled at the thought.

'Dude, you look a bit off colour. I heard of these Peruvian vampire mosquitos that drain humans of their blood. Do you have any bites?'

Viggo's improbable diagnosis forced me to focus on the present. 'I have a lot on my mind. What time is Hope coming?'

He stretched and yawned. I envied his near-constant state of relaxation. 'Two hours.'

He began rummaging through the desk drawers. 'What are you after?' I asked.

'Sticky tape. To wrap Hope's gift. If Gunnar's evil machine doesn't come up with anything, my date tomorrow could be going ahead.'

'What did you get her?'

He frowned, as if I was a hopeless imbecile. 'The Mexican cardigan, dude! The one Brother Cristobal gave us.'

This was going to be a killer date: cheap buffet, bring-your-own-candle, stolen coupon and a moth-infested cardigan. Viggo kept on digging for the sticky tape and, in my humble opinion, for his own grave. I wanted to tell him, but felt utterly underqualified. My only catastrophic date so far consisted of a movie and burger with Emily Lunn – she had brought her sister along and I ended up paying for both. Financially and romantically it had been a total disaster. And the movie had been a major letdown too. 'I'd better find Isabelle,' I said. 'We need to get cracking on our Norway project.'

Viggo made a face. He still believed that we fancied each other and didn't relish the idea of the two of us spending time alone. 'Dude, I'll have to come and check on you. Take it as a friendly warning.'

'There's no need,' I said, aware that she'd rather die than succumb to my charms, 'but if you have to, we'll be in my cabin.'

'Make sure you leave the door open,' he cautioned. 'I know you mean well, but love and hormones work in mysterious ways.'

The Scandinavia map was stretched across my desk; Isabelle's attention was lost in the freezing Norwegian waters. I waved my hand in front of her face. 'Earth to Isabelle, can you hear me?'

She threw a furtive glance at the empty corridor. 'We need somewhere private.'

I paled, the impossible had happened! Fed up with Viggo's lack of interest, she was focussing her attentions on me. 'You're a very nice girl,' I began, exceptionally awkwardly. She arched her perfectly plucked eyebrows. Had I been too stingy with words? I nervously wet my lips and mustered all my courage, ready for my first ever performance of letting someone so good looking down gently. 'You're very pretty and, sometimes, I quite… like you but… not that way.'

At least I didn't think so, I honestly wasn't too sure anymore.

'Oh-my-God,' she said disdainfully, 'it's contagious. You're officially as moronic as Viggo, but only half as good-looking.'

I wasn't sure how to react. All in all, being half as good-looking as Viggo wasn't too bad, in fact, it was nearly a compliment. Isabelle, who had never before come so close to admitting that she found him attractive, regretted her slip up. 'It was meant as a joke, of course,' she said.

'Of course,' I agreed, reinforcing her theory that my intelligence was below average.

Satisfied by my dumbness, she carried on. 'I mean it, Noah, we've got to talk. It's important.' She shut the door, pulled her chair closer to mine and put her hand on my wrist. I didn't pull away and felt a bit guilty for enjoying her touch. 'The conversation I heard between Magnus and Knut was about you. And they also talked about a secret organisation they're part of.'

'Alvastra?'

The stupidity of my answer confirmed that she could be horribly right, I was morphing into my father's aide.

'No, idiot! A *secret* organisation—'

The flimsy door swung open and framed a frustrated Viggo. 'Guys, we had an agreement!'

'There's nothing going on,' I said, painfully aware of how ambiguous things looked.

'Dude, she's still holding your hand!' he said crossly. Isabelle let go of my wrist as if it was on fire. He squeezed himself in the cabin, sat in a squatting position and lowered his voice a notch. 'Look, personally, I don't have anything against young love—'

'*Young* love?' screeched Isabelle. His choice of adjective had hit a raw nerve. She didn't see their four-year gap as an obstacle, but he clearly perceived it as a lifetime. 'You should stop treating us like children, you're not that much older than us.'

'I'm nineteen!'

She huffed. 'Not exactly Methuselah!'

'Whatever, this isn't about my age. Guys, nothing can happen between you on my watch. I know you're bored, but there must be something else you can do with your time. When Knut's gone, I'll speak to your dads and see if I can get you out a bit more. How about that?'

For Isabelle it was a win-win situation, she would get off Valhalla more often and spend extra time with Viggo. 'Fine,' she said, throwing me a fairly credible longing look. 'We'll behave. I'll do my best to fend off Noah's persistent advances.'

'Persistent advances?' he echoed, positively impressed. 'Dude, I didn't know you had it in you!'

'Me neither,' I muttered.

CHAPTER 24

When Hope arrived, Gunnar turned his head by a whole two degrees. We were supposed to complete our second confined dive but, with Knut on board, my father couldn't spare anyone to baby-sit us by the hotel pool. Viggo had come up with an ingenious solution. Valhalla was equipped with its own shark cage – he would lower it into the pristine Caribbean waters and we would practise within the safety of its bars. Gunnar's barely-detectable head-turn hadn't escaped his notice and he was now in a foul mood. While Isabelle and I assembled our diving kits, they had an antagonistic exchange in their native Swedish during which, I presume, they both laid claim to Hope. I took advantage of their altercation and shuffled closer to Isabelle. 'What else did my father and Knut say?' I whispered.

She glanced over her shoulder, the Nordic barking was in full swing. 'Knut doesn't want you around because he fears for your safety,' she said, unaware that she was feeding me old news. 'The secret organisation they're part of has existed for hundreds of years and follows a strict chain of command. They never mentioned it by name, but Knut is the highest authority and your father reports to him.'

'It ties in with what we've seen so far.'

She pushed her face closer. 'Knut wanted you off Valhalla as soon as possible. When Magnus refused, he pulled rank.'

'He what?'

'You heard. He *ordered* Magnus to ship you back to London.'

'I take it my father stood up to him. I mean… I'm still here.'

'That's the thing: he didn't. They're taking this hierarchy thing incredibly seriously – Magnus *begged* him to let you stay.'

'My father? Begging?'

'Yeah, I've known him a long time and I have never, ever, heard him plead with anyone before. And I've listened in on thousands of conversations,' she added, as if she was applying for a phone tapping job at MI6. 'Does the name Fredrik mean anything to you?'

I placed my mask over my head. 'He's my uncle. Why?'

'His name kept popping up. He used to be in the secret organisation too. I think Magnus took his place. Is he dead or something?'

'No, but he was involved in a major accident the year my parents divorced.'

'The *same* year? And it didn't strike you as suspicious?'

Hope's voice cut our conversation short. 'If you're done with your pre-dive safety checks, stand on the gunwale and give me a "giant stride" water entry.'

Isabelle went first. I didn't remember her double-checking my gear, but I stuck the regulator in my mouth, dangled my leg over the side of Valhalla and jumped. I panicked the moment I hit the waves: I was sinking too fast. I should have inflated my BCD to compensate, but I coiled around Isabelle instead and she tried her best to keep me afloat. Viggo leaned overboard in that precise moment and completely misread the scene. None of the words he said contained more than four letters. He spent the rest of the day watching us like a hawk.

The following morning, I woke up later than usual. My alarm clock lay in the middle of the cabin, where I had catapulted it two hours earlier in an attempt to shut it off. I dragged myself to the bathroom and shuddered at my own reflection. The shadows under my eyes could have sheltered a caravan of Bedouins. I had been up most of the night googling Fredrik. I hadn't discovered much, but my parents had filed for divorce exactly three months after his accident. Could Isabelle be right? Were the accident and the divorce somehow related? Had my father truly replaced Fredrik in the Swedish mafia – or whatever mysterious organisation they were part of? I splashed water over my face, got dressed and yawned all the way to the kitchen. A jubilant Viggo was loading the dishwasher. 'Knut's leaving this afternoon,' he announced. 'The facial recognition software didn't generate any hits.'

Checking for fingerprints was pointless, the Russians had never removed their gloves. Viggo rubbed his hands in anticipation. 'Dude, the timing's perfect. With Knut gone, I should be able to get the night off.'

I poured myself a glass of milk. 'What happens with the map?'

'The original will be stored in a secure facility, but Knut has agreed to leave a copy for you and Magnus to work on as a side project. I doubt you'll be making any progress without the Arabic pages, but if you come up with anything, you'll have to notify him immediately.'

'Typical,' I snorted, 'we reach a dead-end and he lets me back in.'

I wasn't proud of it, but I wished I could find the ring just to rub it in my grandfather's stern face. I tried to focus on the positive: with Knut gone, everything could have gone back to normal – whatever normal was. An unknown man walked in and helped himself to the filtered coffee jug. I did a double-take, I had never seen my father in a suit. I was amazed he owned one. Viggo jumped at the chance to tease him. 'Bank loan or bail hearing?'

My father chuckled. 'Cut it out, I'm having lunch downtown with Knut and Miguel. It's a jacket and tie venue.'

'Am I still driving Knut to the airport later?' asked Viggo.

My father nodded. 'I also need you to stop by the dive shop, my new speargun has arrived.'

'Can I have the night off afterwards?'

'Hope?' asked my father. Viggo's grin confirmed the obvious. 'Fine, but you've got to be back in time to cook us breakfast.'

CHAPTER 25

The majority of Gunnar and Moshe's suitcases were hard-shelled and I suspected they contained items that were not usually seen (or even allowed) on commercial flights. I had just found out that Knut would be going directly to the airport without coming back to Valhalla. Officially, the lunch was running late, but I had a feeling that my grandfather wanted to avoid saying goodbye. Viggo would pick him up from the restaurant and drive him to his waiting plane. I loaded the last suitcase in the minivan and wiped some sweat off my face. 'Thanks for helping out, dude,' said Viggo. He climbed into the van and retrieved something from the glove compartment. 'I've wrapped Hope's present, check it out.'

For a moment, I wished I was blind. He had picked the worst gift paper in the world: it was covered in tired lilac flowers and the way they bent to follow the soft shape of the cardigan made them look wilted. He chucked the horrid bundle on the passenger seat, got the engine revving and gave me a fist bump. 'Wish me luck for tonight.'

Judging by his gift, he needed it.

Girls have an overdeveloped sixth sense. I had just started thinking about Isabelle, when she stormed into my cabin and announced that she had reached an epiphany. I indulged her, partly because I was curious, partly because I couldn't be bothered with my homework and partly because I was depressed. Aside from not making any progress on the map, I hadn't heard from Cressida in a while. The hopes that she could be vaguely interested in me were on the brink of extinction. Isabelle loaded a map of Norway on my laptop. 'This is just for show,' she specified, as if being caught doing homework would dent our reputation. My apathy irritated her. 'You could look more excited, you know? Why the long face? Is it about Water-Cressida?'

I hated the nickname she had given her. And I hated that Viggo's unusual name couldn't be easily modified for mocking purposes. I silently cursed his mother for her invincible choice. Isabelle was in a frenzy and flapped around my cabin like a bird facing a strong wind. 'When you hear what I have to say, Water-Cressida will be the last thing on your mind. I did some research and, incredibly, it all makes sense.'

'What does?' I asked, moving my glass so she wouldn't knock it over.

The bird landed on my desk. 'Our clues are 1119, a vermillion cross and a centuries old secret organisation, right?'

'Uhu.'

She pushed my books to one side and flattened the printout of a medieval knight in chain mail armour on my desk. The vermillion cross emblazoned on his white surcoat caught my eye. 'Who's he?' I asked.

'Not *who*, but *what*,' she replied cryptically.

I hated how she was dragging this out. 'I know what he is, he's a knight.'

'Not just *any* knight, a Templar Knight.' She resumed her flapping. 'Don't you find it peculiar that our fathers and Viggo have the Templars' symbol tattooed on their bodies?'

I could sense where she was heading and it was too crazy for words. 'You can't seriously think—'

'Our fathers are Templars!' she said, with a passion I didn't know she had.

I chuckled softly. 'That cross represents millions of other things.'

She hated being contradicted. 'Shut up, there are other clues. The Templars followed a strict chain of command, like everyone on Valhalla—'

'And in most organisations around the world! Try a summer job in a fast-food restaurant if you don't believe me! Look, the Templars were wiped out, I don't remember the exact date, but they were destroyed by King Philip IV. He was French,' I added accusingly.

Patriotism took over. 'I'm sure he had his reasons.'

'Are you for real?'

She huffed. 'We're getting distracted. The point is that, *theoretically*, the Templars were wiped out, but nobody knows for sure. We're onto something, Noah! I can feel it!'

I had serious doubts the Force was strong within her. 'It's a fascinating theory,' I began, 'but can you really imagine Viggo as a Templar? When he's not loading the dishwasher, he's texting our diving instructor!'

She got her face level with mine. 'Do you know when the Templar Order was founded?'

I didn't, but her smugness was more palpable than usual. '1119?' I asked, just to be sure.

Her lips curled in a triumphant smile. Ignoring her ramblings had become a whole lot harder.

Isabelle and I immersed ourselves in medieval times. Since being recaptured by the First Crusade in 1099, Jerusalem had become the top destination for spiritual tourism. The city itself was relatively safe, but the same couldn't be said for the rest of Outremer – a French term used to describe the Crusader states. Once the pilgrims reached the Jaffa Port, they were very much on their own, much to the joy of the local bandits who routinely attacked the ever-present supply of travellers.

In 1119 a group of nine Frankish knights saw a gap in the market and decided to found an order aimed at protecting the Christian pilgrims who were flocking to the Holy City. The knights volunteered their services to the King of Jerusalem, Baldwin II. Since, I'm sure, he wasn't exactly inundated with such requests, he welcomed them with open arms. The order's business plan was more hopeful than practical, its members had no assets and optimistically planned to survive on donations. The first, tangible one came directly from King Baldwin, who let them set up their headquarters on Temple Mount, in the captured Al-Aqsa Mosque which was believed to be directly above the ruins of the Temple of Solomon. And so *The order of the Poor Fellow-Soldiers of Christ and of the Temple of Solomon* (and I thought knights were men of few words!) was officially born.

The knights became widely known as the Knights Templar or, simply, The Templars.

In 1129 the Roman Catholic Church officially endorsed the order and shot the Templars into medieval stardom. Affluent families flooded them with all sorts of donations, from money, to land, to non-inheriting sons that could serve as knights. As if things couldn't get any better, Pope Innocent III issued a papal bull (which, I found out, isn't a devout animal) exempting the knights from obeying local laws and taxes anywhere. The order would report directly to the Pope.

In time, the Templars accumulated vast riches all over Europe and Outremer. Castles, fortresses, the entire island of Cyprus, you name it, they owned it. Their solid reputation as warriors spread to their accounting abilities and soon they were providing high-end financial services to a variety of secular businesses. Within two centuries, the penniless knights had become one of Europe's richest and most powerful organisations.

Unfortunately, all good stories come to an end. The party-spoiler, in this case, was the heavily indebted King Philip IV, also known as The Fair. He borrowed vast amounts from the Templars, but eventually realised that there was no way he could honour his debts. The idea of selling his palace and moving into a one-bed flat probably didn't appeal to him. King Philip wanted more than just to see his debts erased, he wanted a big slice of the Templars' wealth. Regrettably (for the Templars), Clement V, the Pope in charge, was a fellow Frenchman and nothing more than a puppet in King Philip's hands.

On Friday 13th October 1307 (the date is rumoured to have launched the Friday 13th superstition) Philip ordered that the Grand Master of the order, Jacques de Molay, and all French Templars should be placed under immediate arrest. They were accused of anything The Fair could come up with, from financial corruption to obscene rituals, from fraud to heresy, and everything in between. A month later, Pope Clement V instructed every European Christian monarch to arrest all Templars within their jurisdiction and seize their assets. Captured members were charged as heretics and sentenced to death.

In 1312, at the Council of Vienne (where King Philip IV conveniently showed up with his army in tow), Pope Clement V officially disbanded the order. The combined efforts of these two clowns had achieved what no Muslim army managed in two centuries: the destruction of the Knights Templar.

Grand Master Jacques de Molay was burned in Paris in 1314. From his pyre, he shouted something along the lines of "God knows who is wrong and has sinned. Soon a calamity will occur to those who have condemned us to death." His last-minute curse couldn't have been more effective: within a year, Pope Clement and King Philip had joined him in the afterlife.

My eyes were dry, I dug for my first-aid kit where my mother had packed some artificial tears. Isabelle raised a single eyebrow. How did she do that? I could only raise two at the same time or nothing at all. Had I been King Philip and she a Templar, I would have chucked her on the closest pyre, surely only heretics could perform such a trick. 'Is that a monogrammed first-aid kit?' she asked with a hint of disgust.

'Yes, it's a Christmas gift from my mother.'

'Sweet,' said the heretic wryly.

I mentally lit her pyre. 'This is all very interesting, but surely—'

'Look!' she squealed. If her nose got any closer to the I-pad, she could have used it to tap the screen. 'The Templars referred to each other as *brothers*. My father often calls Magnus like that.'

I spread my hands. 'It's a very common term. You're twisting the facts to fit your theory. Did you see this?' I navigated to the right page. 'The Templars were a monastic order. They weren't allowed to marry, they took vows of poverty, chastity, piety and obedience. Our fathers were married and Viggo has been buzzing around Hope non-stop. They're even out on a date tonight – not very monastic, is it?'

'Are they on a *date*?' she asked, a slight quaver in her voice. I cursed my big mouth – despite her snotty attitude, her crush on my father's aide was pretty major. She stood up and grabbed the printout of the knight. 'I'm right about this, I know I am. Have a think about it and let me know, by tomorrow morning, if you want to investigate things further. And for your information, knights were allowed a few horses and a servant who didn't have to conform to a specific civil status. Viggo could fit that role.'

Before I could point out the lack of horses in our marina, she slammed the door behind her. I wasn't sure she knew they could be closed softly. I lay on my bed and mentally re-examined the various clues. As far-fetched as it was, I couldn't completely dismiss Isabelle's theory: could my father truly be part of a modern-day Templar order?

CHAPTER 26

My rumbling stomach woke me at 1:43am. I went to the kitchen, fixed myself a boring cheese sandwich, grabbed a glass of milk and made my way to the main deck, looking forward to my midnight feast under the stars. My heart skipped a beat, a ghostly shape was swaying in the breeze. I gingerly approached – the supernatural being turned out to be Isabelle wrapped in her bed sheet. 'Thank you,' she said, taking half the sandwich from my plate and sinking her pearly whites into it before I had a chance protest.

'You're welcome,' I muttered, noticing the empty tub of ice-cream at her feet. I don't know if there are anthropological studies on the subject, but girls seem to mend broken hearts by eating copious amounts of ice-cream straight from the tub.

'Are you in, then?' she asked, hinting at our earlier conversation.

'I thought I had until tomorrow to decide.'

'It's past midnight. It *is* tomorrow. And that idiot hasn't come back yet.'

Ah! She was guarding the gangway to pulverise any chances of Viggo smuggling Hope on board. I bit into my sandwich, it was nice. I wished I still had the other half.

She did the heretic eyebrow trick again. 'So? Are you in or out?'

'I'm in, but we must call a proper truce on Cressida and you must promise that, if we get caught snooping around, you won't blame everything on me.'

She rolled her eyes and made sure I could see her do it. 'You're as bad as your father. Fine, I promise.'

We shook hands.

'I did some more research on the Templars' symbols,' she said with a troublesome smile. 'One of their most famous seals depicts two men riding a single horse, just like —'

The screeching sound of braking tyres made us jump. A car door slammed. Could the Russians have bypassed the brand-new security system so soon? Incredibly, we began bickering about what to do. Before we could agree on a plan, hurried steps crossed the gangway. We had nowhere to run. We ducked behind the shark cage and covered ourselves as best as we could with Isabelle's sheet. Someone jumped on deck and Isabelle chose that exact moment to sneeze, of all places, on my shoulder. The intruder heard her and was now moving with the stealth of a Ninja. I peered out from under the sheet, only to stare into the tip of a speargun. 'One move and I'll hook you like a tuna!'

I swallowed. Did that count as a move?

Isabelle immediately recognised her beloved's voice and emerged from our canvas fort. 'Put that thing down, Viggo. It's just us.'

He stepped forward. The alarm in his eyes was replaced by sheer disappointment. He shot me an accusing stare which, I suppose, was better than being shot with the speargun. 'You've got to be kidding me!' he yelled, lowering the weapon. 'What are you doing back here at this time? Is that... a bed sheet? Actually, don't answer, I don't want to know. I don't have time for this right now.'

Isabelle threw me a killer look, not that I had brought the sheet in the first place. A strange smell lingered in the air, I couldn't place it, but it was kind of overpowering. Viggo strode towards the stern clutching the abhorrent pink cardigan in one hand and my father's new fishing gun in the other. We trotted after him. 'Did your date finish early?' asked Isabelle, unable to hide her jubilation.

Viggo swung round to face her. 'Yes, not that it's any of your business.'

She wriggled her nose. Ah, he was the culprit! He must have used half a bottle of cheap aftershave. I was a few metres behind, but could have found him with my eyes closed. He resumed walking and she kept on cantering behind him. He reached my father's cabin and began pounding on the door. 'Magnus, open up, it's important.'

'It'd better be.' My father's sleepy voice was followed by the sound of a rusty key turning in a rusty lock. So much for the best security money can buy. He stood in the door frame in his pyjama bottoms, rubbing the sleep from his face and trying to focus on his visitors. 'What on earth is this smell?' he asked, suddenly awake.

Viggo groaned. 'It's my new aftershave.'

My father inhaled and blinked. 'It's making my eyes water. I have a meeting with someone I can't stand tomorrow, can I borrow it?'

'Sure, knock yourself out.'

'Literally.' My father inhaled again. 'What's the essence supposed to be?'

'White musk.'

'More like musk ox!'

'It should have highlighted my uncompromising masculinity,' said Viggo, aware that the aftershave had brutally failed to deliver.

'It does, it does,' said my father, trying to cheer up his deflated assistant, 'in a primal sort of way. I picture a very sweaty warrior after a three-day battle in the scorching heat.'

Viggo was instantly more upbeat. He smelled his shirt without passing out. 'You're right, it's primal!'

Isabelle pulled a face and kept on pinching her nose. The doors of the cuckoo clock sprang open and the mechanism shot out. There was no bird.

'Can I come in?' asked Viggo.

My father stood aside.

'Can I come too?' I asked, hoping that the aftershave fumes, the missing cuckoo and my father's sleepiness would play in my favour.

'The more, the merrier,' he answered from the bottom of a yawn, totally missing Viggo's stare which intimated the opposite. Viggo placed the cardigan on my father's desk and babbled something in Swedish.

'If it's about the map, Noah can stay,' replied my father in English. 'Isabelle, go back to bed.'

'I'm not going anywhere,' she protested. 'If you want me out of this cabin, you'll have to remove me by force.'

My father didn't bat an eyelid. 'Do you prefer to be dragged or carried?'

I felt a bit sorry for her, but not enough to take her side. She huffed and stormed out. Viggo handed my father two folded pieces of paper. 'They were hidden in the cardigan's sleeves,' he said, 'they fell out when Hope tried it on.'

My father opened them up. They were covered in Arabic writing. I gulped. 'Is that what I think it is?'

'The monks must have made a copy of the Arabic pages,' said Viggo. 'The prior wanted them to forget about the book and move on, but Brother Cristobal couldn't. He tried to help us, but we didn't see it.'

I couldn't believe our own stupidity. 'The cardigan wasn't just a ruse to give us the name of the book, it was a way to smuggle the pages out of the monastery.'

'That's right,' said Viggo. 'And Cristobal's reference to the Gospel of Matthew wasn't accidental either. I looked up the Sermon on the Mount. One of its most famous verses is *Ask, and it will be given you. Seek, and you will find. Knock, and it will be opened for you.*'

My father seemed too oblivious to our combined genius. He kept on staring at the Arabic writing, hypnotised. 'How's your Arabic?' I said, trying to break the tension.

'Not bad,' he mumbled, without looking up.

My mouth fell open. 'You speak *Arabic*?'

'Yeah, when you were little I spent a year and a half between Jordan and Israel.'

It was yet another reminder of how disjointed our lives had been. I selfishly hoped that the pages made no sense. Knut would have to be informed and, whenever he came, I was likely to go. 'What do they say?'

'It's a first-hand account by…'

He suddenly let out an eloquent expletive.

'By whom?' I asked, alarmed.

'Arabic is complicated, I'll need some time to translate this properly,' he replied, even though it was perfectly clear that he had grasped more than he was letting on. He asked Viggo for some coffee.

'Will those pages affect my being here?' I asked. His failure to answer fuelled my fears. I didn't want to go to boarding school, I had to fight my corner. 'Whatever they say, the pages are linked to the map, and you promised that—'

He raised his hand to stop me. 'I have never broken a promise and I don't intend to start now. Trust me, I'll work something out.'

Viggo levelled nine tablespoons of coffee and dropped them in the cafetiere. While it brewed, he quietly sent some texts. It didn't take a genius to figure out who the recipient was. 'So, how was your date?' I asked.

He shook his head deliberately slowly. 'Dude, it had so much potential, but everything, and I mean *everything*, went wrong.'

'I'm a good listener,' I offered. 'And it will stay between us... dudes.'

I felt utterly idiotic using that term, but Viggo appreciated the gesture. He pushed the plunger down and imprisoned the coffee granules at the bottom of the cafetiere. 'I picked Hope up from the dive shop. Less than ten minutes into the drive she started to sneeze. It was too early for pollen season, but I rolled up the windows anyway and... things got worse.'

He was mortification personified. 'The aftershave?' I asked sympathetically.

'It obviously over-highlighted my uncompromising masculinity. No girl should be allergic to that, right?'

'Right,' I said, painfully aware that his fragrance could knock out the dead.

'Anyway, Hope's a real sweet girl and didn't want to ruin our date, so we stocked up on tissues and drove to the restaurant. We totally hit it off, dude! She was into me too because, at closing time, she suggested going to the Green Parrot for drinks. Did I mention that she lives right above the Green Parrot?'

'No.'

'Do you get where I'm going with this?'

'To Hope's flat.'

I'm ashamed to say I was a bit jealous. Not that I would have known what to do if she had invited me to her apartment in the middle of the night. He lowered his head, crestfallen. 'I wish I had never given her the damned cardigan. When the pages came out, I immediately put two and two together. I explained that Magnus needed them urgently and that we had to take a rain check on the Green Parrot, but she thought I wanted to wriggle out of the date. She was mad, dude! I asked for the bill and tried to use my coupon, but the stupid manager insisted it wasn't valid and charged me full price. The restaurant didn't take credit cards and I hadn't brought enough money, so I had to ask her to chip in. I offered to drive her home, but she got a taxi instead. Do you think I blew my chances?'

Like leaves in a gale! I struggled to formulate a response that wouldn't dent his morale and he appreciated my silent honesty.

'It's OK, thanks for not lying to my face.' He put the cafetiere on a tray and placed a mug next to it. 'I'd better take this to Magnus before it gets cold. Looks like it's going to be a long night. You should go to bed.'

For a while, I did, but I couldn't shake the feeling of guilt. Viggo was my friend and he was going through a bad patch, I shouldn't have left him alone. I decided to check on him. The kitchen was deserted, but his still-warm empty mug was sitting on the counter, next to his I-pad and one of the sat-phones. I examined the screen: two missed calls from someone called Kostas. And that's when I heard Viggo's voice coming from the control room. Judging by the amount of begging, he had to be talking to either Hope or God. The sound of the sat-phone vibrating against the counter startled me – Kostas again. I picked it up with the honest intention of saying that Viggo wasn't available, but hadn't banked on Kostas firing words faster than a machine gun, without as much as a single breath in between.

'Viggo, this is Kostas from the Legal Department.' I tried to interrupt, but he wouldn't let me. 'I'm calling about Magnus's trip request. My understanding is that he wants to include two young civilians in his team on the basis that a fully-fledged member should be allowed to choose his own crew. Moving minors across international borders is a complex issue, I need to ascertain parental responsibility. Can you confirm that, according to governing laws, Noah Joakim Larsson is his son and that Magnus has temporary custody?'

The prospect of coming clean faded into the background. Who the hell was this guy? Had my father found a way to keep me in his treasure hunt despite the recovery of the Arabic pages? 'Yes,' I said, before my better judgement had a chance to take over.

'And I understand that the girl is Miguel Santiago de Castillo's daughter and that he will also be involved in the operation. Correct?' asked Kostas in a single breath.

His guess was as good as mine. 'Um… yes.'

'I see. As far as I can tell, his request isn't in breach of any governing laws and is compliant with our rules, therefore the youngsters will be allowed to join his team on a temporary basis. Of course, the usual protocols will have to be followed. From a purely technical point of view, the minors can be regarded as adults, therefore standard procedures will apply.'

'The minors can be regarded as adults?' I echoed, wondering which rules he was talking about. 'Seriously? As in… grown-ups?'

I couldn't believe I had just said that, for a moment I thought I had blown my rickety cover. My mysterious caller, in typical lawyer fashion, seemed unperturbed by the stupidity of my question. Lawyers charge by the hour, stupid questions are an essential part of their livelihood. 'Our rules were written in medieval times, back then fifteen-year-olds were of age. They could marry, rule countries and do everything in between.'

I shuddered at the idea of Isabelle ruling a country. The caller continued. 'I'll forward my findings to Operations. Unless there are objections from the higher levels, Magnus's trip request should be approved within the next thirty minutes and he will be granted access to the necessary resources.'

'And if there are objections?'

'Then it's up to Magnus. His request is most unusual, but if he wants to pursue it, he's on solid ground. The rules are clearly in his favour.' For the first time, he paused to breathe. His tone changed from cold efficiency to sincere worry. 'I need you to give Magnus a message, strictly off the record.'

'Sure.'

'From what I can see there is no specific need for the minors to be involved. If anything happens to them, this whole thing would blow up in his face. He should choose wisely.'

I thanked him and hung up. It took my shaky fingers three attempts, but I managed to delete the two missed calls. Hopefully, since my father's request was going to be approved, nobody would ever find out about my conversation with Kostas. I needed to speak to Isabelle, but I couldn't risk being found in her cabin in the middle of the night. Viggo had been gracious enough not to tell my father about our supposedly romantic encounter behind the shark cage, not that there was much to tell, but I had pushed him far enough. I combed my hair and Skyped her from my bed. I filled her in on my call with Kostas and her eyes got as wide as my phone-screen. We were still messaging when my father barged in. He seemed surprised to find me awake, then saw my phone and broke into a knowing smile. 'Girlfriend?'

'Farming game.'

Not that it was something to be proud of, but I was turning into an excellent liar. 'Pack your stuff,' he said. 'This time tomorrow you'll be farming in Sicily.'

CHAPTER 27

The speed camera flashed. 'Dad, you've triggered another one,' I said. He slowed the car down. Marginally. We had flown to Sicily on a commercial flight and our rented people carrier was about to reach the outskirts of a town called Licata. My father had brought me up to speed with his translation of the Arabic pages. I was obviously being fed an abridged version: in 1318 a French knight called Godefroi de Carignan was travelling on the doomed *Nuestra Señora* ship when she had sunk off the coast of Sicily. Despite sustaining serious injuries, Godefroi had managed to reach the shores of Licata, which back then was called Limpiadum. The locals had rushed him to a monastery in Agrigento, where his wounds could be tended to. Unfortunately, infection had set in and it was only a matter of time before Godefroi would succumb to his fate. The knight was carrying the mysterious twelfth ring, a coveted item even in those years. To prevent it from falling into the wrong hands, he had embarked on a final journey to deliver the ring to a secure hiding place. Before setting off, he had marked his intended destination, the approximate position of the sunk *Nuestra Señora* and the towns of Licata and Agrigento on the map in our possession. Pity our map was incomplete and, as luck would have it, the ring's hiding place happened to be drawn on the scroll's missing part. My father couldn't have cared less. Apparently, he and Miguel were good at cracking mysteries and they were certain that an in-depth study of Godefroi's letter would have revealed clues to the ring's location – they couldn't believe that the knight would put all his eggs in one basket. I sincerely hoped their gut feeling was right. Knut, who was adamant to add the ring to his private collection, had hired my father's company to retrieve it and was financing the expedition. I knew there had to be a lot more, but kept quiet and pretended to go along with it. Unsurprisingly, I also kept quiet about my conversation with Kostas.

The plan was to go to Sicily and retrace Godefroi's steps. The knight's only connection to Licata was to have been washed up on its shores, so our stay wouldn't be long – enough to recover from the jet-lag and, hopefully, crack the letter. My father and I had never been on a long-haul trip before and he was determined to make it a bit special. He had pledged to spend an entire afternoon hanging around with me and had even hired a boat to explore the Sicilian coast. If I survived the drive, we would finally spend some quality time together.

We were booked into a private residence in an area known as *Quartiere della Marina*. We parked the people carrier and proceeded on foot through the narrow, winding streets. A bunch of prehistoric housewives took a break from their daily chores and studied us with unwelcome interest. Viggo's passage was marked by a series of appreciative comments and a lady that could have passed for a mummified corpse blew him a kiss. We stopped in front of an arched, wooden door that faced directly into a tiny street. The building was three stories high and its pointy windows had a Middle-Eastern feel. There was no doorbell, no knocker and no post box: the worst nightmare of a door to door seller. My father knocked confidently, the spy hole opened and framed an inquisitive dark eye. 'Open Sesame,' commanded my father with a straight face.

I was too tired to laugh, we were in the middle of Licata and he was quoting a phrase from *Ali Baba and the Forty Thieves*. Isabelle used her last reserves of energy to produce a couple of weary scoffs, which died down as the door creaked on its hinges. We entered a reception room furnished with oriental carpets, floor cushions and round low tables. The shabby exterior did the building no justice. 'Your rooms are upstairs,' said us our host, who hadn't bothered asking who we were.

'Thank you,' replied my father. 'Have you chartered a boat?'

'All I could get at such short notice was The Pearl.'

My father marvelled. 'Is she still around?'

'She's moored in a nearby marina, the details are on the table. Unless you need me, I'll take my leave. Your squire knows how to contact me.'

Isabelle burst out laughing. 'Who?'

The host stiffened and apprehensive glances were exchanged. Miguel ushered the man outside and I explored our temporary home. The reception area occupied most of the ground floor. At the back, a well-equipped kitchenette opened on to a large, square-shaped, internal courtyard that came with its own stone well. The first floor was dominated by a modern wet room, flanked by two small bedrooms. Viggo's and mine contained two single beds which, despite being separated by a night table, were close enough for him to slap me in the face without needing to get up. Isabelle's lodgings were even tinier. She had a window, therefore she couldn't use her claustrophobia as an excuse to get a bigger room.

'Did you hear what that man said?' she whispered. In an impossible quest for privacy, she attempted to drag me inside her room, but the laws of physics prevented it. Entering or exiting that room two at a time, required the flexibility of a contortionist. Viggo appeared from downstairs and stumbled on his own shoe lace. He fell forward and his shirt rode up, exposing a handgun tucked into the back of his cargo shorts. Great, a squire who couldn't even tie his owns shoes had been issued a firearm. Isabelle saw it too, but seemed more mesmerised by the elastic of his boxer shorts.

My father and Miguel's rooms were in direct contrast with our cramped accommodation. They enjoyed panoramic sea views and a joint roof terrace inhabited by the largest prickly pears I had ever seen. In a corner of the terrace, my father, armed with a pen knife, was inspecting the contents of a large cardboard box. He removed two plastic pipes and pushed them together. They clicked into place. 'Aren't you a bit old to play Lego?' I asked.

I had never made fun of him before and nervously awaited his reaction. A light smack on my head was followed by his boisterous laugh. 'These are to build underwater grids,' he said, handing me one of the pipes. 'If Knut wasn't in such a hurry to get to the ring, we could use the geographical, geological and primary source data to narrow down the area where the *Nuestra*

Señora is. Adding in factors such as type of sediment, known earthquakes, currents, man-made interventions and so on, would shrink the area even further. If our pre-disturbance survey highlighted a particular sector, we'd build a grid over it, inspect it square by square with the relevant equipment and identify the coordinates that require further investigation. Then we could proceed with an exploratory excavation.'

His efficiency stunned me. I had never seen him in fully operational mode. For the first time, I got a glimpse of what my mother must have liked about him: competent, logical, dedicated and knowledgeable. I stared at him with a new-found respect. 'What is primary source data?' I asked.

'Direct or first-hand evidence about an event. In our case, Godefroi's account and the map.'

'Did Godefroi explain how he came by the ring in the first place? Did it belong to him or was he carrying it on behalf of someone else?'

I had asked him a few times already – so far, my curiosity had triggered three serious cases of selective amnesia and a sighting of the sea serpent in the Gulf of Bothnia which, I discovered, wasn't a made-up place. On this occasion, he simply ignored my questions.

Later that evening we had a lovely dinner in Licata. The owner of the restaurant was very welcoming and offered the adults a few glasses of *limoncello* (a lemon-based digestive liquor) on the house. Miguel's phone beeped and he realised that he had missed a call from his ex-wife. 'Have you heard from your mother lately?' he asked me, pocketing the phone.

'Not since her engagement.'

'Is Katherine getting married?' Miguel, his second glass of *limoncello* in mid-air, stared inquisitively at my father who bit his lip and nodded back. 'Why didn't you tell me, Magnus?'

'There's nothing to tell,' replied dad curtly, unable to mask his bitterness. He raised his empty glass to the waiter to signal he wanted a refill. 'It had to happen sooner or later.'

Miguel discreetly bumped Viggo's arm, but he shrugged his shoulders. This was news to him too.

'Who's the groom?' asked Miguel, as tactfully as he could.

My father downed another *limoncello*. 'Some doctor. French. Good joints apparently.'

Miguel bumped Viggo again. 'Why don't you guys head back? We'll catch up.'

My father didn't protest, too busy asking for another refill.

God works in mysterious ways. So does jet lag. I had struggled to eat with my eyes open but, by the time we got home, I was wide awake. We decided to continue our evening on the roof terrace and brought up some floor cushions. Ariel declared that he preferred a good book to our lame company and retired to the lounge. We lay underneath the stars that I never got to see in London and did a very poor job of identifying the various constellations. Viggo let out a loud burp. 'Where are your manners?' protested Isabelle.

'No idea,' he replied earnestly. 'I'm Viking and proud. My ancestors were against all sorts of etiquette and I do not wish to insult their traditions.' The paladin of bad manners then elbowed me in the rib-cage. 'Dude, what's up with Magnus and your mother?'

'Not sure.'

'Does he hold a candle for her?' asked Isabelle.

'Of course not.' I was under the same impression and my statement didn't sound particularly convincing. 'Marriages are complicated.'

Or at least they were in *Amor Prohibido*. Isabelle locked eyes with Viggo and smiled as alluringly as she could, unaware that she was sporting a moustache of chocolate ice-cream. 'Viggo, what are your views on marriage?' asked the flirty musketeer.

He scratched his head and stuck out his bottom lip. 'What's not to like? Fanfare, food and bridesmaids – unless you're the groom, it's paradise on earth.'

'That's your idea of wedding parties,' hissed the musketeer. 'I asked about marriage, a union between a man and woman who swear eternal love to each other. Surely even you must think about it sometimes? I mean... there are no impediments for you to get married, are there? It's not like you took an oath of cha... chastity or something, right?'

Poor Isabelle, she was trying to establish whether she had fallen in love with a potential monk. It was dark, but I could feel her blushing from the tips of her painted toes to the roots of her hair. Viggo sat up, a slight frown between his eyes. 'Did you just ask me if I've taken an oath of chastity?'

A commotion from the ground floor saved her from answering. Heavy footsteps echoed up the stairs and a spirited (in the sense that he had drunk too many spirits) version of my father stormed onto the terrace. He reminded me of a skittle, he kept on losing his balance, but he always recovered. Viggo took a step towards him, but my drunken father picked up one of the plastic pipes that was meant for the grid and elegantly extended his arm. *'En guarde!'*

Viggo was momentarily lost, but as my father thrust forward to attack him with his rudimentary sword, he picked up another pipe and started parrying the blows. These two had fenced before, the way the blows were inflicted and deflected radiated years of professional training. Isabelle was totally enthralled by Viggo's neat performance, in the heat of the moment she cheered him on and distracted him. My father jumped at the chance to inflict his *coup de grace* and victoriously rested the plastic pipe against Viggo's throat. His aide threw his makeshift sword to the ground and acknowledged defeat. Where on earth had a marine biologist and a drop out from a Swedish university learnt to fence like that?

CHAPTER 28

We were sitting on one of Licata's most famous beaches and Ariel was recounting the role of Sicily in the Punic Wars. Judging by the crowds, another attack was imminent and the Sicilians were out in force. We had hired a beach umbrella, but the sun was at its peak and I was slowly evaporating. Viggo possessed the stamina of a cactus – beads of sweat ran down his back like mini Niagara Falls, but he seemed not to notice. Ariel had slathered himself in sun protection oil and was shining like the Cullinan diamond. My father had been mercifully left behind on account of his big night. I couldn't understand what the hell was going on. After practically ignoring mum for over a decade, he suddenly bore a grudge because she was getting married. I went for a swim to clear my head. I was floating in the tepid waters of the Mediterranean when a fit girl in a turquoise bikini emerged from the crowded beach and scanned the horizon. I was far enough to blatantly check her out without being discovered. The heat was definitely getting to me: it took me a few minutes of intense ogling to figure out she was Isabelle. We were not supposed to spend time alone, so I was surprised when she swam in my direction. 'Viggo's gone to buy some drinks, but he'll be back soon,' she said when she was close enough. 'Last night I did some checking on the internet, a squire looked after a knight's every need. A mixture between a butler, a slave and a personal secretary.'

I considered the relationship between my father and his aide. 'It sounds about right. Is Viggo of noble descent, by any chance?'

'Why?'

'I did some research too.' She was partially impressed by my modicum of initiative because she waited for me to speak. 'At first squires came from a poor background and were hired as temporary help. As the reputation of the order grew, the position became a stepping stone for young men of noble descent keen to become fully fledged knights. I was trying to figure out if Viggo is a temp squire or a knight to be.'

'I know zilch about his background,' she admitted with an ounce of regret. 'But I could do some digging.'

Snooping in general put her in a good mood, snooping on Viggo was her idea of heaven. She clutched my wrist. 'Were squires required to take vows?'

'No, until they became knights, they led a normal life.'

'So… they didn't have to follow monastic rules?'

'Nope, which would explain why our squire is currently chatting with two German tourists.'

'How do you know they're Germans?' she asked, scouting the beach with the precision of a sniper.

'I heard them talking as I walked past.'

I failed to mention that they were as old as my mother. Isabelle cast her best evil-eye on the two slender ladies chit-chatting with Viggo at the edge of the water. 'I bet they don't even shave their legs.'

I was too far to tell, but I didn't share the same impression. One of the tourists scribbled something on Viggo's arm, presumably her phone number. Isabelle clenched her fists.

'There's one thing that keeps bugging me,' I said, thinking aloud.

She took a break from voodoo practice. 'What?'

'The monastic life.'

'It won't be forever, Noah. You'll get a girlfriend sooner or later.'

I blushed. 'I was talking about the Templars. Military commitments aside, they led a very secluded life. They were not permitted relationships with women and had to pray on a regular basis.' I started counting on my fingers. 'My father has been married, he's been dating and, unless we count Brother Felipe's funeral, I've never seen him set foot in a church.'

'Maybe King Philip IV had a point and the knights were truly despicable men. Your father could be the incarnation of what he was trying to wipe out.'

I ignored her stupid remark, deep down she felt sympathy towards King Philip because she also had a tendency to max out on her credit. Unfortunately for her, she didn't have the manpower to exterminate Visa. 'How about Miguel, has he been dating since getting divorced?'

'Nothing serious, but he did have girlfriends.'

'Lineage?'

'He's of noble descent, but a meaningless title is all that's left. The Santiago de Castillo are the poorest barons on the planet. No palace, no land, not even a limping pony with a scruffy tail.'

I interrupted the list of riches she would never see and pointed at the beach. The German cougars had left and the squire was summoning us out of the water. A familiar figure was standing behind him: my father had graced us with his presence.

The air-conditioned beach bar saved us from the midday heat. The plan was to grab a bite and play some foosball. Before starting the match, my father, who had been fairly quiet, removed his sunglasses and rubbed his bloodshot eyes. 'I need to apologise for last night,' he said to no-one in particular. 'I'm sorry, I don't know how it happened.'

Isabelle snorted and pushed the coin into the foosball table, the balls cascaded into their slot. 'You were drunk. It usually happens by drinking copious amounts of alcohol.'

'Well, thank you for unravelling that mystery,' he replied, his words drenched in jaded sarcasm.

'Why did you get so plastered?' she continued, resting the ball on the serving hole. 'Are you still in love with your wife?'

The ball dropped onto the pitch, none of the players moved. 'We're divorced,' said my father mechanically.

'That's not the answer to my question.'

'Isabelle, that's enough!' thundered Miguel. 'Apologise, now!'

She pouted instead. My father sank a goal in her side and shoved the foosball rods against the table. I had never seen him so furious. 'We're off on our mini-cruise first thing tomorrow,' he said, looking straight at her. 'Until then, you'd better stay the hell out of my way.'

She didn't have to try hard: he spent the rest of the day sleeping on the sun lounger.

CHAPTER 29

The alarm clock shattered the peace of the early morning. Viggo's hand slapped the night table and eventually found the snooze button. In a superhuman effort, we rose to our feet and stood face to face in the small space between our beds, two opponents sizing each other up. We scrambled for the bathroom at the same time. He beat me. And used all the hot water.

Soon after breakfast, we drove to *Marina del Sole*, the harbour where our vessel was moored. My father made a special effort to strike up a conversation with Isabelle and she was smart enough to take it as a sign that hostilities were temporarily over. He had brought his laptop along to work on the letter, but assured me that we would still spend the afternoon together. We reached the marina, which was more upmarket than I had imagined. An army of immaculate yachts looked down on a particular vessel. Our optimistically named The Pearl of Sicily was roughly twelve metres long and painted in three different colours. I doubted that the owner was the artistic type, more likely he was on a tight budget. The Pearl had enjoyed a very chequered career and had been modified to serve a number of purposes. My father defined her as hybrid, but it had nothing to do with her carbon emissions. She was part fishing boat, part salvage boat and part whatever your imagination wanted her to be. When it came to The Pearl words failed me, I prayed her engines wouldn't. We climbed on board. A man of my father's age emerged from the pilot house. 'Magnus, good to see you're still alive.'

'I do my best,' replied dad with a grin. 'Everyone, this is Marco, our captain. Marco, this is Noah, my son —'

'Your son?' gasped Marco. 'You kept that quiet!'

I tried not to look offended, but I don't think I managed. My father failed to notice (or pretended not to) and proceeded to introduce the rest of the group. The captain's posture betrayed military training or a very stiff back. 'I believe you already know Sesame, my second in command,' he said to my father.

The man who had let us into the Licata residence stepped out of the pilot house.

'Seriously?' I blurted. 'Is your name Sesame?'

'My mother loved *One Thousand and One Nights*,' he replied with an air of resignation.

I really had to get a grip on my conspiracy theories.

Marco manoeuvred The Pearl out of the marina and sailed towards the open sea. I had just convinced him to let me have a go at the helm when my father called a team meeting down below. 'There are some things we need to discuss,' he began, as we sat around an oval table with raised edges. 'As you know, Knut has tasked us with retrieving the twelfth ring. If we want this mission to be a success, it's vital that we're all on the same page.' He carefully gauged his next words. 'Knut is a very private person, he doesn't want his affairs broadcasted to the four winds. If you truly want to be a part of the search operation, you'll have to take an oath.'

'An oath?' echoed Isabelle sceptically.

'Like a medieval knight or something?' I asked, picturing myself in a lavish throne room in front of a pretty queen who looked a lot like Cressida.

'Sort of,' replied my father.

Excitement flooded my veins, was I about to take a Templar oath? Twenty minutes later, my excitement had somewhat faded. 'Is that it?' I asked.

My father chuckled at my disappointment. 'Did you expect me to tap you on the shoulders with the flat side of a sword?'

Was I that transparent? My mysterious oath had turned out to be a fairly insipid affair.

I, Noah Joakim Larsson, son of Magnus, solemnly declare of my own free will and accord that I will not share the details of the secret assignment which I am about to undertake with another living soul. I solemnly promise, upon my honour, that I will take all knowledge acquired during the undertaking of this mission to my grave.

Viggo had witnessed the whole ceremony (for lack of a better word) and high-fived me, as if I had reached an important milestone. Isabelle was being sworn elsewhere and I could only imagine how jealous she must be, my witness was Viggo, hers Sesame.

The beauty of the Sicilian coastline soon made me forget the blandness of my oath. Marco lowered the anchor at regular intervals to give us the chance to go for a swim. My father spent the morning working on the letter, but joined us in the afternoon. I was having an awesome time doing all the things we had never had a chance to do together: dive-bombing, swimming, snorkelling, playing water polo and generally joking around. For the first time in my life, I felt as if I was his priority. We were larking about on the paddle board when Viggo, phone in his hand, leaned over the side of The Pearl. 'Magnus, it's Professor Kasper Harket,' he shouted.

'I'll call him later,' replied my father, trying to shake me off the paddle board. 'This afternoon, I'm officially on holiday with my son.'

'It's about Jörmungand,' yelled Viggo.

My father let go of the paddle board. 'Jörmungand?'

'Who the hell is Jörmungand?' I asked.

'A mythical serpent featured in Norse mythology. He's the king of sea serpents,' said my father, taking a few strokes towards The Pearl.

I thrust my paddle in the water and jumped off the board. 'So much for being on holiday with your son!'

He turned around with a guilty look. 'I won't be long. Trust me.'

I did, and in less than an hour we were back at the marina. I was choking on my own rage. I couldn't believe that he had cut our afternoon short to go and visit Professor Harket's archaeological dig on the outskirts of Caltanissetta. My father and Harket, a professor of Viking and Medieval Norse Studies at the University of Oslo, shared a common obsession for Jörmungand, the Midgard Serpent. Sicily had been ruled by the

Normans for decades and Harket spent his summers digging up various sites. One of his students had uncovered a very detailed stone carving of Jörmungand and, as luck would have it, we happened to be in Sicily at the same time. My father sheepishly climbed into the taxi that would drive him to Harket's dig. 'Ariel and I will be late,' he said. 'I'll see you tomorrow. Why don't you guys go out for a nice meal? I'll buy. Miguel, are you sure you don't want to come?'

'Positive, a nice meal beats Jörmungand any time.'

My father waved us goodbye, but I stuck my hands in my pockets and made a point of looking the other way.

I was so furious that I barely touched my dinner. Miguel, on the other hand, devoured his main, polished off my plate and proceeded to stuff his face with an array of Sicilian desserts. At home, he raided the medicine cabinet for indigestion pills and retired to his room to sleep it off. With the roof terrace off limits, Viggo, Isabelle and I had to settle for the internal courtyard. He unloaded the van and placed the contents by the stone well. Three yellow cylinders, approximately thirty-five centimetres tall and with a beak-shaped protuberance at one end, escaped one of the dive bags. I picked one up and pretended to spray it under my armpits. 'Giant-sized deodorant? Hairspray?'

He laughed and reclaimed the cylinder. 'Not even close. Mini scuba tanks. They're pretty handy. If your equipment fails, you stick one of these babies into your mouth and swim to the surface.'

Isabelle appeared carrying some floor cushions and a citronella candle. I couldn't decide if she wanted to keep the mosquitos at bay or put Viggo in a romantic mood, but the candle failed on both counts. We made ourselves comfortable and Viggo cracked open a bottle of beer, I reached for one too.

'Dude, I'm not sure your father would approve.'

I shrugged. 'He can legally adopt the sea serpent for all I care.'

The whole scene would have been a lot more dramatic if I could have actually opened my beer, but the twist cap kept on slipping through my fingers. Viggo took another swig from his bottle. 'Don't be bitter. Kasper Harket is a cool dude. Whenever I visit his digs, I think about switching to archaeology and ditching everything else.'

Isabelle gasped. 'Are you thinking of going back to uni and leaving Magnus?'

She could be so predictable. If Viggo abandoned my father without taking any foolish vows, he could be romantically available for years to come. 'I will have to at some point,' he said. 'I must finish my degree. Magnus made it clear, he would have me as his... helper, as long as I promised to complete my studies.'

I marvelled at my father's unusually responsible approach. He had clearly given Viggo's future some thought, I wondered if he had ever done the same with mine. Isabelle pressed on. 'You should definitely go back to uni, Viggo. And put together a career-plan.'

'I already have one.'

I gave up on the beer. 'You do?'

'Yeah, I'll get my degree and come back and work for Magnus.'

'As what?' asked Isabelle contemptuously. 'A *squire*? Surely you don't need a degree for that!'

His expression suddenly changed. For a moment, I thought that she had hit a raw nerve. 'Quiet,' he whispered. He blew the candle out and pointed at the house. A shiver ran down my spine. Someone had broken in. Light beams were dancing around the ground floor like lights in a cheap school disco – not that I had seen any other types. We frantically surveyed the courtyard for a way out that wasn't there. The internal garden was only accessible via our kitchen's back door and, aside from the one belonging to our house, was enclosed by solid walls. We crouched behind the well. 'Where's the sat-phone?' I asked.

'In the house, recharging,' said Viggo, desolately scanning our open-air cell. He rubbed the side of his face, where some stubble had begun to sprout, and looked up to our bedroom's window. The light came on – the intruders had made it to the first floor. He reached for the handgun at the back of his cargo shorts, checked the magazine, clipped it back into place and removed the safety catch. Isabelle and I were too nervous to protest. 'I've got to go in,' he said. 'Miguel's alone.'

'I'll come with you.' The firmness in my voice didn't extend to my shaky legs.

He shook his head. 'Too dangerous. You must get in the well.'

'*What?*'

'Dude, it's the safest place!'

'Maybe,' I conceded, 'but you can't go alone, they're too many!'

He didn't disagree and re-checked the gun instead. Isabelle pulled me back. 'Let him go, Noah. My father needs him, you'd just be in his way.'

Viggo leopard-crawled over the flagstones and returned with a dive bag. 'Listen to me,' he said, 'I will lower you into the well with the mini-tanks, your masks and an inflatable buoyancy aid. Keep the mini-tanks in your hands and the masks on your heads. If you hear voices, dive under and stay there as long as you can. If the intruders shine their torches down, don't panic. If you're deep enough, they won't be able to see you.' He threw me a nylon rope. 'Double-knot it around your waist. You'll go first.'

I grabbed his arm. 'I'm coming with you, whether you like it or not.'

'Dude, you can't,' he whispered. 'She's claustrophobic. She'll need you down there.'

He turned to Isabelle, cupped her face between his hands and dried her tears with his thumbs. His tender attitude sent her into a romantic trance.

'Princess, look at me,' he said. That wasn't difficult, she hadn't been able to look at anything else since he had started fiddling with her face. 'The well will be a bit scary, but you're strong, you can handle it. All you have to do is sit tight, be quiet and conserve your energies. I'll come and get you as soon as it's safe.'

The well was covered by a wooden lid that folded down the middle. We slid it off and stared into nothingness. Viggo nodded in my direction. I was as ready as I could be. I flung my legs over the side and began to abseil towards the depths of the earth. My feet hit the water and I instantly wished for a wetsuit, it was much colder than I expected. The well was roughly a metre wide, its sides coated in green slime. Within minutes, Isabelle was next to me, holding the inflatable buoyancy aid. Up above, Viggo replaced the lid. I switched on my mask's LED torch and let my eyes adjust to the dim light. Isabelle's teeth were already chattering. Her fingers stroked the side of the well. I had to take her mind off the enclosed space. 'You like Viggo a lot, don't you?'

'That's the most ridiculous thing I've ever heard,' she scoffed, way too defensively.

'C'mon, I see the way you look at him…'

I hoped that discussing Viggo would distract her from our predicament. We had been in the well less than a few minutes and the cold was already seeping through my bones.

'I guess he's… um… very gentle on the eye,' she said, stating the absolute obvious. 'Not so much on anything else.'

I couldn't fault her description. 'He's a nice guy, a bit clumsy sometimes.'

She nodded, or maybe she shivered from the cold. 'What do you like about Cressida?'

What a good question. I didn't know her that well and I wasn't too sure. 'She's very pretty and —'

A gunshot shattered the quiet of the night and silenced a chorus of crickets. Isabelle dug her fingernails deep into my palm, I was too shocked to complain. Two more shots followed. The sound of unfamiliar voices reached our ears. Unexpectedly, she hugged me. 'You have been a fairly good friend, Noah Larsson,' she whispered.

Unbelievable, the worst moment of our lives and she had carefully avoided using a superlative. Nevermind, we had more important things to do, like saving ourselves. I awkwardly returned the hug and opened the valve of the floating aid. The deflating hiss reminded me of my mother's kettle. We popped the mini-tanks into our mouths, lowered the masks, switched off the LED torch and sank below the water edge.

The intruders' light beam pierced the water like a one-eyed monster, but we handled it incredibly well. Nothing puts you in line like a string of gunshots. The mini-tanks had a limited supply of air, so I was pretty relieved when darkness returned.

We quietly ascended, re-inflated the buoyancy aid, clicked on the torch and, for a while, waited in religious silence. We were shivering badly and I wasn't sure how much longer we could endure the well's unforgiving temperature. If our bodies couldn't replenish the heat that was being lost, hypothermia would set in. I checked my watch, we had been in the water for over an hour. Isabelle broke the eerie silence. 'He's a sweet guy deep down, isn't he?'

I presumed she was still talking about Viggo. 'Yeah.'

'Sometimes, when I look at him, I feel... I don't know... it's such an overwhelming sensation... and his eyes... Magnus has nice eyes too... actually you too... you all have the same eyes... the same shade of blue... eyes are the mirror to the soul... do you think that Viggo and Hope have... you know...'

Oh God! One of the tell-tale signs of hypothermia is mental confusion. Her candid confession was a clear indication that her brain was beginning to lose its bearings. Intruders or not, I had to get her out of the well as soon as possible. I looked up, but all I could see were slippery stones and couple of... handles? About a metre above my head, a rudimentary T-bar had been screwed to the side of the well. I shone the torch up and noticed some more, spaced at irregular intervals. They must have been part of a basic access ladder. I interrupted her ramblings. 'I think I found a way out, but I need to step on your shoulders.'

She stared back with a calm expression, as if I had asked her how many sugars she wanted in her tea. 'Sure,' she said, managing to slur the four-letter word.

I swam behind her, counted to three, pushed her down with all my strength and jumped on her shoulders. She kicked upwards in a mixture of shock and survival instinct and propelled me out of the water. My outstretched arms were just about able to grab the T-bar at the first attempt. My feet scraped and slipped against the slimy stones, but I was able to heave myself up. I silently thanked Ariel for all those push-ups, there was no way I would have been able to hold my body weight when I first set foot on Valhalla. I climbed the metal handles at top speed, constantly afraid that they would collapse under my weight and throw me back in the freezing well. My feet touched the ground. I let out a sigh of relief. I glanced at the house. Everything was still. Too still. No lights, no sounds. The place seemed deserted. By the dive bags, coiled on one of the flagstones, was the nylon-rope. I had no time to lose – I had to get Isabelle out before she became too unresponsive. I secured the rope around my waist and dropped the other end into the well. 'Tie it around you, let me know when you're ready.'

'Done,' she replied after an eternity.

I heaved with every muscle in my body and managed to haul her onto the first rung. Using the rope as a safety line, she climbed the rest of the way and made it out of the well in one piece. We were shivering badly, but being out of that dark, wet dungeon had re-energised us. Her eyes gravitated towards the house. 'I think they've gone,' I said.

We were both terrified but, being British, I could conceal my feelings better. Self-denial is a bit of a national trait. We tiptoed into the silent kitchen. Isabelle flicked the light switch. The ground floor was exactly as we left it, not a speck of dust out of place – whatever the intruders were after, they knew where to look.

'I'll get us some towels,' said Isabelle. She stepped out of the kitchen, gasped and clasped her hand to her mouth. I rushed over. Viggo lay slumped at the bottom of the stairs. The deep cut on his forehead had begun to coagulate, but his left arm was bleeding profusely. I tried to remember one of my mother's many lectures on what to do in a medical emergency, but my mind was blank. I knelt beside him and placed two fingers on his neck.

'Is he alive?' mumbled Isabelle, hand still covering her mouth.

'I think so, I've got a pulse.'

She was impressed by my medical skills, which said it all about her state of mind. I found some clean dish towels in the kitchen and pressed them to the wound to stem the blood.

'Shouldn't you give him mouth to mouth or something?' she asked.

'I'm not going to kiss him unless I absolutely have to, but if you want to, be my guest.'

She blushed, he stirred. Slowly, he opened his eyes and blinked at the unfamiliar surroundings. He sat up and rested his back against the wall. It took him a few seconds to register the pain in his arm. 'I think I've been shot.'

I couldn't dispute his diagnosis. 'We need to get you to a hospital.'

He lifted his injured bicep closer to his face and calmly examined his bullet wound. 'No need, I'll be fine.'

'You've been shot!' I yelled in a high-pitched voice which was too embarrassing for words.

'Dude, chill! You sound like a girl! The wound is superficial, it's just a deep graze.' He tested the arm's mobility and grimaced. 'I need to call Magnus, they took Miguel.'

'What?' I screeched, in the same high-pitched voice. 'Why?'

'I don't know, we didn't exactly sit down for tea!' He rubbed his eyes. 'I remember being shot and falling backwards. Next thing I knew, the two of you were hovering over my face.' He sighed. 'Can you get me a phone? I really need to call Magnus.'

I handed him the Iridium. He dialled my father and delivered the bad news. Well, sort of, he avoided any mention of his wound. 'What do you want us to do?' he asked, receiver pressed to his ear. My father barked some instructions at the other end. 'Fine. See you in two hours.'

Isabelle, face streaming with tears, collapsed on a chair. Crying girls have a paralysing effect on most guys. It's not that we don't care, we just don't know what to do, in particular if we're out of tissues, which I was. I waited for Viggo to say something, but he was too absorbed in his wound. I drew a breath and forced myself to speak. 'It's OK. We'll find Miguel, you'll see.'

She was too smart to believe me. She sobbed louder. Viggo got to his feet and elbowed me softly with his good arm. 'Why don't you give her… you know… a hug?'

Wonderful, he was still convinced that we secretly fancied each other and was under the illusion that my hug could somehow make her feel better. She surprised me by spontaneously launching herself into my arms and I couldn't fail to notice the pool of snot that was beginning to collect around her nostrils. 'Don't let him see me like this,' she whispered. 'My nose is dripping.'

Her warm breath tickled my ear. I would have enjoyed the sensation a lot more if she hadn't wiped her nose against my shirt. When she released me from her snot-infested embrace, I changed into dry clothes and hunted around for the first-aid kit to dress Viggo's wounds. Thanks to mum's extensive training, I had developed bandaging skills worthy of an Egyptian embalmer.

'I don't want to scare you,' said Viggo, popping a couple of strong painkillers, 'but we're not safe here. Until Magnus and Ariel get back, we should get to the busy, touristy area and stay in full view. Crowds will minimise chances of the attackers trying anything funny. We have no idea what we're dealing with, keep your eyes peeled.'

CHAPTER 30

Licata's busiest area turned out to be incredibly quiet. Given the late hour, most restaurants were closing and the more resilient nocturnal crowds were heading for clubs that wouldn't allow minors through their doors. Being fifteen is a bit of a limbo, children look at you as if you are an adult and adults look at you as if you are a child. You belong neither here nor there. We had been refused by the umpteenth closing restaurant, when I noticed a movement out of the corner of my eye. 'I think we're being followed,' I whispered. 'Two guys with Marine haircuts.'

Viggo didn't turn. 'Damn it, some of Miguel's abductors had buzz cuts. In here, quick.'

He pushed us through the doors of the nearest hotel. It was a small building and the number of brass plaques outside the entrance vouched for its quality. The duty-manager of the *Italian Boutique Hotel of the Year* came to greet us or, rather, to stop us. His receding hairline was in stark contrast with the handlebar moustache that sat on his upper lip. 'May I help you?' he said, with his chin in the air.

'Ah, yes, where's the bar please?' asked Viggo.

The duty-manager did his best to sound more accusing than helpful. 'Are you guests?'

'No, but we'd like to have a drink at the bar.'

'I'm afraid the bar is for guests only.'

'Look,' said Viggo, 'this is our last night in Licata. It would mean a lot if we could have a drink in its finest establishment.'

The manager was unmovable. 'Licata's finest establishment is for patrons only. Now, if I may ask you to leave—'

'Viggo? Oh – my – God! It is you!'

A slender woman in her mid-forties stared at him as if he had been catapulted from heaven. She had squeezed into an extra-tight black dress and her platinum bob framed a face slathered in heavy make-up, it was hard to tell what lay underneath. I stared at her surgically enhanced lips, covered in a bright shade of red, and wondered if she was a girl-clown on the run. 'Helga and I were hoping you'd phone, but we were beginning to lose hope. Are you staying for a drink?' she asked expectantly.

Viggo's lips curved downwards. 'I'd love to, but the manager won't let me.'

The painted lady glared at the manager.

'You should have mentioned you were a friend of *Fräulein* Ursula,' said the manager with a constipated face. 'Please, do come through.'

On the way to the bar, Viggo put his face close to my ear. 'Dude, I have no idea who she is.'

'Didn't you meet her at the beach the day after my dad got drunk? I remember you talking to two German ladies…'

'You're so smart!'

'Who's smart?' echoed Ursula the clown.

'My… brother,' replied Viggo.

'Oh, your brother,' said Ursula. 'And the girl must be your sister.'

I extended my hand, but Ursula had wrapped both arms around Viggo's uninjured bicep. Isabelle was foaming at the mouth. 'Helga will join us shortly, but *I* saw you first,' said Ursula, carefully marking her territory. 'What can I get you?'

'A coke please,' replied Viggo.

Ursula snuggled closer to him and he tensed slightly. 'I'm sure you can handle something stronger,' she said, squeezing his bicep. 'You look very strong to me.'

Viggo half-smiled, even he could tell that she was hitting on him. We had been able to escape our pursuers, but I wasn't sure he could escape Ursula. He perched himself on a bar stool. 'Just a coke, thank you.'

'Nonsense.' Ursula pushed her stool closer to his. 'Barman, two vodkas and two orange juices.'

Our drinks materialised in front of us and Ursula coiled around Viggo like a snake around a tree. He ignored his vodka, or maybe she was holding him so tight that he couldn't move his arms. Ursula tried to pour the vodka directly into his mouth. 'Have a sip, it will help you unwind.'

'He can't drink, he's on medication,' said Isabelle. The steam coming out of her ears could have powered a train.

'Poor Viggo, where does it hurt?' asked Ursula, oblivious to the big plaster on his forehead. 'Maybe Ursula can kiss it better?'

Viggo promptly leaned backwards and successfully avoided Ursula's pouting lips. Since he had failed to identify the origin of his pain, Ursula decided to give him a shoulder massage which, in light of his recent injury, brought tears to his eyes. She didn't notice, downed her vodka and ordered another. And that's when I saw Helga stomping towards us. She made a beeline for Ursula and spoke as if Viggo wasn't there. 'We saw him together. *He* must decide which one of us he prefers.'

Ursula was unwilling to let go of her prey. 'Why don't you get to know his brother better? He's young, but he will grow as strong as Viggo.'

Helga deigned me with a pitiful look. 'I don't have the time to water him daily.'

I thanked my lucky stars she wasn't into gardening. Viggo's phone rang. He extricated himself from Ursula's embrace and provided my father with the name of the hotel we were imprisoned in.

'Was that your girlfriend?' asked Ursula with a sinister glint in her inebriated eyes.

Viggo slid the phone in his pocket. 'Just a friend.'

Four rounds of drinks later, Ursula was getting harder and harder to deflect. I tried to engage Helga in conversation, but I had met more talkative walls. The sat-phone rang again. Ursula tried to stop Viggo from answering, but the alcohol had made her too slow. He intentionally spoke Swedish to exclude her from the conversation, but I doubted she had noticed he was talking a foreign language. 'Are you sure it's not a girlfriend?' she asked again. 'She's calling a bit too often.'

'Positive, shall we sit on the sofas?'

Ursula jumped at the invitation and Viggo positioned his back safely against the wall, excluding the possibility of further unsolicited massages. He then pointed out that one of her fake lashes was falling off. I had no idea where he was coming up with this stuff, it wasn't even true, but she dashed to the bathroom and took a break from her conquering activities. Viggo dragged me onto the sofa besides him, much to Helga's dismay who was about to jump into the space vacated by Ursula. 'Magnus is at the back of the building,' he said, 'the front is being watched. We must find a way out.'

'Isabelle and I will check the fire exits.'

'And leave me alone with the praying mantis?'

I grimaced apologetically. The mantis returned. Isabelle and I excused ourselves, not that Helga minded or Ursula noticed, and began our exploration. Every single fire exit was alarmed, our escape wouldn't have gone unnoticed. We had to find another way. We returned to our table, Ursula was stroking Viggo's hair as if he was a Persian cat. I sat in front of a fuming Helga and I had a Eureka moment. 'So, is this hotel all it's cracked up to be?' I asked.

'It's nice,' she said without sentiment, trying to fish an olive out of her cocktail.

'The rooms facing the main street must be quite noisy,' I said.

The olive kept on slipping through her fingers. 'I wouldn't know. We're at the back and it's dead quiet.'

'Are you high up?

'First floor.'

Viggo grasped my plan. He stretched into a fake yawn and casually put his arm around Ursula's shoulders. Isabelle went as green as the olive that Helga was now furiously chewing. 'I would love to take a look at your room,' he told her, without breaking eye contact. 'Which number is it?'

The clown smiled suggestively. She fished a key out of her handbag and dangled it in front of Viggo's face. '112. Shall we?'

Seriously? Was it that easy? I struggled to greet Cressida without blushing and he could just invite himself into a woman's bedroom?

'Outside her room in ten minutes,' he whispered, brushing past me. 'Don't make any noise.'

164

CHAPTER 31

Viggo let us into Ursula's room, she was nowhere in sight. He ushered us onto a small balcony overlooking a grassy area. He had tied the bed sheets together to form a rope and secured one end to the balcony's railings. My father and Ariel were waiting at the bottom. I had some reservations about the strength of the makeshift rope, but Ursula's voice, coming from the bathroom, erased my doubts. 'Can I come out now?' she asked from behind the closed door.

Viggo helped Isabelle over the railings. 'Not yet.'

'You're *so* funny, Viggo, I haven't played hide and seek in years! But when I find you...' Her words lingered in the air, either for effect or because she had passed out. I didn't mind, I wasn't sure I wanted to hear the rest of that sentence.

'I need more time, I want things to be perfect,' said Viggo, sounding nearly sincere. He then grabbed my arm and lowered his voice. 'Dude, you can't tell anyone about her! Nothing happened! I swear on my mother's grave!'

His mother had phoned the previous week and seemed well enough, but I nodded and he relaxed. It was my turn to go. I flung my legs over the balcony and safely reached the ground. The hotel deserved another plaque for the quality of its bedding. Viggo was next, he landed on Ariel with the grace of a sack of potatoes. 'What's up with your arm?' asked my father, helping him up.

'He's been shot.' Isabelle made it sound as if he had done it on purpose.

For once even my father was taken aback, he lifted Viggo's sleeve and exposed my neat bandaging. Viggo pulled away. 'Superficial, I'll be fine. I'm a medical student, remember?'

'You didn't even finish your first year,' said my father glumly.

Ariel ran a hand over his smooth skull. 'He'll need antibiotics. A bacterial infection can be deadlier than a bullet.'

Despite her recent engagement, I entertained the notion that he could be my mother's ideal man. My father nervously scanned the area. 'We can't stay here, we're too exposed. Let's go to a safe place where we can talk properly.'

We followed him to a black Range Rover Discovery partially parked on the pavement. 'Where did you get this?' I asked.

'Hertz.'

I was surprised he would do something as normal as hiring a car from a standard rental agency. One of the screen wipers was holding down a fine. Viggo pocketed it in a fluid movement that betrayed regular practice. We clipped our seatbelts. My father kept a watchful eye on the rear-view mirror and doubled-back twice to make sure we weren't followed. 'I want your injury checked over,' he said to Viggo, without taking his eyes off the road. 'Hospitals have an obligation to report gunshot wounds, we'll leave them as a last resort. Get Sesame to put you in touch with a discreet doctor. And ask him to deliver the passports, laptops, I-pads and any electronic devices we left on The Pearl to our new location, he knows the address. We'll also need two untraceable Glocks.'

Isabelle didn't bat an eyelid – her extensive brand knowledge didn't include firearms. Viggo rang Sesame and asked for the Glock pistols as if they were a mushroom and pepperoni pizza. Ironically, securing a doctor was much more complicated. 'How much? You've got to be kidding!' screeched Viggo. He rested the sat-phone on his chest. 'Magnus, Sesame's doctor —'

'Whatever he charges will be cheaper than your funeral. Book him,' said my father, overtaking a speeding Porsche Spyder. He headed south, past Agrigento, and followed the signs to the Valley of the Temples – a UNESCO World Heritage site. We entered the archaeological park and were catapulted back in time. The Doric columns of the Temple of Concordia stood majestically against the night sky, like they had done since the fifth century BC. I was so absorbed with the view that I didn't realise we had come to a halt in a lit parking area. My father left the Range Rover across the line separating two well-defined parking bays and led us to a two-storey villa, the only five-star hotel within the archaeological complex. The night porter rushed towards us and I prepared myself for a spectacular rejection. 'Mr Larsson?'

'Yes.'

'Welcome to Villa Concordia, we've been expecting you.'

'Are you Sesame's friend?'

The porter nodded. 'I understand you need somewhere discreet for the next few days and that you want to be notified of any unusual activity.'

'That's right,' said my father.

'Very well. Your quarters are ready. This way please.'

I wondered how we would be able check-in without passports and discovered that it's done by following the porter straight past the reception desk.

Inside our suite, I collapsed on what may have been an antique sofa, it was very soft. Ariel headed for the minibar. He ignored a pile of coasters and placed his bottle of water directly on the table. Mum couldn't have loved him after all. My father was as tense as a bow string, his frown had turned into a permanent feature. Isabelle curled up on an armchair and wrapped her arms around herself. 'We must call the police.'

My father rubbed his frown with the palm of his hand. 'Not until we figure this out.'

'There's nothing to figure out, Magnus!' she yelled. 'My father's been taken!'

'And I will do everything I can to get him back, but we need to think this through.' He turned to Viggo. 'You said the intruders were a mix of Russians and Eastern Europeans.'

He nodded. 'They spoke English between them, but they shot me before I could place the various accents.'

'The house was untouched,' I added. 'They were looking for someone, rather than something.'

'Are you saying they were specifically after my dad?' said Isabelle. 'Who could possibly be interested in him?'

Old habits die hard. Despite being genuinely worried about him, she made it sound as if he was a total waste of space.

'Yuri's boss,' said my father.

'Yuri's boss?' I echoed. I wanted to lean forward, but the sofa was softer than quicksand and I had irreversibly sunk into its cushions. 'What makes you say that?'

He bit his thumbnail. Did he also bite his nails? Maybe that's why mum couldn't stand it when I did it. He zoomed in on me and Isabelle. 'You do understand that Miguel's abduction doesn't change a thing. You're bound by your oath and—'

'Dad, for God's sake, spit it out!' I couldn't take it anymore. The gravity of our situation was getting more real with each passing minute. 'We took the damned oath and we're going to stick to it. If any of us wanted to renege on our word, we'd be sitting in a police station right now. Viggo's been shot, Miguel abducted, Isabelle and I risked our lives at the bottom of that well! We're in this together, if you have something to tell us, this would be a good time!'

His eyes bore into mine, his scrutiny too intense to bear. I wasn't proud of my tirade, but I felt a lot lighter. 'I'm sorry,' I muttered. 'I overstepped the mark.'

'You haven't,' he said, after a long silence. 'You deserve an explanation. I had a very interesting chat with Professor Harket this afternoon. Sajjad Shareef, a lecturer of Arabic Studies at Cambridge University, has vanished without a trace.'

'So?'

'He had just finished translating an Arabic manuscript for a wealthy private client. The manuscript should have revealed the location of a precious ring, but the text didn't contain any obvious clues. The client wasn't happy and accused Sajjad of withholding information. Soon after that, he vanished into thin air. Yesterday, one of Harket's colleagues, an expert on Medieval Sicily, was contacted by someone called Yuri to interpret a similar letter. He refused.'

I shrugged. 'Yuri will find someone else.'

'I doubt it. News in the academic circles travel fast – nobody will touch a document that may have led to Sajjad's disappearance. Whoever Yuri works for is struggling to make sense of Godefroi's letter.'

'Is that why they took Miguel?' I asked. 'Are they hoping he'll figure out the ring's location?'

'I think so, but if we get to it first, he'll no longer serve a purpose and may be released.'

'Had you and Miguel figured out where they ring might be?'

My father shook his head. 'Not yet. We were supposed to work on the letter yesterday, but I wasted the day recovering from my hangover.'

I sank back into the sofa's jaws. 'I guess Knut was right, the Russians were after the ring after all. What does he have to say about this?'

My father let out a string of Swedish curses.

'He hasn't told him yet,' translated Viggo.

I had never seen my father so edgy, not even when Valhalla was broken into. He got up, went to one of the bedrooms and slammed the door behind him. Ariel leafed through a newspaper, searching for the crosswords page. 'Let him be, he needs to clear his mind.'

That may have been the case, but I was fed up of having to wait for someone's permission to see my own father. How could I get to know him if I was never given the chance? I slid off the sofa with the sinuosity of a black mamba and made a dash for his room. He was on the balcony, eyes glued to the Temple of Concordia, arms crossed over his chest. He didn't seem very pleased to see me. 'What is it?' he said tersely.

'I'm trying to process what's going on. Are you sure that keeping this from Knut is a good idea?'

'Yes, we have zero leads. He would demand that you were moved to a more secure location. It's the logical thing to do but...'

'But?'

'I still believe I can keep you safe. Problems arose when we were separated, when I didn't watch over you properly. The last thing I need right now is having you out of my sight. Next door doesn't count,' he quickly added.

I ignored the hint. 'Isabelle has a point. This would be a good time to call the police. I know Knut wants the ring for his collection, but I'm sure he doesn't want it this badly.'

He snorted. 'You don't know Knut.'

'Agreed, but—'

'Noah, leave it.' He shook his head, forlornly. 'There is *so* much you don't understand.'

'Then make me!' I yelled. I hated being patronised. 'I *want* to understand.'

'Drop the attitude,' he said through clenched teeth. 'I have enough on my plate. I need to keep my promise to you, save my best friend, stick to my mission and stay true to an oath I have taken many years ago.'

I wasn't expecting to be at the top of his weird list and wanted to make sure it wasn't a coincidence. 'Is that in order of importance?'

My question sent him over the edge. 'What does it matter?' he roared.

'It matters to *me*!' I yelled, just as angry.

My answer seemed to temporarily curb his rage. 'Yes, it is in order of importance. I failed you in many ways, Noah, I'm aware of that. This is the one promise I have made to you and I have every intention of keeping it.'

'Why are promises so important to you?'

'Because they are the essence of who you are. Promising something and sticking to it requires willingness, sacrifice, determination and honour.'

I wished he had put that much effort into his paternal duties, but this wasn't the time to bring it up. 'Is there any chance Miguel will figure out the ring's location before you do?'

He chewed his lip and didn't answer. I cleared my throat and raised my right hand. 'I solemnly promise that anything you say to me, right now, will stay strictly between us.'

He stifled an amused smile.

I clenched my fists around the balcony rail. 'Why can't you ever take me seriously? I want to help, I'm not a total idiot, you know?'

He killed the smile. 'Do you mean it?'

'The promise or that I'm not an idiot?'

'The promise, the idiot part is too subjective.'

'I do. I really do.'

He nodded slowly. 'Miguel's got good instincts. There's a very good chance he'll figure things out before me, but he won't reveal his findings.'

'What if his abductors force him to?' Images of the London Dungeon's Torture Chamber sprang to mind.

'He's a strong man, physically and psychologically,' said my father.

'That's not an answer.'

'That's the best I've got.'

'Is he in serious danger?'

'To a degree. I may know who Yuri's boss is, let's nickname this person *The Collector*, are you with me?' I nodded. 'The Collector is dead-set on recovering the ring because it would grant him access to… an inner circle. He wants to be part of it very badly and harming Miguel could be counterproductive. I think he'll keep it as a last resort.'

I filled in the blanks by applying the "my father is a Templar" theory. It worked like a charm. The Collector wanted to join the Templars and harming one of them wouldn't have been a good start. 'What can you tell me about the inner circle?' I asked.

'Nothing,' he replied flatly. 'And it's not because I don't trust you: Knut has sworn me to secrecy.'

'Do you often work for Knut?'

'I recover artefacts for him on a regular basis.'

'Does he pay you?'

'It's not about money, Noah.' His eyes lit up with unbridled excitement. 'It's about the thrill of the search. Nothing makes me feel more alive than recovering something from a distant past. The harder to find, the better. I'm a seeker, and a good one at that. When you first asked to be included in the treasure hunt, I saw the glint in your eyes and I knew we were cut from the same cloth.'

Viggo stuck his head through the door and interrupted the deepest conversation I had ever had with my father. I threw him a silent curse. 'Computers and passports are here,' he announced.

My father stepped back into the room. 'Good. I'll make a start on Godefroi's letter.'

I made to leave.

'Noah?' he called.

'Yes?'

'We should chat more often.'

CHAPTER 32

The doctor, a wiry man with an aquiline nose, bent over Viggo like a witch over a cauldron. 'You will need stitches,' he said in a whiny voice. 'Six, seven at the most. Don't worry, I charge by complete suture, not by single stitch.' He inserted a thread in a semi-circular surgical needle. 'May I?

Viggo flinched. 'Aren't you going to numb the area first?'

'It will cost another two hundred.'

'I thought your price was all-inclusive,' gasped Viggo, who didn't relish the idea of being embroidered on while fully sensitive.

'Anaesthesia is extra,' replied the doctor, curved needle ready to strike. 'Shall I proceed?'

'Go ahead, he'll be fine,' droned Ariel, without lifting his eyes from his crossword puzzle.

Viggo clenched his jaw. '*He* won't be fine, *he'll* be sore. Get him his money, Ariel.'

My tutor folded his newspaper in half and temporarily abandoned his quest for twenty-five across: first wife of Ramesses II. 'We can't use the credit card tonight, it could be traced. Sesame will get us some emergency funding tomorrow. In the meantime, you'll have to grin and bear it.'

'I'll bear it,' grumbled Viggo. 'But I won't grin.'

He didn't bear it either. His selection of moans and grunts snared my father out his self-inflicted bedroom exile. 'Is someone dying?' he asked, sarcastically.

'Hopefully not,' replied the doctor, placing two boxes of amoxicillin on the table. 'And taking one of these pills three times a day will further reduce the risk.'

He let himself out. Viggo popped the first antibiotic pill and massaged his arm. 'It's late,' said my father. 'We should call it a night. Ariel, will stand guard first, Viggo will take over in four hours. I need somewhere quiet to work on Godefroi's letter, I'll take the double-room. You can use the triple.'

Given the underlying issues of our group, a triple wasn't the most ideal arrangement. I felt totally out of place because, regrettably, I had never shared a room with a girl before and Isabelle felt utterly embarrassed by Viggo's shirtless presence. Arm aside, he seemed absolutely fine. He plonked himself on one of the beds, bid us goodnight, rolled onto his side and fell asleep instantly. How on earth did he do that?

When I opened my eyes, Viggo had been replaced by Ariel. I was surprised he slept with both eyes closed. In the lounge, a room-service waitress was transferring our breakfast from her cart to the table. She used coasters. Coasters must have been invented by girls. I bit into a pastry that resembled a donut minus the hole. It produced an ominous squishy sound – dollops of custard rained down on my only shirt. 'Happened to me too,' said Viggo sympathetically, pointing at his own crusty shirt. 'We'll need some clean clothes. Magnus pulled an all-nighter, do you want to bring him some coffee?'

I poured a fresh cup and knocked on my father's door. There was no reply, so I let myself in. My father, his head at a funny angle, was sound asleep in his chair. I glanced at his laptop screen. I honestly didn't mean to pry, but I read the first sentence and I was hooked.

Annus Domini 1318

My condition has worsened; I can tell by the face of the infirmary brother. If he had access to the superior medical knowledge of the Arab physicians, he could probably save my life, but anything coming from the Infidels is treated with contempt and suspicion. I have known the Infidels, I have battled them and I have befriended them. They fought with honour, as we did, they fought in the name of God, as we did, and they fought to protect what was dear to them, as we did. I have come to the heretical conclusion that we are not that different. And it is in their language, which I have spoken for so many years, that I choose to entrust my final words. I hope that the enigmatic Arabic writing will shield my secrets from prying eyes and guide them to those of an enlightened reader, of pure heart and open mind.

My name is Godefroi de Carignan, I am a Knight Templar. I can finally say this freely because by the time my words will be found, I will be long gone on my final journey towards the Kingdom of Heaven. The safety of my brotherhood is paramount and I pray that what I am about to disclose will not fall into the wrong hands. My order has entrusted me with a precious item. My duty was to protect it but, in the light of my injury, I will not be able to do so for much longer.

On the first day of September, I left the port of Valencia, in the Kingdom of Aragon, en route to Cyprus. A few weeks into my journey, the black clouds appeared on the horizon, the breeze turned to wind and the waves became rougher and angrier, as if they wanted to chase us out of the sea. The storm, therefore, was not completely unexpected. Yet, I was not prepared for its strength and fury. As the sea tossed us around like leaves in the wind, the mast collapsed and a shard of wood sliced through my side. I was thrown into the sea. In the distance, I saw the fire of a lighthouse. I clung to a piece of driftwood and began kicking towards it with all my strength. I prayed to the Lord to deliver me safely to dry land and He gracefully listened. I dragged myself out of the water and collapsed upon the wet sand.

When I awoke, a monk was wiping sweat from my forehead. A fisherman had found me on a beach close to the port of Limpiadum, in the Kingdom of Sicily, and brought me to the Monastery of the Holy Spirit in Agrigentum. My wound is not deep, but it is festering. I only have a few days before the infection spreads and claims my life. I must act fast; my time is short.

I asked the fisherman to help me to secure a fast horse and decent weapon. On a parchment, I marked the city of Agrigentum, the beach where I have been found and the location where I intend to conceal my precious item. I also indicated the approximate position of the Nuestra Señora, some parts of which were visible a few days after the sinking. I will be leaving tomorrow. In preparation for my journey, I have asked the monks for a book of prayers to the Virgin Mary. I pray that she will let me live long enough to fulfil my last mission and give me the strength to complete what I have been chosen for, and I pray that she will keep me safe during my last mortal journey in a perilous and unknown land.

As I come to the end of my story, the day is coming to an end too. The veil of night has descended upon the monastery. An owl is hooting outside my window, sheltered by centuries old olive trees, and the candle burning beside me is getting shorter. I will use its wax to attach the letter and the map to the back of the book of prayers. As I entrust my words to the Mother of God, I pray that my brothers will eventually find them and that the item be returned to its rightful owners. Tomorrow I will set off at dawn with Pegasus, my new mount. I trust that the light of Mary, Mother of God and custodian of my knowledge, will guide me, shield me and deliver me safely to my destination.

I lived my life with courage, dignity and integrity. I am proud of being a Knight Templar and I look forward to re-joining my brothers in the afterlife.

Godefroi de Carignan, Knight Templar.

As I struggled to come to terms with the implications of what I had just read, I was overcome by an uncomfortable sensation. Yoda would identify it as a disturbance in the Force. I gingerly turned my head. My father's gaze was tearing through me: I was going through his things without permission. 'If you weren't my son, I'd knock your head off in a single blow!'

'I didn't mean to—'

'Snoop? Pry? Betray my trust?'

I found the barrage of accusations disproportionate in relation to the crime. He definitely wasn't a morning person. 'I came to bring you some coffee and your computer was on.'

He snorted. 'I expected better from you.'

For someone who had abandoned his son in favour of a sea serpent, he could be incredibly judgemental. 'Don't be a hypocrite. It's not as if you've never made a mistake,' I blurted.

He didn't deny it. But he didn't admit it either. 'That coffee had better be good,' he said instead.

I pushed the cup forward. I couldn't believe how exhausted he looked. 'The Templars were active after 1307,' I said.

I nervously waited for his reply. He yawned in my face, stretched his arms to the sides and gulped the coffee in one go.

'Is that all you have to say?' I asked.

He inspected the bottom of his empty mug. 'I haven't said a word.'

'Exactly, I was expecting a bit more from a... seeker.'

He slurped the last drop of coffee. 'Such as?'

'An opinion?'

He waved his hand. 'There are countless theories about what happened to the Templars, but nothing's been proven. It's just centuries-old gossip.'

'Cryptozoology relies on gossip.'

'Ouch! You sound just like your mother.'

He was trying to change the subject, but I wasn't going to let him. 'You cannot dismiss Godefroi's letter as mere gossip when you flew all the way to Sicily to look for his ring.'

He bit his lip.

'Dad,' I continued, 'there are many Templar organisations scattered all over the world. Godefroi's letter proves that one of them is the real thing. If you google them —'

'*Google* them? Do you think that after staying undercover for seven hundred years, the Templars would suddenly launch a website and tweet the whereabouts of their missing fleet? C'mon Noah, you're a smart kid.'

'Am I?'

'Right now, I have some strong reservations.' Mincing his words had never been his style. 'If the Templars were still around, there isn't a chance in hell we could find them, unless they wanted to be found. An order that survived that long, undetected, would know how to cover its tracks. Plus, there isn't much for them to do right now, is there?'

'Meaning?'

'Nowadays pilgrims get proper insurance and travel in air-conditioned coaches.'

He had a point, what would the order's mission be in this day and age? Had they evolved and adapted or had they remained fossilised in their beliefs, whatever they may be? If they existed, they must have a purpose of some kind. He probably knew, but I couldn't ask him. He went to the bathroom and turned on the shower. 'Get out of here,' he said as neutrally as he could. 'You've done enough snooping for one day.'

CHAPTER 33

Ariel, Glock securely lodged in his shoulder holster, was busy loading bullets into the spare magazine. We desperately needed clean clothes and Viggo had just returned from the briefest shopping trip in history. He dumped some unbranded bags on the sofa and pointed his thumb at my father's room. 'Is he still in there?' he asked in disbelief.

Right on cue, my father emerged with an empty coffee pot in his hand. He was unrecognisable: the bloodshot eyes, the dishevelled hair, the half-braided beard, the eye bags that would have attracted a charge from RyanAir... He was a zombie-version of himself. If he had gone trick or treating in his current state, he would have been inundated with sweets. 'I need more coffee,' he rasped.

'You need some sleep,' said Viggo firmly.

'The location of the ring is somewhere in that letter,' replied my father. 'I have to figure it out.'

Viggo took the empty coffee pot from his hands. 'And you will, but you must take a break.'

'Not yet.'

'Why don't you let us help?' I asked.

My father yawned in my face. Twice. He still had his tonsils.

'He's right, Magnus,' said Viggo, while my father leaned against the doorframe. 'You don't have to do it all on your own. If we put our heads together, we may come up with something.'

My father's eyes slowly began to close. 'Sleep deprivation is used as a form of torture,' said Ariel, waking him up. 'Putting yourself through it won't bring you any closer to finding the ring. Or Miguel.'

Isabelle opened her mouth to say something, but Viggo had taken off his shirt to try on his latest purchase and she missed her chance.

'You're right, I'm a wreck,' conceded my father, sinking further into the doorframe.

'I'm not usually one for sympathy, but I could knock you out for a couple of hours,' said Ariel.

'Thanks for the offer, but I'll stick with the traditional methods. Wake me in an hour. We'll work on the letter together.'

He swapped the door frame for the bed and was asleep before he hit the pillow.

Isabelle could hardly contain her excitement or, more precisely, her arrogance. She hadn't seen the letter yet, but was already talking as if *she* would break the enigma and figure out the ring's hiding place. My self-confidence had never been my strongpoint, but hers was way above her abilities. I went for a shower just to get out of earshot. I towel dried my hair (my need of a barber was more evident with each passing day) and inspected the contents of the shopping bag that Viggo had given me: a multi-pack of underpants, three plain t-shirts, ankle socks and a pair of military-green cargo shorts with matching belt. I checked my reflection in the mirror – I was dressed exactly like him.

I was vegetating in front of the TV when Isabelle stormed out of the bedroom. I fought really hard not to laugh, Viggo had bought the exact same clothes for everyone. The oversized t-shirt hung on her tiny frame like a sheet on a thin ghost and the cargo shorts reached right below her knee, where the ankle socks began. She could have been awarded an honorary membership in a Latino street gang. She marched up to Viggo. 'These clothes are too big.'

'It's the smallest size they had,' he replied defensively.

'They're men's clothes,' she said, pulling at the empty fabric.

'I went shopping for necessities, not fashion items, the shop only sold men's clothes.'

'And it didn't occur to you to walk into a different shop?' she screeched.

He tried to keep a straight face, but the result of his blunder was too hilarious for words, we burst into fits of laughter. Between gasps, I realised that we had developed the sort of camaraderie that I had never enjoyed with any of my school friends. Not even with Tom. It felt good. Really good.

Two reality-shows later, a human-looking version of my father joined us in the lounge, laptop under his arm. 'Are you really getting the feeble minds to help?' asked Ariel, pointing at me and Isabelle.

My father twitched his face. 'It's worth a shot. I've read the letter over and over and I cannot find a way in. Hopefully you'll pick up on something I've missed.'

'So, where is this letter?' asked Isabelle with an air of superiority and more dignity than her attire allowed.

My father looked her up and down but kept his comments to himself. 'Not so fast,' he replied. 'You must understand that the letter contains some speculations. I expect you to concentrate solely on clues that could lead us to the ring and disregard everything else, are we clear?'

We all agreed. With the legal bits out of the way, my father distributed copies of Godefroi's memoirs around the table and set the timer on his watch. 'I want you to study the letter carefully for the next hour,' he said. 'When the time is up, we'll discuss our impressions.'

This was the best homework I'd ever had. I sharpened a pencil that didn't need sharpening because I was too excited and I desperately needed to fiddle with something. Fifty minutes later my pencil was lethally sharp. The same couldn't be said of my mind, I hadn't found any obvious clues. Isabelle's brain hadn't delivered either – she was too subdued. Ariel had gone back to twenty-five across, Viggo was drawing flowers on the coasters and my father's letter had turned into a plane. A sensation of utter failure swamped the room. The watch beeped. 'Any epiphanies?' asked my father expectantly.

Our silence spoke a thousand words.

Viggo took the lead. 'The first paragraph is useless. After years in Outremer, Godefroi learns to appreciate the ways of the Infidels. He fights them, but he respects them. It's all very interesting, but I cannot see how his personal impressions could be linked to the ring.'

My father flattened his plane to its original shape, grabbed a black marker and deleted the first part. 'I like this approach. Any comments on the second paragraph?'

'The Templars were still in existence,' trilled Isabelle, as if she was the only one who had figured it out.

'That's irrelevant,' said my father curtly. She wanted to reply, but he cut her short. 'Let's move on. Godefroi gets taken to the monastery in Agrigento and realises that his wound is infected.'

'Poor dude, all he needed was some amoxicillin,' said Viggo, popping one of his antibiotics. He swallowed the pill without water. It got stuck in his throat.

'How about the monastery?' I asked, while Viggo produced some rasping sounds in the background. 'Should we check it out?'

My father smacked Viggo's back and dislodged the pill. 'It could be worth a visit, but the ring's not there, Godefroi said so.'

'The last part is quite convoluted,' said Viggo. 'He was probably feverish. He rambles on about the olive trees outside the monastery, prays to the Virgin Mary to keep him safe, waffles about the owls, hopes that the ring will be returned to the Templars, reveals that his new horse is called Pegasus...'

'Who gives a fig about the name of his horse?' Isabelle's input didn't generate any reactions, other than Viggo suddenly yearning for figs.

'It could be a hidden clue,' I said, for the sake of contradicting her.

My father unconvincingly scribbled down the horse's name. 'Anything else?' he asked.

A hopeless silence descended on the room. I involuntarily cleared my throat.

'Yes?' said my father. His voice was charged with anticipation, I felt I had to come up with something.

'He... um... he had a change of heart half way through the letter.'

My father skim-read the various paragraphs. 'I don't see it.'

'At the beginning Godefroi prays to the Lord, but in the end he seems a lot keener on the Virgin Mary.'

'The Templars built many churches in her honour and held her in the highest regard,' said my father, jotting down my thoughts.

'He may be onto something,' mumbled Viggo, without looking up from figheaven.com. We waited for him to continue, but he added two jars of homemade jam to his cart instead.

'For God's sake, shut that website down and elaborate!' roared my father.

A startled Viggo quickly complied. 'One of the paragraphs bugs me,' he said, running his finger down the page until he found what he was looking for. 'The sentence *I trust that the light of Mary, Mother of God and custodian of my knowledge, will guide me, shield me and deliver me safely to my destination* leaves me a bit disoriented.'

'Nothing new there,' said Isabelle, as stony-faced as Queen Elizabeth during her Christmas speech.

Viggo exploded. 'If you don't have anything nice to say, shut the hell up!'

She threw an eraser at his face, and missed. 'That's not how the quote goes!'

'I know! I was being intentionally rude! And you throw like a girl.'

'I *am* a girl!'

'Stop it, right now,' thundered my father. 'We don't have time for this. We must work together, as a team, or we'll never find the ring. Viggo, focus, what bugs you about the sentence?'

He sighed and rubbed the stubble on his chin. 'Godefroi says that the Virgin Mary is the custodian of his knowledge. What on earth is he on about? I mean, praying for guidance and protection makes sense, but this knowledge thing seems, I don't know, out of place.'

183

We re-examined the sentence, but nobody spoke or volunteered further theories. Silence was followed by more silence.

'Is that it?' My father's voice was soaked with disappointment. No-one met his gaze. 'All the five of us could come up with is that Godefroi's horse was strangely named Pegasus and that, in his final hours, he favoured the Virgin Mary over God?'

He shook his head dejectedly. Unless we were hit in the head by a heavy stroke of genius, Miguel and the ring were slowly slipping away.

'We could adopt a scientific approach,' said Isabelle, for once speaking instead of scoffing. 'Godefroi only had a few days left. If we get a map of the Agrigento area, calculate the average speed of a horse and allow for forage stops, we can create a chart with concentric circles. Then we could see which suitable hiding places were within galloping reach.'

'Is this a real-life mathematical expression?' I asked dumbfounded. I had always considered maths as an abstract form of torture. I never thought it could be applied to our dimension.

My father considered Isabelle's theory. 'Give it a go, we have nothing to lose. We'll keep trying to break the letter.' He turned to face Viggo and I. 'Let your minds flow, pursue any leads, no matter how far-fetched. We're running out of time.'

Out of desperation, I checked the website of the monastery where Godefroi had spent his last days. 'Dad?'

'Uhu?'

'The Holy Spirit monastery was founded in 1299.'

'So?'

'How could Godefroi see centuries old olive trees outside its windows barely eighteen years later?'

My father pulled a clueless face. 'People built next to accessible resources back then, maybe the trees were there from before. An olive tree was pretty much a guaranteed income.'

I scrolled through the pictures. 'I'm looking at the Holy Spirit gardens and I can't see any olive trees.'

'Why don't you phone and ask? Monasteries never throw anything away. If they produced oil in medieval times, they'll have a record of it.'

I picked up the phone and spoke to a very helpful monk. He agreed to check the monastery archives and confirmed that they had never had any olive trees. My father made a note of the information. 'Interesting. My list now reads: Pegasus, Virgin Mary/God change of heart and olive trees. Isabelle, how are you getting on?'

Considering that her equestrian knowledge went as far as Black Beauty, she had surpassed herself. She had calculated the average canter speed of a horse at approximately twenty kilometres per hour. The figure allowed for terrain changes, environmental factors, forage stops and resting time. She estimated that Godefroi's injuries would have prevented him from galloping fast and that he could have handled one to two days' travel at the most. She began drawing concentric circles around the Holy Spirit monastery. 'Each circle represents one hour. Or twenty kilometres,' she began condescendingly, as if she was addressing a convention of imbeciles.

Viggo wasn't convinced about the speed. 'He must have gone slower,' he said. 'He only had one horse, I'm sure he didn't want to wear it out and risk being stranded in the middle of nowhere.'

Isabelle set her pencil down. And huffed. 'Are you an expert on horses now?'

'As a matter of fact, I am. I've been riding since I was five. I really miss my horse,' he added nostalgically.

'What's his name?' I asked.

'Dude, I'd rather not say.'

'For you to be embarrassed, it's got to be pretty lame.'

He grimaced. 'It is.'

'You've kindled my curiosity, shoot.'

He exhaled. 'Pegasus.'

I slapped my thigh and began to laugh. 'Like Godefroi's?'

'Yep.'

I flapped my arms in the air. 'Was he white and winged?'

He laughed along. 'Yeah, I flew him to uni every day.'

'Seriously, what possessed you to call him Pegasus?'

'I got him on my thirteenth birthday, at the time, I had a major crush on Athena, the Greek goddess.'

I laughed some more. 'It keeps getting better…'

He feigned offence. 'Stop teasing, I'm baring my soul here!'

'She was pretty average,' said Isabelle acidly, scrolling through images of Athena.

'C'mon, she's the goddess of war *and* wisdom,' he replied. 'It doesn't get much cooler than that! I wanted to honour her by having a giant owl tattooed across my back, but by the time I was old enough for a tattoo, my love for Athena had somewhat dwindled.'

I frowned. 'Why an owl?'

'Athena is often represented as an owl, or accompanied by one.'

'I thought her symbol was an olive branch,' I said, confused.

'That too, but it's hardly tattoo material.'

I couldn't disagree.

'How could I miss it!' said my father, in a mixture of shock and triumph. 'The owl, the olive tree, the shield, the knowledge: Athena!'

He dragged a chair next to Isabelle and began studying her circles. 'How far is the city of Syracuse from Agrigento?' he asked.

She fed the question into the computer. 'Two hundred and fifteen kilometres.'

'Based on your calculations, could Godefroi have made it there?' pressed my father.

'If he rode for eleven hours, yes.'

'Riding that long would be harsh on the buttocks of a fit man,' said Viggo. 'Godefroi was injured.'

186

'But he was pressed for time,' countered my father. 'Ariel, in your army days, have you ever been on a horse for eleven hours?'

'I was in the Israeli Special Forces, not chasing buffalos in the Great Plains.'

'Believe me,' said Viggo, 'riding for eleven hours requires buttocks of steel.'

While they bickered about posteriors, I studied the route between Agrigento and Syracuse. 'Two hundred and fifteen kilometres is the driving distance,' I said. 'Godefroi was on a horse, he didn't have to stick to paved roads. And if he lived long enough, he may have split the ride over two days.'

Google Maps offered a variety of ways to calculate a distance between two places. I selected the walking option. By cutting out all the major roads, the itinerary instantly shortened. 'One hundred and eighty-eight kilometres,' mumbled my father, doing some calculations in his head. 'Sore buttocks or not, he could have made it. Pack your stuff, we're off to Syracuse.'

CHAPTER 34

Syracuse lay in the South-East corner of Sicily and enjoyed a very particular layout. It was made up of two parts, separated by a narrow stretch of sea and connected by three bridges. The oldest part was located on a natural island called Ortigia, the other on mainland Sicily. All the Greek temples and the historical buildings, including our hotel, were on Ortigia.

The Discovery was by far the comfiest car we had travelled in and Isabelle had fallen asleep after our latest refuelling stop. Her head rested on my left shoulder and I tried to keep as still as possible not to wake her up. Why did I have to be so nice? Having her so close generated a strange feeling, not at all unpleasant, and I tried to imagine how cool this moment would be if she was Cressida instead. The navigator yapped some more instructions. We crossed the Umbertino Bridge and entered the historical heart of Syracuse. My father struggled to squeeze the Discovery through Ortigia's narrow streets.

'We lost a mirror,' droned Ariel.

'We're nearly there,' replied my father, ignoring the variety of rasping sounds coming from the outside. He turned into a panoramic road, overlooking the Ionian Sea.

'That's it, Grand Hotel Ortigia,' said Viggo, pointing at a two-storey structure with a series of flags hanging over the entrance. 'The only hotel on the island with a private car park.'

My father killed the engine and handed the car keys to the hotel valet. Our interconnecting suites were on the ground floor. One had been set up as sleeping quarters, the other as a work hub. One of its walls was dominated by a smart board. 'This is the Cathedral of Syracuse,' said my father, uploading images of an impressive church to the smart board. Its façade was so intricate that it was impossible to absorb everything in one go. 'In the past, converting temples into churches was common practice and the Cathedral of Syracuse used to be the Temple of Athena.' He paused. 'I believe this is where Godefroi hid the ring.' He reaped a few gasps and continued. ''Battle of Himera, does it ring a bell?'

It didn't ring a thing, I hoped it was a rhetorical question.

'Yes,' said Viggo, while peeking under his bandages. 'Gelon, the King of Syracuse, and Theron, the Tyrant of Agrigento, defeated the Carthaginian army.'

'That's right,' said my father. 'And to commemorate the victory, Gelon built Athena a fitting temple. Over time, the pagan gods were abandoned and the temple was turned into a Christian church which, in 878, fell into the hands of the Arab invaders. It was used as a mosque until 1093, when the Norman king in charge reinstated it as a Christian church dedicated to the cult of the Virgin Mary.'

'What makes you think Godefroi hid the ring there?' I asked.

'His choice of words. The owl and the olive trees aren't the only references to Athena. As Viggo pointed out, referring to the Virgin Mary as a custodian of knowledge sounded strange, but the definition fits Athena like a glove. Godefroi also mentions that the *light* of Mary will *guide* him and *shield* him.'

His hopeful grin told me I should have made a connection, but I had that foggy algebra feeling seeping through my brain. 'I have no idea what you're talking about,' I confessed.

Isabelle welcomed my public display of ignorance, so she wouldn't have to parade hers.

'OK,' said my father, 'let's start from the beginning. The temple's original structure included a very tall, square-based tower. Affixed to it was Athena's fabled *shield*.' He let the word sink in. 'In the right conditions, the sun reflected off the copper shield and made the temple visible from a considerable distance. The shield acted as a beacon, as a *guiding light*. Are you with me?'

I nodded. 'Do you think Godefroi hid the ring in the tower?'

'I hope not! It was destroyed in a major earthquake in 1542. But the clues he gave us definitely point towards the Temple of Athena.'

'So where is this ring, exactly?' asked Isabelle.

'Not sure,' replied my father. 'Let's go to the cathedral and figure it out.'

CHAPTER 35

We left the Discovery in the hotel car park and walked the
short distance to the town's main square. The stone-coloured
piazza was dominated by the imposing cathedral. It was hard to
believe that the indisputably Christian façade, dotted with
statues of saints and angels, housed a pagan temple on the
inside. A figure of the Virgin Mary presided over a massive
arched entrance, flanked by two smaller doors. I climbed six
marble steps and stepped inside – the church was huge. To be
fair, given its front, it had to be expected, but the optimist in me
was hoping for some type of shrinking effect that would have
made our search a lot more manageable. The cathedral was split
into three naves and the original temple columns were still
visible along the left-hand side. 'We'll be here forever,' moaned
Isabelle, dipping her fingers in the holy water and smoothing
her hair. An annoyed worshipper emerged from her prayer
book and urged her to be quiet.

'My father said to concentrate on the areas which belonged
to the original temple and disregard the more modern
additions,' I whispered. 'That should narrow the search a bit.'

'Umph.'

'What?' I had actually understood her grunt perfectly, why
did she have to be so unpleasant?

'Umph,' repeated Isabelle.

'Stop being so negative.'

'Easy for you to say, your father's prancing around limestone
columns without a care in the world; mine has been kidnapped!'

'That's not fair. He's very worried about Miguel.'

She was grumpier than a camel. 'But he's more worried about
the ring. Today he hasn't mentioned my father once.'

Viggo crept up behind us. 'Don't be like that. Magnus isn't
used to kids. If he knew you were so upset—'

'I am not a *kid*,' she screeched. 'I am a woman! Why can't you
see that?'

'Because you dress like a man,' replied the worshipper,
snapping her book closed. Isabelle turned into a verbal volcano,

abuse flowing like lava. Viggo grabbed her by the elbow and dragged her into the left nave. She attempted to dig her heels in, but her trainers inexorably slid across the floor. He squeezed her between the statue of Saint Catherine and an original Doric column. He wasn't happy, I couldn't speak for Saint Catherine. 'Princess, I know you're going through a tough time, but acting like you're possessed is not going to do us, or Miguel, any favours. You can call yourself whatever you like, I really don't care, just don't let your foul mood put the whole operation in jeopardy, OK?'

She stared at him with a mixture of blind rage and pure infatuation. 'It's just… I'm worried about my father.'

The way he leaned a muscular arm against the Doric column, made it look as if he was supporting the whole building single-handedly. 'I understand that, so I'll make you a very special deal. If you behave, I'll let you and Noah wander around the church on your own. How's that? But no holding hands and no smooching, we're in a place of worship.'

I cursed his poor judgement and watched her face silently fall. Oblivious to our unhappiness, he cautioned us to stay within the perimeter of the church and sauntered off. 'Shall we check the chapels along the right nave?' I asked, my voice polite, but devoid of emotions.

'Yes,' she said, equally unenthusiastically. 'The moment we find that bloody ring, I'll demand to be taken shopping. This outfit is in breach of my human rights.'

I had a feeling Amnesty International would reject her case. We crossed the main nave. The right side of the cathedral was guarded by a row of columns and flanked by four chapels: *Battistero*, *Santa Lucia*, *Sacramento* and *Santissimo Crocifisso*. Wrought iron gates and smooth wooden fences separated them from the incessant flow of tourists. We tried our best to explore the explorable, but the endless number of visitors made it virtually impossible.

Two hours later we got an outside table at a posh café right across from the cathedral. A large, white parasol sheltered us from the Sicilian sun. A young, dark-haired waiter came to take our order. Judging by the amount of pomade he had used on his hair, enough to style a whole gorilla, he wasn't the parsimonious type. He fiddled with his retractable pen. 'What can I get you, *signori*?'

I casually ordered my first-ever espresso. Mum never let me drink coffee – apparently, it was the first step towards substance abuse – but my father didn't object. He joined me on the road to perdition and asked for a cappuccino. 'I knew the ring's hiding place wouldn't be obvious,' he said, while we waited for our drinks, 'but I was hoping for an epiphany or two.'

'What if Godefroi never made it here?' asked Viggo, checking out a tourist in a very short skirt. 'We cannot fully discount that possibility.'

'We'd be back at square one,' replied my father, glumly.

The oily waiter returned with our order. Viggo attacked his overflowing chalice of ice-cream; Ariel downed his espresso in one go. I couldn't fight like my tutor, but maybe I could drink like him. I took a deep breath and gulped the contents of my cup. The bitter flavour hit my taste buds almost immediately – I couldn't tell if I liked it or not. Maybe it was one of those acquired tastes that adults often talk about. Oblivious to my coffee degustation exercise, my father was racking his brains about the ring. 'Every single item related to Athena's original temple was a dead-end. We must have missed something.'

'Maybe we're getting distracted by this whole Athena thing,' I blurted, fresh on the wave of my caffeine shot. 'The Athena clues were supposed to lead us to the cathedral, but maybe Godefroi hid the ring somewhere which has nothing to do with her.'

'Keep going,' said my father, inadvertently dunking his beard in his cappuccino.

'Templars were big on symbols, weren't they?'

'They were,' he conceded, drying his beard with a napkin.

'Is there anything in the church that is obviously Templar?'

He thought for a moment and stuck his bottom lip out. 'Nothing obvious.'

'I didn't pick up on anything either,' said Viggo, between noisy slurps. His table manners didn't elicit a single vitriolic comment from Isabelle.

'No vermillion crosses, no two men on a horse, no Holy Grail?' she asked apathetically, looking in the direction of the waiter. He blew her a kiss and she smiled demurely.

'Nope,' replied my father. 'The only chalice I have seen today is on this very table and Viggo is eating ice-cream out of it.'

We all laughed, Isabelle too, or maybe she was giggling at her greasy suitor. He wasn't her type, but her oversized ego was basking in the attention. I studied Viggo's chalice with a feeling of déjà-vu. All in all, it was quite plain: short base, wide cup and two semi-circular handles measuring a third of the cup's height. 'Dad, does the Holy Grail look like Viggo's chalice?'

'It's never been found. Nobody knows for sure.'

'But it could?'

'I guess. Where are you going with this?'

'There is a huge chalice in the cathedral. A Templar could view it as a Holy Grail symbol and deem it as the perfect hiding place.'

My father stared at me as if I had just come out of a lamp. 'Where?' he asked urgently. 'Where did you see this chalice?'

'In the Baptismal Chapel. It's not a chalice per se, but the baptismal font is shaped just like one.'

He was on his feet before I could finish the sentence. 'Stay here, I'm going to have a look.'

He dashed across the square. Ariel planted a light smack at the back of Isabelle's head. 'Stop encouraging the waiter.'

A crimson tide washed over her face. Viggo homed in on the waiter, me and, finally, her. 'Unbelievable!' he muttered. 'Flirting with the waiter right in front of Noah!'

'What do you mean by right in front of Noah?' probed Ariel.

Great, my love life hadn't properly begun and it was already a mess. My father rushed back and chucked some money on the table. 'Let's go back to the hotel. We must do some digging on this baptismal font.'

Two tables away from us, a man in sunglasses and a baseball cap lowered his camera and asked for the bill. I bumped Viggo's elbow. 'That guy took a picture of us.'

He scanned the myriads of camera-toting tourists jamming the square. 'Which guy?'

'He's… gone.' I pointed at an empty table. 'He was sitting right there.'

'Don't be paranoid, dude. We're standing in front of the cathedral. Everyone's snapping away.'

I should have listened to my gut feeling.

CHAPTER 36

My father had photographed the baptismal font from every possible angle and was busy uploading the images to the smart board. The font was nothing special: a huge marble chalice, resting on a round stone pedestal. Surrounding its base were seven identical bronze lions. Their right paws were lifted in the air, talons pointing downwards, as if they were about to shake someone's hand. Their mouths were closed in a smile as enigmatic as the Mona Lisa's – my theory that she may have been toothless had got me an F in Art History. 'The font and the pedestal are made of one solid piece of marble,' I said, studying the images. 'I can't see any obvious cracks or crannies that could conceal the ring.'

'Nothing beats a hands-on examination,' said my father. 'We need to go back to the church when it's quiet and check the font inch by inch.'

'You'll have to break in at night time, the cathedral is permanently teeming with tourists!'

My sarcasm was met with an ominous smile. 'Great idea,' he said. 'Check what time the cathedral closes. We'll need darkness and suitable clothing.' Before I could recover, he turned to Viggo. 'Make some calls. Get me the blueprints of the building adjacent to the cathedral. We need a way in.'

We parked in front of a large sport store in mainland Syracuse and headed for the running section. Isabelle filled her basket with anything she could lay her hands on, including a kettlebell that she could barely lift. Viggo handed me a pair of black Lycra leggings. 'There you go, try them on,' he said.

'B-b-but… these are t-tights!' I stammered, horrified.

'*Running* tights,' he corrected. 'They're for dudes too.'

I reluctantly followed him to the fitting rooms where my father had already changed into his black running tights and long sleeved shirt. The Lycra garments stuck to him like a second skin, leaving absolutely nothing to the imagination. He was a fit man, but the look was way too revealing for my British roots. I grudgingly changed into similar clothes and checked my image in the floor to ceiling mirror. On the plus side, the Krav Maga was paying off, I was getting more muscular and my chest finally had some definition; on the downside, despite being fully dressed, I had never felt more naked. My father and Viggo seemed more worried about our bulging hips – boxers and leggings didn't mix well. After a surreal discussion on burglar-friendly underwear, we reluctantly agreed that we should wear Y-fronts for the raid. I took one last look at my figure hugging ensemble and exhaled. This was going to be an interesting evening.

Ariel and Isabelle were waiting by the tills. She was cradling her overflowing mesh basket. 'I got her what she needs for church,' barked my tutor, 'but she demanded a lot more. Including a kettlebell that she managed to dump on my foot.'

She held the basket tighter. 'I need a new outfit. Or at least a pair of shorts that won't fall down as I walk.'

My father briefly considered his options. 'Isabelle, I need you fully-compliant this evening. If you do exactly as I say for the next eight hours, the basket's yours. Do we have a deal?'

'I love being bribed,' she gushed, shaking his hand.

Back at the hotel, Ariel was in a terrible mood. It had nothing to do with the kettlebell and, for once, it wasn't my fault either. He was still bugged by twenty-five across, the first wife of Ramesses II remained nameless and he refused to google her. As we walked through the lobby, the receptionist rushed towards us waving a cardboard tube, the word "urgent" stamped across it in bright red letters. 'Mr Larsson, this just came by courier.'

My father took the tube. 'Thanks, I was expecting it.'

The receptionist didn't move.

'Is that all?' asked my father.

She stared at him with a smitten expression. 'What? Oh yes, that's it. Have a nice day, Mr Larsson.'

Unlike Viggo, my father could immediately tell if someone was besotted with him. He rewarded the receptionist with one of his best smiles, read her badge and thanked her by first name. Alessandra fluttered back to the reception desk with the grace of a butterfly. Viggo gave him a mischievous look. 'If the raid goes well, you should invite her for a drink.'

'She's too young for me,' replied my father. 'I bet she's never seen a rotary dial phone.'

'Maybe not,' said Viggo, 'but if she likes you in your tights, she's a keeper.'

His teasing earned him a playful smack on the back of the head. 'Cut it,' said my father, unlocking our bedroom door, 'we have work to do. These are the plans we were waiting for.'

Inside, he stretched the tube's contents across the desk. The blueprints of the three-storey palace located next to the cathedral came into view. Aside from the episcopal offices, the palace housed a seminary and a library. 'Excluding the main doors, the cathedral is accessible via two passages,' said my father, peering at the plans. 'The first connects the priest's house to the *Santissimo Sacramento* chapel. The second links the episcopal offices to the Baptismal chapel. The priest is likely to be in, so the offices are our best bet.'

'We could access the episcopal offices via the seminar or the library,' suggested Viggo.

'The seminar has a very strict visitor policy,' said my father. 'The library can be viewed by appointment only and there is a long waiting list.'

'Don't you have any friends who could pull some strings?' I asked. After all, he had just got the palace's blueprints out of thin air.

My father scratched his temple. 'I do, but we may need to inspect the font beyond standard methods. I don't want my name attached to it.'

'*Beyond* standard methods?' I gasped. 'As in damaging the font?'

'I hope it won't come to that, but I can't discount it, there is too much at stake.' He refocused on the blueprints. 'Entering the episcopal palace from the front is not an option, too much exposure. Any usable windows at the back?'

'Yes,' replied Viggo, 'but they're probably alarmed.'

'Wouldn't it be easier to get locked inside the cathedral at closing time and come out when we're ready?' I asked. My plan was neither fearless nor epic, but at least it didn't involve storming through unknown buildings decked in figure-hugging outfits.

My father thought about it and nodded. 'Basic, but effective. We should definitely get you espresso more often!'

CHAPTER 37

We wanted to be in position before the church got too empty, so we got to the cathedral an hour before closing time. Our running gear was neatly packed into a pair of inconspicuous backpacks, Ariel was carrying one, Viggo the other. One by one, we sneaked into our designated hiding places: two medieval pulpits at the back of the main nave. My father, Viggo and I would share the first, Isabelle and Ariel the second. I made my way up – stomach tied into a quadruple knot – and joined my partners in crime on the pulpit floor. Their composure was reassuring and disturbing at the same time – I couldn't believe that they had actually brought books along. And I couldn't believe their titles either: *"Amputation for dummies"* and *"Unicorns: legend meets science."* At 7:30pm the priest urged the few remaining tourists to leave. Minutes later, the front doors creaked on their hinges and locks slid into familiar places. There was some movement over the next few hours, then everything went quiet. Viggo stuck his head above the pulpit's parapet and rotated three hundred and sixty degrees. The coast was clear. He unzipped the backpack and removed our tragic outfits. The pulpit was a tight squeeze, it was never meant for a crowd, so we had to change one at a time. A few contortions later, we all got into costume – for lack of a better word – and descended into the main nave. Nobody spoke. My father, Viggo and Ariel were completely at ease in their second skins, but Isabelle and I didn't know where to look. I had seen her in a bikini before, so her toned shape was no big news, but she had never seen me this bare. There was no escaping the feeling of awkwardness, just like my clothes it was mercilessly attached to my skin. 'Damn it!' whispered Viggo. 'I forgot the Y-fronts.'

'At least you remembered the boxers,' I said.

Isabelle instinctively glanced at his bulging hips. Realising that she was staring at his buttocks, she hurriedly averted her eyes. Viggo misjudged her reaction. 'Does it look that bad?'

'N-no, I mean, I don't know, I… d-didn't look,' she stuttered.

'But you did,' he insisted. 'I saw you.'

'You're wrong. I was looking at Noah.'

'Uh,' grunted Viggo with tangible contempt. 'You should have looked at him earlier, when he was sitting right in front of you, but you were too busy flirting with Mr Cappuccino.'

My father threw us a curious look and I wished I could sink to the bottom of the Mariana Trench. Thankfully the *Battistero* chapel came into view and priorities changed. The baptismal font sat on a raised platform, flanked by two golden mosaics. A large glass panel surmounted by three stars dominated the back wall. The wooden doors leading to the episcopal palace were visible on the right. We climbed over the low gate that separated the chapel from the nave. My father switched on a small torch and visually inspected the font. He then stuck the torch in his mouth and ran his hands all over it, including the pedestal. 'Solid marble,' he concluded. 'Let's check the lions.'

We crouched down. The bronze lions were also subjected to a visual inspection. 'Are they hollow on the inside?' I asked.

Viggo banged his torch against the closest lion, a loud clang reverberated across the empty church. 'Yes.'

My father smacked him on the head and shot him a reproachful stare.

'I'm surprised his head didn't make the same sound' scoffed Isabelle.

Viggo took both hits without complaining. My father grabbed each lion by the head and jiggled them around. None of them budged. 'We need to detach them,' he said.

While he selected his first victim, I noticed a dent in the marble surface. Given the font's illustrious age, some wear and tear was to be expected, but the dent was a bit too round, a bit too perfect to be accidental. I pushed my finger inside it, secretly hoping for a concealed mechanism that, amidst strobe lights and confetti, would reveal the hiding place of the ring. All I got was a condescending stare from Isabelle. Yet, the dent intrigued me. It sat above the head of one of the lions, like a halo carved in stone. I pointed it out to my father. He put his safari on hold and examined the recess. 'It is a bit too smooth,' he agreed. 'What the hell, let's take it as a sign and start from this lion. Scalpel!'

Viggo unrolled a leather pouch packed with various implements, selected a sharp tool and passed it over. My father began vandalising the font as delicately as he could. An hour later, he was brandishing a lion figurine. He shone his torch inside the bronze cast. Nothing. He shook it, still nothing. He grabbed a long, thin screwdriver and pushed it all the way inside the statuette. And that's when a loud noise, as if something had been knocked over, resonated throughout the church. It had come from the altar's end. We froze. We weren't alone. Isabelle was so scared that she found the courage to snuggle up to Ariel. My father brought a finger to his lips and urged us to be quiet. We didn't move a muscle, nerves on edge, ears ready to pick up the slightest noise, but the church was as silent as a grave.

'Ariel, with me,' whispered my father. My tutor nodded and removed the Glock's safety catch. My father pushed the lion into Isabelle's arms and reached for the other gun. He handed it to Viggo and dragged him to one side. 'Don't let Noah and Isabelle out of your sight. We talked about this, you know what to do. Keep your head screwed on and stick to your orders. We'll be back before you know it.'

The main nave was flanked by two rows of large columns. Using them as cover, my father and Ariel began to make their way towards the altar. Viggo selected the correct tools from the leather pouch and started picking the lock of the doors leading to the episcopal offices. If we made it out of here in one piece, I was going to ask him to teach me. Isabelle, a tight bundle of nerves, was standing next to him, lion clutched to her heaving chest. 'How are they doing?' asked Viggo, without turning.

I cautiously leaned over. My father and Ariel were level with the *Sacramento* chapel, from which the priest's house could be accessed.

'Hands in the air,' shouted an unfamiliar voice, in a Russian accent. Beads of sweat ran down my back like an avalanche down a mountain, my throat felt drier than the Sahara Desert on a hot day and I thought I was about to be sick. Viggo threw a worried glance over his shoulder, but kept working on the lock with measured movements. I inched forward. My father's and Ariel's hands were raised, the Glock nowhere in sight. Ariel had somehow managed to tuck it at the back of his tights. I couldn't see their opponent, all I got was the sound. Listening to an action movie isn't much fun.

'Magnus Larsson, what an honour!' said the voice.

'Who are you?' asked my father, betraying no fear.

'My name is irrelevant—'

'*Irrelevant*? I take it your mother didn't like you.'

'Very funny, Mr Larsson,' said Irrelevant, without sounding particularly amused. 'First things first, get the rest of your team to come out.'

'It's just the two of us.'

'Drop the act. We've been watching you very carefully. Five of you entered this church, three are missing.'

'You should have paid more attention, the others left early via the side door in Via Minerva.'

'You're lying.'

'Do you really think I'd be breaking and entering a cathedral with such an incompetent crew?'

Irrelevant seemed to weigh his reply. He obviously didn't hold us in high regard either. 'Where's the ring?' he barked.

'I don't know what you're talking about,' replied my father.

'Don't play dumb. Your replacement led us here, but he wasn't able to find the ring either. If you sneaked in after closing time, there must be a reason.'

'Replacement?'

'Haven't you worked it out yet? *You* were the original target of the Licata break-in. My boss thinks very highly of you, Mr Larsson. He was sure you would be able to decode the letter and guide him to the ring's location. In your absence, we had to do with Mr Santiago de Castillo who, I may add, proved just as worthy. Threatening to harm his daughter was the tipping point. Pavel, bring him out.'

The door to the priest's house squeaked open. Despite my mounting curiosity, I didn't dare stick out a millimetre further. 'I'm sorry I led them here,' said Miguel's voice. 'They threatened to harm Isabelle. I didn't know whether they had her or not, but I couldn't risk calling their bluff.'

'They played you,' said my father. 'She's been with me all along. She was never in any danger.'

The last sentence was definitely debatable. Upon hearing her father's voice, Isabelle frantically scrambled in his direction. I wrapped my arms around her just in time. I had often pictured myself hugging a girl this tight, but in my version of the events she wasn't trying to run away from me. Judging by her laboured breathing, a panic attack was imminent. I hoped my next close encounter with a girl would be less dramatic. I pulled her back and gently steered her towards Viggo who had worked his magic on the lock: the double-doors stood open. Irrelevant's voice boomed across the church. 'Where is the ring?'

'I don't know,' replied my father. Ironically, he wasn't lying.

'You obviously need some leverage,' hissed Irrelevant. 'Have a look at your associate's chest and let me ask you again: where is the ring?'

This time I had to peek. A red dot was shining on Ariel's chest. 'He must be a bad shooter if he needs mechanical help at such close range,' droned my tutor.

'You won't be so smug when you're dead. If you don't give me the ring, I'll—'

All hell broke loose: Ariel had reached for the Glock, but his swift movement hadn't escaped his opponents who immediately opened fire. My father dived for cover behind a column, Ariel fell to the floor. Despite being hit he kept on shooting. He shouted to my father to get the hell out. I raced towards Viggo. He grabbed his backpack and pushed a lion-clutching Isabelle through the double doors. We closed them behind us, pushed a heavy desk against them to block access and sprinted along foreign corridors. The passage we were running along had doors at either side, we tried every single one – none of them budged. The episcopal offices were closed for the night, their secrets safely locked away. We came across a set of French doors overlooking a large, well-tended, internal garden. 'Through here,' said Viggo.

The opening mechanism was the same as any standard window, no locks. I pulled Isabelle behind me. 'We have to go back for my dad, we have to go back for my dad,' she repeated on a loop.

'Be quiet,' I urged, 'someone may hear us.'

We crossed the internal garden and reached another set of French doors. Viggo smashed the glass with his elbow, inserted his hand in the opening and reached for the handle. 'This is the seminary,' he said. 'According to the blueprints, we can go through here and come out in Via della Conciliazione. Then we'll… we'll make a plan.'

'He doesn't even have a plan,' said Isabelle, between loud sobs. Her wails wouldn't have gone unnoticed in a busy square, let alone in a silent seminary in the middle of the night.

Viggo grabbed my arm. 'Forget anything I said before, this is an emergency, do what you've got to do.'

I frowned, confused. 'What the hell are you talking about?'

'You've got to calm her down and shut her up, dude! Kiss her or something.'

His bizarre suggestion should have come earlier. The prospect of locking lips with me immediately silenced Isabelle. I was pretty relieved. Call me old fashioned, but kissing my fake girlfriend inside a seminary just to keep her quiet wasn't my idea of romance. From what I knew of Viggo's dating habits, he may have thought differently. The seminary's lack of security provided a near-welcoming feeling. We took refuge in the first accessible room. 'Before we leave, we should get back into normal clothes,' said Viggo. 'We'll be less conspicuous.' He stripped down to his boxers and rummaged through the backpack. 'Damn it!'

I really couldn't take much more. 'What now?'

'This is Ariel's backpack, Isabelle has a change of clothes, but we don't.'

'What happened to Ariel's clothes?' I asked bewildered.

'Don't know, they're not here.'

'They may be on the pulpit's floor,' said Isabelle sheepishly. 'I didn't want mine to get creased.'

Viggo clasped his hands to his face. When he emerged he shone his torch around the room. We were in the seminary's laundry, a bunch of freshly pressed cassocks hung neatly from a clothes rail.

'You can't be serious,' I said, taking the cassock he was handing me.

'Dude, it's the perfect disguise, they're not looking for a pair of priests. C'mon Princess, get changed, we must get going.'

'Turn around,' she said haughtily, dumping the lion on an ironing board.

We complied. For the first time, she was ready before us. Putting on a cassock is harder than it looks. Maybe they made it hard on purpose. Getting into that thing every morning must require the patience of a saint. It took me forever to do up the thirty-three buttons that ran down along the front. Judging by the variety of Swedish imprecations, Viggo wasn't faring much better. 'I'm done,' he eventually announced.

The sight of Viggo in a priest's robe was too much for Isabelle. She had to lean against the wall for support. She didn't give me, or my cassock, a second look. Or a first for that matter. 'Let's get out of here,' said Viggo.

I reached for the lion on the ironing board. 'Wait!'

'We must ditch it, dude. It would place us at a crime scene.'

The screwdriver was still lodged where my father had inserted it. 'The lion's hollow,' I said. 'The screwdriver must be holding onto something.'

Viggo stepped closer. I wrapped my hand around the screwdriver and jiggled it around. 'Can you feel anything?' asked Isabelle.

'It's weird,' I replied, 'like stirring… crystallised honey.'

I removed the screwdriver – its tip was covered in sticky residue. Viggo rubbed it between his fingers. 'Not honey. Wax.'

Isabelle frowned. 'Why would anyone fill a bronze cast with wax?'

I scratched my head. 'To make something stick?'

And then it hit me – maybe Godefroi had used wax to secure the ring inside the lion's head! I re-inserted the screwdriver and subjected the poor animal to a full lobotomy. Waxy curls rained down on my cassock. I kept going and eventually scraped against something hard. Undiluted adrenaline surged through my veins. A few not-so-gentle digs later, an object rolled out and landed at my feet. I collected it with quivering hands: a large silver ring, tarnished after centuries of neglect. Its round emblem was engraved with a Templar cross. The curved inscription underneath it read "MCXIX." The emblem rested on the hilts of two identical swords, their blades joined together to form the ring's band. I ran my fingers over it, completely mesmerised.

'Oh my God!' squealed Isabelle. 'The twelfth ring! You found it! Can I try it on?'

Whether Cartier, medieval jewel or pure piece of junk, she couldn't resist shiny trinkets. In a past life she must have been a magpie. Viggo clasped my shoulder. 'That's awesome, dude! Now we'd better make a move. I think I heard voices.'

CHAPTER 38

We sneaked out of the seminary and reached a nearby piazza. Police sirens blaring in the distance forced me to deal with the enormity of our situation. We may have got the ring, but at what cost? My stomach was tied into a quadruple knot and I was physically sick by the side of a magnificent fountain. Viggo patted me on the back. 'It's OK, dude. It's a lot to take in. At least we have the ring.'

I splashed water over my face and looked up. 'Who cares? Ariel's been shot! I saw him fall to the floor, I saw blood *on* the floor!'

Images of my father scrambling for safety flashed through my brain. I sniffed, my eyes were teary from being sick and my throat was on fire. 'Do you think my dad's OK?' I asked. 'He must have made it out, right?'

Viggo sat on the edge of the fountain, his back to the water, and dived into his hands. His body language didn't exactly fill me with hope. 'I don't know, I really don't know,' came the muffled reply.

'You're useless!' screamed Isabelle, her face a waterfall of tears. She wiped her nose on her forearm. 'You don't know anything! You don't even have a plan! We're doomed, we're so doomed!'

'For God's sake, woman, shut the hell up!' he yelled. 'I *do* have a plan, but you won't like it one bit!'

'What did you just say?' she asked incredulously.

'I'm sorry,' he mumbled. 'I didn't mean to shout.'

'It's OK,' she replied, with a stupid smile on her face. In spite of the circumstances, she had just hit the stratosphere. He had called her "woman" for the very first time. I was much more worried about the rest of his sentence.

He had placed Ariel's backpack on his lap and was busy rummaging through it. 'Car keys, Glock, some cash, hotel keys… ah, here's the phone.'

'What's this plan we won't like one bit?' I asked him.

He rubbed his eyebrow, as if he wanted to obliterate it from his face. 'My instructions are to keep you safe, and I cannot do it effectively on my own.' He grimaced. 'Dude, I really wish there was another way, but…'

'But what?'

He sighed. 'I need to phone Knut. He'll know what to do.'

I gulped. 'You can't do that!'

'I *have* to. Yuri's gang will stop at nothing to get the ring. If they pick up our scent, we're dead meat.'

My chest tightened. Kostas's worst fears had come true. My father's plan had blown up in his face. 'If you get Knut involved, I'll never see my father again, whether he made it out of the cathedral or not. Knut never wanted me around in the first place, he'll use this whole mess as an excuse to ship me back to London. Why are we even wasting time talking about this? We should be looking for my father.'

'We're not going back, it's too dangerous,' he said firmly.

'There must be something we can do.'

He shook his head. 'My hands are tied. I know this won't make any sense to you, but there are rules I must obey, protocols I need to follow. Magnus wants you safe, dude, he's the one who said to escalate to Knut if things got out of control. I'm sorry.'

I stepped away from the fountain to reassess my situation. I had no intention of surrendering to Knut without knowing what had happened to my father first. It didn't feel right. Jörmungand aside, we had only just connected and I wasn't going to give up on him so easily. With a determination I didn't know I had, I rotated on the balls of my feet, homed in on Viggo on the edge of the fountain and charged like a bull down the streets of Pamplona. I launched myself through the air and pushed him into the fountain. It was like watching a scene in slow motion – his mouth fell open in surprise and his eyes searched mine for an explanation that never came. We hit the shallow water and I buried him under a deluge of Krav Maga hits that he easily deflected. I kept going, rather than a Krav Maga fighter, I looked like a professional water splasher.

'What was that for?' he asked bewildered, pinning both arms to my sides in spite of his injured bicep. I didn't answer and tried to unpin my arms instead. He caught me glancing at the backpack perched on the side of the fountain and saw through my plan. He let go of me and began scouting the shallow water. The sat-phone was squashed under my foot, where it had been for the last few minutes. No Iridium, no Knut.

'Princess, is the phone there?' he asked, mildly panicked.

'No, it was in your hand when Noah... attacked you?'

'Is everything OK, Father?'

The question came from a fat, uniformed policeman. He was standing on the edge of the fountain, arms resting over his large belly.

'Um... yes, thank you,' replied Viggo nervously.

'Mind telling me what's going on?' asked the policemen.

'I... was showing my student an ancient baptismal rite.'

'This a public fountain, Father, not the river Jordan.'

'Of course, how inconsiderate of me.'

The policeman sighed. 'Bathing in public fountains is forbidden. I should fine you, but if my mother finds out that I issued a fine to a priest, I might as well go straight to hell. Get out of the fountain, will you?'

Viggo climbed out.

'Father,' continued the policeman, 'if I let you off, you wouldn't mind saying a few prayers for me, would you? I've been playing the lottery a while now...'

'Sure,' mumbled Viggo, wringing water out of his cassock.

'Everyone calls me Beppe, but I was christened Giuseppe. Better stick to the official name in your conversations with God, right?'

'Giuseppe it is. Now get the hell out of... I mean... go forth and multiply.'

'But I'm not married, Father.'

'Then multiply when you do.' He brazenly blessed the policeman and sent him on his way. With Giuseppe gone, Viggo strode to the edge of the fountain and demanded the Iridium. I didn't put up a fight, the phone's circuits were completely fried. 'Dead,' I said, with the same sympathy my mother displayed when she addressed relatives of deceased patients.

'Dude, how could you?'

'I'm sorry, you left me no choice.' He gave me a frosty stare. I got out of the fountain. 'My father is a resourceful guy, you know he is, for all we know he may have followed the Russians and managed to free Miguel. Why don't we give him twenty-four hours to make contact before rushing into something we may regret? What if he shows up two hours from now and you've already dragged Knut into the equation?'

'Do you really think he may have freed my father?' asked Isabelle hopefully.

'Maybe,' I replied.

'He's leading you on, Princess. This is about him, not us.'

Unexpectedly, she sided with me. 'But he has a point, Magnus *is* very resourceful. Maybe we could wait a bit…'

I could have hugged her, but my priority was to fix things with Viggo. 'We'll keep a super-low profile and check the news in the morning. If my father is… dead or if he doesn't make contact by this time tomorrow, I'll walk into a police station and contact Knut myself. That's a promise.'

'Twenty-four hours,' he said, still giving me the arctic treatment, 'but you will do as I say, when I say it. And there is one more non-negotiable condition.'

'What?'

'Magnus had a plan B in case I couldn't get hold of Knut. We're going to execute it.'

CHAPTER 39

The hotel was likely to be watched. With no credit cards and no documents, our chances of finding a secure place for the night were grim. We stepped into a deserted internet café. Absolving the owner from a number of sins in exchange for free computer time wasn't one of our best moments, but beggars can't be choosers and the mysterious Plan B we had agreed to couldn't be kick-started without Google Maps. Viggo sat in front of a monitor and looked up the distance between Syracuse and Palermo, another Sicilian city. 'The main objective of Plan B —'

'Viggo? I can't believe it!'

I couldn't believe it either, of all people Ursula had walked in from the street. What the hell was she doing in Ortigia? She was a bit unsteady on her towering heels and I suspected she had visited a variety of local bars before spotting us from the window. Viggo stood up, unsure how to justify his untimely departure from her bedroom. If Ursula's eyes got any wider, they would have picked up a satellite signal. 'Oh – my – God! Are you a *priest*? I knew there had to be a reason for your sudden disappearance in Licata! Wait 'til I tell Helga, she left for Hamburg yesterday.'

Viggo's outstanding improvisation abilities came to his aid. In my opinion, he should abandon university altogether and join a theatre company. 'I'm so sorry,' he said to Ursula, with the best puppy eyes I had ever seen. 'I never meant to lie to you. When our paths crossed, I was in the midst of a mystical crisis. I've only just taken my vows and meeting you made me question my choices even more...'

'But the faith is strong with this one,' said Isabelle, unashamedly rephrasing Darth Vader's quote. 'Viggo found his way again, and he will soon find his way to his new parish in a remote African village. You should say your goodbyes now.'

'I had forgotten about your "lovely" sister,' said Ursula, unashamedly turning her back to Isabelle. 'So, *Viggo*, what are you doing here? Making the most of the internet before being shipped off to your desolate parish to be?'

211

The way she stressed his name implied that Isabelle should keep her gob shut. 'Actually, we're here because we have nowhere else to stay, money's tight and I'm in trouble,' he answered frankly.

'Are you in trouble with the Vatican?' asked Ursula, overstressing each syllable.

'Probably.'

Considering we were wearing stolen cassocks and posing as clerics, his words weren't far from the truth. Ursula rested a sympathetic hand on his bicep. 'You don't want to go to this remote African village, do you?'

He shook his head. 'I'm a very bad priest.'

That was indisputable. Ursula withdrew a key card from her silver clutch bag. 'I cannot help with Vatican troubles, but you can stay at my aparthotel for tonight. It's just around the corner. Helga's already left, so there's space for everyone, even your awful sister.'

He accepted the key card and instinctively pushed it in a side pocket that wasn't there. 'Will you be… around?'

Ursula didn't miss the quaver his voice. 'Don't worry, I won't lead you further into temptation. Helga and I had double-booked our accommodation and missed the cancellation deadline, I'll stay at the other hotel.' She stepped closer, slipped him her card and gave him a peck on the cheek. 'Goodbye handsome Viggo, if you have another mystical crisis and happen to be stranded in Hamburg, look me up.'

Ursula's self-catering apartment was stifling hot. The air-con unit wasn't working. I debated whether to take my cassock off, but decided against it. There was no way I could sit in front of Isabelle wearing nothing but a pair of uncool Y-fronts. I copied Viggo and undid the top buttons. He was still off with me and I hoped that my recent actions wouldn't permanently dent our friendship. Isabelle busied herself in the kitchen and surprised us with some sandwiches, which we ate in religious silence. 'I need to get you to Palermo,' said Viggo out of the blue, undoing a few more buttons.

'You agreed to give my father twenty-four hours,' I reminded him, unable to get past button number seven, which was particularly hard.

'I know, but I never said we'd stay here. Plan B's objective is to get you to a safe place in Palermo as quickly as possible.' He shot me a reproaching stare. 'And if you're thinking of pulling another one of your stunts, think again because there is no Plan C. I really can't tell you more, so you'll have to trust me, I'm in charge and—'

'Oh Viggo, cut it,' erupted Isabelle. 'If you give yourself any more airs, there's going to be a tornado! You're nothing but a lowly squire, not even a fully-fledged knight!'

Her outburst caught me completely unaware and I feigned sudden interest in button number eight. Viggo went down the same route and finished unbuttoning his whole cassock before he found the nerve to look up. We noticed the empty bottles of Heineken on the kitchen counter at the same time. While making sandwiches, Isabelle had sampled Ursula's beer and was now as drunk as a skunk. Viggo, cassock open down the front like a robe, walked to the sink and filled up a glass of water. 'You've been drinking,' he said, placing the glass in front of her.

She definitely had, because she didn't flinch at his half-naked passage. 'I only had a few beers,' she moaned, as if he was a party spoiler. 'Hey, your cassock's open.'

Yep, unquestionably drunk. She got her face embarrassingly close to the elastic of his boxer shorts and tried to identify the brand. Such intense concentration was usually devoted to Teen Vogue. 'Who's Björn Borg?'

He put some decorous distance between them. 'A Swedish tennis player, five times Wimbledon champion. He's got his own line of underwear.'

'Wow! For a squire you do know a lot of stuff!' She concentrated on his boxers again. 'Hey Noah, did you know about this Björn Borg guy? His underpants are pretty cool.'

I wasn't sure I wanted to be part of this conversation. I pretended not to hear. Viggo sighed. 'Princess, drink your water.'

'I'm not taking orders from a squire,' she replied haughtily.

He nervously shifted from one foot to the other, open cassock flapping back and forth. 'Give it a rest, Sesame's squire thing was just a joke.'

'This whole thing's a joke!' she screamed, gesturing towards the nearest piece of furniture, which happened to be the sofa.

'What *thing*?' he asked, struggling to follow the boozy meanderings of her mind.

'You, a squire! Magnus and my father, Templars! Knut, God knows what! I may not have all the facts, but I'm not stupid! Did you really think I wasn't going to figure it out? The matching tattoos, the hierarchy, the international web of contacts… Noah, stop fiddling with that button and tell him! Tell him we've known all along!'

Great. She had blown my cover with the subtlety of a dynamite stick. Viggo retreated behind a wall of silence and I had a feeling that she had dug us into a very deep hole. 'That's complete madness,' he eventually murmured unconvincingly.

'Is it? So, tell me, squire, why are you obsessed with fighting techniques? Why do you all have matching tattoos of the Templar cross? Why do you need contingency plans for a holiday and, most importantly, why aren't you married?'

He glowered at her, particularly bewildered by the last accusation. He opened his arms. 'I'm only nineteen.'

I was too slow to avoid his gaze and my embarrassed face confirmed his worst fears: I knew everything, or at least as much as she did.

'I'm only nineteen,' he repeated to no-one in particular. 'And this is the worst day of my life.'

Sometimes I forgot that he wasn't that much older than us. This was probably his first time in charge of an operation and Isabelle and I weren't making things easy. It hit me that failing to deliver the ring, or save us, could have tarnished his reputation forever. His Templar dream, like Jacques De Molay, would go up in smoke. I shuddered at my own imagery, tasteless, completely tasteless. 'Viggo,' I said, 'for the record, it's nothing you've done. At first it was just a theory, then—'

'*My* theory,' boasted Isabelle. She hadn't registered that her glass was empty and kept on bringing it to her lips. I quietly replenished it and saved her from drinking more air.

Viggo sat across the table from me and raised his hand. 'Dude, stop right there, I don't want to know. The less you tell me, the less I have to lie if… when Magnus makes contact.'

'But—'

'I'm the eldest and I'm in charge,' he said confidently. 'Tomorrow I'll deliver you and the ring to a safe house in Palermo. Afterwards, if you think it's a smart move, you can discuss your theories with your father. If I were you, I'd think long and hard about how you're going to handle this alleged information. The same goes for you, Isabelle.'

She raised a challenging eyebrow. 'Alleged?'

'Alleged. You have no proof.'

'You're so defensive,' she said airily. 'Why don't you come clean? You can trust us. If you don't want to trust Noah, trust *me*, just *me*. You can trust *me*, Viggo.'

I guess she wanted to be enticing, but her inebriated attempt reminded me of the snake from *The Jungle Book* trying to hypnotise Mowgli. Viggo didn't seem particularly mesmerised and the timing of her escaping burp couldn't have been worse. He leaned backwards to escape the fumes and she fell forward into his arms. Had she been sober, she would have turned crimson but, despite being half on her chair and half on him, she searched for an impossible comfortable position. She squashed her face against his naked chest, mumbled in French for a few more minutes and fell asleep. 'We should put Snoring Beauty to bed,' he said, looking down at her. 'She's going to have a major hangover tomorrow. And she's dribbling on my chest.'

I went to the bedroom, switched the light on and pulled the sheets back. He carried Isabelle over and gently laid her to sleep. His tenderness was rewarded with a second burp. He sat at the edge of the bed, elbows on his knees, and slowly sunk into his hands. 'I'm sorry about the phone,' I said, stepping closer.

He spread his fingers over his face and looked up. 'I'm not happy about it, but you were in a tight spot.'

'About the rest…'

He didn't speak, but didn't interrupt me either.

'Your secret's safe with me,' I said. 'I have no intention of landing you in any trouble with your… superiors.'

He scratched the nape of his neck. 'Thanks. Let's hope Magnus makes contact. If he doesn't, this is going to be my last assignment anyway. And if your theories had to reach the wrong ears, this would most definitely be my last assignment.'

In my head, it was as good as an admission. Probably in his too. 'I know we're in trouble,' I said, 'and I can tell you're not very… experienced.' I waited for him to stop me. I didn't want to push it if my help wasn't wanted.

He wet his lips. 'Go on.'

'If you need a wing man you can trust, I'm here.'

He scanned me so thoroughly I thought I was going to turn into a PDF. 'A wing man? You? I would need to interview you. How tall are you, a bit under 1.80?'

'And still growing,' I specified.

'Ah, the perks of being fifteen. Have you started shaving yet?'

'Yes. Once. For Christmas. I plan to shave again next Christmas.'

'Academic titles?'

'Zero, my academic career is a work in progress.'

'Progress rate?'

'Slow. Bordering on the undetectable.'

He pretended to be impressed by my answers. 'Job's yours, the only other unsuitable candidate has drunk herself into a stupor.'

Our one-to-one had put us into a better mood and I briefly wondered what his interview with my father must have been like.

'Seriously, dude, I could do with some help. This is just me and you though, no superiors involved, is that clear?'

'Crystal.'

'OK, here's conundrum number one. The best way to get to Palermo is by car. We can't hire one, my credit card and driving license are at the hotel which is likely to be under surveillance. We have the Discovery keys, but the car is cocooned in the hotel parking lot. Even if we manage to get it out, petrol is very expensive and we have roughly four hundred euros. I have no idea how much the Discovery guzzles, but I'd say on a par with Ursula, and Palermo is over three hundred kilometres away. Any ideas?'

CHAPTER 40

Viggo, freshly shaved and respectably styled, slowed his pace down Viale dei Mille, around the corner from the Grand Hotel Ortigia. He was about to run a hand through his sticky hair, then thought better of it. His combed-back wavy curls lay flattened under half a tube of gel – I sincerely hoped it was gel, I couldn't read German and Ursula's bathroom had more potions than the Harrods beauty department. 'Are you ready?' I asked him.

He straightened his cassock. 'Yes.'

'Isabelle and I will wait for you here,' I reminded him. 'All you have to do is walk into the hotel, as if you were a guest —'

'I *am* a guest, I never checked out,' he said with a serene look on his face. I couldn't fault his logic.

'The doorman will not stop a priest,' I continued, wishing I could be as chilled as he was, 'and the goons aren't watching out for a cleric. When you're inside, go to our rooms, get our stuff and make your way to the parking lot. Take the Discovery, exit via the back and come back here to pick us up.'

'Fine. If I'm not out in ten minutes —'

'I'll contact Knut. I promise.'

He jerked his thumb in Isabelle's direction. 'Is she OK?'

She was suffering the consequences of her drunken episode: splitting headache, sensitivity to light, queasiness, overall grumpiness and generic mortification. We had made her drink enough water to make a desert fertile and forced her to wear a pair of Ursula's sunglasses. 'I'm fine,' she grumbled unconvincingly, parking herself on a public bench. She looked like a three-dimensional black-and-white photograph, her skin had taken on a slight tinge of grey. I had no idea how much she remembered from the night before and I think she was too afraid to ask.

'I'm off then,' said Viggo.

He gingerly made his way to the hotel and I joined Isabelle on the bench. All we could do was wait. 'Did I do anything stupid last night?' she murmured, after a long silence.

'Other than getting plastered?'

She sighed. 'Yes, other than that.'

Tormenting her was more enjoyable than I thought. 'What makes you think you did?'

'I had this really strange dream. Have you ever heard of a Björn Borg?'

'He makes Viggo's boxers.'

A shade of red took over the grey.

'You seemed to like them,' I added casually.

She yanked her sunglasses off. Deep frowns deformed her pretty features. 'I liked his b-boxers? H-how…?' she stammered.

A familiar Range Rover Discovery pulled up next to us, the driver's window framed Viggo's chiselled cheekbones. 'Why don't you ask him?' I said, opening the door for her. She shot me a half-hearted death stare and climbed in. I joined Viggo in the front and scanned the empty seats. 'Where's our stuff?'

He glanced at the rear-view mirror. 'Don't know. Our rooms were wiped clean. They took everything.'

I gaped. '*Everything*? Including personal phones?'

'Everything.' He checked the mirror again and got into first gear. 'Let's get out of here. I'm pretty sure one of the goons was hanging around the reception area.'

My chest tightened. 'Did you manage to check the morning papers?'

'Dead-end, but it was to be expected. By the time Ariel got shot, they had already been printed. We'll give it a couple of hours and check real-time websites.' He turned into a quiet side street and parked in front of an electronics shop to input our destination details in the satnav. The shop's window was crammed with hoovers, blenders and switched-on TV sets. A stiff anchor lady was mouthing the news. Suddenly, Ariel's face flashed across the screens, surrounded by some paramedics who tried to push the cameraman out of the way. I dug my elbow in Viggo's side, he looked up from the satnav and let out a very unpriestly exclamation. 'We've got to find him,' I said. 'He'll know what happened to my father!'

Viggo grimaced. 'No detours until we know more. If he's under arrest, we'd better stay clear.'

I pointed at a small café next to the electronics shop. 'I bet the barista is an authority on local gossip.'

He pulled the hand-brake and winked. 'I like your plan, wing man.'

The tiny bell above the café's door tinkled. I wasn't sure why they had bothered hanging it there, the place was no bigger than a caravan and couldn't handle more than five standing customers at a time. We were on an economy drive (in the sense that we were saving all our money for petrol) and only ordered three espressos. Isabelle checked out the sweet rolls. 'Stop dribbling over those pastries,' said Viggo. 'They're staying put behind the counter.'

Unsure about the events of the previous night, she complied without a peep. Her meekness worried him. 'Is she alright? Did you two have a fight or something?'

'Nope, all rosy,' I answered with the enthusiasm of an octogenarian convict nearing the end of his life sentence in solitary confinement.

Viggo focused on the barista. 'I heard a lot of police sirens last night. Any idea what happened?'

'Two separate incidents,' said the barista, depositing the espresso cups on their respective saucers. 'A tourist was shot right next to Piazza Duomo and our cathedral, our beautiful cathedral, was desecrated by the Russian mafia. They had the audacity to settle some business right in the Sacramento Chapel.'

Viggo theatrically crossed himself. 'Any casualties?'

The barista wasn't the charitable type. 'Don't think so, but if anyone died, they got what they deserved.'

'What about the tourist?' I asked, downing my coffee in a single gulp. If espresso was an acquired taste, I had acquired it.

'He's in hospital,' said the barista. 'An Israeli teacher. Found it too hot to run during the day, so he jogged at night. Poor man!

Shot, concussed and left for dead. I bet he'll never come to Sicily again.'

If Ariel had had the presence of mind to get out of the cathedral and justify his outfit, he couldn't be truly concussed. And if he had passed himself off as a victim, he wouldn't be under arrest either. We paid for our coffees and jumped into the car.

Umberto I, Syracuse's only hospital, was a five-storey block that favoured practicality over elegance. Inside the main entrance, a large sign listed the hospital services. We grouped in front of it, trying to determine the correct wing for victims of gunshot wounds. 'You're a med student, what do you think?' I asked Viggo.

He pensively rubbed his forehead. 'We can exclude maternity and gynaecology…'

'Do mankind a favour, stick to archaeology! You can't kill what's already dead!' snorted Isabelle, jostling him out of the way. She ran her finger over the list of departments. 'They must have taken the bullets out. He'll be recovering in General Surgery.'

Without waiting for our opinion, she approached a nurse and asked for directions to the surgery wing. 'It's on the fourth floor,' replied the nurse in fluent English, 'but visiting times are over.' She then noticed our cassocks and presumed the worse. 'Oh *mamma mia*, are you together? I hope you're not here to administer any last rites.'

'Have no fear, child,' replied Viggo, even though the nurse was at least double his age, 'we're here in a chaperoning capacity.'

The nurse narrowed her eyes. 'Aren't the two of you a bit young to be priests? I've seen older altar boys!'

I wished I could sprout a beard on command and straightened my back in an attempt to gain a couple of centimetres. Viggo pushed Isabelle forward. 'This is the daughter of the tourist who was shot last night,' he said. 'She just flew in from Jerusalem.'

Isabelle tried to smile and removed her sunglasses. '*Shalom.*'

The hangover, Miguel's kidnapping, Viggo's lack of interest and the Björn Borg mystery had taken their toll. She was a wreck. The nurse instantly felt sorry for her and escorted us to Ariel's room.

Not many people can look scary from a hospital bed, but Ariel was the exception. An I.V. was securely planted into his wrist and the regular beeping of the vitals machine confirmed, once and for all, that he was human. He recognised us immediately and switched off the TV. 'Father,' he said to Viggo, 'I'm glad to see you.'

'The pleasure is mine, child —'

'Cut the performance short. My head's very sore,' barked Ariel, as soon as the nurse left.

The thespian's lips curved downwards. 'I was just getting into character!'

'Who did the feeble minds come as?'

I thought my disguise was pretty obvious.

'Meet Noah,' replied Viggo, 'a young seminarian, and Isabelle, your daughter.'

'*My daughter*? I must have died and gone to hell.'

With the niceties out of the way, Viggo dragged a plastic chair next to Ariel's bed and sat down. 'How bad is it?'

'He was a poor shot and missed my vital organs.'

Ariel sounded disappointed at having been shot by such a novice.

'Surgery?' probed Viggo.

'Last night, two bullets removed. They sent them to the police.'

'Damn it, if they match them to the discarded shells in the cathedral, your story will crumble. Why didn't you stop them?'

'I was under general anaesthesia.'

It was the most infallible excuse I had ever heard.

'How long will you be here for?' continued Viggo.

'Seven to ten days; if you need me faster, I can discharge myself.'

'You just had surgery, let's not push it. How are you handling the police investigation? Is your cover tight so far?'

'It's not tight, but it's not blown. My presumed concussion is buying me time and my contact at the Israeli embassy is buying me a clean passport that will match the name I've given. Magnus will get a bill for it.'

'Is he OK?' I asked. My Adam's apple went up and down my throat a few times and I braced myself for the worst.

Ariel snorted. 'He made it out. Unscathed. Typical Magnus. Last I saw him, he was sprinting towards the side door that leads to Via Minerva.'

I was so relieved, I thought my heart was going to explode, good thing I was already in a hospital. I spontaneously hugged Isabelle, but she was as stiff as a pizza crust reheated too many times. I didn't take offence, her stiffness had nothing to do with my (possibly unwelcome) embrace. I knew exactly what she was going through. I squeezed her hand for support. It felt natural. 'My father?' she whispered.

'As far as I know, still captive,' said Ariel. Her eyes filled with tears, he took no notice and turned to Viggo. 'What's your next move?'

'Ever been to the Palermo safe house?' he asked.

'No. Plan B then.'

Viggo gently squeezed Ariel's I.V. and tried to read the label. 'Yes, Plan B. We're off to Palermo. With the ring.'

'Leave the I.V. alone. Did you say *with*?'

He grinned. 'I most certainly did.'

Ariel grimaced. Or smiled back. 'Magnus will be impressed. When he makes contact, I'll send him your way.'

'How will he find you?' I asked, keen to see my father in the flesh.

'Same way you did,' he droned, reaching for the remote control. 'I'm a TV star now.'

CHAPTER 41

Viggo rang the bell of an unremarkable building in Monreale, a small town on the outskirts of Palermo. A security camera trained its lonely eye on us and a polite voice spoke through intercom. *'Desidera?'*

'Um… we don't speak Italian,' began Viggo.

The faceless voice switched to Cambridge English. 'How may I be of assistance?'

'Is Mr Baldwin home?'

I made the connection with King Baldwin of Jerusalem. 'Access code?' asked the voice.

'This is an impromptu visit, there wasn't time to request one.'

Some static buzz came through the intercom. 'One, two, zero, three,' recited the voice.

Isabelle and I traded quizzical looks. 'Philippe de Plessis,' replied Viggo, without missing a beat.

'One, one, eight, three.'

'Arnold de Torroja.'

'One, two, nine, zero.'

He clasped his hand to his forehead.

'One, two, nine, zero,' repeated the voice.

'Thomas… no, wait! Guillaume de Beaujeu.'

The door buzzed open. The voice was reciting calendar years and Viggo had successfully passed the Grand Masters bingo. We entered a windowless and poorly lit reception area. The dark panelling of the walls added to the general gloom. A stern looking man indicated a burgundy sofa. He was taller than average and extremely pale, not surprising given that he was working in an upmarket catacomb. His pointy face was elongated, as if he pulled it every morning before brushing his teeth. He reminded me of Christopher Lee in the 1970's version of *Count Dracula*. The safe house was the opposite of welcoming, no newspapers, no refreshments, not even a teeny-tiny mint. Dracula's presence didn't help. He summoned Viggo closer to the desk and produced a fountain pen and a clipboard. They kept their voices low, but it was impossible not to overhear. 'I need to check some details,' said Dracula.

'Check-away.'

Dracula stiffened. 'Pardon?'

'I'm sorry. Yes, sir.'

'I presume you have a good reason for bringing your charges in here? I'm certain they don't belong.'

'I do, let me explain—'

'Name?' asked Dracula curtly.

'Viggo Gustafsson.'

The Count put the pen down. 'Gustafsson?'

'Yes, sir.'

Without a word, Dracula reached for a fingerprint scanner. Viggo placed his index on the reader. The machine sent some information to Dracula's terminal. Our ghostly host picked up the phone and babbled something in Italian. All I got was Viggo's name. A door swung open and, before I could make a sound, I was being crushed by my father's embrace. 'I thought I'd lost you,' he said, letting go of me and then hugging me again. He eventually released me and pulled Isabelle to his chest. Viggo had to make do with a series of energetic slaps on the back. 'You did well, Viggo, you did *very* well.'

'Thank you.' He grinned and clapped my shoulder. 'I had the best wing man I could have wished for.'

My father, still in his running gear, took a step back and pretended to admire our cassocks. 'Ariel warned me you had gone for a more mature look. It suits you.'

We all chuckled, apart from Dracula.

'How did you get here so fast?' I asked.

'Long story. Tell me, do you really have the ring?'

Isabelle lifted her hand. We had purchased enough cheap bling to decorate a rapper's entourage and her fingers were encrusted with a variety of tacky trinkets. The priceless medieval seal was happily sitting amongst all the other junk. She slipped it off and placed it into my father's open palm.

'The three of you have surpassed yourselves,' he said, closing his fist firmly over it. 'I'm so proud of you.'

We followed him through a side door. The rest of the building was as gloomy as the reception area. We reached a windowless basement illuminated by industrial neon lights. State of the art safes lined the entire perimeter of the underground chamber. My father programmed one of them to recognise his retina and placed the ring inside. He then turned to us. 'I need to call Knut. Let's meet in two hours. There is a lot we need to discuss.' He summoned one of the guards who was standing by the entrance and asked him to escort us to our rooms.

The safe house was Spartan, essential and, most of all, shrouded in secrecy. Getting from one area to the other required clearing various checkpoints and inquisitive CCTV cameras monitored the guests' every move. I was dying to explore, but an impassive sentinel – I didn't know how else to describe the watchmen planted all over the place – advised me to return to my room until further notice. I showered and inspected my tiny wardrobe. It was stocked with a selection of anonymous clothes in various sizes. I dumped my cassock in favour of a pair of grey jogging bottoms and a white t-shirt. The bedroom's phone rang. My father, Viggo and Isabelle were waiting downstairs.

After a short drive, we arrived at a deserted pizzeria where my father had the nerve to ask for a quiet table. We all wore grey jogging bottoms, apart from Viggo who had managed to source a pair of cargo shorts. Our starters arrived together with a jug of home-made lemonade and two ice-cold beers. 'How did you beat us to Monreale?' I asked my father, while stealing a grilled aubergine from under Viggo's nose. 'When we saw Ariel, you hadn't made contact yet.'

'I missed you by an hour.'

'You got here really fast, did you steal a car or something?' My joke was met with an embarrassing silence. I nearly choked on the aubergine. 'You did?'

My father spread his palms upwards. 'It was an emergency. You didn't exactly purchase your cassocks, did you?'

'Point taken. What did you do after the shooting?'

'I left the cathedral through a side door and kept a low profile.'

I was fine with his explanation, but Isabelle's female intuition detected something fishy. 'And *where* exactly did you keep this low profile?' she asked.

Another embarrassing silence followed. My father pinched the bridge of his nose, as if he had superglued it to his face and wanted to make sure it stuck. Viggo put two and two together and teased him in a deep, Darth Vader voice. 'I sense you misused your powers of seduction. Do we know her?'

My father took a sip of his beer and unsuccessfully tried to look unfazed. 'A gentleman never tells.'

I was incredibly embarrassed, this type of conversation never happened with mum. The day we had "the talk" had been one of the most excruciating of my life. Thankfully, she had never touched on the subject again. I was a bit curious about this woman's identity, but the prospect of hearing about my father's romantic interlude was beyond awkward. Isabelle leaned towards him, fists clenched. 'You're despicable! Spending the night with a mystery woman while my father is at the mercy of his captors!'

He got his nose closer to hers. 'Let me assure you, *that* woman wasn't an experience I'd like to repeat!'

Irrespective of my ignorance in such matters, I doubted it could have been such a traumatic episode. My father didn't exactly come across as a shrinking violet. 'I returned to the hotel straight after the shooting,' he continued, 'but the Russians had beaten me to it. They went to our rooms and wiped them clean. Miguel was with them, as far as I could tell he was unharmed. I couldn't challenge them by myself, but I managed to delay them.'

'How?' I asked.

'I slashed the tyres of their people carrier.' The line between seeker and vandal seemed to be a thin one. He carried on. 'No mechanic would come out at that time of night so they ordered two taxis through the reception desk. I waited for them to leave and went in, Alessandra was on duty —'

'So your lady-friend was Alessandra the receptionist?' Isabelle's tone couldn't have been more condemnatory.

'I wish!' replied my father, clearly no longer bothered by Alessandra's unfamiliarity with rotary dial phones. 'Anyway, Alessandra had booked the taxis for the Russians and eventually, as long as I promised to leave her out of it, agreed to give me the destination address. The place where they're keeping Miguel isn't that far from here.'

'That's great!' I said. 'When are we going?'

He sighed. 'Noah, Isabelle, there is something I need to tell you. Something very important.'

I held my breath. Was he finally going to come clean about his Templar associations? I braced myself for the official revelation and offered a smile of encouragement. 'I'm listening.'

'You must go home.'

The smile died on my lips. *Go home?* I had no home! Mum was in Lebanon, so home was supposed to be with him! I wasn't even upset, not yet, just stunned. 'Excuse me?'

'You must go home,' he repeated.

I looked at Viggo for support, but his eyes were conveniently glued to his feet. Isabelle seemed mildly relieved. Going home wasn't as much of a tragedy for her as it was for me. 'I don't get it, what did I do wrong?' I asked.

'You didn't do anything wrong,' replied my father. 'But *I* have.'

'Here we go again!' I huffed. 'You make a mistake and I pay the consequences!'

'Those are pretty harsh words!'

'But true.'

He fiddled with the tablecloth. Viggo cautiously looked up from his feet, but only to reach for the last aubergine. My father turned to him and Isabelle. 'Can you give us a few minutes?'

Viggo stood up and offered her his arm. 'Come Princess, I'll show you the lobster tank.'

Destination aside, they could have passed for a loved-up couple. My father turned his piercing eyes on me. 'Noah, I'm doing this for you. You're a smart kid, by now you've figured out that my life is very... unusual.'

'And I adapted. I even found the twelfth ring!'

'You have,' he said, with a faint smile. 'And I couldn't be more proud. But I'm afraid Knut was right, I can't protect you. I thought I could, I truly did, but last night proved me wrong. I put you in harm's way and I nearly lost you. I've never been so scared in my whole life. And I don't scare easily.'

I scowled. 'So that's it? You'll return me like an unwanted package because your stint as a father was more complicated than expected?'

He exhaled. 'Noah, if anything happened to you, I wouldn't be able to live with myself.'

'It's all about you, isn't it? It doesn't matter how *I* feel.'

'That's not fair!'

'You're damn right it's not!' I yelled.

'Calm down, I'm trying to have an adult conversation here.'

'Really? Because I don't feel like an adult at all, you're making all the decisions and my opinion counts for nothing.'

'I wish things were different...'

'Then change them for God's sake! With you it's always one step forward and ten steps back, but the bottom line is that you always have, and always will, come first. You waltz in and out of my life when you feel like it and I have to put up with it.'

'*Put up* with it? Is that how you really feel?'

'Yes, whenever I think we're making progress, you pull the rug from under my feet. This emotional drain is getting harder and harder to handle!' My heart was pumping pure bitterness. 'In fact, you know what? We should stick to seeing each other once a year.' I smacked the table with the flat of my hand, it was harder than I expected. 'I'm such an idiot!'

'Why?' he asked, without contradicting me, which would have been nice.

'Because I believed you cared. Did you know that one of my best moments was seeing you go against Knut to keep me with you? And do you know why? Because that's what fathers do, they stand by their children, they don't abandon them at the first hurdle or to chase fantastic creatures.'

He snorted. 'And what could you possibly know about fatherhood?'

'Thanks to you, absolutely nothing.'

My words hit home. He went eerily quiet and bit the nail of his thumb. His other hand was curled into a tight fist, I hoped it wouldn't fly in my face. The waiter brought our pizzas, I shoved my plate to one side. 'When am I going?' I asked emotionlessly.

'Let's talk about this—'

'Just tell me when. I really don't want to hear any more platitudes on how you want to change the world, but you can't.'

There was a long pause.

'A couple of weeks from now,' he said softly. 'I doubt your mother will be able to return any sooner. First thing tomorrow, I'll take you to a secure location. Later in the day, Viggo and I will extract Miguel. Whether we succeed or fail, there's no telling about possible repercussions, so staying with me for the next few months is no longer an option. If all goes well, I'll join you at the secure location until it's time for you to go back. Then I'll return to Valhalla and wait for the dust to settle. Or unsettle.'

'And if all *doesn't* go well?'

'Then Knut will take care of everything. And I'll no longer be around.'

'So, either way, it makes no difference to me.'

I knew my words were caustic, but I didn't care. I hoped they burned through his soul, like his perpetual rejection was burning through mine.

'Noah, it doesn't have to be this way. I'll speak to Katie about the custody arrangement, I'll visit more often.'

'Don't bother.' I could feel my lip trembling, but there was no way I was going to cry in front of him. 'I need some air, I'm going for a walk.'

I pushed the chair back and made for the door. I walked at a deliberately fast pace, in an attempt to leave my excuse-for-a-father behind. Someone was running after me, I walked faster. 'Dude, wait up,' shouted Viggo.

I swirled to face him, furious and hurt. 'Did you know about this?'

'No. I only knew you were not coming on the Miguel thing because Magnus asked me to submit the details of the extraction plan with the relevant... um... office. I had no idea you were going home.'

My father's silhouette appeared in the background, Isabelle by his side. He was taking his time. No doubt the coward was hoping that Viggo would fix things for him. I barely registered the battered Ford Transit van until it suddenly braked and the side door slid open. Five armed men stormed out. My father sprinted forward. The yellow pointer on Viggo's chest was followed by a short, buzzing sound. He collapsed to the floor, his body twisting and jerking. Isabelle screamed. I turned. My father's body was on the asphalt next to her, also writhing madly. What on earth... I felt a hand over my mouth, someone grabbed hold of me and dragged me into the van. Despite all her kicking, Isabelle was next. One of the captors rolled duct tape around our wrists, the others collected the unconscious bodies from the street and dumped them into the van.

CHAPTER 42

My father and Viggo were unconscious, but alive. Their chests were going up down, following the universal rhythm of life. The abductor in charge of duct taping had finished an outstanding job on my father and was busy restraining Viggo. He was the provident type and had brought a spare roll, mum would have praised his forward thinking. My breathing was laboured and my mouth dry, funnily enough I could still taste the lemonade. In an attempt to dominate my fear, I concentrated on the citrusy flavour. I couldn't figure out what the hell had happened until Isabelle mouthed "Taser guns." A newspaper article about the Met Police being issued with weapons which incapacitate, rather than kill, their victims, flickered through my head. My father stirred.

'Sergei, he's waking up,' said the Duct-Taper.

Sergei abandoned the front seat and climbed into the back. 'Mr Larsson, we meet again.'

His face wasn't familiar, but I immediately recognised his voice. He was the man who had been threatening my father in the cathedral. How on earth did he manage to track us down so quickly? My father was just as mystified. 'How did you find us?' he asked, grimacing in pain.

I'm sure he was referring specifically to how he had located us in Monreale, but Sergei was in show-off mode and started from the very beginning. 'Our contact at Interpol monitored your passport since you left Nassau. After the Licata break-in, you covered your tracks pretty well, switching car was a good move, but I bet you didn't know that Italian hotels abide by strict anti-mafia laws. They have a duty to report their guests' passport details to the police on a daily basis. The moment you resurfaced at the Grand Hotel Ortigia, we kept you under surveillance and put a tracker in your car. When your aide picked it up yesterday, it led us straight to Monreale.'

I prayed he hadn't seen us slip into the safe house. When we had first reached Monreale, Viggo had insisted on parking the Discovery two streets away from it, on the off chance that we had been followed. I wished he had been as paranoid when he had parked the bugged Discovery right in front of the pizza place.

'We couldn't believe you were so close to our base,' continued Sergei, 'we're practically neighbours.'

'I'll pop in to borrow a cup of sugar then,' said my father. His impertinence cost him a smack in the face.

'You won't be so smug when we finish with you. Where's the ring?'

Good, he had no idea about the safe house.

'I already told you in the cathedral,' replied my father, 'I don't know. Let the kids go, they have nothing to do with this and would only be in your way.'

'Nice try, Mr Larsson. Until your memory recovers, these kids will keep us company.'

'Let them go and I'll get you a copy of the map,' said my father. Technically, he was cheating – the map's missing corner made it completely useless – but this wasn't a time to be pedantic.

Sergei laughed in his face. 'We already have a copy. Yuri got it off your scanner the day he broke into Valhalla.'

'That's impossible,' I blurted. 'Viggo and I were responsible for scanning the map and we never left any hard copies lying around.'

'You didn't have to,' said Sergei. 'Your scanner has a built-in memory feature which enables it to recall the last ten documents that have crossed its glass screen. All Yuri had to do was press print.'

My father tensed. The scanner had seen its fair share of confidential documents. 'What else did he get?' he asked, alarmed.

'Just faces,' replied Sergei, with palpable frustration. 'Map aside, it was like printing a bloody art gallery.'

I paled – the prehistoric selfies had found their way into the real world. My father frowned. 'Faces?'

'Why don't you ask your son?' said Sergei, tilting his head in my direction.

I glanced at Viggo, hoping we could share the mortification, but he was still out cold. For a brief moment, I wished I had been tasered too. 'I... um... may have scanned my own face.' I paused. 'Repeatedly.'

My awkward confession reaped a selection of chuckles from the other captors. And a disdainful scoff from Isabelle. Sergei leaned towards me and lowered his voice to a hiss. 'Vladimir kept one of your self-portraits.'

I doubted he wanted to display me on his mantelpiece. I nervously glanced around the van. 'Where is he?'

'Moscow. Getting his jaw fixed.' I let out a loud sigh of relief. Sergei smirked. 'Did I mention he's my brother?'

The van eventually came to a halt. Its door slid open and revealed a remote farmhouse surrounded by various outbuildings and a vast expanse of countryside. My father, still a bit wobbly on his legs, was immediately frog-marched to the farmhouse. I was very worried about Viggo. He had never regained consciousness and the Duct-Taper was hauling him into one of the outbuildings. 'Shouldn't he be awake by now?' asked another captor, picking at the long scar on his cheek.

'Maybe electric charge in your gun too high,' replied the Duct-Taper in a thick accent.

Scarface gaped. 'Is it adjustable?'

'It is in *Star Trek*.'

The Duct-Taper and Scarface shared similar features and, I suspected, a single brain. Their square jaws and deep-set eyes were complemented by Marine haircuts which clearly did nothing for their weapon-handling skills.

Isabelle and I were ungraciously dumped in the same outbuilding. Before locking us into our cell for the night, the Duct-Taper deposited a bottle of water and a tower of plastic glasses on the floor. He then removed a large knife from a brown leather sheath. 'You behave, I cut restraints. No screaming, no shouting. Yes?'

I agreed, we were in the middle of nowhere, shouting would have been a pure waste of energy. He put the blade too close to my wrists for comfort, I shut my eyes and hoped he had a firm hand. Within seconds, I was massaging my forearms and peeling off sticky residue. After cutting Isabelle's ties, the Duct-Taper shone his torch on the water and then on a plastic bucket standing in a corner. 'Drink and toilet. Food tomorrow.'

At the prospect of using a proxy-toilet in my presence, Isabelle plucked up the courage to speak. 'Excuse me, sir, you must be joking!'

Diplomacy had never been her strongpoint.

'I no joke. Never.'

'Well, that is your prerogative, but I'm a girl and I will need my own toilet. I'm sure the Geneva Convention stipulates that male and female prisoners of war are entitled to separate facilities.'

'You no prisoner of war, you hostage.'

'But you must adhere to some kind of humanitarian manifesto,' she spluttered, 'every organisation does!'

'I ask boss,' said the captor, who probably had never had such an argumentative hostage. He locked the door and left. Our cell, a bare room of four metres by four, was an unfinished storage area. Its glassless window was too high to reach and the only piece of furniture was an uninviting double-mattress. Isabelle sat on it and pulled her knees to her chest. We had been given a candle, but it was burning quickly. 'What do you think they'll do to us?' she murmured.

'Not sure.'

I was being devoured alive by the sense of guilt. If I hadn't stormed out of the restaurant in such a hurry my father and Viggo would have been more vigilant and this whole mess could have been avoided. Now my friend lay unconscious next door and my father was in the exact position he had wanted to avoid all along: having to choose between me and the ring. 'Do you think they're going to kill us?' she asked bluntly.

'Of course not,' I replied, even if the thought had crossed my mind more often than I cared to admit. I joined her on the mattress and lay down. The flickering flame died and the room was plunged into total darkness. 'Noah?'

'Yeah?'

'Are you scared?'

'A bit.'

'Are you thinking about Cressida?'

I was actually thinking that Isabelle smelled nice, but there was no way I was going to tell her. 'I am now.'

'Do you miss her?'

'Kind of. It's hard to miss what you never had.'

'When you go back to London, you should get together with her. I know she's way out of your league, but you look much better than when you first came. You're fitter and less pasty. You may have half a chance.'

I snorted. 'Thanks, I feel so much better. You should be a motivational speaker. Was I *that* pasty?'

'Cadaver pasty.'

'So my courtship will have to be quick, if the tan disappears, I'm done.'

She giggled. '*Courtship?* Where do you come up with these ancient words? Do you watch period rom-coms before going to sleep or something?'

I chuckled softly. 'The last book we read in school was *Wuthering Heights*, some of the lingo stuck.'

I kept quiet about Carmen's soaps. If this was going to be my last night on earth, I wanted to go to my unmarked grave with a modicum of dignity. She laughed again, that rare, sweet laugh that she kept for special occasions. I leaned on my elbow but, in the obscurity, she didn't see it. 'The last book we read was *The Old Man and The Sea*,' she said. 'Seriously, who would go through all that trouble for a marlin?'

'I'm surprised you read something other than *Teen Vogue*. Do you read it or do you just look at the pictures?'

She laughed again and leaned forward. The idea was to pretend-smack me, because I did get a light slap on my shoulder, but she didn't expect my face to be so close. The unthinkable happened. Somehow, and totally unintentionally, our lips brushed. The accidental gesture completely spoilt our carefree moment. *Had we just kissed?* Surely, if it was involuntary, it didn't count, right? I couldn't see her face, so it was hard to figure out what to do next. Was she shocked? Horrified? Happy? OK, I knew it couldn't be the last one, but the fact that she hadn't delivered further blows confirmed that she was as befuddled as I was. Why did I always have to end up in these pathetic situations?

'Well, goodnight then,' she said stiffly.

'Goodnight.'

I rolled over to my side. She hadn't accused me of anything, so I went with the assumption that she didn't know what the hell had happened either.

The rooster's crow woke me with a jolt. Isabelle was lying on my left arm, her back turned, and I was holding her the same way I used to hug Bruno, my giant teddy bear. She felt a lot nicer, definitely less hairy. I had never woken up next to a girl before. Despite wishing that the circumstances, and possibly the girl, were different, it was a fairly pleasant experience. She stretched in her sleep and rolled over, draping one of her arms around my shoulder. She was now facing me and our lips were less than five centimetres apart. There was no way I was going to repeat last night's clumsy performance, so I pushed my head as far back as it would go. While I realigned my vertebrae, I studied her pretty face: the long lashes, the cute freckles, the black ant scouting her forehead... Suddenly, she opened her eyes. 'What are you doing?' she shrieked.

Sometimes the best defence is a direct attack. 'Nothing, I woke up and you were hugging me.'

'Liar!'

I poked her right arm, which was still draped over my shoulder. 'This sweaty scarf belongs to you, doesn't it?'

Before she could think of a suitable insult, the key turned in the lock and Viggo stumbled in. He leaned against the wall, moaning that he wasn't feeling so good. We rushed to his aid and helped him onto the mattress, where he whinged for another couple of minutes. The captors ignored him and left. 'You guys OK?' he asked, in a normal voice, as soon as their steps faded away.

Isabelle immediately stopped stroking his forehead. Being nice to him on his deathbed was acceptable, being nice to him because she fancied him was unthinkable. That's girls for you. I was confused by his miraculous recovery. 'We're fine, you're the one who's supposed to be in pain.'

'Nah, just pretending. I never blacked-out, I've been conscious all along.'

I should have been happy he was alive and well, but all I could feel was mounting anger.

'Dude, what's with the hypercritical look?' he asked.

I threw my arms in the air in a fit of rage. 'Nothing, absolutely nothing! I was torn apart by guilt for the whole of last night and you were fine all along! Everything's hunky dory, Viggo!'

Isabelle shrank away from him. Resorting to a possum surviving technique wasn't exactly heroic. 'You played *dead*?'

He clearly resented her vocabulary. 'I played *harmless*. I figured that if I looked out of it, they wouldn't see me as a threat. And it worked. I've been locked up with Miguel all night.'

'How is he?' she asked, forgiving the possum on the spot.

'Fine, worried about you though. His door is secured by a simple external latch which is impossible to open from the inside. Even if he managed to, they check on him every fifteen minutes, so he couldn't get very far. Hey, you've got a window.'

'We've considered it,' I said. 'It's too high.'

'How often did they check on you?'

'Not once. They threw us in here last night and we didn't see them again until this morning.'

He got to his feet and assessed the distance between the floor the window. 'How's your balance?'

'Constantly in the red,' replied Isabelle gloomily.

'I meant your physical balance. Ever done circus skills?' We shook our heads. 'Pity, it would have made it much easier. Princess, you're the lightest, if you balance on my hands, I could extend my arms and push you out of the window.'

'And splatter me on the other side? No thanks, I'd rather die pretty.'

I could have told her that worms are blind and would have feasted on her either way, but decided not to. 'Nobody's going to die,' said Viggo. 'There's a huge pile of hay at the other side. I saw it while they brought me here. If you land on it, you'll be fine.'

'Says who?' she asked defiantly.

'Me, Viggo.'

'I was being sarcastic, you idiot!'

The insult washed right over him, he was too engrossed with his plan. 'Listen to me, I'll push you out of the window under the cover of darkness. You'll land on the hay, make your way to the nearest village and raise the alarm.'

'*Which* nearest village? We have no idea where we are!'

If she yelled any louder, our captors could have given us directions. He removed his diver watch and gave it to her. 'It's got a built-in compass. Head North-East, towards the coast. You're bound to find villages on the way.'

She took the watch and drew a sharp breath. 'Even if I survive the plunge, I'll be a sitting duck in the Sicilian countryside. Forget it, your plan sucks!'

He crossed his arms and sulked. I couldn't help but notice that she had kept the watch. I had been the catalyst of this mess, the least I could do was put things right. 'I'll do it,' I blurted, before I could change my mind.

CHAPTER 43

I spent the morning balancing on Viggo's shoulders. Despite a couple of bad falls, it wasn't long before I could stand on his upturned hands. Pushing me up towards the window was a different matter. I wished Isabelle would change her mind. She was the lightest. Pushing her up would have been much easier. Viggo's muscles were beginning to shake under the strain and we decided to take a short break. Incredibly, we began bickering over toilet customs. Isabelle had forbidden Viggo from using the bucket and he was feeling quite resentful. He didn't think that her inhibitions should have interfered with his bodily functions. For once, I publicly sided with her. He took offence and called me a prude from Victorian times. Our surreal fight was cut short by the unmistakeable sound of rotor blades. Could Dracula have noticed our absence and organised a rescue operation at such short notice? Viggo crushed my hopes. 'The safe house isn't a baby-sitting service,' he said, 'people come and go at all times. Ariel is our only hope. If he realises that we've disappeared without a trace, he may get suspicious and get things moving.'

'It's a long shot, he's still in hospital.'

'I know,' he said glumly. 'Essentially, we're on our own.'

The helicopter touched down somewhere on the farm. 'Who do you think it is?' I asked.

Viggo sat on the dirty floor and leaned his back against the wall. 'I don't know, but it could explain why we've been here over twelve hours and nobody came to interrogate us. They were waiting for the big shots. I have a bad feeling about this.'

I did too. I was now more determined than ever to put Viggo's plan into action, even if it meant leaving my fingernails embedded in the wall. I wished that darkness would come faster, the waiting around was driving me insane.

Early in the afternoon, the Duct-Taper and Scarface paid us a visit. As per Isabelle's appeal, and possibly in accordance with the Geneva Convention, we had been granted proper toilet breaks. Irrespective of the machine gun buried in my back, I made the most of my lavatory tour. In daylight, the farm proved larger than expected. The stables and a pig sty were behind the main farmhouse, the helicopter – not that I could fly it – was next to a derelict barn. There was no sound coming from the stables. Unlike the pig sty, they had to be devoid of animals. The van was parked under a canopy and seemed to be the only driveable vehicle apart from a once-red tractor. Both had seen better days. Plenty of them. I made a mental note of the layout and tried to memorise any tree, bush or building that could provide cover during my escape. I returned to my cell, keen to compare my findings with my fellow-prisoners. Unfortunately, one of them failed to return. 'He'll be here soon,' I said to Isabelle, even though I feared the contrary.

She looked up from the dusty floor. 'It's been over an hour. Something's wrong.'

'Maybe they moved him to another cell.'

'Umph.'

I hated that sound. 'What's that supposed to mean?' I asked as non-confrontationally as possible. I didn't want to ignite an argument that could lead to discussing our alleged kiss.

'That they had no reason to split us up. We're small fishes, and that includes Viggo. In their eyes, we're so harmless that they hardly bother to check on us.'

'How about we prove them wrong? Viggo's not here, but his plan is worth a shot.'

She raised a critical eyebrow. 'His plan was sketchy and simplistic.'

'Agreed, but it's all we've got, and you're not completely against it or you wouldn't have kept his watch. I'm stronger than you—'

She shot me a defiant look, some people are born argumentative.

'I'm *taller* than you,' I rephrased, 'so I'll have to push you out. I know you don't want to be a sitting duck in the Sicilian countryside, but surely it beats being a sitting duck here!'

She pursed her lips and weighed her options. 'Crouch down, let's show them what we're made of.'

I did. She began to climb on my back. 'Ouch, I think you just kicked me in the kidneys.'

Everyone else would instinctively apologise, but she was in a league of her own. 'Impossible.'

'It really hurts. You're not wearing heels, are you?'

'My father won't let me. You're just sore from falling off Viggo earlier. Stop wriggling or I'll fall too.'

She kicked her legs over my shoulders. I pushed her calves against my chest. They felt nice, and I felt them a bit too long. 'Aren't you supposed to stand up or something?' she complained from above.

'Um... yeah, I was about to. Ready?'

'Yes.'

I stood up and let go of her legs. She slowly positioned her feet on my shoulders.

'Take your time' I said. 'Small, measured movements.'

Once she was stable, she placed her feet in my upturned palms and I closed my fingers over them.

'I'm steady,' she said. 'Push me up.'

My arms were shaking, but I ignored it and concentrated on my task. Her balance was much better than mine, I pointed it out and she revealed that she did gymnastics twice a week. 'And you didn't think to mention this earlier when Viggo asked about circus skills?' I grunted through clenched teeth.

'Shut up and push me a bit higher, I'm nearly there... just a little bit more...'

We heard voices outside and she jumped to the floor with the agility of a flying squirrel. The key turned in the lock and the Duct-Taper, who preferred to be called Miroslav, handed me a first-aid kit. I failed to understand why, until he and Scarface dragged a shirtless Viggo onto the dirty mattress and made a swift exit. The image of my friend beaten to a pulp will stay with me forever. Isabelle went a whiter shade of white and, at first, all I could do was clutch the first-aid kit to my chest. I forced myself to snap out of it and knelt beside him, trying to assess his injuries. He had a swollen eye, a bloody nose, a cut upper lip and various abrasions. Countless bruises were starting to form pretty much everywhere on his body. His old forehead cut had opened up again and the blood was flowing freely. The skin around the base of his wrists was raw, a clear sign that, during his ordeal, he had been tied up. I checked his arms, wrists, fingers and legs. As far as I could tell, he had no broken bones. I was scared to touch his chest because it was covered in large bruises that were going redder before my eyes. I used the bottled water to wash the blood from his face.

'Viggo, can you hear me?' I said, struggling to keep my voice steady. He nodded. Good, at least he was conscious. I reached for the first-aid kit and began to fix the fixable.

'Who did this to you?' I continued. It didn't really matter, but I wanted to make sure his cognitive functions were intact.

'Sergei,' he mumbled. 'It was Sergei. He knows how to hit. He's sick, he… he enjoys it.' He spat some blood. 'I think I bit my tongue.'

Isabelle gave him some water to rinse the blood from his mouth. He leaned forward to spit the red-tinged liquid on the floor and hit her jogging bottoms instead. With his good eye, he threw her an apologetic glance and readied himself for a barrage of remonstrations. And right then I discovered that girls really do have a weakness for beaten up guys – as long as they were good-looking before the beating started – because she didn't make a sound and offered him more water instead. 'It hurts every time I breathe in,' he said, trying to sit up.

I helped him up as gently as I could. 'Sounds like a cracked rib.'

He ran his hand over his face. 'Does it look as bad as it feels?'

'I've seen worse.'

I really had, in a heavyweight boxing match.

He produced the stupidest horsy grin. 'Do I have all my teeth?'

'Open up… I count thirty-one.'

'I'm waiting on a wisdom tooth.'

'Then you're fine.'

'Do you think Hope will still like me?'

Even in his mashed-up state, he could have walked into a bar and scored more than the average guy. 'Sure.'

'Dude, ever been punched?' he murmured, trying to find a comfortable position.

'Once. Outside the language lab, but it wasn't my fault. I walked straight into a punch that was meant for Tom Wright.'

'That was lucky…'

His sarcastic comment was accompanied by a pained expression.

'Tom thought so too.'

'Did Ariel cover how to take a punch?'

'You mean the Inside Defence technique?'

'No, not how to block. How to absorb if you cannot block.'

I had an inkling his topic of conversation wasn't accidental. 'He said to pull my abdominal muscles over my core to protect my internal organs and to exhale to disperse the energy.'

'That's good advice, keep it in mind.'

'What are you trying to say?'

'Nothing.'

Isabelle had exhausted her tiny reserve of patience. 'Spit it out, Viggo! Or I swear to God I'll punch you in your good eye and tell Hope that you were in Ursula's bedroom!'

And so amongst exhales and grimaces – and prompted by Isabelle's occasional threats – he told us how Sergei and Scarface had taken him to the stables, tied his hands above his head and suspended him from the ceiling's central beam. Then, without asking him a single question, Sergei had proceeded to beat the hell out of him. I didn't want to believe that Sergei would beat someone to a pulp just for the sake of it. 'Why would he do something like that?'

Viggo's answer floored me. 'To show Magnus and Miguel what you can look forward to if they keep on denying any knowledge of the ring.'

My face fell, and the grim future that lay ahead wasn't the only reason. 'My father was *there*? And he let this happen?'

Loyal as ever, he immediately jumped to his defence. 'There was nothing he could do. His hands were tied, and I'm not talking metaphors.'

'He could have told them where the bloody ring was!'

'He couldn't, he's taken an oath! We all did! Dude, you cannot go back on your word!'

'I don't want to, but it may be our only option.'

'Look at my face! What do you think they'll do to us if we give them what they want on a silver plate?'

I pictured a variety of scenarios. None of them looked good, in fact they got progressively worse. The ring was our only bargaining chip. I just wasn't too sure that my father would be willing to bargain.

'Are they going to torture us too?' asked Isabelle, her voice barely audible.

There was an uncomfortable silence. We all knew the answer. 'We've got to get out of here fast,' I said. 'All of us.'

Viggo's cerebral cells kicked into action. 'If we time it right, there may be a way, but it's going to be more dangerous than my original plan. If they catch us, things will turn ugly.'

In my book, they already were. 'Shoot.'

'I push you out, same as before, but instead of running to the nearest village, you stay put until the guard checks on Miguel. Then you let him out.'

'Are you sure the door is secured by a simple latch?'

'Positive, I was there for a whole night, remember? The key is getting the night patrol out of action before he notices that Miguel is gone. If he raises the alarm, we're done.'

'There's no way I can take out the night guard, you've seen my Krav Maga…'

'Leave it to Miguel. He's been locked-up for days, he'll have a lot of pent-up energy.'

I hoped he was right. 'And then?'

'The night patrol has the keys to our outbuilding. Come and get us. The van is so old that it probably has a cassette player. We can hot-wire it and get the hell out of here.'

'And my father?'

'Dude, aside from the night guard's gun, we'll be unarmed. We don't know how many they are. Taking the farmhouse is suicidal.'

'I'm not leaving without him.'

'If we're not here, they'll have no leverage. You'll be doing him a favour.'

Not for the first time, I marvelled at how brilliant he could be under that apparent layer of asininity. The thought of leaving my father behind gutted me, but Viggo's plan made sense. 'Can you really hot-wire a car?' I asked him.

'As long as it's pre-1990 or thereabout. Modern vehicles are too sophisticated for hot-wiring. Without a laptop to interrogate the on-board computer, you don't stand much of chance…'

'Will you teach me?'

'Sure, but not tonight.'

CHAPTER 44

I cursed the long summer day and wished the sun would make an exit. Judging by the colour of the sky, we were missing out on a glorious sunset. In a few hours, we would finally be able to put our plan into action. Suddenly, the Duct-Taper barged in with a nylon rope coiled under his arm. It couldn't be good news. 'You, with me.'

Couldn't he be more specific? There were three of us for God's sake! Viggo made to stand up, but the Duct-Taper shook his head. 'Haven't you had enough for one day? I'm talking to the boy.'

Isabelle stared at me with terrified Bambi eyes. I was relieved she wasn't going to get hurt, but I certainly wasn't looking forward to my own destiny. I felt incredibly heroic for saving the girl and totally unlucky for drawing the short straw. A cross between Superman and Wily Coyote.

Viggo had been subjected to his savage beating in the stables, so I was surprised to be taken to the farmhouse. I was even more astounded to find a table set for dinner. My father, hands tied behind his back, was sitting on a chair and studying a large roast-beef with a certain interest. He saw me and made to speak.

'Quiet, Larsson,' said the Duct-Taper, pushing me down onto one of the empty seats. Theoretically, I was a Larsson too, but this wasn't the time for clever remarks.

The other Larsson didn't disappoint and immediately disobeyed. 'Are you hurt?'

'No. You?'

'Another peep and I hit the boy.'

The Duct-Taper switched to butler mode and, oblivious to minimum age restrictions, filled our chalices with red wine. A silver-haired man, whom I had never seen before, walked into the room and sat at the head of the table. He exuded authority and arrogance. My father smirked.

'Good, you know who I am,' said the man. 'We can dispense with the official introductions.'

My father sneered. 'Andrei Dragomirov. I should have known it was you all along.'

'You should have,' replied Dragomirov, unfolding his napkin. I had heard his name before. He was the man Knut was paranoid about. Dragomirov had green, lifeless, reptilian eyes, devoid of any emotion. He noticed my father's restraints. 'Where are my manners? Miroslav, untie Mr Larsson.'

The Duct-Taper removed my father's bindings. Dragomirov continued. 'May I call you Magnus?'

'It is my name.'

A statement, rather than a permission. Dragomirov remained unperturbed. 'I sense hostility.'

'You sense correctly.'

My father massaged his wrists, his usual collection of bracelets had been replaced by angry tie marks. Miroslav, the Duct-Taper, took up position behind him. 'Before we proceed,' said Dragomirov, 'you should know that Miroslav has a gun trained on you and won't hesitate to pull the trigger.'

My father didn't flinch. 'Shooting an unarmed man in the back isn't particularly honourable.'

Dragomirov adjusted his cufflinks. 'Not everyone can afford honour, Magnus.'

'I beg to differ, it is free, after all.'

'It's easy for you to say, honour, together with everything else, was handed to you on a silver plate.'

'Honour cannot be *handed*,' said my father, holding Dragomirov's gaze. 'Being honourable, or dishonourable, is a personal choice.'

'Please, have a drink.'

'You first.'

Dragomirov took a sip of his wine. 'As you can see, it is not poisoned.'

I was happy to be left out of the conversation. I felt like a dwarf among rivalling titans.

Dragomirov set his chalice on the table. 'Conversing about honour is most pleasant, but we have more pressing matters to discuss. Let's cut to the chase.'

My father nodded once. 'Let's do that.'

'You have something I want, don't insult me by denying it.'

'The prospect of insulting you is hard to resist.'

Dragomirov ignored his jibe. 'Out of respect for your position within the brotherhood, I would prefer to solve our matter civilly. We will soon be on the same side, it would be a pity to start on the wrong foot. It is not my wish to harm you,' he paused. 'Or your son. Sergei gave you a taster of what we are capable of and I'm sure you'd want to spare young Noah unnecessary pain. Your cadet is alive, by the way. He is a cadet, is he not?'

My father didn't answer. A part of me was dying to hear more of their conversation, but the other wished I could spirit myself out of the room. It wasn't out of cowardice or fear, but out of guilt for putting him in such an impossible position. Dragomirov beckoned for someone to come over and a youngish man stepped out of the shadows. I would never forget his unremarkable face: Yuri, the guy who had broken into Valhalla. Dragomirov fixed his soulless eyes on my father. 'You will be allowed a knife and a fork, but Yuri will stand behind Noah. Any sudden moves and the boy dies. Is that understood?'

'Yes,' muttered my father, slowly reaching for his cutlery.

The Duct-Taper slung his Uzi machine gun over his back and dished the roast and the trimmings. Dragomirov raised his chalice into the air and gave my father the phoniest smile. 'First of all, congratulations on locating the ring. Such an accomplishment deserves to be celebrated. Is the vintage *Chateau Margaux* to your satisfaction?'

'It's passable,' replied my father, unimpressed by a bottle of wine that probably cost as much as a small car.

Dragomirov didn't appreciate his answer and let out the faintest sigh. 'Magnus, I know the ring is in your possession, admit it and we can move on to the next phase.' My father remained silent. A hint of impatience flashed across the reptilian eyes. 'I have a proposal for you.'

'I'm not interested.'

'Don't be so hasty. Listen to what I have to say —'

'Do I have a choice?'

'Indulge me.' Dragomirov topped up his glass. 'You tell me where the ring is, proclaim your allegiance to me and I will personally make sure you have everything you ever wished for. We can join forces at the Council of Twelve —'

'You're talking to the wrong man,' snorted my father, before throwing me an uncomfortable glance. 'I have no place at that table.'

'Oh, but you will,' said Dragomirov. 'And thanks to the ring, I will too. I want in on the most exclusive brotherhood in the world and I will not be denied such a privilege because I wasn't born into the right blood line.'

I briefly wondered which blood line he was referring to. My father seemed completely uninterested and helped himself to some more trimmings.

'Would you say your son is worthier than mine?' asked Dragomirov out of the blue.

'I can't answer that,' replied my father sensibly. 'I know nothing about your son and there is no accurate way to quantify someone's virtue.'

'And yet your son is entitled to a place at the top table of the brotherhood and mine isn't. Just like you are and I'm not. There may be no accurate way to quantify virtue, but success is easily measurable. I have proven myself to the world, Magnus. I came from nothing, I had to fight my way to the top using any means necessary. I didn't let anything, or anyone, stand in my way. My accomplishments, unlike yours, speak for themselves. I should be welcomed into the order with open arms, rather than being forced to use a backdoor.' He gulped another chalice of wine, before resuming his rant. 'I have accumulated enough riches to support a small country, and yet my peers look down on me as if I was the scum of the earth! Do you know how humiliating that is? But things are about to change. I will become the most powerful man on earth and those who scorned me will soon regret their actions.' Dragomirov's glassy eyes converged on my face. 'How old are you, Noah?'

I swallowed, but my mouth was dry. 'Fifteen.'

'Are you enjoying your training?'

I gaped, a potato fell off my fork and landed on the roast-beef, splattering gravy on my already dirty t-shirt. The reptilian eyes looked momentarily puzzled. 'You haven't started yet?'

I hung my head. Dragomirov turned to my father, the creepy eyes briefly inhabited by sheer shock. 'Isn't this boy your first born?'

He took a sip of his wine. 'I think so.'

'You *think* so?' I gasped.

He dished some more potatoes and avoided my gaze. 'I've had a chequered life.'

Dragomirov pursed his lips. 'Is he your first born or not?'

My father's shrug wasn't exactly reassuring.

'Yuri?' said Dragomirov, hardly opening his mouth. He would have made a great ventriloquist.

Yuri put on his genealogist hat. 'According to official records, the boy is his firstborn. My investigator didn't uncover any prior or subsequent sons.'

Dragomirov was perplexed. 'Then why hasn't he started his training? I understand that firstborns are groomed from the age of thirteen.'

The drinkable wine was beginning to grow on my father. He reached for his chalice and didn't offer any explanations. Dragomirov pressed on. 'Don't you want your son to be a part of history? Don't you want him to carry on the centuries old tradition? Don't you want him to follow in your footsteps, like you followed in your father's?'

My father's apparent calm was annihilated by a fit of rage. 'He will follow whichever path he chooses,' he roared, 'regardless of an ancient curse he never signed up for in the first place.'

The vitreous eyes danced in their sockets. 'Ancient *curse*? Is that how you define being part of the brotherhood? Are you truly stripping your firstborn of the opportunity to become a Knight Templar and continue the family tradition?'

The room went silent. I dropped another potato. How could a potato make so much noise? I looked at my father, somewhat expectantly, but he looked away. Dragomirov noticed. And sneered. 'Oh, I see… the boy doesn't know, does he? I knew you were unpredictable, Magnus, but I never expected this. You *never* told him what's in store for him?'

Deep inside, I was more excited than nervous. 'What is he talking about?' I asked my father.

He didn't answer, but he held my gaze. And his eyes were filled with immeasurable sadness.

'You are Templar royalty, Noah,' announced Dragomirov. 'The Larsson family has been in the inner circle of the order for centuries. Your destiny is pre-ordained.'

CHAPTER 45

Dragomirov leaned towards me. 'Tell me, young Noah, what do you know about the Templar Knights?'

My academic reputation had never been something to be proud of, I decided to uphold it. 'Not much.'

'Surely you must have heard of them. Everybody has.'

'Um… yes. They were a medieval order of warrior-monks.'

'They were until 1307, when they were attacked by King Philip IV.' Dragomirov kept on playing with the butter knife, at least he had opted for a blunt piece of cutlery. 'It was the order's darkest hour and one of your ancestors played an instrumental role in keeping the brotherhood alive. Were you truly never told about it?'

I shook my head. I had only recently discovered who my grandfather was. Family history, together with algebra, was clearly one of my weakest points. My father was holding his knife at a funny angle. It took me a few seconds to realise that he was using it as a mirror to check on the Duct-Taper. He tightened his grip and his blue eyes briefly turned to ice. For a moment, I thought he was going to take the Duct-Taper out, then I remembered about Yuri standing behind me with a loaded weapon. If the Duct-Taper was despatched to Saint Peter's gates, I would be right behind him. My father must have come to the same conclusion, because he blinked, loosened his grip and rested his knife on the plate. I didn't know whether to feel relieved or disappointed. The night guard walking past the window distracted me. It was the van driver. The Duct-Taper nodded to him and he nodded back. As quickly as he had come, he was gone. 'I think it's time for a history lesson, young man,' Dragomirov's voice brought me back to the room. 'Make yourself comfortable.'

I would have but, tension aside, the chair was very hard.

'In October 1307,' began Dragomirov, 'the Templars got wind of their imminent demise. They assigned twelve knights the task of delivering the Templar treasure to secret locations scattered across the known world. The chosen knights had proven themselves to be humble servants and excellent warriors. Their devotion was absolute, their intentions pure and they could be trusted to be true to their oath until the very end. Each of the Chosen Twelve was issued with an identical seal ring. The knights were also provided with new, streamlined rules which had to be implemented immediately. One of the most drastic changes was that they would no longer be a monastic order. The new articles also stipulated that the privilege to serve the order, as well as the honour to bear the ring, could be passed down from generation to generation. Each firstborn son would bestow it upon his firstborn son, and so forth. If a knight failed to produce a son, or if his son wasn't deemed worthy or able, the honour would be bestowed upon the second born or a carefully chosen cadet. Upon your grandfather's death, his ring will be passed to your father. Isn't that right, Magnus?'

My father bit what was left of his thumbnail and continued to remain silent.

'Every year,' continued Dragomirov, 'the Chosen Twelve would hold a secret council to review the order's strategy. At the end of each meeting, they would choose the date and location of the next council. This information was highly classified and only the Chosen Twelve were privy to it.' He dusted some imaginary dirt off the crisp tablecloth. 'To be admitted to the secret council, each knight had to produce his ring. Those were hard times; each time they parted, the knights knew they may not see each other again. They had no way of being pre-introduced to each other's successors, so the rings were the only proof of their legitimacy. Luckily, for me at least, one of them went missing in 1318. It belonged to a French knight named Godefroi de Carignan. He was last seen in the port of Valencia, boarding the *Nuestra Señora,* one of the ships of the Templar fleet. Sadly,' he added with a gleeful smile, 'Godefroi and his ring vanished somewhere along the way to Cyprus. When he failed to attend the next council, or send someone in his place, a stand-in knight was elected in accordance with the rules. The stand-in knight agreed to renounce his position if

Godefroi, his bloodline, his chosen cadet or his chosen cadet's bloodline ever returned to claim their rightful place.'

'Godefroi, his chosen cadet or their bloodlines?' I asked incredulously. 'But... if Godefroi died and his bloodline ended, anyone who happens to find the ring could claim to be a descendant of his unknown chosen cadet and demand to join the inner circle. The order would have no way to disprove his claim. How could they agree to such a stupid rule?'

Dragomirov let out a soft chuckle. 'In their eyes, it wasn't stupid at all. Officially, they no longer existed, therefore the risk of outside infiltration was minimal. As far as they were concerned, only a legitimate descendant could have been aware of the ring's significance and such knowledge could only have been passed on by a member of the Chosen Twelve.' He paused. 'According to the existing Templar code, Godefroi's ring entitles me to his place amongst the Chosen Twelve, therefore the order will have no choice but to allow me into the brotherhood as a fully-fledged member. The rules are clear.'

'Surely these rules can be amended...'

Dragomirov laughed. 'You would have to speak to your grandfather about that. Unfortunately, as Grand Master, he has sworn to abide by and enforce the original rules. He cannot change them to suit a purpose, no matter how noble such purpose may be. Creating a precedent of that sort would be very risky.'

'How did you come by this information?' asked my father, breaking his wall of silence. He bit his thumbnail again, he was nervous.

'Don't worry, your systems haven't been hacked and your security measures are as sound as they could be,' replied Dragomirov, before curling his lips into a victorious smile. 'I have someone on the inside.'

Blood drained from my father's face. 'That's impossible.'

'Not all brothers are as virtuous as you are, Magnus. There are a few disgruntled members among the brotherhood. The order's strategy is no longer to everyone's taste.'

'Which strategy?' I blurted.

Dragomirov seemed to appreciate my interest. 'The order's tentacles reach everywhere. Politics, finance, science, religion, the arts… The senior members rub shoulders with the world's most influential people. They keep track of everything, from political developments to medical discoveries, from experimental research to obscure archaeological digs. Nothing gets past them. They could control the world if they wanted to, and yet they will only use their power for what they perceive as a greater good. Having that much power and not exploiting it to its full potential is a crime. Under my leadership, the order will no longer hide in the shadows. We will become the richest, strongest, most powerful brotherhood in the world.'

CHAPTER 46

So it was true. The confirmation that Isabelle and I were not totally crazy, that our inklings were right, that our fathers were modern day Templar Knights, had come from a ruthless Russian man I had just met. 'Amuse me,' he was saying to my father, 'because I do find this situation most peculiar. My understanding was that only special circumstances would absolve a firstborn from fulfilling his duty. Death, permanent injury, mental disorders or… repudiation.'

My father's jaw twitched slightly and Dragomirov appeared briefly disconcerted. 'Repudiation? He is your son, is he not?'

'Noah and I are not close, we've never been,' replied my father, slicing a potato in half. I hoped there was a reason for his callousness, because his words hurt like hell. 'His mother has sole custody. I'm his father on paper, but I don't have any rights or responsibilities. And it suits me just fine.'

Repudiated? Had he *repudiated* me? How could a father *repudiate* his legitimate son? Was it even possible in our day and age? Was it legal? Abandoned was bad enough, but… *repudiated*? The word implied absolute rejection and total lack of love. Dragomirov intertwined his long pianist fingers and rested them on the table. 'Well,' he said coldly, 'if you are so disconnected from the boy, witnessing his demise will be a lot easier for you.'

My father wet his lips. 'Demise?'

Dragomirov broke into a sly smile. 'I wasn't born yesterday, Magnus. For reasons which I cannot comprehend, you pulled out all the stops to ensure Noah won't follow in your wake. Whether you want to recognise him as your heir or not, remains your choice, but I want the ring and you're not being particularly forthcoming. If Noah means so little to you, then he is of no value to me. If, on the other hand, you would be willing to exchange his safety for the ring, it could be the beginning of a most successful venture. Did you know that, a long time ago, I asked your father to allow me into the order? I'm not used to asking, it wasn't easy, but I wanted to prove my humbleness and—'

'You wouldn't recognise humbleness if it slapped you in the face. Spare me the details.'

Dragomirov's mounting rage made him look even more sinister. 'As you wish. After dinner, we'll find out if you are also willing to sacrifice your firstborn for the good of the order.'

Dad raised an eyebrow. 'Also?'

'Oh, didn't Knut tell you?' Dragomirov feigned surprise. 'When he turned me away, he underestimated my threats. Do not make the same mistake. Fredrik was lucky to survive his accident, but I'll make sure that Noah isn't granted the same blessing.'

My father didn't move; I wasn't even sure he was breathing. 'It was *you*?'

'It was,' said Dragomirov proudly.

Wild rage, deep hatred, sheer pain and pure disbelief distorted my father's features. 'Fredrik was innocent,' he yelled. 'He was in the prime of his life! And so is Noah! Knut was just following protocol! You cannot expect centuries old rules to be amended for your benefit! That's not how it works!'

It was the closest he had ever come to admitting the order's existence. Dragomirov waved his hand, as if my father's remonstrations were nothing but an irritating buzz. 'I will be part of the Templar Order with or without your help. The rules are clear, the ring entitles the bearer to a place at the Council of Twelve. Stop fighting me, side with me before it's too late. If he could turn back time, I'm sure Knut would act differently.'

Dad's breath was shallower. 'You know *nothing* about my father.'

'I know enough.' Dragomirov smirked. 'I know that his dedication to the order surpasses everything else, including his family. I know that despite nearly losing a son to the brotherhood, he didn't hesitate to surrender the other. I know that he expected you to come through for the order even if your life was going in a very different direction. And I know that even though Fredrik was the predestined one, he made you complete your training and kept you as a reserve, a perennial second best. How did that make you feel, Magnus? Don't tell me that a part of you doesn't hold some resentment towards your father. Side with me, help me pave the way for the Council of Twelve to welcome me with open arms and you have my word that your son will be unharmed. Whether he joins the order or not will be entirely up to you. As for Knut, you won't have to answer to him anymore, he's an old man, accidents happen… And then his ring will pass to you and you will sit at the Council of Twelve. And you will support my candidacy for Grand Master, of course.'

'You haven't even made it through the door and are already running for the top spot?'

'I'm a man of vision.'

'You're a man of delusion.'

Throughout their conversation, my father didn't acknowledge me once. It was as if I didn't exist. Right now his rejection was the last of my worries. The Duct-Taper had begun to clear the table and, if Dragomirov was a man of his word, my torture would soon begin. I reached for the *Chateaux Marguax* and gulped it down.

Dragomirov delicately dabbed the sides of his mouth and threw his napkin on the table. 'I would offer you coffee, but the sight of what Noah is about to endure should be enough to keep you awake.'

CHAPTER 47

The stables were long and well lit. A thick rope was dangling from the central wooden beam and I was pushed right underneath it. Dark blood stains smeared the unfinished cement floor. My father was ordered to sit next to Dragomirov, their chairs facing my direction. Yuri, Scarface and the Duct-Taper took position behind them. I felt like a gladiator in the arena, except my emperor had already pointed his thumb down. I couldn't read my father. He was as still as a statue, as inscrutable as a sphinx, as impenetrable as Fort Knox. He was looking at me, but avoiding my gaze. My chest seemed far more interesting than my face. Sergei tied the rope around my wrists and hoisted me up. He secured the hauling line to a metal hook protruding from the floor. My feet no longer touched the ground and my shoulders felt like they were going to pop out of their sockets.

'It doesn't have to be like this, Magnus,' said Dragomirov, in his best salesman tone.

I waited for my father to see sense, to propose a solution, to fight my corner for God's sake! He remained as silent as a tomb which, ironically, was going to be my final destination if he didn't come up with anything.

The first blow caught me completely unprepared. Sergei's knuckles made contact with my stomach and pretty much rearranged my internal organs. My father closed his eyes. Sergei turned his head and waited for Dragomirov's signal. The second blow was even harder than the first, but this time I remembered to tighten my core muscles. Sergei noticed and sneered. Viggo was right, this guy knew what he was doing. He hit me square in the jaw. I tasted blood and saw stars. I was still floating in the Milky Way when he sank a blow in my lower back. I wanted to scream, but I was in too much pain. Yuri held my father's face up to force him to watch. A faint gesture from Dragomirov and my torturer took a break. 'You can stop this at any time, Magnus,' he said, 'all you have to do is give me the ring.'

'No.'

Naturally, I resented his answer.

'Sergei, continue,' barked Dragomirov. Sergei raised the corners of his lips in a vicious smirk and knocked all the air out of me. I couldn't breathe. It felt as if my lungs had been deflated and couldn't fill up again. I think my father's eyes were moist, or maybe it was a mirage caused by the pain. Sergei sank a hit into my solar plexus. The network of nerves sent raw shots of pain across my entire body. Dragomirov was getting more impatient by the second. 'Where is the ring?'

My father blinked, but didn't speak.

'Harder, Sergei.'

Sergei hit me twice more. I wasn't even bothering to keep my abs tight anymore, it was useless. Before my body could deal with the pain, the next surge was already coming. Sergei's fist made contact with the side of my face and a trickle of warm blood ran down my temple. It joined the other stains on the cement floor in a sort of gruesome, abstract painting. 'It's getting messy,' said Dragomirov to my father. 'Are you sure you don't want to cooperate?'

'I'm sure,' he said softly, staring at the emptiness in front of him.

I was too hurt to cry. The only thing that kept me going was the realisation that I hadn't seen the night guard in a while. I didn't dare to raise my hopes.

'You weren't lying,' said Dragomirov to my father, with misplaced admiration. 'You don't care much for the boy after all.' He turned to Sergei. 'Crush his throat, let's get it over and done with.'

Much to Sergei's annoyance, my father sprung to his feet. 'Wait!'

The Duct-Taper positioned a precautionary finger on the trigger and Dragomirov beamed expectantly. 'Yes?'

My father cleared his throat. 'Stop. I...'

I hoped Sergei had a mop, because Dragomirov was practically drooling. 'You...?'

My father swallowed hard. 'I... I'll...'

I couldn't wait to hear the rest of that sentence. Would he give up the ring to save my life? Would he break the promise that defined his very existence for my benefit? Would he really put me first, before the Templars, before himself, before his word, before his honour?

And then it was pure mayhem. The doors of the stable were kicked off their hinges and bullets were flying like snowflakes in a storm. The captors ran for cover. Viggo crouched behind my father with a knife between his teeth, pirate style, and freed him. They both dived behind a pile of firewood. 'Hang in there, Noah,' shouted Viggo.

Thanks! Where else could I hang? I was attached to a beam in the middle of the stables and bullets were flying right, left and centre. A well-aimed shot rang above my head and the hauling rope snapped in half. I fell on the blood stains, but managed to get up and free myself. Viggo winked in my direction, the gun still in his hand. I made a sprint for him, but Sergei caught me by the waist and dragged me back. I thrashed and writhed, but I was weak from the beating and he had the upper hand. I kicked myself (figuratively speaking, given my recent beating I deserved some compassion) for thinking about Cressida during Ariel's lessons. I knew there was an elbow technique I could use, but my mind was blank. 'Let him go,' said my father, leaving the shelter provided by the firewood.

'You must be joking, he's my insurance,' replied Sergei. 'Stay where you are. One step and he's dead.'

Everyone stopped.

'What did you do with the helicopter pilot?' asked Sergei.

'He's tied up in the pig sty,' replied Miguel.

'Get him.'

My father nodded to Viggo, who grumpily made his way to the pig sty and returned with the terrified pilot.

'We are going to walk to the chopper and take Noah with us,' said Sergei. 'Any sudden moves and I cut his throat, clear?'

His threat elicited a few reluctant nods. Using me as a shield, he began walking backwards towards the stable doors. He had discarded his empty gun in favour of the military knife that had been hanging from his belt. I could feel the cold of its blade against my throat. Scarface and the Duct-Taper lay unconscious on the floor, blood pouring from their wounds. Dragomirov and Yuri crept out of the woodwork and joined the fleeing party. 'Put your weapons down,' said Yuri, Uzi pistol in his hand. 'If you care for the boy, put your weapons down.'

Guns clattered to the floor, but my father and his unarmed team kept up with us as we walked to the helicopter. The sound of the rotor blades filled the night. 'Leave Noah,' shouted my father.

Dragomirov briefly emerged from behind Yuri's shoulder. 'The boy for the ring.'

'I don't have the ring here,' yelled my father over the sound of the rotor blades.

I gulped. Had he just admitted to having the ring *and* implied that he was willing to bargain?

Dragomirov gave a triumphant smile. 'Retrieve it and return to Nassau. I'll be in touch. Until then, no harm will come to your son.'

Dragomirov climbed into the helicopter. With the corner of my eye, I saw Miguel reach behind his back and withdraw a small gun. I didn't hear the shot, but Yuri fell forward holding his side. His fall took Sergei by surprise, he relented his grip and I was able to summon all my strength into the *Krav Maga Elbow Strike Number Five*. I pushed my bent arm up and forward, then drove the elbow back and upwards, smashing it into his chin. Sergei was only slightly stunned, but it was enough to make my escape. I ran for my life, Miguel discarded his now empty gun. I spun on my feet to see how much distance I had put between myself and Sergei. Yuri was scrambling into the helicopter, but Sergei was still on the ground, his arm deliberately folded backwards. I failed to grasp his intentions, but his hateful stare promised nothing good. 'For Vladimir,' he said.

My father shouted to duck, but I didn't react fast enough. And then, as if in slow motion, I saw the knife travelling at top speed in my direction. I froze on the spot. The blade must have been a metre and a half from my face when my father flew diagonally across the trajectory and stopped it. Sergei clambered on board, the chopper lifted off and my father collapsed at my feet, clutching his shoulder. He pulled the knife out and tried to stem the bleeding with his bare hands. Viggo rushed over and bent over him. He peered at the wound with a worried look on his face. He applied more pressure, but blood kept on spurting through his fingers. My father grabbed his wrist and said something in Swedish. 'Of course I'll get him to safety,' said Viggo, 'but you'll be fine. This is just a scratch. You're 0 positive, right?'

Dad gave him a faint smile. 'You really have to work on your bedside manner.'

The noise of the helicopter returned, why had they come back? My first thought was to run back to the stables and scan the floor for weapons we could use. 'It's a different chopper,' said Miguel, eyes glued to the sky. 'It's not Dragomirov's.'

The helicopter landed by the disused barn and Isabelle rushed out of the farmhouse brandishing something. 'I've found more weapons,' she shouted. She saw my father on the ground, shirt drenched in blood, and stopped in her tracks.

Three people emerged from the chopper and ran towards us, well two were running, the third was more of a limping buffalo. Miguel's torch shone on his bald head, I had never been so happy to see Ariel. Minutes later we lifted off, my father was slipping in and out of consciousness. Viggo kept on pressing fresh bandages to the wound, the moment they touched the shoulder, their colour switched from pristine white to vermillion red. 'Is there anything you can do?' asked Miguel frantically.

Viggo reached for the last pack of bandages. 'It's a nicked artery, man! He needs a hospital, he's bleeding out! Are there any HemCon patches?'

Ariel shook the content of the first-aid box to the floor and handed Viggo a small foil packet. Viggo extracted an average looking plaster, stuck it to my father's shoulder and kept on applying pressure. 'What's that?' asked Isabelle.

'HemCon patches were developed for the military,' droned Ariel. 'They are fabricated from a bio-compatible polysaccharide. Its positive charge attracts the red blood cells' negative charge and forms a very tight seal.'

Engine aside, the helicopter went momentarily silent. Viggo translated for the masses. 'The patch should stop the bleeding. The wound will seal more quickly and blood loss will be minimised, but he has lost a hell of a lot already.'

Miguel conferred with Marco and the Italian radioed a request for an emergency landing in a Palermo hospital. 'He's going to be OK, isn't he?' I asked.

Viggo double-checked that the magic patch was in place. 'I hope so, but…'

'But what?'

He sniffed and looked away. Isabelle squeezed my arm for support, I turned and buried my head in her shoulder, tears streaming down my face.

'Pull yourself together, dude,' whispered Viggo, as softly as you can whisper in a flying helicopter. 'He needs you.'

CHAPTER 48

The landing pad was marked with a huge "H." The medical team transferred my father to a waiting stretcher and rushed him inside the hospital building. We sat in the relatives' room, which was bare and depressing. The vending machine offered a selection of hot drinks that tasted as bad as they looked. A doctor in green scrubs stepped in and cleared his throat. 'His condition is very serious,' he said, removing his latex gloves. 'He'll need emergency surgery. We will do all we can, but I would advise you to contact his family. He is conscious at the moment. He's asking for Noah and Viggo.'

We stepped forward. The doctor discreetly assessed our swollen eyes and various contusions, but kept his comments to himself. He led us to the trauma unit and warned us that we only had a few minutes, the operating theatre was practically ready. My father, paler than an anaemic corpse, lay on a stretcher surrounded by an army of medical staff. 'Don't call Knut, not yet,' he said to Viggo. Each word seemed to suck some life out of him.

'But—'

'This is Fredrik all over again, I'm not going to put him through it. If I make it, I'll tell him myself. If I don't, you have my instructions.'

One of the doctors unhooked two I.V. bags and placed them on my father's chest, together with a portable monitor. 'We must go.'

'Wait,' said my father.

'We can't,' replied the doctor, pushing the stretcher out of the room.

My father tried to sit up. 'Noah,' he shouted.

'Stay down Mr Larsson,' said the doctor, 'you're in no condition to—'

'Shut up! Noah?'

I ran to my father's side, he grabbed my hand. 'The stuff I said earlier, I didn't mean it.'

He grimaced, the doctors exchanged nervous looks. One of them tapped his watch, time was ticking.

'I know,' I replied, trying to keep a brave face. 'You must go now, do as the doctors say.'

He looked for my eyes and dug his fingers into my hand. His stare was deep and sincere. 'None of this is your fault. I love you, son.'

The portable monitor emitted a long, uninterrupted beep. A green line went flat. A doctor jumped on the gurney and began CPR, the others rushed the stretcher towards the operating theatre. Someone pulled me back. I broke down.

Viggo and I shared a cubicle in the emergency department. A young nurse was applying ointment to his swollen eye, another was stitching up the side of my face. 'There will hardly be a scar,' she said.

I tried to smile, but I was numb inside. The last thing on my mind was my physical appearance. My father's parting words were playing through my head on a loop. He loved me. He loved *me*. And he had proved it beyond my wildest expectations. As I faced certain death, he had willingly and readily taken my place.

'You know he'd do it all over again if he had to, right?' said Viggo, softly.

'If he dies—'

'He won't. You Larssons are a tough breed.'

I hoped we were. 'I never thanked you.'

'For what?'

'Risking your life to get me out of there.'

He gave me sheepish grin. 'Dude, I'm no hero. As it turned out, I couldn't hot-wire the van…'

He was being modest, deep down we both knew that he wouldn't have left me behind anyway. I clapped his shoulder and let out a soft chuckle. 'Isabelle is going to throw it back in your face until the end of days.'

CHAPTER 49

Two and a half weeks later, on a sunny, humid afternoon, we touched down in Nassau International Airport where my adventure had begun. My father had been discharged from hospital and Knut's hefty donation to their neonatal unit had provided enough incentive to sweep the circumstances of our impromptu admittance under the carpet. Medical notes had gone missing, computers had crashed and brand new, state of the art incubators were on the way.

I stepped onto Valhalla's sun-baked deck and felt at home. My father had resorted to a barrage of excuses to avoid discussing the conversation with Dragomirov, but I was more determined than ever to get to the bottom of it. Shortly after unpacking, we sat down in his cabin to Skype mum. She gave us an update on her Lebanese adventure, which was as exciting as a Foreign Office bulletin. It covered the weather, political unrest, field hospital survival rates and two strategically placed compliments for her husband to be. Considering that she believed compliments to be a deterrent for self-improvement, Jean-Claude must have occupied a very special place in her heart. So special that they had decided to bring the wedding forward. My stay in the Bahamas would be cut short, I would leave next month. 'I don't want to go back,' I said firmly, closing the laptop down.

'You must, staying with me was always going to be temporary,' replied my father.

'In Monreale you said that you would speak to her about the custody arrangement.'

He stroked his beard. 'Did I say that before or after you told me to go to hell and stormed out of the restaurant?'

'Before,' I admitted.

He chuckled. 'I'll speak to her. I meant what I said, Noah, I'll visit more often. Of course, before I broach the subject with Katie… maybe… if we could agree…'

I sighed and smiled, sometimes he could be so predictable. 'What happened in Sicily will stay strictly between us. Our secret's safe.'

'Oh, is it *our* secret now?'

He sounded light hearted, but his eyes told a different story. There was one particular thing that had been bugging me since our conversation with Dragomirov, something I didn't want to take back to London with me. 'Did you really repudiate me?' I asked.

He sniffed and crossed his arms over his chest. 'It sounds worse than it is, it's just an antiquated word —'

Excuses, excuses. 'Did you?'

'Yes.'

'Why?'

He shook his head. 'There was no other way.'

'Dragomirov said that I'm entitled to —'

'No.'

Hell, if there was a chance I could become a Knight Templar, I wasn't going to let go of it so easily. 'Dad, I *want* to join the order, I *want* to begin my training. I'm old enough, I heard what Dragomirov said.'

'You're not old enough to drive a car. Or fly alone, or —'

'Don't change the subject, why won't you let me? It's my birth right.'

He massaged his chin, as if it was suddenly sore. 'We're talking hypothetically, of course.'

'Of course.'

'Well, hypothetically speaking, I stripped you of that right when I repudiated you.'

'Can't you reinstate it or something?'

He bit a random nail and didn't rule out the reversibility of his verdict. 'It wasn't the type of life I wanted for you.'

'Why not?' I protested. 'What could be better than that?'

'Everything. Pretty much everything. When the time comes, you will be free to make your own decisions, pick your own destiny, live your own life.'

'But my destiny chose me! And I like it! It suits me perfectly!'

'Don't even go there, I will stand by my choice. I love you, I will come and visit as often as Katie lets me, but you'll remain repudiated.'

'That's insulting!'

'You'll get over it.'

OK, he wasn't going to budge, but he wasn't the only stubborn one in the family, I had no intention of budging either. 'Be honest with me, was everything Dragomirov said true?'

Silence.

'Dad?'

More silence.

'This is as honest as I can be,' he replied.

'You haven't denied.'

'You catch on quickly.'

'Let me start my training,' I begged, 'let me be one of you.'

He produced a chuckle that was either bitter or patronising. Or maybe both. 'You don't even know what we do! I know how exciting it sounds at first, but somewhere down the line you'll meet a girl, you'll fall in love, you'll have a family and you'll have to lie to them day in, day out. Your oath will always come before you, before *them*! It will follow you wherever you go, it will be a part of you for as long as you live. And then, at some point, you'll begin to wonder if it was such a good idea in the first place.'

I reflected on his words. 'Did you love mum?'

'Very much.'

'Do you still?'

He gave me a faint nod. 'I will never forgive myself for hurting her the way I did.'

'Does she know that you—'

'Of course not.'

'If Fredrik hadn't been hurt, would you have stayed with us?'

He half-smiled. 'I like to think so, unless Katie got too jealous of Jörmungand.' He grabbed a chair and sat in front of me. 'I was a second born, Noah, I wasn't expecting to be called into active service. Fredrik's accident changed everything. Believe me, leaving you nearly broke me, I missed you every single day, but it was the right thing to do.'

I could have disputed his choice, argued until I was blue in the face, but it wouldn't have changed the past. What I wanted to change, was the future. 'If being a Templar is so challenging, so demanding, so punishing, why are you letting Viggo train? He's being trained, isn't he?'

'I won't discuss Viggo with you. Let's say he ticks the right boxes. I already told you much more than I should have.'

He hadn't asked me to take any oaths of secrecy, my father was beginning to trust me. I would gain more of his trust, I would prove myself worthy of his expectations and I would not give up on my birth right just because he had decided it was the best thing to do. I would fulfil my destiny: I was a Larsson, I was a fighter. 'Dad?'

'Last question, OK?'

'It's not a question. I'm proud to have you as my father.'

And I truly was.

CHAPTER 50

It had been nineteen days since that conversation and we hadn't discussed birth rights or secret orders again. We had spent our time swimming, kayaking, surfing, studying and... searching for the sea serpent. Ariel had made a full recovery and, apart from a triumphant smile when he remembered that Ramesses II's wife was called Nefertari, returned to his usual impassive self. Mind you, he had never been anything else, not even with two bullets in his body. Viggo was enjoying a well-deserved break with Hope. Isabelle hadn't taken too kindly to it, but the prospect of an imminent return to the Parisian high streets was cheering her up. We had never discussed our alleged kiss. Hidden by constant bickering, barrages of insults and omnipresent huffs and puffs, our weird friendship was somehow growing. People don't go through what we had gone through without establishing some sort of bond.

We were in the departures area of Nassau International. Isabelle and Miguel were due to board an Air France flight and I had been booked on the British Airways door-to-door-prisoner-service again. My father entrusted me to a steward named James. 'I'll see you in a couple of months,' he said, waving me off.

'Say bye to Viggo for me,' I replied.

My father checked his watch. 'He said he'd be here...'

'He is,' said Viggo's voice. He was jogging in our direction. He joined us and gave me a slap on the back that nearly dislodged my shoulder. 'I wouldn't have missed it for the world. Keep in touch, dude.'

I gave him a fist bump. 'I will.'

He grabbed Isabelle and kissed her on both cheeks, continental style. 'Bye Princess, don't spend too much on the Champs Elysees.'

She produced an unintelligent giggle and pushed every hair she could find behind her ears.

Suddenly, Viggo bent forward and covered the side of his face. 'Who are you hiding from?' I asked, bewildered.

'I think I just saw Ursula,' he muttered, keeping his hand firmly in place. 'She's coming this way.'

'Relax, that's not Ursula,' said my father, as a platinum-blond woman walked past us. He then gave Viggo a curious look. 'How do you know Ursula?'

Viggo straightened, hands on his hips. 'How do *you* know Ursula?'

My father's expression was one of pained embarrassment. 'We... I... I met her in Syracuse.'

My jaw dropped. 'Oh my God! When you kept a low profile after the shooting, did you... spend the night with Ursula?'

He opened his mouth to speak, to defend himself, but his face told us all we needed to know. Viggo and I exploded in fits of laughter.

I was still laughing when James led me through the security checks. I was about to enter the British Airways lounge when Isabelle called after me. I waited for her to catch up. 'I hope all goes well with Cressida,' she said sincerely.

'I hope so too. And I'm sorry about the way things turned out with Viggo.'

'He accepted my friendship on Facebook,' she squeaked, as if she had won the lottery. 'And I'll see him again soon. Are you coming back for the Easter holidays?'

'Don't know yet.'

'Alright, well, until then, *bon voyage*.'

I smiled. 'You have a safe trip too.'

James nudged my arm. 'We must go.'

It was goodbye kiss time, one as in England or two as in France? I had no idea what etiquette dictated on these occasions, I leaned forward to kiss her left cheek and she headed for the right side of my face. A collision was inevitable and our lips accidentally brushed. Not again! She quickly retracted, mumbled something about being late for boarding and disappeared without making eye contact. Had we just kissed?

THE END

I hope you enjoyed *The Twelfth Ring*, the first book of the Noah Larsson series.
If you have a few minutes, I'd really appreciate a review on Amazon, Goodreads or both.
Even a line or two makes a tremendous difference, so thanks in advance for your help.

To receive Noah Larsson's next adventure at a discounted price, please sign up at:
www.samclarkeficiton.com
or follow me on:
www.Facebook.com/SamClarkeFiction
www.Twitter.com/SamClarke777
www.Instagram.com/samclarkefiction

I promise not to share your email address with anyone and you can unsubscribe at any time.

ABOUT THE AUTHOR

Sam Clarke wanted to be a pirate, but her literacy skills were too advanced and she had to settle for writing instead. She is addicted to rock music, coffee and Japanese manga. Her gardening skills are abysmal and she is rumoured to have killed a potted cactus. She currently lives in London next to a very noisy bar. This is her first book.

Manufactured by Amazon.ca
Bolton, ON